MEAN EVERGREEN

Mercy Watts Mysteries Book Twelve

AW HARTOIN

Mean Evergreen

Mercy Watts Mysteries Book 12

This book is a work of fiction. Names, characters, places and incidents either are products of the author's imagination or are used fictitiously. Any resemblance to actual events or locales or persons, living or dead, is entirely coincidental.

ALSO BY AW HARTOIN

Historical Thriller

The Paris Package (Stella Bled Book One)

Strangers in Venice (Stella Bled Book Two)

One Child in Berlin (Stella Bled Book Three)

Dark Victory (Stella Bled Book Four)

A Quiet Little Place on Rue de Lille (Stella Bled Book Five)

Young Adult fantasy

Flare-up (Away From Whipplethorn Short)

A Fairy's Guide To Disaster (Away From Whipplethorn Book One)

Fierce Creatures (Away From Whipplethorn Book Two)

A Monster's Paradise (Away From Whipplethorn Book Three)

A Wicked Chill (Away From Whipplethorn Book Four)

To the Eternal (Away From Whipplethorn Book Five)

Mercy Watts Mysteries

Novels

A Good Man Gone (Mercy Watts Mysteries Book One)

Diver Down (A Mercy Watts Mystery Book Two)

Double Black Diamond (Mercy Watts Mysteries BookThree)

Drop Dead Red (Mercy Watts Mysteries Book Four)

In the Worst Way (Mercy Watts Mysteries Book Five)

The Wife of Riley (Mercy Watts Mysteries Book Six)

My Bad Grandad (Mercy Watts Mysteries Book Seven)

Brain Trust (Mercy Watts Mysteries Book Eight)

Down and Dirty (Mercy Watts Mysteries Book Nine)

Small Time Crime (Mercy Watts Mysteries Book Ten)

Bottle Blonde (Mercy Watts Mysteries Book Eleven)

Mean Evergreen (Mercy Watts Mysteries Book Twelve)

Silver Bells at Hotel Hell (Mercy Watts Mysteries Book Thirteen)

Short stories

Coke with a Twist

Touch and Go

Nowhere Fast

Dry Spell

A Sin and a Shame

Paranormal

It Started with a Whisper

For the real Grandma J

CHAPTER ONE

Some people say waiting is the hardest part and I'm one of them. At least I was until that snowy Tuesday when I sat in a frigid, windswept parking lot at Missouri Eastern Correctional Center. I hated waiting, and I'd been doing it for forty-five minutes. Dad said to get there at eight sharp and I did. Well. Okay. Ten after eight. But I was only late because I didn't want to do it. Nobody would. Freezing your butt off with the grand view of razor wire, a guard tower, and the brown buildings of a correctional center wasn't high on anybody's list. Why do they call it a correctional center anyway? Does it actually correct anything or anyone? I had serious doubts on that because I'd been roped into picking up Stevie Warnock and he was beyond correcting.

Stevie was the dimwitted son of one of the smartest men I knew, Big Steve Warnock, a brilliant lawyer and long-time friend of my family. It doesn't sound like a big deal to pick up one felon from a minimum to medium security prison, but it was. Stevie had been a problem all his life and specifically for me. The moron liked me and that's why I got the pleasure of dealing with him. My dad and Big Steve said I had a good track record with the nitwit, but that was just luck. Something was going to go wrong with this assignment and I resented it. I was supposed to be in Germany on a case. A real case. A paying case.

About two weeks ago, I'd been kidnapped by Anton Thooft and had then been hired by his sister Kimberly to find out why a fifty-something teacher working in Stuttgart, Germany at a Department of Defense school had suddenly flown back to his home state of Missouri, knocked me out with a chemical agent, and thrown me in a trunk. Nobody thought hiring me, the victim, was a good idea, except Kimberly, but I did it. I found out that Anton had been blackmailed over a family secret, which, as he might've predicted, tore his family apart. But Kimberly wasn't done. She wanted to know who did the blackmailing and why. I was all set to hit the road until my mother got wind of the plan and, as all loving mothers do, she ruined it. "It's Christmas. You have to rest."

It wasn't Christmas, yet, and I didn't want to rest. I wanted to know why Anton had targeted me, not to mention I had a bet with my boyfriend Chuck over the culprits and I intended to win. Bathroom cleaning was on the line and I take that very seriously. But when Mom couldn't prevail upon me to stay home, she called in reinforcements and the rest of my family piled on. My grandparents, aunt, cousins even. They all had something to say about my trip. They all said that Kimberly didn't care if I went before or after Christmas as long as it happened. That was true, but I cared. It didn't feel right to let it lie. I was still going until my father, the great and bossy Tommy Watts, got into the act. Dad thought I should stay home and take it easy. "Rest, bake, relax," he said.

I should've known he was up to something. My dad doesn't relax. He doesn't understand the urge. The man couldn't watch a movie with my mom without a case file on his lap or a phone in hand to answer emails. It's just not who he is. I will admit he'd been trying and he'd even been described as calm recently. Once. And that's why I fell for it. Dad was going to be a regular dad. He was going to do Christmas like people do. Yeah, right.

Seventeen hours after he said, "Relax, baby girl"—That's right, I counted—I got the swell job of picking up Stevie Warnock from prison. I protested. I really did. "It's for the family," Dad said. Not our family obviously, but Dad didn't make distinctions like that. Big Steve and his long-suffering wife Olivia were like family and that was the end of that discussion.

I knew all about the legal maneuvering Big Steve had done to score a sweet deal for his son. Four years for whatever he did. I'm sure Dad told me what the charges were, but I wasn't paying attention. It was probably a laundry list. I wouldn't put anything past Stevie, except violence. He was never violent, more like accident-prone, and if there was an accident, Stevie was going to have it. The guy just rolled with whatever was happening. He never thought about it. If someone happened to cross his path and said, "Hey, drive this coke to New Jersey and bring back a crate of Uzis. You got nothing else going on." Stevie would say, "You're right. I don't." And there he'd be driving drugs and guns across state lines.

How the dufus was so consistently in the wrong place at the right time to do something bad was a mystery. It just happened. I'd asked Stevie and he had no idea. To be fair, no idea was the story of his life, but now I was involved in it again. The last time I'd seen him was in New Orleans, a lifetime and a half ago when he was on the run from the Costillas after stealing sixty-two stereos from them and leading a blood-thirsty Richard Costilla to my grandparents' house where I ended up shooting him in the face. Not a good time and I still wasn't over it. Mom said I should forgive Stevie, but how do you forgive someone who never apologized and probably had forgotten all about it. You can't. You just can't.

I wasn't going to forgive him for freezing my butt off either. I felt bad about running the engine and wasting gas, so I kept turning the car off, but then my hands and feet would go numb and I'd have to turn it on again. What was taking so long? It's not like Missouri wanted to keep him.

Get your little bag of crap and get out.

I kept an eye on the visitor's entrance with its snowy walkway, but there was nothing to see. The prison seemed like a ghost town in the middle of nowhere, even though it was very close to the Hwy 44 corridor. If I got out of the car, I could probably have heard the traffic and it was in-between Pacific and Eureka, two bustling small towns. All sorts of things were happening just a mile or two away, but right there it felt like Siberia with mounds of snow so high I could barely see the top of the sign for the prison when I drove in. Honestly, if you didn't know it was there, you might miss the whole shooting match as my grandad would say. Just a little blue sign with gold lettering, oddly friendly for a prison. I didn't miss it. I wish I had because the waiting turned out to be the best part of my day.

Just when I picked up my phone to call Dad and report that Stevie had apparently not scored early parole for reasons unknown, the door opened and the dufus ambled out. His brown hair was shaved and he wore a white tee shirt and a pair of sweatpants that were brand new but way too short. He'd gained a little weight and wasn't quite as spindly as before, but it was the same old Stevie, goofy as hell and totally confused, which was probably why a guard came out with him. I'd seen a few other prisoners leave when I arrived. But they were alone for their reunions. Stevie was the only one who rated an escort. She probably wanted to make sure he left. With Stevie, there was a possibility that he'd wander around the parking lot until he got frostbite or maybe she thought nobody wanted him back and he'd need a ride to his parole officer to check-in.

Whatever the reason, a large black lady with rosy cheeks and an air of exhausted resignation pointed the way down the walk to Stevie and then accompanied him to the edge of the parking lot where she stopped to watch him wander around. I took a breath and got out to wave. Stevie spotted me and did a fist pump.

"Hey, Mercy. What you doin' here?" Stevie gave me an unwelcome hug and I gave him one of Chuck's jackets. It engulfed him like he was wearing his dad's clothes.

"I'm picking you up," I said.

"I know. I requested that you get me."

Then why did you ask?

"Swell," I said.

"Yeah, it is." Stevie grinned at me and I felt a twinge of affection for the idiot. He wasn't mean-spirited. I had to give him that.

"Why did you ask for me?" I asked.

"You and me. We got a thing going on."

I stared for a second, trying to get his meaning. He couldn't mean a *thing* like a *thing thing*, even Stevie wasn't that stupid.

"We don't have a *thing*," I said.

"Oh, yeah. I told all the guys about you and me." Stevie waved an arm at the prison and a pit formed in my stomach.

"You told a bunch of prisoners about me?"

"About you *and me*. They already knew about you. You got a lot of fans on the inside."

Awesome. Just what I don't need.

"I hope you told them that I have a six-foot-two cop boyfriend who likes to shoot people for sport," I said.

"Hell, no. Nobody wants to hear that," said Stevie. "I told them about how much fun we had in New Orleans and how hot and cool you are."

"Thanks. That's just great."

I started to open the passenger door for him and he said, "See, we got a thing."

"If by *thing* you mean you do something stupid and I have to help out with it, then yeah, we have a thing."

"Exactly," he said.

I opened the door. "Whatever. Get in and let's get this over with."

"Where are we going?" He held up a small paper bag. "My bags are packed."

"I see that. Get in."

"Don't you get it? That's a movie quote. I'm the crazy prisoner."

I covered my eyes for a second. "Yes, you're the crazy prisoner. Please, get in. We've got a lot to do. I have to take you shopping, get you cleaned up and presentable for your mother and your parole officer. This could take a while."

"*The Green Mile*. I'm Wild Bill. That's what the guys called me."

"That's not a good thing, Stevie," I said.

"It's my first nickname. I always wanted a nickname."

"You have a nickname. Stevie's your nickname. Your name is Steven."

"That's no good. Stevie." He blew a raspberry. "I wanted something cool. Call me Wild Bill."

"That's a hard pass," I said, pointing to the passenger seat.

"Why not? Come on. Call me Wild Bill."

"That guy was a deranged child rapist and killer."

"Other than that, he was pretty funny and we look alike," said Stevie. Always the one to miss the big picture was our Stevie.

"Get in," I said. "I'm supposed to take you to Macy's."

"Ooh, I like Macy's. Let's go. My bags are packed." He grinned at me again and I rolled my eyes.

And that's when it happened. It was all fine. I mean as fine as it gets with Stevie and then it went to crap. Just like that. Stevie started to duck into the passenger side and I saw the back of his head for the first time.

"Oh, my god!" I lunged for him, dragging Stevie out of the seat and throwing him against the car. Not bad, considering I still had one arm in a cast. "What the hell is on your head?"

"What? What?" Stevie slapped his hands over the back of this head and started spinning. Think dog chasing his tail as if he could see the back of his head if he just went fast enough.

I watched for a second in amazement and then grabbed him, shoving him back against the car. "Stop that!"

"What is it? What is it?" he asked in a panic. "Do I have fleas?"

"Probably, but no." I turned him around to get a better look, hoping I'd seen it wrong. A mistake. A trick of the light. "Crap on a cracker. Are you insane? Have you lost what little mind you had?"

"What is it?" Stevie started feeling the back of his head again.

My heart was pounding and my vision got a little misty. I had to fix it. How was I going to fix it? "A tattoo."

Stevie slumped against the car and patted his chest. "Oh, Jesus. You scared me. I thought something was really wrong with me."

"Something is," I said.

"Huh?"

I'm not gonna lie. If I'd had a weapon, it wouldn't have looked good for Stevie. But since I didn't, I buried my face in my hands.

"Dude, it's fine," he said. "Just a tattoo. Everybody has tats."

I didn't look up. I couldn't. I wasn't ready. "Everybody doesn't have *that* tattoo."

"Jeez, I didn't know you were a drama queen. You gotta do what ya gotta do."

"You didn't have to do *that*."

"I did. You see, I joined this club and you got to get tatted up. Don't worry. Chaz did it for free. Didn't cost me nothing."

I looked up and stared into his blank face as he glanced around looking just as happy as all get out. "What are you planning on telling your parents?"

Stevie shrugged. "Nothing. Who cares? My hair'll grow. I got hair, Mercy."

"Not right now you don't," I said.

"A couple of weeks and presto, it's gone."

"But it will still be there."

"Nobody will know," he said, and I could see his interest in the situation fading. Not that he was much interested in the first place.

"You'll know. I'll know, and it's right there *on your head*. Didn't Big Steve and Olivia visit?"

"Sure. Dad came a few times, but he's mad about something. Mom came every week. She loves me."

Not for long.

"How'd you hide it?"

"Huh?"

"That...that thing on your head, Stevie. How'd you hide it?" I asked.

"I didn't. They probably didn't care."

My fists clenched, even the one in the cast. "They would care. I care. Everybody in the whole damn world would care."

"Don't get excited about nothing, Mercy," said Stevie.

That's when I got excited. I got super excited. I snatched his little brown paper bag right out of his hands and started smacking him with it. A debit card, razor, and toothbrush all went flying.

"Hey!" Stevie ran and I chased him, right around the car in a circle.

"Come back, you moron. I'll smack that thing right off your head."

"You're crazy! What's wrong with you?" Stevie yelled and put on a little speed to dash out of my reach.

"Come back here so I can kill you!" I yelled over the roof of the car.

Stevie looked at me totally bewildered. "I didn't do nothing."

"I will get a gun and shoot you if you say that again!"

There was a loud slap on the hood of the car and we looked over to see the guard standing there with her hands on her hips. Even in my fury, I could see she'd expected this and was ready. "I can't have that kinda talk now."

"Have you seen that?" I was still yelling. I couldn't stop.

She nodded. "I've seen it."

"What?" Stevie asked, still bewildered.

"You have a swastika on your head!" I yelled.

"Huh?"

The guard shook her head slightly and sighed. "It takes all kinds."

"Of idiots," I yelled.

"Hey!" yelled Stevie. "Who you calling an idiot?"

"You've got a swastika tattooed on your head!"

Stevie's forehead puckered into a frown. "A what?"

"A swastika. A Nazi Swastika. On your head."

"Nah." Then he chuckled. "I just got the club tat."

"The club tat is a swastika."

He looked up to the sky and thought about it. "Oh, yeah?"

"Yeah, Stevie," I yelled. "You let someone put that obscenity on your head. Permanently."

"I didn't know."

"It's your job to know what some white supremacist douchebag is tattooing on your head!"

"Calm down. I'll just grow out my hair."

I gripped the top of the car for support. "When? Today? Before your *Jewish* parents see it?"

The guard whistled. "Stevie Stevie Stevie."

"I didn't mean nothing by it," said Stevie.

"That's the problem!" I yelled. "You never mean anything by anything, but you still do it. Your mother. What am I going to say to Olivia?"

"Mom won't care."

"Yes, she will and your father. This'll kill your father. Are you trying to kill Big Steve?" I asked. "Maybe you want him to kill you. Is that it? Is that the plan?"

"It's not that bad." Stevie looked like it might just be dawning on him that he could be in trouble. He looked at the guard with raised eyebrows.

"You've got a huge problem," she said. "Whatever this woman tells you to do you better do it."

"Yeah?"

"Oh, yeah."

I looked at that swastika and whipped the poofball hat right off my head. "Put this on."

"It's a girlie hat," protested Stevie.

I marched around the car, grabbed him by the shoulders, and faced him toward the guard. She slapped the hood again and said, "What did I just say?"

Stevie pulled on my hat and I shoved him in the car with a boot to the butt for good measure. I slammed the door and stomped over to the driver's side. Murder was on my mind and it must've shown.

"Miss Watts, you aren't going to take him out and shoot him, are you?" she asked.

"Call me Mercy and probably not. I'm sorry. I didn't ask your name."

She smiled and pulled open her parka so I could see her name tag. "Officer James, but Stevie knows me as Noreen."

"Thanks," I said. "You may have saved his life."

"I thought we'd be having a problem, but I admit I was glad to see you instead of his father or yours," said Noreen.

"That would've been bad," I said, taking a breath. "You're very calm about this."

"Same shit different day. It's not unusual."

"Stevie has got to be unusual."

"Yeah, well, they usually know what's on their own heads, but Stevie, he's not typical in a lot of ways." Noreen gestured to the prison. "There's a lot of *innocent* men in there but not him. He owned it from day one."

"Only 'cause he's too stupid to deny it," I said.

"That and he is who he is and he's not ashamed."

"He should be. I'm ashamed of him."

"For what it's worth, I don't think he had any clue about that ink or the so-called gang that gave it to him."

"That's the problem," I said. "He's always been like that."

A look of consternation passed over Noreen's face.

"What?" I asked.

"Well, I'm not supposed to say this or even know it, but..."

"But...?" I asked.

"It's confidential, you understand, and you didn't hear anything from me."

Ah, crap.

"What is it?"

"I think he's got a diagnosis."

"Diagnosis? For what? He's sick?"

"From the therapist. We offer therapy and counseling to our inmates. We are trying to rehabilitate them and it helps."

People always surprised me. Nasty seemed to come out of nowhere, but so did kindness.

"Do you think Stevie will tell me about it?" I asked.

"He seemed to like therapy and if he remembers, you'd be the one he'd tell," said Noreen.

"Me?"

"He's got great affection for you."

I leaned over and looked through the windshield. Stevie grinned and waved at me. "I don't understand that."

"It is what it is," said Noreen. "I've dealt with enough nasty bastards to appreciate the good-hearted idiots."

"You're not upset about the tattoo?"

"Mercy, I've seen it all in there five times over. Stevie Warnock's idiot ink comes as no great surprise. He's lucky they didn't put it on his forehead."

"You don't get paid enough," I said.

"Amen." Noreen gave me a wave and strolled back to the prison. I was sorry to see her go.

I turned down a back alley in the Central West End of St. Louis and Stevie leaned forward squinting. "Where's Macy's?"

"We're not going to Macy's yet," I said, squeezing my mother's car between a dumpster and recycling cans. "This is first."

"How come we're parking back here?"

"We're near Hawthorne Avenue and I'm not taking any chances."

Stevie frowned and asked, "Chances of what?"

"Somebody seeing my mother's car at a tattoo shop. Nobody is going to know about this. Nobody."

"Who's getting a tattoo?"

"You."

He did a fist pump. "Yes. I've been thinking about getting a sleeve. What do you think about my mom's favorite flower?"

I put my forehead on the steering wheel. "A tattoo to cover up that abomination on the back of your head."

"Oh. That's not as much fun," said Stevie. "And the first one hurt bad."

"Good," I said.

"You're mean to me."

"I'm saving you from certain death or would you like me to drive to my parent's house and let them get a load of your latest bad decision?" I asked.

"Mercy?" Stevie's voice was soft and a little pleading.

"Yeah?"

"I don't have any money."

"Don't worry about it." I got out and Stevie obediently followed me to the front of Black Heart Ink. I'd texted the owner, Charming Velázquez, before we left the prison parking lot. If anyone could be understanding of Stevie, it was her.

I'd known Charming forever. We went to school together. She was the only daughter of a pair of nice but uptight radiologists. She was supposed to go to medical school and make up the fourth generation of Velázquez doctors along with her brothers. Charming went a different way and I heard her mom was still taking anti-depressants over it.

Being the family outlier gave Charming a soft spot for those of us that didn't quite fit and Stevie certainly qualified. Plus, she wasn't easily spooked. She did penis piercing, for crying out loud. I did catheters in my normal life as a nurse, but piercing was beyond the pale for me.

The door dinged when I opened it and Charming's small but snazzy studio appeared empty, but I could hear chatting from behind the black and chrome partition.

"Be right out!" called Charming from somewhere in the depths of her studio. It was a great location and Charming was doing well for herself, but that wasn't helping her with her mother.

I went over to look at the books. Something to cover up a swastika wasn't going to be easy. Flowers? Something geometric? I found a cool tribal pattern that might work and said, "What do you think of this?"

No answer.

I turned around to see Stevie hovering by the door, still wearing my poofball hat and wringing his hands.

"What are you doing?" I asked.

"Nothin'."

"Come over here and look at this."

"Do you know them?" he asked.

"Who?"

"The shop people."

"I do. I texted her about your situation. I told you that."

He looked confused. "Did you?"

"I did."

"What'd she say?"

I shrugged. "Come over."

"Was she mad, too?" he asked, and my frozen solid heart melted just a tad.

"She's not mad at you, Stevie. She doesn't know you," I said.

He was unconvinced and stayed by the door. Charming popped out from the back about three minutes later with a customer who was gingerly putting on a jacket. She greeted me, rang up the customer's enormous bill, and chatted happily about his next section, which I gathered was quite ornate. When he turned to go, he got a load of

Stevie in his prison togs, Chuck's huge jacket, and my pink poofball and to his credit, he hesitated but then just nodded at me and then Stevie before leaving.

Charming came out from behind the counter and hugged me. We'd never been friends in high school but since then we'd formed a casual friendship. We had disappointing parents in common.

"How's the arm?" she asked.

"Better, thanks."

She took a look at my face. "Rash is better, too. That was wicked. Are you sure you don't want me to do some eyeliner? I could totally give you the Marilyn cat eye."

"'Cause that's what I need," I said with a laugh.

"It would look great."

"I know, but I'm trying to blend not stand out more."

"Girl, you're the spitting image of Marilyn Monroe. When are you going to embrace it?" Charming asked.

"Never."

"I give up."

"Finally."

We laughed and then turned to Stevie who was now pressed against the plate glass window.

"So, who do we have here?" Charming asked and she was as her name implied, charming, but Stevie looked absolutely terrified.

I waited to see what he'd do until it became clear that nothing was the answer.

"This is Stevie Warnock. He just got released this morning."

"Don't tell her that," he said and then clamped his hand over his mouth.

"What is up with you?" I asked.

"Nothin'," he said behind his hand.

Charming waved him over. "Come on. I don't bite and I don't give a damn about your previous incarcerations, either."

Stevie didn't budge and Charming shrugged. "We've got to get a move on. I've got a sleeve coming in and he's a wrastler."

"A what?"

"Never mind. I've got the time right now," said Charming. "Just barely."

"Give us a minute," I said. "I'll get him squared away."

Charming smiled. "A minute. I'm counting."

She went into the back and started chatting with someone. I pointed at Stevie. "What is your deal? We've got to fix that thing."

"I don't want her to see it," said Stevie.

"She has to see it."

"You think it's bad and—"

"It is bad and it's awful. How can you even question that?"

He shrugged. "I don't know."

"What about your family?" I marched over, grabbed Stevie and dragged him in front of a mirror. Then I whipped him around and held up a hand mirror so he could see the back of his head. There it was in black and blue. Weird, I know, but some of it was blue. Maybe the scumbag ran out of black. It wasn't a great tattoo and only about three-fourths finished, but it was definitely a swastika. No doubt about it.

Stevie frowned. "He didn't finish. He told me he got it done."

"That's what you're worried about?" I whacked him with the mirror. "What about your family? How could you do this to them after everything they went through. I just...I can't even." I was yelling again and Charming ran out, took one look at Stevie's head, and her pretty face turned to thunder.

Stevie slapped a hand over the back of his head. "Don't look."

"Too late," she said.

"That's right. It's too late!" I yelled. "I'm done. I tried. When Big Steve kills you, don't come crying to me."

"He'll forgive me. He always does," said Stevie backing away slowly.

"Not this time. She was his mother, Stevie. Do you think he's just going to get over that? He's not over it. He'll never be over it. You've been nothing but trouble and now this. This! Of all things. It's an insult to your grandparents, not to mention millions of other people."

"My grandparents?"

"Yes." I grabbed him by the tee shirt and twisted it. "The people who fought to survive and gave you your life."

Stevie's eyes were wide and for once not empty. "What are you talking about?"

I shoved him away from me and Charming ran over, wrapping her arms around me.

"You know!" I yelled. "You just don't care enough to remember."

"I don't know. What about them?"

Charming held me back and it's a good thing, too. I had a foot back. I was going to start kicking. No thought went into that. I was going to start kicking the stupid out of Stevie Warnock. As far as I knew, kicking hadn't been tried yet, and I was willing to give it a go.

"He doesn't know, Mercy," said Charming.

"He does!"

"I don't!" Stevie yelled. "I don't know anything. Nobody tells me anything about anything!"

"Tell him," said Charming.

"Your grandmother was in the resistance during the war. She was a child, but she ended up in a concentration camp where she nearly died. But she married your grandfather who was also in a camp and they had your dad. The strain of having a child was too much for her and she died. Constanza gave her life only to have her only grandchild get a swastika on his head!"

Stevie dropped his hands. "How do you know all that?"

I took a breath and then said, "I've been investigating your family, trying to find out what happened to Constanza."

"Does my dad know?"

"Of course, he knows."

"All of it?"

"He's known about his parents for forever. I found out about the resistance part and I told him."

"I didn't..." Stevie wandered over to the books and began flipping through the sketches and pictures. Charming let go of me and sat down next to him. "If you have any ideas that aren't in the books, let me know. We can work it out."

A huge guy with every inch of him tattooed came out of the back. "Charming? You alright out here?"

"Sure, Darius. Can you call my eleven o'clock and cancel?"

"The wrastler?"

"Yeah."

"No problem. That guy's a nightmare," said Darius. "What should I tell him?"

"Family emergency."

Darius looked the three of us over, nodded, and went into the back.

"Sorry if you're losing a customer," I said.

"He's not going anywhere. He loves my work and nobody else will put up with him. He passes out and then tries to punch me. We've taken to strapping him to the chair, so in a way you've made my day easier."

Stevie didn't look up. He kept flipping through pages, but I had the feeling he wasn't seeing any of the art. "Where were they?"

"Auschwitz. Your grandfather was in the main camp and your grandmother was in a satellite camp," I said.

"Why? What did they do?"

"They were Jews, Stevie."

"I know, I mean in the resistance, what did they do?" he asked quietly.

"He wasn't in it that I know of and we're still working on how Constanza was involved."

"Dad never told me." Stevie looked up and his eyes were sad and had a loneliness to them that I'd never seen before. "Why didn't he tell me?"

"Maybe it was too hard to talk about," said Charming.

"He told Mercy."

I sat down on the other side of him. "Actually, he didn't. I found out through some other stuff I was working on and he confirmed it."

"He probably thought I was too stupid to understand," he said. "I am too stupid."

I took his hand and said, "You don't have a good track record, but maybe you can tell me what the therapist said."

"Huh?"

"In prison. You saw a therapist, didn't you?"

"How'd you know?" he asked.

"Everybody does, don't they?" I asked.

"Not everybody. Some guys think it's bullshit, but I liked it. Misty was nice. We talked and I felt better. I got techniques."

"For what?"

"Concentrating and thinking about stuff. I'm supposed to keep a notebook so I can remember stuff by writing it down." Stevie closed the book and asked, "Do you do lilies and sunflowers?"

"Sure." Charming got up and went behind the counter. "I've got a special book back here."

She brought the book out with a sketch pad and two of them went through the book and designed the most beautiful tattoo I'd ever seen. Intertwined lilies and sunflowers with a dragon peeking through the leaves and stems.

While they worked, I asked questions. Stevie, as usual, didn't remember exactly what Misty the therapist had said. He didn't even remember what her last name was. He did know that she thought he needed pills and he was supposed to see a doctor who could give him the pills, but he got paroled before that happened.

"What were the pills going to do?" I asked.

"Help me to think," he said. "I think I think just fine, but she said I don't."

"Sounds like ADD," said Charming. "My stepson Liam has that. He takes Concerta. It helps a lot."

"What does he do?" Stevie asked.

"He can't concentrate. He's impulsive and does crazy stuff like he forgets to use a potholder and burns his hand. He does his homework but can't remember to turn it in. Last week, his mom forgot his med on accident and some kid dared him to eat a rock and he did it. Liam just doesn't think without his meds. His doctor says he suggestible."

Stevie looked up from the sketch and said, "I ate stuff."

"I know," I said, suddenly feeling flipping terrible. ADD. Was that the problem?

"What did you eat?" Charming asked.

Stevie frowned and looked at me like I'd been there. I wasn't, for the record. Stevie was five years older than me.

"Worms and rocks," I said.

He made a face. “Oh, yeah. Why in the hell would I want to do that?”

“We never knew why.”

“Maybe pills will change that,” said Charming. “You should call the therapist, Mercy.”

“She won’t tell me anything. He’s not my kid.”

“Stevie can give her permission.”

I got out my phone and went through a huge rigamarole to find out who Misty was and how to contact her. You’d think Misty was a state secret. In the end I had to call on my new prison connection, Noreen. She gave me Misty’s name and number, but I didn’t hear it from her.

By that time, Charming was almost done with the drawing, but Stevie wasn’t quite satisfied. “I need my grandpa in there.”

“Did you know him well?” I asked.

“He talked to me and he was really nice.”

“He talked to you?”

Charming looked up from the shading she was doing. “Is that weird?”

“Kinda,” I said. “Big Steve said he never talked, that he couldn’t really communicate at all.”

“That’s so sad.”

“He talked to me,” said Stevie.

“About what?” I asked.

He frowned. “I don’t know. He was really quiet and nice though.”

“Gentle,” said Charming. “Something gentle.”

I pointed at the dragon. “Who’s this?”

Stevie laughed. “I just like dragons. I think Grandpa liked them, too.” Then he frowned. “He did. He gave me dragon books. I think they’re still at home.”

“And the sunflower is who?”

“Mom. It’s her favorite.”

“What about the lily? I asked.

“I just...I can’t remember. I think I just like lilies.”

Charming grabbed a second sheet of sketch paper and quickly drew a sweet little mouse. “Gentle, sweet, a survivor.”

“And it works with the rest of it,” I said.

"Do you think he'd want to be a mouse though?" Stevie asked. "He was a big guy like Dad."

"I have no idea," said Charming. "The biggest guys can have the sweetest souls though."

"He'd be happy that you remembered him. He could be the dragon, if you want," I said.

"No," said Stevie. "He wasn't the dragon. I think the mouse is good. He was super quiet. You hardly knew he was there. Let's do the mouse."

Charming worked the mouse into the final image and it really worked.

"It's going to go away completely, right?" Stevie asked. "The swastika will be gone. Mom and Dad'll never know?"

"With the shading and lines, it will disappear," said Charming.

"But it will still be there, like Mercy said," he said sadly. "I'm an idiot."

"Don't think of it like that," I said. "It's still there, like what happened to them is still there, but they're the bigger part of the picture. Surviving and going on is the most important part."

"Yeah, that's good." He grinned. "Let's do it."

Charming and Stevie went down to a room so she could get to work and I got on calling Misty the therapist. After some wheedling and getting Stevie on the line, she agreed to talk to me. This was the one time when my so-called celebrity status worked in my favor. She knew who I was and for some reason decided I was more trustworthy because of it.

"You understand that I didn't do formal testing on Stevie?" Misty asked.

"Got it, but what is your opinion?" I asked.

"He's got ADD off the charts. I'm surprised he can drive."

"He's wrecked four cars and lost his license."

"Well, there you go," said Misty.

I went into another room, closed the door, and curled up in the chair, surrounded by beautiful artwork and needles. Needles I was used to. Artwork not so much. "So, I have to ask. How did you know he had ADD? Nobody ever mentioned it before that I know of."

"His handwriting. It's terrible."

"That's half the people I know."

"His is different. If you watch him writing, he's just having a terrible time. Not that he can't write. He can, but it's an effort to stay focused and do it well. He has to slow down and he struggles with that. Then I started watching his eyes. He fades out and looks away, like he's gone for a few seconds and then comes back. He misses out on what happened in that time period."

"And you think meds will fix that?" I asked.

"Fix isn't the right word. It will help. If he slows down his brain, he'll be able to drive down the street, see a stop sign, and then continue driving and remember it's there."

"He can't remember stop signs?"

"Well, it's not that he doesn't remember them exactly. His brain will have bounced off to something else."

"What a nightmare."

"I'd say so. Don't get your hopes up too high though. Stevie's no genius. He's not going to get on meds and suddenly be analyzing Shakespeare and get totally into physics."

"Nobody will think that's a possibility," I said.

"You'd be surprised with parents. They will get ideas about their kid and it's hard to let go of them."

I wondered what Big Steve would think. Olivia would definitely get her hopes up. "Why didn't anyone catch this before?"

"I couldn't really say, but it wasn't hugely popular to medicate kids when Stevie was young, and even when they did it was mostly for hyperactivity. Stevie's not hyper. They probably just thought he was dumb."

"He kinda is," I said.

"I assessed his IQ as average. He's not an idiot. He's average."

"Seriously?"

"I swear to God. Stevie Warnock is average," said Misty.

"Holy crap," I said. "Do you get this a lot at the prison?"

"I do and let me say Stevie's lucky. He came from a good home with kind parents with no abuse of any kind. If you combine Stevie's ADD with violence and/or neglect, you've got a real problem."

"You think he'll be alright then?" I asked.

"He's got a better chance than most."

I thanked her and went back to Stevie who was lying down prone with his eyes closed while Charming inked his head.

"Well?" she asked me.

"He's got ADD, a whole lot of ADD," I said. "But he's not crazy or anything. Meds will help."

Charming continued to work and then asked, "I know I said I didn't care, but what did he do to get into prison?"

I named a few things that Stevie had done and Charming got thoughtful. "Nothing violent?"

I laughed. "Nope. Can you imagine Stevie violent? No way."

"Liam's doc is great and he treats adults. I've got a card in my wallet. Why don't you get it out and call him?"

I got out the card. Downtown office. Convenient enough to get there easily. "Is he taking patients?" I asked.

"Tell him I sent you and I think he'll squeeze Stevie in," said Charming. "He's a good guy. I just didn't want to send him a psycho."

"Not a psycho," I said with a laugh.

"You know I was thinking..."

I leaned over to look at the swastika that was rapidly disappearing into something gorgeous. "That you wish you could post this transformation?"

"No, but that would be nice," she said.

"What then?"

"He'll need a job," said Charming.

Stevie's eyes popped open. "Did someone say job?"

She gave him a little smack on the shoulder. "Don't move."

"I'm not. You hiring?"

Charming gave him an evaluating look. "Maybe if you get medicated and stay medicated."

"You'd do that for me?" he asked.

"You remind me of Liam. I'd want someone to give him a chance."

"Who's Liam?"

"My stepson."

"You've got a stepson?"

Charming rolled her eyes. "You really need those meds."

Stevie gave her a thumbs-up. "I'm on it."

I poked him. "You mean, I'm on it."

"Same thing. We got a thing, you and me. We help each other."

I couldn't remember Stevie ever helping me, but I was willing to go with it under the circumstances. "Sure, why not?"

"I'm gonna get a job and remember stuff," said Stevie. "Dad'll be so happy."

He will. He really will.

CHAPTER TWO

Twenty-four hours, a migraine, and three pounds later, I tried to wake up in the world's longest, hottest shower. Beet red and it wasn't really working. I'd forgotten how exhausting Stevie could be.

He was in the chair with Charming for three hours and the miracle did occur. Hate symbol gone. Love symbol beautifully in place. Then we went to Macy's and strolled the mall for a good long while because when you've been locked up everything is fantastic and amazing. We ate four times. Twice at the Cheesecake Factory and they are not fans of mine. The last time I'd been there I had Fats Licata in tow or maybe she had me in tow. That seems more accurate. Either way, Moe was with us. You're not supposed to have dogs in the Cheesecake Factory, but Fats doesn't do no and the employees were made to understand that. I was hoping nobody would remember me. They remembered real well and I was pretty sure that if someone had to sneeze it would be in my food. So I had to beg for forgiveness, promise fab tipping, and remind them that Fats and Moe behaved heroically at The City Museum. Moe bit the shooter's crotch, for crying out loud.

The crotch biting did it and we got seated. I was moderately confident that nobody phlegmed our food either time. After all that, I was done for the day, Stevie wasn't. He insisted on visiting friends in West County. They had his duffel bag. I know what you're thinking, 'cause I was thinking it, too. But there was nothing in that bag except dirty underwear, cheap toiletries, and Terry Pratchett paperbacks. It turned out Stevie read, but only Terry Pratchett. He was the only writer that could hold Stevie's attention.

Then with the smelly duffel, we went bowling and got pedicures. Prison had taught Stevie the value of foot care. Don't ask. I don't know. After all that, we went back to my apartment, ate again, and watched three *Die Hard* movies. It was the hardest babysitting job of my life.

Of course, it was my own fault. I decided with Stevie's agreement that he wouldn't go home until his head bandage came off and he got on meds. Stevie would've agreed to having a skunk stapled to his butt he was so happy about the job and didn't want to jeopardize it by causing a fuss, but that meant I had about forty-eight hours of Stevie total. It was exhausting. He got me up to play hearts at two in the morning. I never realized how little he slept or how little I would be sleeping while he was around.

I would've snoozed all day, but I had things to do. Regular things. Mercy things. So I rolled out of bed and poured myself into the shower with good intentions. They didn't last long. I was seriously considering laying down in the shower when someone came in the bathroom.

"Get out! I will kill you so hard you'll wish you'd never been released!" I yelled. If Stevie pulled back that curtain, so help me God.

"What the hell?" my boyfriend Chuck asked.

"Oh, it's you," I said.

"Who'd you think it was?"

"Stevie."

"Stevie's in prison. Are you okay?" he asked.

"He's on parole," I said.

The bathroom door opened and closed. I decided sleeping in the shower wasn't a good option and rinsed the conditioner out of my hair.

The door opened again and Chuck said, "What the hell is Stevie doing on our sofa?"

"You tell me," I said.

"No. You tell me. You put him there."

"I don't know what he's doing right now."

Chuck heaved a sigh. "Why are you causing me a problem? It's been a long damn night."

I peeked out from behind the shower curtain and saw my handsome cop boyfriend sitting on the toilet, lid down I'm happy to say.

"How's the case going?" I asked.

"Terrible. I think we got a connection between those two rapes."

"Rapes? I thought you were on that carjacking."

He put his head in his hands. "I was. That guy's mom turned him in so Sidney and I got the rapes."

"A connection is good."

"Yeah, but one happened in an alley. It has to be the worst, most contaminated crime scene I've ever worked. We've got blood and semen in multiple areas, not to mention spent casings, and a human finger. A finger!"

"Oh, my God. He cut off her finger?" My time babysitting was starting to sound better.

"No. It's not her finger and according to our victim he had all of his. We've got a random finger."

"I don't even know what to say," I said.

"Don't say anything. Just come out here and hug me."

I sniffed and I could smell it, even over the fruity soaps and shampoos I'd been using.

"Do you still have alley all over you?" I asked.

Chuck slumped. "You can smell that?"

"You didn't mention the vomit."

"There might've been vomit."

"And urine?"

Head back in hands.

"Did...someone throw it on you?" I asked, already knowing the answer.

"He didn't throw it. I was interviewing a transient and he decided to pee. Right then. Right there. The splatter got me."

"That was a terrible night." I whipped back the curtain and finished rinsing. "I'll get out and you can get in."

Nothing from the downtrodden detective.

"I'll make you some food and take that suit into the cleaners."

Still nothing.

"Do you want an omelet? Aaron says my omelets are no longer an insult to eggs," I said, turning off the water.

"Chuck?" I pulled back the curtain to find Chuck slumped over, his head propped against the wall and dead asleep. That's when I knew he was truly exhausted. He never misses a chance to watch me get out of the shower. It's one of his favorite things. It doesn't matter if I'm bloated or have a casted arm wrapped in plastic, he thinks it's sexy as hell. I don't get it, but there we are.

I grabbed my towel and dried off, watching to see if he'd take a peek. Nope. He was really out, so I dressed and got some gloves. One thing about nurses, we always have gloves and it's a good thing, too. Chuck's suit was gross. The stink of so many things was in it and that transient had terrible aim. Both pantlegs. Both shoes and socks. So gross.

"What are we doing?" Chuck asked as I eased his jacket off.

"You're getting in the shower and I'm bagging this stuff like it's evidence."

"I'll just go to bed."

"Take a shower or go to your apartment," I said, using my mother's tone that she used on my dad. He used to have to change in the basement if he had to sit in on an autopsy or something equally gross. If we had a basement, that's where Chuck would be.

"You're mean to me."

"Yep. Now get in the shower."

Somehow, he had the strength to waggle his brows at me. "You want to get in with me?"

"Tempting but no."

"Mean."

"I've got stuff to do," I said.

Chuck stripped the rest of the way and dropped his underwear in the garbage bag I held out to him before climbing in the shower. "What stuff?"

"I'm supposed to go into the attic today."

"Oh, yeah. Man, I wanted to do that," he said.

"You can meet me over there later," I said.

"Can't. I get four hours and then it's back on the finger and blood."

"Don't forget the rape."

"Not a chance," Chuck said. "We're all over it. It's looking like a pattern."

"Swell."

"I know. Just what this town needs. A serial rapist."

I blew dry my hair and slapped on some lip balm. "Well, let me know if you need anything."

"I'm just going to bed."

"No omelet?"

"What omelet?"

"I offered an omelet when you were on the toilet."

He laughed. "That makes us sound so classy."

"We're super classy. Everybody thinks so," I said.

He pulled back the curtain. "Nobody thinks that. The best we get is smelly cop and Marilyn Monroe."

"Could be worse," I said with hands on hips.

"How?"

"We could be running around missing a finger."

"It's not much of a bright side but I'll take it." He stuck his face farther out. "Kiss me or is my mouth too dirty."

"Always, but I'll chance it."

I kissed him and he said, "Take Stevie with you."

"Really? I won't be long," I said.

"Babe, I have got to sleep. There's no way he's going to let me do that."

I sighed. "Fine. I'll take him."

"He might be useful."

"Useful is something Stevie has never been."

"The Bled attic is huge. You could use a second pair of hands," he said, ducking back in.

"Are we sure we want to do this?" I asked.

"You must be kidding? The Girls said we could have anything we wanted up there. It's a flipping treasure trove."

"Is it though?"

"Mercy, our furniture is discount IKEA and hand me downs. They've got all kinds of stuff up there. A hundred years of no holds barred spending. Millicent said there were some beds and dressers. Bona fide antiques. We can't afford anything half as good."

"Fine, fine. I'll do it," I said.

"And you'll take Stevie?"

"I will take Stevie."

"About that omelet..."

"Stevie," I said as I walked into my living room through a warren of boxes. Chuck was halfway moved in and my apartment was in full disaster mode. The move into our apartment over the Bled garage/stables couldn't come fast enough, but the renovations that The Girls insisted on were taking forever.

"Stevie."

No response from the lump on my sofa and it was a big lump, too. Stevie was stretched out with Chuck's poodle Pickpocket sleeping on his chest and Skanky curled up next to his head, purring like a rusty buzzsaw. The animals were deeply in love with Stevie and the feeling was mutual. He played and brushed them, clipped toenails with no hissing or snapping, and played a rather raucous game of hide and go seek. I didn't know cats and dogs did hide and go seek, but they do when Stevie Warnock was leading the game and they were worn out after. If Stevie wasn't a felon, he'd be the world's best pet sitter.

"Hey, varmints, get up." I climbed over a box of Chuck's high school trophies and put my hands on my hips. "Up. Come on. Up."

Pick opened one eye, wagged twice, and went right back to sleep. I didn't even get that much from Skanky. He continued to purr. I was no longer consequential to my own cat. My feisty feline was usually full of love when I came home to feed him and provide scratches, but last night he showed me his hind end and cleaned Stevie's arm for one full *Die Hard*. I couldn't even get a meow and Pick, who was an attention whore, acted like I spit in his kibble. I'm not gonna lie, it hurt a little. I could've used some love after that day.

"Come on, Stevie." I poked him. "We have to go."

"No way. Sleeping."

"Get up."

"I'll hang out with Chuck."

"He's sleeping and he wants to be left alone," I said.

Stevie turned his head away. "He doesn't mean it."

"He does. You're going with me."

"Nah."

I was tempted just to book it out of there, but Chuck might not forgive such a betrayal. If I knew Stevie, he'd probably wake up five minutes after I left and be raring to go. He was just that perverse. But he, like my varmints, was food driven, so I went into the kitchen and got to work on the Aaron omelets. Aaron was my sometimes partner and full-time foodie. He bought me a De Buyer omelet pan, forced me to season it properly, and then gave me omelet lessons. I did not get a choice in the matter and I ate so many omelets during my training that I thought I'd never want another one, but like so many food-related aversions, I got over it. Mostly because Aaron left me to my own devices and I got to do things like put cheddar and ham in my omelet, something he considered pedestrian and beneath me. You'd think that as long as he'd been hanging out with me he'd know nothing is beneath Mercy Watts. Nothing.

I turned to latte making once the first omelet was going, cheddar and sausage; no fancy-pants herbs snipped with my herb shears. Yeah, I have those. Not my idea.

When I turned around who was standing at the breakfast bar salivating? Stevie. And Pick, but he's practically always juicy.

"Whatcha got there?" he asked.

"I thought you were sleeping."

"Now I'm hungry."

"Shocking," I said. "Get dressed. We're going to the Bled mansion."

He held up his arms like a toddler. "I'm dressed."

"Not in your I-just-got-out-of-prison clothes. Your new stuff."

"This is comfortable."

I gave him the stink eye, which he was impervious to.

"Do you have a sty?" he asked. "Your eye looks weird."

"I do not have a sty. Wear your new clothes. You're going to the doctor to hopefully get meds and therapy."

Stevie picked some curly black poodle hair off his not-so-white tee. "Maybe these clothes will help."

"How would they help?" I asked.

"I'll look more crazy."

"Trust me. That is not a problem."

"You sure?"

"Misty sent your records over to him. He knows you're plenty nuts," I said.

He did a fist pump. "Awesome."

I rolled my eyes and pointed at the Macy's bags piled up by my front windows. "Get on it."

He did, unfortunately. I made him a coffee, slid his omelet on a plate, and then looked up to see his naked bony butt in the middle of my living room.

"Stevie!" I yelled. Big mistake.

He turned around. "Huh?"

"Oh, God damn." I slapped a hand over my eyes. "I'm never gonna unsee that."

"Gimme a break. You've seen millions of wieners."

"I have not and I don't want to. Put some underwear and pants on."

"Such a prude."

"Yes, I'm a prude. Get dressed!"

Stevie laughed and told Skanky about how uptight I am. My disloyal cat yowed in agreement.

"I'm dressed," he said.

"Thank goodness." I put his breakfast on the breakfast bar and shuddered.

"Jeez. You would never make it in prison."

"You say that like it's a bad thing."

"With your track record, it is. You gotta end up in jail at least," said Stevie through a mouthful of omelet.

"Thanks."

"It's a fact."

"Not a fact. I don't traffic drugs," I said.

Stevie snorted. "Yeah, you do. I know all about Colorado."

"That was different. It was for a child in need."

He guzzled his coffee and said, "Keep telling yourself that."

I blew a raspberry at him and finished Chuck's omelet. "Will you feed the varmints while I feed the Chuck."

Stevie saluted me and I went back into the bedroom where Chuck had collapsed, still wet and wearing a towel, on the bed. "Hey. Wake up and eat this." I put the plate on his incredibly taut six-pack.

He sniffed. "What is it?"

"An omelet."

"What's in it?"

"Cheddar and sausage. I had some leftover andouille."

"I'm on a diet. You know that," Chuck said with consternation.

"Well, I'm over your diet. Stop eating weird crap and gassing me out of bed every night."

"I don't."

"You do."

"I have to get bulked up before I get too old," he said.

"Fine. It's a good thing we're having separate bedrooms in the new place."

I marched out to the sound of "Hey what did you say?"

Stevie looked up from giving Pick a bacon treat and asked, "So separate bedrooms, huh? I guess being that guy isn't everything."

"It's separate until he stops eating a dozen boiled eggs a day." I grabbed my coat and tossed Pick's leash to Stevie. "You ready?"

He put on a tailored black wool coat that I picked out with his mother Olivia in mind and clipped on Pick's leash. "My bags are packed. Where are we going?"

"Okay. If you want to convince your parents it's going to be different this time, lose the Wild Bill references," I said, going out into the hall.

"Are you sure? It's funny," he said.

"Nobody wants to think their kid is Wild Bill, especially a guy who just defended a similar douchebag."

"Did Dad get him off?"

"Off death row. Life in prison. No parole."

"Is that good?" Stevie asked.

"Depends on who you ask. The guy was one of the killers from the Kansas graveyard."

The Kansas serial killer graveyard was now so infamous, even Stevie didn't have to ask me what I was talking about. My connection to mass murderer Kent Blankenship had led the authorities to a plot of land where a group called Unsub buried their victims. Dozens of investigations came out of the site with more to come.

"Why did Dad do it?" Stevie asked. "Those guys should freaking die."

"Somebody had to. Defense counsel is required."

"Why him though?"

We went out the front door of my building into icy December air and watched as Pick had a sniff and a pee before heading down the street.

"Don't you know?" Stevie asked. "You gotta know."

"Big Steve was suggested because he's done so much death penalty work, but he did say no. Probably because I was involved and your mom was pretty freaked about it."

"She was always scared about those guys Dad defends. She hates it." Stevie stuck out an arm for me to hold onto when we passed over some ice.

"I know."

"So, why'd he do it?"

"The victims' families came to him and asked him to do it," I said.

"What the hell? Why?"

I slid around and clutched Stevie's arm. "There was a real fight about who was going to do it in the public defender's office. People quit over it. It was a ten-foot-pole kinda situation. So a couple of the parents came and asked Big Steve so it could get done quickly. Your dad is known for working fast and getting the best out of a bad situation."

"Like me," said Stevie softly. "He got me a great deal and I got paroled quick, too."

"It pays to have a great lawyer," I said. "In this case, Big Steve said the families had suffered enough and having to wait additional time was just another agony on top of more agony, so he did it."

"How long did it take?"

"Three weeks. He knocked it out quick, a deal the families could live with and info out of the guy."

"So, it's over," said Stevie.

"It's not over by a long shot."

Stevie stopped walking and turned to me. "You're out though, right?"

I shrugged. "I'm out as much as I can be."

"What does that mean?"

"It's going to go on for years, all the trials and stuff. Some of the perps won't do a deal."

"You're not going to do anything else though."

I laughed. "Not if I can help it. Why?"

"The guys, you know in prison, they talked about you and that Blankenship."

The pit in my stomach came back. "Oh yeah?"

"They think he's not done with you," said Stevie.

I started walking again as much for a distraction as a way to get somewhere. "Why's that?"

"People know people in the system. One of the guys has a brother in Hunt. He said Blankenship has a thing for you and he wants you back."

"Kent Blankenship is in solitary. He's locked down to only communication with his lawyer. That's it. Your friend's brother wouldn't know anything about what Blankenship wants."

Stevie's eyes were darting around and for a second I thought he'd lost the thread, but then he said, "He's not cut off, Mercy. Nobody's totally cut off. He's talking to somebody."

We turned onto Hawthorne Avenue and despite the beauty of the Christmas decorations, I felt like I couldn't see anything, even though it was right there shiny and joyful.

"If your source is at Hunt, he's criminally insane," I said after we passed a couple houses done up in their finest, tasteful best.

"That doesn't mean he's wrong," said Stevie.

"What did he do?"

"Rapist."

"And?"

"My guy was kinda weird about that," he said.

Imagine that. Weird about your brother locked up in Hunt.

"Did he tell you anything?" I asked.

"He wouldn't, but another guy..." Stevie started watching a pair of squirrels, dashing around an oak.

"Focus," I said. "What about this other guy?"

"Oh. Huh?"

"Hunt. Crazy brother. What did he do?"

"Yeah, yeah. James said he was a kind of cannibal, but not the bad kind," said Stevie and I have to say he said it with conviction.

"There's a good kind of cannibal?"

"He didn't eat other people."

I turned to the front of the Bled mansion and keyed in my code for the gate. "I'm not sure I want to know, but who did he eat?"

"James says he ate his own foot." Stevie said it like it was an everyday thing and didn't appear to be terribly shocked. I, for one. was nauseated and picturing it.

"Well, that'll do it," I said when we got to the door.

"That doesn't mean he doesn't know stuff."

"Stevie, the guy ate his own foot. I'm not taking his word for the weather."

I reached up to key my code into the front door pad, but Stevie grabbed my arm. "You got to be careful. There's a lot of weirdos out there."

There's at least one right here.

I pulled out a cord hidden under my sweater and coat. "I'm careful."

"What's that?"

"A panic button," I said.

"Cool." Stevie proceeded to push the button.

"Stevie!"

"It's a button. I got to push it."

"Oh, my God." I keyed us into the mansion and shoved Stevie through the door as my phone went berserk. "This is how you ended up in prison. Impulse!"

"Ya think?"

"Yes!"

Stevie got instantly distracted by a bench with Egyptian dogs' heads as armrest and started petting them. I unclipped Pick, who sprinted down the hall, his nails clicking on the hardwood. Then there was a frantic clicking followed by a thump. The dog never learned.

"Pickpocket, you silly dog!" called out Joy the housekeeper. "Mercy!"

"I'm here!"

"Have you been kidnapped?"

Holy crap! Is anyone not on the alert list?

"I have not been kidnapped!"

"Call your father!"

"On it!"

I called back the security company, both of The Girls, my dad, my mom, Uncle Morty, and Chuck, who'd been woken up to think I'd been kidnapped again.

"Are you sure you're okay?" he asked, panting.

"I'm fine."

"Why'd you push it?"

"Stevie pushed it, not me," I said.

"Why?"

"Do you really need to ask that?"

"Never mind."

I hung up and gave Stevie the stink eye again, but he just patted a dog head and said, "This is the coolest thing ever. Where'd they get it?"

"1922."

"Huh?"

"It's an antique," I said. "Come on, we're going up."

"To where?"

"The attic."

"What for?" he asked.

"I'm looking for stuff for my new apartment," I said, taking off my coat and then his. "You are going to write down a list of questions for the doctor." I handed him a little pad and pen."

"Do I have to?" he asked as I led the way up the long curved staircase.

"Yes, you have to be informed about the medication and everything." I started in about side effects and got up to the second floor before I realized Stevie wasn't behind me. He'd gotten distracted by the photos on the wall and I had to tromp back down to get him.

"Is that you?" he asked, pointing at a photo of a pig-tailed me having a snack on a grave.

"That's me. Come on."

"Why are you having lunch on a grave?"

"It's a long story," I said.

"I got time."

I grabbed his arm and dragged him up the stairs.

"Come on, tell me," said Stevie. "I'll remember."

"Whatever." We got up to the attic staircase, a set of double doors built into the woodwork and so well-hidden I passed them twice before I spotted the telltale cracks in the paneling.

"That's so cool," said Stevie. "Like Scooby-Doo."

I grinned. "It is. Kinda."

"Kinda? This house is rad." He dashed up the attic stairs and through an enormous spiderweb without hesitation. Better him than me. "Whoa! This is incredible." Stevie grinned down at me. "Come on. What's you waiting for?"

I climbed the stairs, cheered by his enthusiasm. Thoughts of Hunt Hospital were fading, but they wouldn't quite leave me. They never did, if I'm being honest. That place and Blankenship had gotten under my skin, just the way that evil bastard wanted. I'd never admit that though. Saying it out loud would only make it worse.

"Look at this." Stevie spun around on the landing of the attic, the only place that wasn't filled with stuff. The attic covered the entire house, except for the conservatories, so it was enormous. What it wasn't was tall. The attic height was only six foot. I'd forgotten about that. Chuck would be happy he didn't have to spend hours crouching over. Stevie and I had no issues though.

Light slanted in through the small windows on either end of the attic, but it didn't help much. I groped around for the light switch while Stevie oohed and aahed over the horde of treasures. He sounded like me when I was a kid. If The Girls wanted to entertain me for a few hours while they had meetings or hosted a tea, they'd put me in the attic. It sounds like a punishment, but it was a treat. The world's most interesting treasure hunt. Sometimes they would give me a goal. "Now Mercy dear, do go up and find Balthazar's broken walking stick. It's got a Saint Bernard's head on it." And off I'd go to find the walking stick and Victorian clothes, hoop skirts, piles of petticoats, games circa 1911, photos needing to go into albums, dress mannequins and books on everything from cooking to Egyptian mummification. Once I found a set of canopic jars tucked into the bottom drawer of a dilapidated dresser. They were complete, organs and seals intact. Nobody knew how a set of Egyptian artifacts from the Nineteenth Dynasty ended up there. Brina Bled, Elias the Odd's mother, had a keen interest in archeology and traveled to Egypt several times, so she probably had something to do with it. Another time, I discovered a set of ivory chopsticks wrapped in a silk kimono inside a broken vase. How'd that happen? Beats me. But they were now on loan to the Smithsonian as part of some Hong Kong exhibit.

I started working my way through the attic in search of a bedroom suite Myrtle was sure was up there.

Stevie stuck his head under a sheet and asked, "Why are we up here?"

"I told you. Furniture."

"Furniture for who?"

"Me. New apartment."

"I remember."

No, you don't.

"How about you write your questions for the doctor?" I asked.

"That's no fun." He pulled off the sheet and revealed a cracked full-length mirror in the Craftsman style. "You want this?"

"I wonder where that came from. The Bleds don't like Craftsman."

"Servant furniture?" he asked, and I gave him a second look.

"Maybe. That's a totally reasonable idea."

"I can have good ideas, ya know," said Stevie. I must've looked incredibly doubtful because he said with a big grin, "I just can't remember them."

"Dufus."

"At least I never ate my own foot," he said.

"Not much of a claim to fame, but yes, you are not a foot eater. Now, we're looking for an Art Nouveau bedroom suite. Fancy and expensive."

"What's it doing up here?" Stevie ducked behind a precarious pile of crates full of old records. I always meant to go through those. Probably some great stuff in there.

"The Girls' parents got it for their wedding, but they didn't like Art Nouveau, only Art Deco."

"I don't know what you're talking about, but it sounds nice."

I pulled a sheet off a group of boxes on top of a couple of steamer trunks. Who knew what was in there? Could be a mummy for all anyone knew.

"How come they don't just give you your furniture?" Stevie asked.

"My furniture?"

"You got a bedroom here, don't you?"

"I do, but it's not my furniture," I said.

"Whose is it?" he asked.

"It's part of the Bled Collection." I couldn't resist. I took down a crate of records and started going through it. Original Sinatras. Early recordings.

"I thought that was art and crap."

"And furniture. That furniture anyway. It's the only set in the collection."

Stevie opened a trunk and pulled a feather boa out. "Who are they collecting it for? You?"

"No. They're not actively collecting it. It was already collected during the war by Stella Bled Lawrence."

Stevie put on a top hat. "What do you think? Steven Tyler?"

I grinned at him. "Very Aerosmith."

"So what are they doing with the collection if they're not giving it to you?"

"Do you remember that picture of me on the grave downstairs?" I asked.

"Yeah. That was weird."

"It's about the collection. The Girls are trying to find the owners of the pieces. Graveyards hold clues, family names and stuff."

"So, they're trying to find the owner of your bedroom set. That stuff's old. Are they alive?"

"No, I'm sure they're dead," I said, thinking of the names so neatly printed on the label under my bed. Two parents. Four children. Gone.

"What happened to them?"

"The Holocaust happened to them." I got another crate down and found to my joy a crate of Billie Holiday albums. "Do you like Billie Holiday? I think this crate has every one of her albums. I wonder why they put them up here."

Stevie didn't answer and I looked up from Billie to find him gazing off into space. That wasn't unusual, but his expression was. Sad. Stevie was never sad. My mom always said he had a happy soul despite everything he did to himself.

"What?"

"What you said about my grandparents, was that true?"

"Absolutely. I wouldn't lie to you," I said.

"Is some of their stuff in the Bled Collection?" he asked.

"No." I explained about Stella and how she smuggled people's art, jewelry, and precious possessions out of Germany, France, and other countries. We were trying to find the relatives of those people so we could give the belongings back.

"How did you find out about my grandma?" he asked.

"Start writing down your questions and I'll tell you." A little bribery goes a long way and Stevie sat down on a rocking chair missing a spindle and poised a pen over the little notepad. He didn't write much, but he did give the appearance of listening.

I told him how Stella's father went to Switzerland after the war and got Constanza out of hospital after she left Auschwitz. Then I showed him the pictures on my phone of Big Steve's mother that he had and the one we'd found from Bickford House in England. Then I told him how Constanza sold some belongings in 1947 and that was how she funded her life in America.

"That's it?" he asked. "That's all you know about her?"

"We're working on it," I said. "Are you upset?"

"I think so. I don't know. It's weird. Like all the sudden I have a family I didn't know about. Dad doesn't talk about them. He never says anything about when he was a kid."

"It wasn't easy."

He nodded. "I don't know. I don't know anything."

"You know this is your grandmother." I showed him the picture on my phone again and Stevie frowned.

"What?" I asked.

"She seems kinda familiar, but I never saw that picture before. Maybe I did and I don't remember. I don't know." He went off and quietly began looking through the attic, lost in his thoughts. I went back to looking for the bedroom set. After an hour, I came up with a dresser and a side table, definitely Art Nouveau, all flowing lines with flowers and inlaid glass. Stevie made his list of questions that were completely unreadable and found five trunks of random uniforms. They could've been dress uniforms or maybe some weird elevator operator wore them. I had no idea.

"Did you see these paintings?" he called out from the far corner next to the left conservatory. I'd never made it that far in my childhood explorations.

"What is it?"

"Paintings."

"Really?"

"Is that collection stuff up here?"

"I don't think so." I climbed over boxes of old dishes and squeezed past a collection of spinning wheels to find Stevie standing in front of a stack of canvases of all sizes. Some were taller than both of us and a few were the size of Stevie's hand, but only a couple were finished. They were rather beautiful in their way, flowers intertwined with nudes or nudes as part of a building. Then there was a child in some, a tiny little hand here or a newborn's smile there. Some of the paintings gave off an angry and isolated feeling. Others were gorgeous with passion and adoration. A man's face was repeated several times, but his features were muted like they were a distant memory that couldn't quite be accessed.

"Are they any good?" Stevie asked.

"I don't know. I think so. Kind of," I said. "They aren't by anyone I recognize, but I'm not an art historian."

"Do you know any art historians?"

"I do actually." I took pictures of the finished canvases and Stevie pointed out the corner of the biggest canvas. It'd been slashed and stabbed. It might've been signed there, but the signature was gone.

"I like these," said Stevie.

"Me, too. Why do you like them?"

"I can't stop looking at them."

"That's as good a reason as any."

Stevie cocked his head to the side. "Pick's coming."

Sure enough. Toenails clicking away. I was used to hearing that sound, but for some reason, I got a feeling, a bad feeling. Something was about to be a pain in my butt. I covered the canvases with a sheet and turned to face whatever was coming up the attic stairs.

CHAPTER THREE

I knew who it was before they got to the top of the stairs. The creaking gave it away. My cousin Tiny Plaskett made stairs suffer like no one else. At six six and three hundred pounds, a small man he was not. Tiny was also one of my favorite people but not on that day.

Tiny's footsteps slowed and he emerged only to the point that I could see his dark eyes over a box of dress patterns. I stared at him and he at me. Not a good sign.

"So you coming up or what?"

"Yeah." Tiny watched me for a second and then sighed before trudging up the final few stairs.

"Hey," called out Stevie. "Did you come to help?"

"Get real," I said. "My dad sent him or forced him to come is more like."

Tiny smoothed his tie and glanced away. Yep. I was dead on.

"How do you know?" Stevie asked.

"Look at that handsome face. He does not want to be here," I said. "Spill it, Gigantor."

Tiny crossed his arms and his biceps bulged so much I feared for his seams. "So now I'm a robot."

"I meant that you're huge and fighting crime."

Tiny wrinkled his nose. "I forgive you."

"Swell. Will I be forgiving you?" I asked.

"Don't kill the messenger."

"So that's a no." I crossed my arms and my cousin came into the attic. He began looking around, stalling.

"Go ahead," I said. "What does he want?"

"Who?" Stevie asked.

"My dad."

"Oh, yeah. Ya know, I used to think your dad was better than mine."

"What do you think now?" I asked.

"It depends on what you got to do," said Stevie."

I turned to Tiny, who'd discovered the Sinatra albums. "Just tell me."

"He wants you at the house," said Tiny.

"Now?"

"Right now."

"Is my mother there?"

Tiny grimaced and said, "She's at her speech therapy with Tenne."

"That's what I thought," I said. "So what is it? Tailing a suspect? Pointless paperwork? Find the dingbat lover of an idiot husband?"

"None of the above," he said. "It's an interview."

"So that's a hard no. Tell my loving father to stick it."

"I'm not gonna do that. Come on, Mercy. Just go. You know you're gonna go."

"Give me one good reason I should do it," I said.

"You'll make my life easier."

"Low blow."

He grinned at me. "Thanks."

"Still not going."

"Alright. I'm authorized to carry you, drag you, whatever I got to do."

"Are you kidding?" I asked.

"Nope. You're goin'."

"Tell me what it's about then. I deserve that at least."

Tiny considered it and I was pretty sure Dad had told him not to tell me, which didn't bode well. Dad knew me. It was something I was not going to agree to.

"He's got a couple of FBI agents over there," he said.

I relaxed. "Is that all?"

"That ain't all."

"Gordan and Gansa? The rookies?"

"New agents," said Tiny.

"From the Kansas investigation?" I asked.

"Kinda."

"Just tell me. I'm going to find out."

Tiny bit his generous lower lip.

"How about this? I'm definitely not going if you don't tell me what I'm walking into without my mom's backup. I'm supposed to be resting. That's why I'm not in Germany right now," I said.

Tiny bowed to the inevitable and told me that two female agents were parked in my parents' kitchen. They were from the Behavioral Science crew and were there to interview me, but the way Tiny described them, it sounded more like they wanted to study me. I knew from experience that whenever anyone wanted to find out how I did what I did, it wasn't a compliment to my skill. It was an investigation into how a moron like me got lucky.

"Why would I want to do this?" I asked.

Tiny shrugged his broad shoulders. "It's for the family."

"Not you, too." I pointed at Stevie. "That's for the family. I'm already on family stuff."

Stevie stared at us blankly. "Huh? What?"

"Tommy said you wouldn't go if he asked you," said Tiny.

"No kidding," I said. "He might be over the FBI's bullshit when Mom was attacked, but I'm not. They can bite my butt. I knew he was up to something with that whole 'Relax, Mercy,' 'Take it easy, baby girl' and I still fell for it. I'm the idiot in this attic."

Stevie did a fist pump. "Yes. It's not me."

Tiny and I rolled our eyes in unison. We might be distant cousins, but we were a lot alike. Dad should've known Tiny would tell me what was up. Deep down, my cousin was on my side no matter who signed the paycheck.

"What are you doing with Stevie?" Tiny asked.

"I'm getting him straightened out before his mother sees him and hey, hey, hey I've got to take him to the doctor so darn it all, I can't go see the FBI agents. So sorry. Buh-bye."

"Don't make me haul your little ass over there," said Tiny.

"Little?"

"Yeah."

"You're a liar, but I like you," I said.

"Who wants a small ass?" he asked.

"I'd like to try it out and by the way, you have not won me over. I do have to go to the doctor with Stevie."

"What's wrong with him?" Tiny eyed my charge as he opened a trunk and put a woman's gold turban on top of the top hat and added another boa to the collection around his neck.

"ADD for starters," I said.

"I was thinking traumatic brain injury," said Tiny.

"It's on the menu. We'll see."

We looked back at Stevie just in time to see him lick a crusty silver fork.

"That's ADD?"

"I have my doubts," I said.

Tiny went over and whipped the hats off Stevie's head. "Stop that. You look crazy."

"I'm not crazy and my head is cold," said Stevie.

"What the hell happened to the back of your head?" Tiny asked.

"I got a tattoo."

"On the back of your head the day you got out of prison?"

"It was a swastika. Now it's flowers."

Tiny looked at me and I shrugged. "That was my day yesterday and you still want me to do the FBI thing?"

"You got to."

"You want to take *that* to the doctor and explain the head?" I asked.

Tiny looked at the rafters. "I don't get paid enough for this."

"You get paid plenty. You make a hell of a lot more than me and you're the new head of stuff and things."

"I'll put that on my card. Department head. Stuff and Things."

"Seriously, the Head of Genetic Research and Related Crime is a big deal," I said.

"And I like it. That genealogy stuff is fascinating."

Tiny had been thrown into the quagmire of DNA during the Thooft investigation when we found out about the baby adoption scam that a certain doctor had going in St. Sebastian. We were overrun by people wanting to know who they really were and where they came from. Dad put Tiny in charge and he was working fourteen-hour days, working his way through birth certificates, DNA profiles, and family trees, but he'd found a passion for it.

"Aunt Willasteen is very proud of you," I said. Willasteen was Tiny's imperious aunt and the only person as scary as my Aunt Miriam. Those two weren't related, but they seemed like they were.

"You told her?" Tiny asked.

"She told me."

"How'd she know?"

"How does she know anything? She's Willasteen."

"Good point. Do we have a deal?" Tiny asked.

"You're going to take Stevie to the doctor? Really?"

Tiny heaved a huge sigh that sounded like enormous fireplace bellows. "Why not? I can work while I'm there." He checked his phone. "I've got thirty-two emails to return and sixteen phone calls."

"Holy crap. I'd rather deal with the agents."

He shooed me to the stairs. "Good. Get 'er done."

I gave him the doctor's details and told him, "Just so you know I'm not doing what those agents want."

"I know," he said with a chuckle. "And I told Tommy that. But he doesn't believe me. He thinks he can get you in a tight spot."

"I'm great at getting out of tight spots."

My cousin grinned at me. "Yes, you are. Watch out, Tommy. Mercy's gonna bring it."

I was and I did.

I went in the front door of my parents' house, avoiding the side alley. I still wasn't recovered from Mom's attack that happened there. My therapist said it would fade with time and it was but not fast enough. For now, it was safer to go in the front.

"Tiny!" Dad yelled from the back of the house. "You got her?"

"I've got myself!" I yelled back and tossed my coat on the bench in the receiving room before I strolled back to the kitchen. I didn't have a plan. When do I ever? But I didn't need one. I wasn't doing it. Period.

Sitting at the kitchen table were two women, looking both snotty and irritated. I guess waiting wasn't their usual thing. Or maybe it was waiting for me that was the problem. I did have a rep for being difficult. Well deserved, I'm happy to say.

Dad grinned at me from the espresso machine and asked, "Latte?"

"Absolutely."

Dad pressed a button and leaned on the counter, looking just as gangly and goofy as a man could get. I caught the agents giving him sidelong glances. They knew all about Tommy Watts. Who didn't? He'd been a famous police detective before they were born and despite his recent much ballyhooed breakdown had come back into the FBI fold with a vengeance, thanks to me. I'd worked a deal that got my dad back in and it was like he never left, but I could tell they were having a hard time relating the reputation with the man grinning at them with his graying red hair sticking up and two day's worth of scraggly beard on his chin. I did, too. My father's appearance did not belie his mind or ability in any way.

"Here you go, baby girl." Dad gave me a lovely latte. "I take it you know why you're here."

"I do," I said.

"But you came."

"I did."

Dad took that as a sign of cooperation. It was not.

"This is Agent Kelly Ladd and Agent Katerina Owens."

They showed me their badges. Whatever. Do not care and not impressed.

I sipped my latte and calmly eyed them over the rim of my cup.

"We're here to interview you about your recent interactions with various criminal elements," said Ladd as she tucked her dishwater blond hair behind her ears.

I said nothing and they seemed surprised.

Then Owens started in and she spoke slower than Ladd. Maybe I was as dumb as I looked. Maybe I just didn't get it. "We are from Behavioral Science and we will be working up in-depth profiles of the criminals you've had contact with."

"Good luck with that," I said.

Ladd put her phone on the table and started recording. "To start, please, state your name and tell us why you think you have been so attractive to criminals."

I'm attractive to criminals? What does that even mean and is it really about what I think?

I didn't respond and Dad came over and clicked off the recording to Ladd's surprise. "My daughter is attractive to most people and what she thinks about her attractiveness is not relevant to this discussion."

Ladd and Owens regrouped and went into telling me what they were after. In short, everything about me that worked for criminals. How did I talk? Smile? They thought I worked it somehow and that meant it could be replicated. The whole thing was insulting. As far as I could tell, they thought I was a flirt and my success with solving crimes was really about sexuality. They should've been as insulted as I was. The FBI sent two very attractive agents to learn how to turn on psychos. That was their value.

"So you want to talk to Blankenship and he won't see you. Is that it?"

Both agents froze and a smile flickered across my dad's face. The whole pointless exercise was worth it just for that. "I told them you were sharp," he said.

"And they didn't believe you," I said.

"Seeing is believing."

"I'm not interested in being studied or used," I said. "If you want in with that bag of crap, figure it out. See ya, Dad."

Dad's pleasant expression switched off and we were back to Dad, Demander in Chief. "Mercy, you need to do this."

"*Need* is such an overused term. I don't need this, Dad."

Ladd leaned forward. "The bureau needs this."

"And that's supposed to move me? I don't think so and I'm not going back in to see Blankenship. I'm simply not."

"We didn't—" started Owens.

"You didn't have to. That's always next. You couldn't get in so you want me to do it. Sweet talk him. Intro you. Heads up. He can't be sweet-talked. He doesn't give a crap."

"You can tell us how you survived—"

"When I clearly shouldn't have," I said. "I know. You don't get it. I've had no formal training. I look like I look so I must be a drug-addled nitwit like they say on the news." I stood up and put my cup down.

"Mercy, they're not giving you an attitude," said Dad.

"They are. You see it. You just don't care."

"I care. We just have to—"

"What? Go in with Blankenship one more time? No thanks. Been there. Done that to freaking death."

"How about Shill?" Ladd asked.

"Will you go in with him?" Owens asked.

"You go in with that sleaze. I just got him washed off."

The agents clenched their jaws and I threw up my hands. "Are you kidding me? He won't talk to you, either?"

Dad put a hand on my shoulder. "He won't talk to anyone, including his lawyer."

"Don't say it," I said.

"He's asking for you."

"Son of a bitch."

"He says he will only talk about the murder of Cassidy Huff with you," said Ladd.

"Why?" Back to yelling. It was a wonder I wasn't hoarse yet.

"We don't know and we have to figure it out," said Owens.

"And your plan is to toss me in there and see what happens?" I asked all screechy.

"We have to start somewhere."

I glared at them. "Then you're going nowhere." I turned around and stalked out. It was worse than I thought. Studying me was bad enough. Studying me under glass with Blankenship and Brian Shill was another matter.

Dad chased me down the hall to the front door. "Mercy, God damn it! Stop!"

"Leave me alone," I said, yanking on my coat.

"It's for the greater good."

"Not my greater good. That's why Mom isn't here. She'd beat you to death with a rock if she was."

"She'd understand that we have to do these things to learn and get better."

"You mean *I* have to do these things," I spat at him.

"You're the one they want," he said. "If the FBI can learn something from you, then we have an obligation to cooperate."

"We? Give me a break."

Dad adopted a soothing tone and said, "You'll be getting a nice consultant fee. Think of the publicity."

"Do you know me at all? I hate publicity," I said.

"You'd never know it."

"I'm not doing it."

"Why not? You've got nothing else going on," said Dad.

"So much for resting," I said.

"Resting." Dad snorted. "You don't need to rest. You can do this."

"What would you tell Mom?"

Dad crossed his skinny arms and the look I was so familiar with came over his face. The sneaky bastard. "Nothing. You're resting like we said. She doesn't watch you like a hawk and Christmastime is busy. You're busy."

"Busy resting?"

"Whatever. It's fine."

"And you think I should do Christmas by going to Hunt Hospital for the Criminally Insane and talk to someone who bit me on the face?"

"That won't happen again," he said with utmost confidence. He probably believed it. My dad had a very selective thought process.

"You said the same thing about my first stalker, not to mention everything else that's happened," I said.

"It's for the family."

"You always say that, too."

"Well, it is. We're rebuilding a brand here and helping society at the same time. It's a good thing," said Dad.

"I'm not doing it and you can't make me."

"You sound like a child."

"Your child. Try to remember that for a change."

The front door opened and Leo Frame walked in, carrying a laptop and a bunch of case files. "Hey. Oh, what's happening here?"

"My father's trying to pimp me out to the FBI," I said.

"Jesus, Mercy," said Dad.

"I'm not doing it."

"Why not? Give me one good reason."

"I don't want to."

Dad straightened up and said, "That is not a valid reason. The agents and I will pick you up at eight sharp tomorrow morning for Hunt. End of discussion."

Unbelievable. Did he hear anything I said?

"No."

Dad spun around and headed back to the kitchen. "Don't forget the dinner at Uncle George's tonight. It's not negotiable."

Just like my whole life.

Leo put down his stuff and slipped off his jacket, his old weathered face warm with concern that my own father had rarely shown. "So that went well."

"It did not," I said. "He doesn't listen."

"Your father has a focus that's hard to deny," said Leo.

"I'm denying it."

"Maybe it won't be so bad this time."

"I've heard that before," I said.

Leo hugged me and said, “I know and I hope it’s true.”

“I’m not doing it.”

“Better find an escape route then and fast,” he said.

I zipped up my jacket. “I already have one.”

“Oh, yeah?”

“Germany, here I come.”

CHAPTER FOUR

I drove to Uncle George's house that night with Chuck snoring on the passenger side. How and why he decided to come was a mystery. I would gladly have ditched it, but my mother called me twice to remind me. I didn't have the heart to say I wanted to wring Dad's neck and why, so I complied.

It was fine, really. I would be out of the country in the morning. I hoped anyway. Flights were booked, but I talked to the Bled travel office and Petra said she'd work her magic if she was allowed. I told her I had tons of frequent flyer miles and I'd take anything. The jump seat, if necessary.

Petra gave The Girls a call and got the green light to use the corporate pull. I told them what Dad was up to and Millicent said they'd stay mum until after I left. Now all I needed was a seat. Just one. I was going it alone for the first time. It was kind of a thrill. I never went anywhere alone and not for lack of trying. I'd literally never been on an airplane alone. Not very adult, but that was all about to change.

I parked in front of what my mom privately called the beige bungalow. It was humongous and done in what Aunt Christine called shades of sand. It was beige. All beige. Inside and out, furniture included. I sat there, looking up at the house that our house could fit neatly inside and tried to figure out how I was going to avoid Dad for the next two hours. He wanted to talk. He'd called me four times since I'd left the house and that was the tipping point. Two was okay. Maybe three. But four? No, he'd had an idea. A normal father would see if I was okay. Was I upset or something? Tommy Watts had moved on. He left messages about my schedule for every day up until Christmas, including Christmas Eve. The man had a plan and I didn't call him back.

"Chuck."

"Five more." Chuck snuggled into the passenger door and blew out a deep breath.

"We're here."

"Where?"

"Uncle George's," I said.

"Oh, my God, why?"

"Dinner. You didn't have to come."

He straightened up and yawned. "Yeah, I did. We're a thing."

"Like me and Stevie," I said with a laugh.

That woke him up. "What?"

"Stevie says we have a thing."

"He's cracked."

"Less cracked than you'd think. Average IQ," I said.

"Must be the low end of average. I once caught him trying to ride a push lawnmower. He couldn't figure out why it wasn't moving."

"He's been tested. It's ADD, severe apparently."

"Where is he? Tell me he's not in the apartment," said Chuck.

"One more night."

He groaned.

"We're giving him his first med in the morning and Tiny agreed to take him home," I said.

"Tiny?"

Uh-oh.

I got out quickly and said, "Come on. Time's a-wasting."

Chuck jumped out of the car and chased me up the walk. "Why aren't you taking him?"

"Tiny offered."

"No, he didn't. Tiny is a department head now and the man is busier than a one-legged man in an ass-kicking contest."

"Have you been spending time with Grandad again?" I asked.

"Don't change the subject, Mercy."

"I'm not taking him. I don't want to take him." I rang the doorbell and prayed Aunt Christine would answer. She was the easiest person in my family to deal with. She didn't pry and she liked that I was a nurse. She'd been an RN when she met Uncle George but gave it up to build their medical supply company.

Please. Please.

The door flew open and there stood my cousins, the Troublesome Trio, Weepy, Snot, and Spoiled Rotten. They were gorgeous, tall and slender with the Watts red hair and blue eyes, the better side of the family tree. The side that got things right and never had nutcases obsessed with them. The side that never had to diet because they didn't really like to eat and working at their father's company, which they had all done and Jilly still did, entailed accounting, not criminals.

They stood there looking at me, posed in coordinated winter white outfits and looking like they were being shot for Vogue. Why did I wear a puffer coat and a baggy sweater, leggings, and snow boots? What was I thinking?

Sorcha dapped her eyes. "Oh, Mercy. Where have you been? You look terrible. Are you sick? We thought you got lost. Oliver couldn't come. I miss him so much." Weepy spun around and started dialing. "I have to call him. It's Christmas."

Bridget, aka Snot, turned up her nose at me. "What are you wearing?"

"Did you bring a hostess gift?" asked Jilly.

"She doesn't need a hostess gift," said Sorcha over her shoulder. "We're family."

"I think she should bring a gift."

"You just want a gift."

"It's Christmas."

"Talk to Oliver."

"He didn't answer."

"You're driving him crazy."

"It's appropriate to bring a gift."

"This was supposed to be a nice dinner. You couldn't wear a skirt?"

I turned around and headed back to the car. Chuck chased me down. "Where do you think you're going?"

"Anywhere."

"Mercy!" Aunt Christine called out.

Then there was a spirited discussion about what was wrong with me, the late, gift less, underdressed cousin.

Chuck turned me around. "If I can do it, you can do it."

"They love you."

He grinned at me. "Naturally."

"Here they come."

The Troublesome Trio came out and took Chuck over and I had a serious moment of envy and not just for the skinny thighs and dislike of brie. As much as my cousins fought and complained, they did it together. I was left on the walk, the only egg in Tommy Watts' basket and he was watching me from the living room window, ready to pounce. If I had siblings, it would be better. We could share Dad and gang up on him the way the trio was on Chuck. I followed him into the house and watched them strip off his jacket and scarf, get him a drink that they thought he should have, and start feeding him things they wanted him to eat. It was like a circus act and so well done, Chuck didn't know what hit him. He didn't even like sushi, but he was eating it.

"Mercy." Aunt Christine took my coat off. "I'm so glad you're here."

"Yeah?"

"Of course. Did you hear about Sorcha?" She took me into the living room and got me a Manhattan. I don't know why. I'd never had one before.

"What's up with Sorcha?"

"We think Oliver is going to propose."

No. Don't say it.

"Interesting. I need the bathroom. Gotta poop."

Aunt Christine ignored that and said, "And you did such a good job as Bridget's Maid of Honor," she raised her glass to Bridget's newly minted husband on the sofa, "that we think you should do it again with Sorcha."

Ah, yes, the wedding weekend from hell. Let's do that again.

"We'll see."

Aunt Christine gave me a big hug. "So glad you're on board. The way you handled that caterer when he threw up on the amuse bouche and flower thing and Bridget's dress. I didn't know you could sew."

Neither did I.

"I need to...something," I said, looking around for an escape route. Why couldn't there have been a flight tonight before dinner?

"Are you alright, dear?" she asked. "You look a little clammy."

If I throw up, I can leave. Think spoiled crab. Think spoiled crab.

"If I could just go to the bathroom—"

"Hello, sweetheart." Dad came over and wrapped a bony arm around my shoulder. "I just need to steal my daughter for a minute."

"Of course. Dinner in just a few," said Aunt Christine, beaming at me.

"You don't need to steal me." I ducked under Dad's arm and ran right into Sorcha.

"Did Mom tell you?" she asked. "I think it's going to happen on Christmas or Christmas Eve. What do you think about bridesmaid dresses with stripes? It's very in and full skirts. No columns. We should take another girls' trip."

Jilly grabbed me. "I think Las Vegas. It's so cliché it's cool."

"I think we want something totally different this time," said Bridget. "A beach. Break out the bikinis."

I'd rather let Blankenship bite me again.

"We can talk about it later." I tried to slip away, but there was Dad, waiting like some kinda skinny vulture, so I turned around and dashed into the front room, but there was Grandad with my uncles. He had his broken ankle propped up on a stool and a stack of case files. He wasn't supposed to have those, but there they were. Grandad was my dad thirty years on.

"Mercy!" Grandad called out. "Your dad wants me to talk to you."

"Busy. Talk later." I turned around and bumped into Mom.

"What are you doing?" she asked. "Come in and talk to Aunt Celeste and Uncle Joe."

"I don't feel good," I blurted out.

She touched my forehead. "You don't feel warm. Did you and your dad have a talk today? He says you want to work, but you must listen to me. You need to rest."

Seriously, Dad?

"Don't worry about it. I'm just going to go get an...antacid," I said.

"It's not your head?" Mom asked.

"Head's good."

"I'm still worried about that chemical and those headaches."

"It's better."

"Really?"

I hugged Mom and said, "Just going to the bathroom. Totally fine."

"Mercy," called out Dad, but I darted away toward the front of the house. I bypassed the stairs and trotted down the hall to the kitchen. Chocolate. Aunt Christine always had a chocolate stash. She let me in on the secret a few years ago during a similar crisis. The green tea tin sitting on the counter was filled with chocolate. Nobody in her part of the family liked green tea, but they loved chocolate, so she had her own hidden stash. She couldn't keep it in supply otherwise. The red-headed Watts might not like to eat, but they couldn't resist chocolate.

I burst through the kitchen door and stopped midway to the green tea tin. "I knew something smelled good."

My partner Aaron stood at Aunt Christine's six-burner Viking with all the burners going and both ovens, too. The little weirdo didn't turn around. He held out a tasting spoon and I obediently came over to take it.

"That is fabulous." I licked my lips. "Béchamel? But it kinda tastes like...champagne."

Aaron looked at me, well, he looked to the left of me and asked, "You hungry?"

"More than I can express," I said.

He picked up a little pot and poured me a thick hot chocolate and added a dashed of spiced rum.

I took a sip and put my forehead on his low, rounded shoulder. "Thanks. I really needed that."

The kitchen door creaked and I groaned inwardly. That was the shortest reprieve ever.

"There you are," said Chuck.

"Oh, it's you."

"Don't sound so excited."

"I'm excited that you're not anybody else," I said.

Chuck came in and leaned over the stove. "Thank God you're cooking."

Aaron nodded and bumped him out of the way and we both retreated to let him work his magic. I was more than grateful for it. Aunt Christine was great but not a cook. Aaron needed to give her lessons, but I don't think it was her fault. She had four people who didn't like to eat. It's hard to get good at something when nobody cares.

"So," said Chuck, "I gotta ask you something."

Swell.

"Go ahead," I said.

"I think Jilly might have a thing for me."

"That's not a question."

"She was, ya know, talking about my abs and stuff," he said with his forehead creasing. "Do you think she does?"

"Every woman I know has a thing for you," I said.

Chuck puffed up and started checking his biceps. "It's the new muscle mass."

There's no new muscle mass.

"They've always had a thing for you. Women. All of them."

"The eggs are working. I'm going to eat more eggs."

I slapped his shoulder. "You're getting perilously close to me *not* having a thing for you."

His eyebrows shot up and he asked in all seriousness, "Why? I look great. My plan is working."

"First, egg farts. I'm not a fan. Second, my boyfriend going on an extreme diet to attract other women is not a winning strategy," I said.

"I'm dating you. I have to look good," he said.

"And smell bad."

"It's fine."

"Perfect. Keep with the eggs and green smoothies and what all and the idea of separate bedrooms will become a reality," I said.

"I don't like that," said Chuck.

"I don't like—"

My father's voice rang out in the hall, "Has anyone seen Mercy?"

I jumped behind the kitchen door a split second before it opened.

"Hey, Chuck," said Dad. "What are you doing in here?"

"Um...talking to Aaron about...steak," said Chuck.

"Are we having steak?"

"Maybe."

"Oh, well," said Dad, "have you seen Mercy?"

I put my finger to my lips and Chuck said, "Not lately. Why?"

"I've got to talk to her about the plan."

"Plan? What plan?"

Dad lowered his voice. "This is just between you and me."

"Okay," said Chuck.

Dad went on to say that there'd been a development in Clinton State Prison in New York. Ben Solomon, a serial killer from the seventies, may have had contact with Brian Shill and had mentioned me in a letter to his court-appointed lawyer.

"So what?" Chuck asked. "Mercy's big in prisons."

Did everyone know that except me?

"She is," said Dad. "But this guy never gave the locations of his victims."

"How'd they get him?"

"The body of his seventh victim was in his trunk when he was pulled over for speeding. Officer smelled it. A search of his cabin turned up trophies from four missing women and two men."

"What do you expect Mercy to do about it?" Chuck asked.

"Ladd and Owens are here to interview her and we're going to Hunt tomorrow," said Dad.

"Who's going to Hunt?"

"The four of us. Blankenship has agreed to see Mercy again."

Chuck frowned and crossed his arms. "I bet he has."

"Don't give me that look," said Dad. "You know we need this. He has information on the other burial locations and he won't talk to anyone but her."

"You think Blankenship has info on Solomon?"

"Unrelated. We're booked on a flight to New York on Friday."

"So the plan is to throw Mercy in with Blankenship and this asshole Solomon? She has a head injury, Tommy. She's recovering."

Dad snorted. "Head injury? Please. She's fine and this is big. Those six families have been waiting since 1974. This is an *in*. We have to take it."

"What about Mercy?" Chuck asked.

"You think my daughter doesn't want to solve murders? She broke the Kansas case. Why do you think Ladd and Owens are here. Sightseeing? They're here for her. Mercy's a key. We have to use it. She's flipping great with the crapbags. The taskforce is getting nowhere with the Kansas suspects we've got in custody. We have to do something."

"I know that. It's frustrating," said Chuck.

"Glad you're on board," said Dad. "Now don't tell Carolina about this. She doesn't need to know."

"She's going to notice Mercy's gone on Friday."

"The official story is we're going to Quantico for a tour."

Chuck rolled his eyes. "Come on. Carolina's not going to buy that."

"She will if you back it up."

"Where does she think you're going tomorrow?" Chuck asked.

"Shopping."

"That'll work," Chuck said sarcastically.

I guess my dad missed the tone. He just said, "Great. I'm going to find Mercy. She's a little skittish, but don't worry, I'll talk her down."

"Sure."

The door closed and I said, "I'm not doing it."

"I don't want you to."

My eyes filled up. "Really?"

"I never want you in with Blankenship ever again," he said. "And Solomon, screw that guy. He probably just wants an eyeful of you."

"There is the possibility that I could get something," I said.

"I know. But this is just...I met Ladd and Owen."

"Not a fan?"

"They're good, but they don't think you are. I say screw 'em until they get a clue," he said. "But the problem is what to do. Tommy won't stop and he does have a point. I don't know how to get you out of it."

"I do. I'm leaving for Germany in the morning," I said, ready for a fight.

"That's supposed to be after Christmas."

"Not anymore. If I'm in Germany, I can't be in Hunt. Besides, I've been hired to do that job and I actually want to do it."

"You do still have a head injury and a broken arm," he said.

"I've dealt with worse," I said.

"I can't go with you."

"Nobody's asking you to."

Chuck came over and hugged me. "You can't go alone. Even if you weren't a little iffy health-wise, I still think The Klinefeld Group is behind Thooft and your kidnapping."

"And I don't. It's somebody else."

"They could be worse," he said.

"I don't think so. Blackmailing a teacher to do the dirty work? Nope. No way."

"Can Fats do it?" he asked. "She's dying to go to Europe."

"No. She's a lot better with the morning sickness, but she's weak."

"Fats weak? That still makes her stronger than me."

"I'm not going to ask and Tiny wouldn't want me to." I looked past Chuck's shoulder. "Hey, Aaron. Want to go to Germany tomorrow?"

Aaron gave me a thumbs-up and kept on cooking.

"Mercy, I love Aaron, but he's not enough with you at half speed. Maybe I can do it. I've got time off coming to me."

"You're on a serial rapist. That's important."

"Not more important than you," he said.

My eyes filled up and tears rolled down my cheeks. I didn't know how long I'd been waiting to hear that until I did.

"Why are you looking at me like that?" Chuck asked.

"I think I might want to marry you someday."

"Might?"

I laughed and wiped my cheeks. "Maybe, if you quit the eggs."

"My future happiness hinges on eggs," he said. "Who'd have thought it. But in all seriousness, Aaron's not enough. He'll run off and make schnitzel or something. No offense, Aaron."

Aaron shrugged. It was true. Aaron would stick with me to a point and he'd been great in the past, but food would lure him away.

"I'll be fine. I think I can take the cast off and my head's good."

"You still get blurry. I'm not taking any chances. I'll call my captain."

"I'll do it," said a voice from the breakfast room and we turned to see Grandma J stand up.

My heart about stopped. Grandma J was my dad's mom and what she was going to do was hardly predictable. She was super proud of Dad's success as she was of Grandad's. But she, like Aunt Christine, had liked my now-defunct nursing career and didn't cheer my getting a PI license.

"Hi Janine," said Chuck hesitantly.

"Hi yourself and before you ask, I heard everything." Grandma J walked over and I saw where my cousins got their style. She was the most fashionable granny ever in a bias-cut eggplant-colored sweater, black leather leggings, and knee-high suede boots. Her silver pageboy haircut showed off her chunky earrings and skillful makeup. Grandad's first wife, Dr. Dorothy Watts, called her "the luscious Janine" and she was dead on.

"What did you hear?" I asked.

"Don't be coy." She came over and kissed my cheek. "I heard your father being a work-obsessed, blinders-on jerk, just like his father."

My mouth dropped and so did Chuck's. This was not my grandmother. I'd never heard her talk like that, not with all the crap Grandad pulled and he pulled a lot. He'd even come out of retirement again to work for my dad against her wishes. Grandma J kept trying to spend time with her husband, but he was a husband who had no time to spend and he liked it that way.

"I've had it with him. It's the last straw." Her hands were balled up and her face filled with fury.

"What happened?" I asked. "He's already out of retirement. What's left?"

"One week," Grandma J said. "One week and I'm not going to get it."

My grandparents had never been on a vacation together. They went to Vegas once because there was a woodworking convention happening and that was Grandad's third career. But they never went on a cruise or to Europe or Florida. They didn't buy a camper and see the national parks like my friends' grandparents did. Grandad worked and Grandma waited. That was how it was. I was used to it. I guess she wasn't.

"Where were you going?"

"Napa Valley. Wine tasting with our friends, Doris and Frank, over New Year's. We were going to be warm and go to spas and be together. But your grandfather just canceled it. He didn't even tell me. He canceled it himself and informed me. There's a big case, you see."

"What's the case?" Chuck asked.

"I don't know and I don't care. There will always be another case. Always another reason. I don't know where I went wrong with Tommy, but I'm absolutely thrilled that you aren't like him in the most important way," said Grandma J and she kissed both of Chuck's cheeks. "I'll do it."

"What?" I asked, still confused.

"I'll go to Germany. I'm obviously not going with your grandfather and I've been waiting for Europe for fifty years."

"Oh, well, Grandma this is work, not a vacation."

"Will I be in Germany and not in my living room alone and angry?"

Should I do this? Somebody tell me. I don't know.

"Yes," I said slowly as I saw her swollen red eyes for the first time.

"Perfect." She held up her phone to show me a Christmassy picture. "Did you know that Stuttgart has one of the biggest Christmas markets in Germany?"

"I did not."

"Will we have time for that?" Grandma asked. "It says three hours. Will we have three hours to go to a Christmas market?"

"I..."

"Yes," said Chuck, squeezing my hand. "You'll totally have time for that."

Grandma J looked at me and I nodded. "We will do it. I just hope you enjoy it. I mean, there will be a lot of running around."

"As opposed to sitting around? That's exactly what I want. A life." She hugged me again and then Chuck.

"What will you tell Grandad?" I asked.

"Exactly what you are going to tell my son. Nothing. If he's lucky, I'll leave a note."

"I hope you won't be disappointed," I said. "I mean Stuttgart isn't a tourist city."

"Don't worry. If I want more when you're done, I'll stay," she said.

"Stay?"

"I'll stay and tour on my own. I can do that. I'm a grown person."

"Of course, you are," said Chuck quickly. "But wouldn't it be more fun with someone else?"

Grandma J tapped a polished finger on her dimpled chin. "I see your point. When we land, I'll call Isolda. She's always up for a laugh."

My mind went through Grandma J's friends and I came up blank. "Who's Isolda?"

"How many Isoldas could you possibly know? Isolda Bled. Imelda's daughter. She's in Germany right now. We're friends on Facebook and I'm following her travels. She always tells me I should up and go where I want. Now I am. I can travel with her. She won't mind. She's been asking me for years."

Isolda Bled was one of the Bled cousins, but a rarely seen one. I pretty much saw her at funerals and on the holidays. Occasionally, she turned up out of the blue to tell stories about traveling in the Middle East or Botswana. She was the best babysitter ever and would somehow get backstage passes to the elephant house at the zoo or take me to The Muny in Forest Park. I got to see *Wicked* and *Beauty and the Beast*. Then she'd be off again and I wouldn't see her for a year. She came off as a bit nutty, but she wasn't one of *those* Bleds. Her mother was though. Imelda was in and out of psychiatric hospitals her whole life and I couldn't help but think it scarred Isolda. She never stayed in one place for long. It was like she was trying to outrun her mother's demons.

"Sounds like a plan," said Chuck. "You'll watch her? Mercy's slippery."

"Hey!" I exclaimed.

"Please," said Grandma J. "I know slippery. I'll stick to her."

Aaron came over with a mug of hot chocolate and gave it to Grandma. She took it and kissed his cheek. "We are going to have the best time."

"Finding the crazies behind a kidnapping plot?" I was dripping with doubt.

"And being not here."

I raised my mug. "To the best time."

Clink.

CHAPTER FIVE

The airport was hopping and by that, I mean totally insane. Everyone and their mother's brother had decided to fly that Thursday. I didn't think people flew out for Christmas so early, but I guess they did. We were lucky to have the Bled pull and got seats.

Aaron and I wheeled our bags over to the Delta kiosks, weaving between happy couples off to skiing, angry businessmen, and families with wailing kids cranky about being at the airport at seven in the morning. I was with the kids, but it was worth it. We were there and no one named Tommy Watts had come out of the woodwork to stop us or at least try to stop us. I considered that a major victory and a minor miracle. My father, famous for his feelings, hadn't smelled a rat. He did corner me after dinner at Aunt Christine's and laid out his plan for Hunt and the medium security jail known as The Workhouse where Brian Shill was awaiting trial having been denied bail.

Stevie had once told me that The Workhouse was total hell and detailed some things that were better left unsaid. I hoped Shill was enjoying every terrible feature The Workhouse had. I know that says something about me and my desire for vengeance, but I'm okay with it. The guy put Cassidy Huff through a wood chipper. Nothing was bad enough for him as far as I was concerned.

Dad went on to inform me about my civic duty and flying to New York, how many interviews I would have to endure with Ladd and Owens, and what to expect from Solomon. I told him no that I wasn't doing it. He said be ready at eight. I said I would not be ready at eight or at any other time, but Dad just kept bulldozing through like he always does. I finally gave up and just sat there until he took a breath.

During that all-important pause, I saw Sorcha and called out, "Sorcha, what do you think about Costa Rica for our bridal trip?"

I never saw Dad again. The Troublesome Trio completely took me over and we had half the wedding planned before Chuck dragged me out of there. I was definitely the Maid of Honor again. No regrets.

"Mercy! Mercy!" Grandma J waved frantically from the middle of a line.

It was not my imagination when every security guard turned around to look. I was kinda infamous at Lambert, being put on the terrorist watchlist and whatnot.

I pulled my cute little paisley biker's cap down to my sunglasses and hustled over before my grandmother gave someone an idea.

"Shush," I said. "Don't draw attention to me."

Grandma J got all squirrelly and looked around. "Do you think he's here?"

"Dad? No. If he knew, he'd never have let me get this far."

"What's the problem?"

"Don't worry about it," I said.

"Alright." She did a spin. "How do I look? Now I tried to be practical. No high heels. Plenty of pockets and I've got this." She pulled up her sweater and revealed a weird beige pouch thing tied around her waist.

"What's that?" I asked.

"My Rick Steves money pouch. He says it's essential," she said. "Do you have yours?"

"I have a purse, pepper spray, and Great Grandpa's Mauser. I'm good."

"You can fly with that?"

"I've got all the paperwork and I'll check it under sporting equipment."

"You've done this before."

"I have."

Grandma J looked at me for a moment. "This is not what I wanted for you."

"I figured," I said.

"But it's who you are."

"Apparently so."

A smile bloomed on her wide lips. "I am so excited. It's my first time."

"For Europe, right?"

"For everything," she said. "I've never done any investigating. Ace always kept me away from it and your father, too. Great Grandpa Elijah said I was too delicate and it stuck."

"You don't seem delicate," I said.

"Thank you. I married Ace Watts and raised three just like him. How delicate can I be?"

"Good point."

Grandma practically vibrated her way up to the counter and chatted the ears off the agent. Her joy did make everything smoother. Herbert the agent barely looked at my paperwork and Mauser, instead of wanting to pat me down and be obnoxious. We sailed through and ended up at security in record time. It was all going so well, I should've known it couldn't last. We even got through the line in record time. Aaron brought breakfast sandwiches and we got coffee at the gate while we waited to board. That's when I got a feeling. That something isn't right feeling. No, not exactly that. It was the somebody's watching me feeling. I tried to shrug it off. It wasn't exactly unusual, but it just kept nagging at me.

The announcement system crackled to life and said louder than I would've liked,"Mercy Watts and party, please come to Gate 31A. Mercy Watts and party, please come to Gate 31A."

Crap on a cracker. There it is.

"What's happening?" Grandma asked. "Are we in trouble?"

"If there's trouble, it's me, don't worry," I said.

We tucked away our sandwiches and went to the desk. If the FBI got wind of my trip and ruined this for Grandma, I would kick somebody's butt and I don't mean maybe.

"Hi. I'm Mercy Watts and this is my party," I said with dread in every fiber of my being.

"It really is you," said Marcy at the desk with a bright smile. She didn't seem devious, but you never know.

"It's me. What's happened?"

"Okay. We've got your upgrades all set. Four in first class."

"First class?" I asked. "We got Comfort Plus." It took a bunch of my miles to upgrade us out of the main cabin, but for Grandma's first trip, it seemed like a good granddaughter thing to do.

"Those tickets have been refunded. Your party is now in first class."

"How'd that happen?"

"You and your party are special guests of Delta and you will be boarding immediately," said Marcy.

The guy in the line next to us leaned over. "How'd you swing that? They're treating me like I've got syphilis and I bought my tickets six months ago."

"I have no idea," I said. "Usually I'm the one with syphilis."

He chuckled and went back to eyeballing the gate guy that was telling him that he and his wife were not sitting together on a long-haul flight and he should be grateful that they weren't next to the toilets.

"We're in first class?" Grandma asked.

"I guess so," I said.

Marcy beamed at us. "I've got your boarding passes all ready. Is there anything that I can do that would make your journey with us more perfect?"

I glanced over at syphilis guy and said, "Let him sit with his wife."

"Well, I..."

I lowered my sunglasses. "You know you can do it, so just do it for us, the special guests of Delta."

Marcy bit her lip and slid over to her compadre, who quickly said, "It looks like we have some seats together in row fourteen. They just came open."

Syphilis guy's wife came over and said, "You are a saint. Thank you."

"Merry Christmas."

Marcy slid back over to us and said, "Anything else?" She sounded a little nervous, so I gave her a break. "That'll do it."

She went back to beaming and said, "So here they are. Four tickets. First class." She put four boarding passes on the counter.

"Four tickets? There's only three of us."

She frowned. "There are four in the Mercy Watts party and you're all here. Perfect. Antonio will let you board now."

"What the..." I turned around and there he was, Moe Licata, giving me a little finger wave much like his niece Fats.

"What in the world?" I asked.

Moe whipped off his flat driving cap and bowed to Grandma. "Moe Licata, at your service." Then he kissed Grandma's hand and winked his right, bulging, moist eye at me. "Glad to see me?"

"Shocked is more like it," I said. "What are you doing here?"

"Fats can't go, so you got me," he said.

"I didn't tell Fats."

"Didn't tell Fats." He put his palms up. "Like that's necessary."

"Um...I thought it was," I said.

He tweaked my chin. "So young and so pretty." He looked at Marcy. "She seems dumb, but she's not. Ticket, please."

An astonished Marcy handed Moe a ticket and watched as the ancient mobster herded us to Antonio at the gate. "It's a good day to be assigned to you. Fats is going to be pissed, but it's not my fault she's knocked up and puking."

We got through the gate and Moe led the way down the long gangway with Aaron. Grandma took my arm and whispered, "Who is this person? He's very odd-looking."

Moe was about the oddest-looking person I knew. His short-cropped hair was sort of brindle patterned like a dog, his eyes were moist and bulging, he had two hairy warts on the side of his nose, and a slightly humped back. I think he was seventy, but he looked ninety-five. He worked for the Fibonacci family in various capacities and my dad had arrested him for racketeering back in the day. I suspected Moe did a lot more for Calpurnia Fibonacci than simple racketeering. If someone said he was the family exterminator, I wouldn't have been surprised. He had that kind of feel about him.

"He's Fats' uncle," I said.

"And he's...going on our trip?" Grandma asked.

"Apparently."

"Why?"

"Well, you know how Fats helps me out, I guess he's going to do that for this trip," I said.

"He's your bodyguard?"

It sounded so stupid I couldn't even say yes. Fats was a bodyguard. The woman scared people by breathing in their direction. I'd seen people on chemo that looked stronger than Moe.

"I don't know."

"That's not a good idea. He looks ill."

We got to the jet and Moe turned around. "Ladies, don't worry about me. I know my business. Calpurnia wouldn't have sent me if I didn't. I've got this. Mrs. Watts, I have got to say those are the most beautiful earrings."

"Thank you," Grandma said, staring a little.

"You're welcome." He held out a liver-spotted hand and helped her over the threshold. "This is going to be a great trip. Did you know that Stuttgart has one of the largest Christmas markets in Germany?"

"I did know that," she said. "I'm so excited."

"So am I. I'm in 2a. Perhaps Mercy will switch with me and we can sit together. Did you know that your husband arrested me in 1977?"

Grandma looked at me with wide eyes and I shrugged. She wanted an adventure. It was now guaranteed.

We stood at baggage claim for what seemed like six years and I kept a hand on Grandma's elbow. The lady was buzzing from the excellent and plentiful espresso in first class. I was afraid she'd dart off in the Stuttgart airport and I'd spend half the day tracking her.

"This is taking a long time. Isn't this taking a long time?" she asked.

"Nope," I said. "This is normal."

"I don't think it's normal. How can this be normal? Normal is an interesting term, isn't it? Who decides what's normal? Who's in charge of that?" With that, my grandmother made a break for it, juking to the right, and I lost my grip. Aaron's arm shot out and he got her without his eyes ever leaving the stationary baggage drop.

"You've got skills, my friend," said Moe.

Aaron gave a slight nod and the baggage carousel made a grinding noise.

"Here we go." Grandma went up on her tiptoes and clasped her hands. "We're almost ready to see Germany."

Moe smiled at her and then whispered to me. "Let's get our stuff. She's not going anywhere now."

"What stuff?" I asked.

"You checked a weapon, didn't you?"

"Sure."

"Alright then." Moe steered me away from the placid Aaron and the thrilled Grandma to the special luggage pick up where there was a short line of people getting skis and whatnot. We waited a few minutes and then presented paperwork. I hadn't thought about Moe Licata packing, but, of course, he was. Fats didn't go to the bathroom unarmed.

The agent and guard checked our paperwork twice with raised eyebrows at my lame disguise of hat and sunglasses and then she retrieved our boxes.

"I can tell it's you," she said.

"Swell."

"You could try a scarf over the lips."

"Noted. Thanks."

The agent handed over my little travel case and then hauled up a big-wheeled one for Moe, plus a rifle case.

He thanked the staff and extended the handle. "Ready?"

"I guess." I thanked the staff and noted that one immediately picked up a phone. Awesome.

I chased Moe out to the baggage claim and asked, "What did you bring?"

"Not my full complement, but it should be sufficient," he said.

"Sufficient for what?"

He smiled at me. "You never know." He eyeballed my puny case and asked, "What did you bring?"

"My Mauser."

"The antique?"

"Yeah."

"That's adorable," he said.

"It fits my hand," I said.

"Good enough.

Our bags came around and Grandma grabbed hers, practically swinging it over her head. Aaron had to snag her again so she wouldn't run off while we collected our luggage. Then there was no holding her back. Grandma was off and running with no clue where we were going. She tried to go up the escalator to the check-in area, but I yanked her off in time.

"We're going to get our rental," I said, panting.

"It's up there."

"It's not."

"Okay. Where? Where?" Grandma asked. I pointed and she shook her head. "I'm getting fuzzy. I need more coffee."

"No more coffee for you."

"You're not in charge. I'm your elder."

God help me.

Aaron came over and took her other elbow.

"Aaron, you'll get me an espresso. I love espresso. I didn't know. It's very good though."

"No," he said.

"Mercy, let's get a real European pastry. We can split it."

"No airport pastry," I said. "It's a rule."

"Since when?"

"Since it's bad. Don't worry. Aaron will explain the food rules."

She leaned over to me. "But he doesn't hardly talk."

"He does when motivated...by food."

"I don't think—"—she pointed—"there's a Mercedes. Right here in the airport." Grandma got away from us and started ogling the

Mercedes on display. I tried to get her past it and then Moe was gone.

We're never getting out of this flipping airport.

"Come on," I said. "Rental car and we lost Moe."

"Oh, my God," she exclaimed. "We can't lose him. He's never been to Germany before."

Aaron pointed and I should've known. He was checking out the sex shop because it's an airport and you got to have a sex shop. I have a few nightmares and looking at a sex shop window with my grandmother is one of them, but you just couldn't avoid that shop. Big, red and black, and filled with mannequins. Awesome. My day just got better.

"Look at that." And Grandma was off and ogling just as much as Moe.

I'm not going to hell. I'm already there.

"Alright, people," I said. "Moving on."

"They have a lot on display," said Grandma.

"They do indeed."

"You'd look good in that nurse outfit, Janine," said Moe.

Kill me now.

Grandma slapped his arm. "Oh, Moe. You are so bad, but not wrong. I have the legs for it."

I'm out.

I hoofed it down to the rental car area and happily the rest of my crazy crew followed. Grandma J grabbed my arm. "Are those in every airport?"

"I don't know," I said. "Here we are. Rental cars."

We got in line and happily, Moe started talking about our Christmas market choices, so I felt free to call Chuck as requested.

"Hey," said someone, not Chuck.

"Who's this?" I asked.

"Mercy, it's Stevie."

"Why are you answering Chuck's phone?"

"I'm animal sitting. How's Stuttgart?"

He remembered Stuttgart. Holy crap.

"Still in the airport. How are you feeling?"

Stevie didn't answer for a minute and then said, "Quiet."

"Is that good?" I asked.

"Yeah. I can see stuff. Did you know you have four coffee makers?"

"Five actually. One's under the sink."

A cabinet door opened and Stevie said, "There it is. You probably don't need that many coffee things."

"Take it up with Chuck," I said. "How'd it go with your parents?"

"Good. Mom loves the tattoo. She cried, but in a good way. Dad didn't say much. He's waiting for me to screw up."

I can't believe you know that.

"They'll come around if you work at it," I said.

"I'm definitely gonna take the pills. Mom said I was good to talk to, so that's nice."

We were next in line, so I said, "Excellent. Can you tell Chuck we got here okay?"

"He's awake. You want to talk to him?" Stevie asked.

"Sure."

Chuck got on and said, "I wish I'd come with you."

"I'm fine. You need to get some rest."

"I can't get you off my mind," he said.

"That's sweet," I said.

"I sent you to deal with The Klinefeld Group on your own."

I rolled my eyes. "It's not them and I'm not alone."

Chuck scoffed. "You've got Aaron and your grandmother."

"And Moe."

"You brought Fats' dog? Why in the heck? She's tiny. What's she going to do? Bite their ankles?"

"She bites crotches, too, but it's not the dog. It's Uncle Moe."

Chuck went quiet and the rental agent waved us up. Moe dashed ahead of me, all smiles and ready with his passport. I don't know what he was going to do. The reservation was in my name, but I let him go for it. Big mistake. He went for a Mercedes.

I elbowed him. "We didn't book a Mercedes."

"I don't drive Opels," Moe said.

"You're not driving."

He looked at me with those moist, bulging eyes and raised his palms. “Come on. What am I for?”

“I don’t know,” I said.

“What don’t you know?” Chuck asked.

“What Moe’s for.”

Moe tapped his American Express card on the counter and said, “We’ll take the Mercedes.”

“S Class?” asked the agent.

He winked at her. “Naturally.”

“We don’t need an S class,” I said.

Moe pushed me away from the counter and Grandma said, “Oh yes. That’s the big one. We should have the big one.”

I walked away. What else could I do?

“So...when you say Moe...” Chuck said.

“Moe Licata.”

“Oh, thank God. Now I can sleep.”

“Are you serious?” I asked.

“Moe Licata has skills,” he said.

I looked over at Moe. His pants were sliding down to reveal the top of a hairy butt and he was putting on Coke bottle glasses to read the rental contract.

“Oh, yeah? What are they?”

Chuck yawned. “I feel so much better. I’m going to lay down. Love you.”

“Okay. Love you,” I said.

Moe turned to me, holding an enormous Mercedes key, his eyes huge and distorted. “All set.”

I do not feel better.

CHAPTER SIX

I was scared to death that Moe would kill us with his stellar eyesight and the fact that he remained hunched over while he drove didn't help. But Moe knew Mercedes and had learned to drive in Italy, so he was both aggressive and reacted quickly. We made it to the hotel near the main train station in record time. Grandma insisted we share a room as a cost-cutting measure, even though German hotels don't do the American thing of two beds per room. We'd be sharing.

"Slumber party," she declared to the desk clerk. "We will get to know each other better."

The clerk looked at me and I said, "I guess that's a thing we're doing."

We dropped our bags and were out the door in record time since Moe was Christmas market motivated. The faster we got working the sooner we got to a market was his plan, so we sped out of Stuttgart proper and raced through the dreary countryside that was both cold and somehow still very green. No snow, unfortunately. Grandma started to complain about the lack of snow but fell asleep mid-sentence. She and Aaron sat in the back. Grandma had her nose pressed against the window and Aaron was eating a sandwich that he'd produced from somewhere. I could've used some coffee, but there was no way I was chancing it with Grandma finally settled down.

"So what do we know about this guy Thooft?" Moe asked.

"Other than he was a teacher and pretty normal until he tried to kidnap me, nothing much."

"He didn't try. He succeeded. You need to work on your reaction time. I can help you with that."

"I got out of the trunk, didn't I?"

"The idea is to never get in the trunk," said Moe, so hunched that he was practically looking through the steering wheel instead of over it.

"I think I did pretty good," I said.

"Pretty good against a middle-aged teacher isn't good enough. What are we looking for in this guy's apartment?"

"I don't know. Something from whoever was blackmailing him. Anything that shows who he was in contact with. Friends we don't know about. Receipts for hotels."

"The sister didn't know the friends?"

"Kimberly knew about his teacher friends, but my guys have been keeping track of their financial activities," I said. "It looks like Anton was paying someone off, but none of the friends from the school have any suspicious deposits or unusual spending."

"How much did they take him for?" Moe asked.

"About seven thousand over the two months," I said.

"Was he drained?"

"No. He had another two in savings. Most of his money went into his retirement funds and wasn't liquid."

Moe nodded. "They wanted cash."

"But I don't think it was his money they were after," I said.

"They were after you."

I looked out at the beautiful rolling hills, dotted with farms. "But they took that money. It was pretty penny-ante considering they had a jet on standby to fly me out of Missouri. I don't get it. If you've got a jet and goons to fly it..."

"Why blackmail a teacher?" Moe finished for me.

"Yeah and why bother with the little sums of money at first. Anton was taking out just a hundred euros here and there at first, then it went up to three hundred every other day."

"Something escalated them. Any ideas what it was?"

I shook my head, but I knew. The withdrawals cranked up a couple days after I found out about the liquor cabinet in my parents' butler's pantry. It was the secret I'd been searching for, the object that Stella Bled Lawrence sent back from Europe in 1938. We got the shipping receipt from my great-grandmother Agatha's purse. It survived the crash that killed her and her husband Daniel.

We'd searched the liquor cabinet, only to discover it was empty of anything from 1938. Josiah Bled had left a page out of *Where the Sidewalk Ends* by Shel Silverstein inside. There were some clues associated with that page and the book it came out of, but I had no idea what they meant.

Moe gave me a sidelong glance and I knew he knew that I knew what happened, but he didn't push it. "What else have you got?"

"He bought books on negotiation."

Moe snorted. "You can't negotiate with a requirement."

"What does that mean?" I asked.

"They, whoever they are, required you. Nothing else was going to do."

"Do people try to negotiate with you?"

"Sure and I'm flexible to a point," said Moe.

"What's the point?"

"Different for every situation. If they owe money, I want it. I'd be willing to go on installments if it gets me where I want to go. But you can't be taking the wife to the Bahamas and slipping me five hundred bucks, acting like it's breaking you. If you owe, it's bologna and hot dogs till you're paid up."

"And there are no installments of me," I said, feeling exhausted and icky. All that was going on as I was living my life. I had no idea Anton Thooft was trying to wriggle out of something that could cost me my life.

"My feeling is that they took the money because they could," said Moe. "Probably making him feel like he had hope when he didn't. Then they hit him with the big guns."

"Big guns?"

"Whatever they used to get him to do it."

"But they must've already used Kimberly's adoption to get the money," I said. "Why else would he start paying them?"

"So why'd it take two months?" Moe asked as we passed a dairy farm and sped around a long curve into the little town of Waldenbuch, passing a car dealer and some nondescript buildings. The town wouldn't have been charming in the least if you didn't bother to look up. High over the town was a small castle and medieval wall. Charming didn't quite cover it.

"They had to work Anton up to it or get the plan going with the plane and whatnot," I said.

Moe shook his head. "Possibly."

"You don't like it?"

"I think Anton didn't like it and they had something else that got him moving."

"There's nothing else," I said. "Anton's mother switched his sister at birth and gave away her son to strangers so she could have a daughter. You don't think that was enough to get Anton going? He spent his whole life hiding that secret. He gave up his dream of politics for it and he made Kimberly give up singing, too."

Moe drove through a traffic circle and we headed to the old part of town. "Maybe. I'm just wondering why it took so long. You blackmail someone you want results. If it's money, you get the money. If it's a kidnapping, why wait around?"

"I don't know," I said with a yawn. "But when we find them, we'll ask."

Moe nodded grimly and I got a bad feeling. Fats was one thing. Moe was another. I didn't know what he'd do. I didn't know what he really was. A low-level enforcer for the Fibonaccis? Did he run a business for money laundering? The possibilities were endless.

We drove slowly into the *Altstadt* and Moe whistled. "Would you look at that? Beautiful. Not Italy. But beautiful."

It was beautiful. I looked up a street and there were half-timbered buildings and a church steeple rising behind the roofs. Very picture postcard, even with the drizzle. We passed a building that looked like it had been there since the Middle Ages and went down a street to a more modern section, passing a tiny police station and alteration shop to find an ancient mill that was apparently still in business.

"The parking is terrible." Moe drove around the block for ten minutes until a spot in front of Anton's building opened up. The Mercedes parked itself and I looked back at Grandma. I could let her sleep, but she'd miss the investigation and not get on the right time zone. But then again, she wouldn't run off and buy gallons of espresso.

"She'll leave the car," said Moe. "This town's too adorable to resist."

"Good point."

I woke her up and found the keyring Kimberly gave me in the bottom of my purse. I pictured her face when she pulled the keys out of the evidence bag. The cops gave all of Anton's effects back when the case was closed and they released the body. There was blood on them. She didn't see it until it was too late.

"Is this it?" Grandma asked, looking up at the plain, fairly modern building.

"This is it."

Aaron put a hand on my shoulder. If he'd had hot chocolate, he'd have given it to me. Since he didn't, I went to the apartment building door, passing the mailboxes. The name Thooft was still on one. I was kinda surprised nobody took it off.

I led the way up the stairs to the top floor and found Anton's apartment on the left. I was so tired and jet-lagged. The thoughts of Kimberly's sorrow wasn't helping and I prayed that there would be something inside my assailant's apartment that would make this easy.

I hesitated. My hands wouldn't quite go to the lock. I wanted them to, but they didn't go. He was in there. Anton. The man rushing at me and putting a smelly, wet rag on my face. I'd kept him at bay so far, but I couldn't in there. I'd be surrounded.

Aaron took the keys and opened the door, revealing a dining room with a high timbered ceiling. We walked in and before I could say that it didn't look like a kidnapper's apartment, a scream burst out from nowhere and Moe pulled a Glock.

She was sitting on the sofa in Anton's living room, eyes wide in shock and clutching an enormous tuxedo cat. A torrent of German burst out of the girl and I understood a little. Something like who the hell are you or something along those lines. Before I could formulate a rudimentary reply, two streams of German came from behind me, Aaron and Grandma. I didn't know what they were saying, but the girl relaxed.

"Since when do you speak German?" I asked Grandma.

She shrugged. "I guess my high school German stuck. I wonder if I can speak French."

What the...?

"Oh, you're Americans," said the girl with relief.

I pushed down Moe's Glock and asked, "Are you? Your English is flawless."

"My dad's American and my mom's German." She stood up and it wasn't that far to go. The girl was about five feet tall and maybe fourteen years old. She seemed faintly Asian with beautiful almond eyes and flawless skin. If she was worried about Moe's weapon, she hid it well. "You're the one, aren't you?"

"The one what?" I asked.

"Mercy Watts. The one Mr. Thooft..." Her face changed from bright and beautiful to sad and wilted.

"Yes. I'm the one."

"I didn't know *you* were coming. I'm Ella by the way." Ella sat, pulling the fat cat onto her lap again and he began a loud purr.

Grandma went past me, walking down a couple of steps into the sunken living room. "We must've given you quite a shock. I'm sorry about that. We didn't know anyone would be here."

"I'm the cat sitter. Mr. Thooft said I only had to watch Porky Boy for a few days, but then he died and I couldn't just not feed him."

"Of course not. Thank you for doing that," said Grandma.

"Did you know someone was coming?" I asked.

"My dad said Mrs. La Roche said someone was coming about the apartment, but it was after Christmas," said Ella.

I went down into the living room and went to the large bookcases by a beehive-shaped fireplace, checking out the books. "There was a change of plans. You should call your dad and let him know we're here."

"Oh, yeah. He freaks easy." Ella texted her father and then said he was coming.

"Who's your father?" I asked.

"Simon McWilliams. He's a teacher. That's how we know Mr. Thooft."

"Do you know Sherri La Roche?"

"Oh, sure. Mrs. La Roche is my English teacher. I'm a Freshman," said Ella.

"Why aren't you at school?" Grandma asked.

"Teacher workday."

"So I've heard that Mrs. La Roche and Anton were good friends," I said. "I'd like to talk to her."

Ella looked out the windows at the cloudy skies over suburban Waldenbuch and clutched Porky Boy tighter. "Why? Aren't you just coming for his stuff?"

"No. There's a company that's going to do that. I'm investigating what happened."

Her eyes flashed back to me. "I don't believe any of that stuff. It's not true."

I sat down on a cushy armchair and glanced up at Moe, who'd holstered his weapon and was gazing out the window, seemingly disinterested. "You don't believe the stuff about me?"

"I know he did that but not that other stuff. There's no way. Mr. Thooft was super nice."

"What other stuff?" Grandma asked, giving the cat a scratch.

"That he was some kind of 4chan freak that hated women. There's no freaking way," said Ella and a pink tinge lit up her cheeks. "He was always super nice. He never did anything to me. It's all lies."

Wait what?

"So there are a lot of rumors going around," I said. "And...something about you?"

"And other people." Her fists were balled up and the pink had turned to rose. "Aren't you a detective or something? It's not true. You know that, don't you?"

"Well, I know he wasn't a 4chan freak as you say," I said. "He didn't hate women. All that stuff was planted on his computer."

Ella's lower lip quivered and she burst into tears. "I knew it, but nobody believed me. He wouldn't hurt me." There was a loud buzzing sound and she said, "That's my dad at the door."

Moe went over and buzzed Mr. McWilliams in. The father was up the stairs in a flash and practically flew in the door when Aaron opened it. "It really is you," he said and then bent over breathing hard.

"You didn't have to run, Dad." Ella rolled her eyes and then hastily wiped the tears off her cheeks, but not hastily enough.

"Why are you crying?" Mr. McWilliams asked. "What's going on?"

I gave him my card and introduced Moe and Grandma. Aaron was in the kitchen rustling around and I decided to leave him out of it.

Mr. McWilliams said hello to everyone and looked down, his high forehead wrinkling. He resembled Ella, only more Asian with darker hair but the same lovely complexion.

"So you're..."

"Investigating Mr. Thooft's case," I said.

"I heard about that on the news," said Mr. McWilliams. "Why would you want to do that?"

"I wanted to find out what happened and Anton's sister did, too. She hired me."

He kept looking at my card. "But that's over. You found out why he did it. The adoption thing, right?"

"Somebody blackmailed him, Dad," said Ella. "He didn't want to hurt her."

"That's what the news said." He looked at me. "Is it true? You never know with the news."

"It's true," I said.

"Then why are you here?"

"To find out who blackmailed him."

Mr. McWilliams went down into the living room and stood in front of the fireplace. "We don't know anything about that."

Mr. McWilliams didn't know Anton well, which didn't surprise me. Nobody did. His was a life lived in hiding, doing his best not to let anyone see what his mother had done. Mr. McWilliams liked Anton but knew absolutely nothing personal about him, not that he had a sister or even a family period.

"He was a great teacher. Totally dedicated," he said. "I don't know what else I can tell you."

"How about the rumors?" Moe asked and Ella flinched.

Mr. McWilliams frowned. "Rumors about what?"

Ella pushed the cat off her lap and stood up. "I need to go home. Kelsey's coming over."

"Hold on," said her dad. "Rumors about what? Anton?"

"Just that 4chan stuff, Dad," said Ella. "She said it's not true."

Her dad turned to me. "It wasn't?"

"No, but I'm more interested in the rumors about your daughter," I said.

Ella made a break for it, but her dad turned all stern. "Stop. What are we talking about? Ella?"

The girl returned to the sofa and sat noticeably closer to my grandmother. I didn't blame her. Mr. McWilliams looked like he was ready to bite someone.

"Nothing," she complained. "Just stupid stuff."

It was not stupid stuff. My stomach hadn't felt so knotted since I first heard Anton was on 4chan. That turned out to be a plant. This might not. Rumors were rife in the high school about Anton Thooft and kids. He was a little too interested in them. Ella had been a prime target because she knew him in his personal life and spent time in his apartment.

"Ella?" Mr. McWilliams looked like his stomach was in knots, too.

"No, Dad." Ella did the hardest and longest eye roll I'd ever witnessed. "He didn't do anything to me. There's no way."

"You're sure?"

"Like I wouldn't know. I'm not an idiot, Dad. I'd know if some guy tried to diddle me. Jeez."

Her dad's shoulders relaxed. "Thank God for that. Does that answer your question, Miss Watts?"

"Not really," I said. "Where'd that rumor come from?"

"I don't know," said Ella. "It started going around right after he died."

"What did they say?"

She pursed her lips and thought about it. "Just that he was doing too much tutoring and meeting kids in coffee shops next to hotels. Stuff like that. It was stupid."

"That's not true," said Mr. McWilliams. "Anton tutored in the school library or the hotel if it was being used."

I raised an eyebrow and Moe asked, "Somebody let their kid get tutored by a guy in a hotel?"

"It's not like that. It's the post hotel, right down the road from the school. People use the breakfast room for all kinds of stuff, book clubs, meetings. It's convenient and has free coffee. Ella got her French tutoring there because nobody wants to come all the way out to Waldenbuch to tutor."

"You felt comfortable with that?" I asked.

"Yes, of course. We're talking an army post here. It doesn't get much safer." I must've made a face because he quickly said, "This isn't Fort Hood, Miss Watts. This group of posts is mostly officers and high command kind of people. It's very secure."

"The army gets a bad rap," said Moe.

"They do, but we don't have those problems here," said Mr. McWilliams. "What happened with Anton...it was a total shock and we were so grateful that you were okay."

I thanked him and asked, "So you never saw anything to make you suspicious of Anton?"

"No. He was a favorite with the kids. He went above and beyond. Great test scores."

"Not social?"

Mr. McWilliams thought about it. "Friendly and helpful. He wasn't a talker, but I'll tell you this. Kids filled up his room at lunch. He made them feel comfortable. You could hear them in there talking a blue streak. Kids that wouldn't say a thing to me, Anton could get them to talk."

"How?" Moe asked.

"I don't know. Ella?"

The girl sat back on the sofa. "He was just nice. He didn't talk down to us and didn't say stupid stuff about how hard everything was going to be all the time. He said we could handle college. It wasn't that bad. Stuff like that."

"I know people thought he might be gay," said Mr. McWilliams.

"He wasn't gay, Dad," said Ella. "He like loved Mrs. La Roche."

"She's married."

"That doesn't matter. He loved her. I could tell."

Anton Thooft was gay, but there was no way I was going to say it. If the rumors were wild about him already, the kids would go berserk if I added that to the mix. The waters were already muddied enough.

"Did he ever say anything about me?" I asked.

"We went through all this with the Army and the *Polizei*," said Mr. McWilliams.

"I'm a little different."

"I can see that."

"Dad! Don't be creepy," said Ella.

"I'm not creepy. I'm observant." He looked at me. "They asked about you. If he talked about you, but Anton Thooft didn't talk about anything, except teaching and the kids."

"Neither of you had any clue?" I asked.

"He seemed okay when he gave me the key," said Ella.

"But not himself," said Grandma.

"Well, no. He was usually more chatty about Porky Boy. He'd tell me how he was doing. If he'd been stealing food. Stuff like that. And he always went over the vet stuff."

"And he didn't this time?" I asked.

"Nope. He just gave me the key and said he'd be back in a few days," said Ella.

"Did he say where he was going?" Moe asked.

"Just a trip. He said he was in a hurry and thanked me. That was it."

"You should talk to Sherri La Roche," said Mr. McWilliams. "She and Anton were tight. They traveled together and were part of a foodie group."

"See," said Ella.

"They were just friends, Ella." Her father sighed. "Sherri's husband is a notorious crab. He doesn't want to do anything but watch football or hockey."

"Whatever, Dad."

Mr. McWilliams waved Ella up and said, "We do have to go. If you have any more questions, we're happy to help."

I shook their hands and then asked Ella, "Were there any kids that seemed particularly clued in with those rumors?"

She shrugged. "They were all over school. Everyone was talking about it."

"Will you give some thought and let me know if there was anyone in particular?"

"Sure."

"Were there any hotels mentioned by name?"

"No," she said. "Just hotels. Totally stupid."

I nodded. "Most likely, but I have to follow every lead."

Ella gave Porky Boy another scratch and left to meet her friend. Mr. McWilliams and I went to the door and he hesitated on the threshold. "She's more upset than she seems."

"I know that," I said.

"Nothing like this has ever happened before. A teacher being shot to death, not to mention the rest of it and with what he did to you, we can't even mourn him."

He didn't want to say it, but I could see it in his eyes. Here comes Mercy Watts stirring the pot. Fantastic.

"I'm not trying to kick up a fuss. I'm doing my job," I said.

Mr. McWilliams looked away. "I'm not blaming you, but you being here..."

"It's not about what he did to me. It's about what was done to him."

His eyes darted back to me. "You consider him a victim, not a suspect?"

"The two aren't mutually exclusive," I said.

He got out his phone and sent me his number. "I'll call Sherri La Roche and see if she's up to talking to you."

"Having a hard time?"

"I'd say she's shattered and blaming herself. Other people are blaming her, too."

"What for?" I asked.

"They think she was running around with an Incel and should've known it. Total BS, of course."

"On several levels."

He pocketed his phone and said, "I'll call you after I talk to her."

I thanked him and Mr. McWilliams went down the stairs. I turned around and just about jumped out of my skin. Grandma, Moe, and Aaron were standing there. Aaron had a carving knife and a bottle of ketchup. Grandma had the cat and Moe was clearing the Glock's chamber. It was like the weirdest superhero poster ever.

"And now we tear the place apart?" Grandma asked.

"What? No," I said.

"That's what your grandfather always says."

Moe holstered his weapon. "I think that's hyperbole."

"Really?" Grandma asked. "I was going to make a mess like on TV."

"We're not wrecking the apartment. We're searching it." I turned to Aaron. "And what are you going to do?"

"The kitchen's dirty," said Aaron.

"Alrighty then. Aaron will clean the kitchen and we'll search for something related to stuff we care about."

Grandma put down the cat and smacked her hands together a lot like Grandad did. "And what would that stuff look like?"

Moe elbowed her. "It's like porn. You'll know it when you see it."

"Ooh. There might be porn?"

Gross.

"Let's just see what we see," I said. "You two in the living room and I'll start in the bedroom."

Grandma raised her hand. "I want the bedroom. That's where the porn will be."

What's happening?

"Okay, Grandma. Go find the porn."

"Janine, you surprise me," said Moe.

Grandma smiled so wide her lipstick cracked. "I've always thought of myself as boring, predictable Janine. This is new and I like it."

"So do I," said Moe.

This does not bode well for Grandad.

"Let's just get to searching and cleaning, for some reason," I said.

We all went to our separate areas. I hit Anton's office and dug through mounds of lesson plans, random papers on random subjects from the Peloponnesian War to Andrew Jackson to indoor gardening on a budget. Anton liked to print things a lot. He also liked to keep things. There were three old laptops stacked up in a corner along with two old cellphones, and a basket of tangled cords that went to who knows what. I found the self-help books he'd ordered from Jamie his former love at Black Heart Books. They were marked up with highlighter and had several bookmarks in each one, especially *Getting to Yes: Negotiating Agreements Without Giving In*.

From looking at that, I started to think there was something to Moe's theory. Anton was stalling, trying to wriggle his way out, but something got him going. Maybe there was something else. The vague accusation about inappropriate behavior with the kids would do it, but would Anton fall for that if there was no proof? I didn't find anything about that in the office. Not a scrap of anything remotely questionable. He did have notes to himself about kids in his classes, but they were sweet. "Remind Dorian to turn in second paper." "Tell Maddie her speech needs more documentation." "Make homework packet for Logan." I got the notes off his multiple bulletin boards and out of the trash to arrange them by date. The notes were pretty steady until about a week before he flew out. There were none after that.

On the desk, I found a stack of Christmas cards and letters from former students and teachers from both the school in Germany and back in Missouri. They ranged from simple signed cards to "You were the best teacher ever." I know I shouldn't be influenced by what Anton left behind. I should have an open mind, but I just wasn't feeling it. If that guy was inappropriate, I'd eat a bag of crab.

Once I got through the office, I moved onto the guest bedroom. Practically empty. And the bathroom. Neat and minimalist.

"Mercy," Grandma walked in as I was rummaging through a bin filled with arthritis creams, "I didn't find any porn, not even the bad kind."

"You're disappointed?" I asked.

"Well, I wanted to find some evidence for you, but this man was pretty dull, like me."

I finished the bathroom and we walked through the bedroom. A little messy and a full laundry basket, but nothing about kids or people blackmailing him. Grandma stood in the middle of the room and stamped her foot. "There's nothing. No threatening letters and his Kindle is full of Sci-Fi and biographies."

"The bastard," I said with a smile.

"That's right. He runs off to attack my granddaughter and doesn't have the decency to leave any clues behind. How is that possible? He wasn't a criminal mastermind."

Moe walked in. "He did leave something behind."

He showed me a book where Anton kept the receipts from all the money he'd withdrawn over the last two months before he came after me. It was stuffed full.

"*Catch-22*," said Grandma. "That says something, doesn't it?"

"It says he was trapped," Moe said.

I took the book and went to the dining room table to spread the receipts out. "Let's see what we've got." I went through all of them and they were right, except for two extras for fifty euros each. They weren't taken out of the same ATM, either. The large block of withdrawals was from one ATM in Sindelfingen. Those two extras were from Weil der Stadt and they were first before any of the other withdrawals.

"Lower amounts," said Grandma. "Maybe he was just shopping."

"He saved them for a reason," I said.

"To keep track of what he'd paid," said Moe. "You gotta know or you'll overpay."

"There's overpaying with blackmail?"

He scratched his chin and looked off to the right. "No, but there is with gambling and women. We could be looking at a debt here."

"And he paid it off by kidnapping Mercy?" Grandma asked.

"Wouldn't be the first time, Janine."

"I'll take your word for it."

Moe gave her a wide smile and said, "You should."

I checked the time and it was only one o'clock. I couldn't be calling my hacker Spidermonkey yet, but I needed those receipts checked. Did Anton go to Weil der Stadt often or ever? There must be a reason that it started there and changed later.

"I'm going to call Novak," I said to no one in particular.

"Who's that?" Grandma asked.

"Hacker."

Her hand fluttered over her chest. "You can't do that. Morty will be so hurt."

"Uncle Morty is recovering. I'm not supposed to stress him."

She picked up a receipt. "Would this stress him?"

"He'd yell," I said.

"Morton yells at you?"

"Where have you been?"

Grandma looked genuinely puzzled. "I don't know."

"Well, anyway, Uncle Morty will already be pissed, because my dad is pissed." I held up my phone to show the eighteen thousand messages I'd gotten from my father since I didn't turn up to do his bidding. I'd read a couple. It wasn't pretty. Words like betrayal, fired, and out of the will were bandied about, but I just replied once with one of Dad's old chestnuts. "Not now. On a case." There were a whole lot more texts after that. Dad's thumbs must be cramped.

"Your poor mother," said Grandma.

"She went to The Girls," I said.

"Your mother left your father?" Moe asked, his eyes so wide and bulging, I thought they might pop out of their sockets. Very disturbing.

"She didn't leave Dad. She took a vacay from his fury. Tiny went to Minneapolis. They are all scattering to the winds."

"Tommy has messaged me a few times," said Grandma.

"Oh, yeah? What did he say?"

Grandma crossed her arms. "I didn't read them. I want to be happy. Call that Novak person and let's get this show on the road."

With Grandma's blessing, I called and left a message for Novak. The guy was seriously busy and pretty odd, so he'd get back whenever he got back. Spidermonkey he was not.

"Well, I guess that's it," I said. "Unless you found something in the kitchen, Aaron."

Aaron stuck his head out of the minuscule kitchen and said, "Mold."

"Not what we're looking for."

He went back to washing dishes and Moe said, "I've got something that isn't something."

"Cryptic," I said.

"Check this out." Moe led me back into the living room and opened the glass front on the fireplace. "He burned a lot of papers before he left."

"That's where all the clues went." Grandma slammed a fist into her well-manicured hand. "He is a bastard."

I squatted in front of the grate and poked around. "Nothing left. Could just be paper from starting a fire."

"That much? No way," said Moe. "And look here. Anton had these handy little fire starter sticks. There's no paper piled up with the wood or kindling."

I smiled up at him. "You're not half bad at this."

"I've got a history of finding people that don't want to be found."

"I bet." I dug around and found a scrap of paper at the back. There wasn't anything on it. Can't be that easy. I mean, come on now. But it was notebook paper, college ruled. I held it up. "Definitely not fire starter."

"Maybe that was the blackmail letter," said Grandma.

"On notebook paper?" Moe asked.

"You think blackmailers have stationary for doing their business?" I asked

"I see your point."

I closed the fireplace and called out to Aaron, "Are you about done?"

The little weirdo ran out wearing yellow rubber gloves and asked, "You hungry?"

"Flipping starving," I said.

Without a word, he went back into the kitchen and I followed in case I was supposed to. The kitchen was immaculate.

"Looks like Kimberly's going to get the deposit back."

Aaron stripped off his gloves and laid them over the gleaming faucet. "Brewery?"

"Yes, please," I said, and I went back into the dining room to find Grandma with her coat on and holding Anton's cat.

"Um...what are you doing with that?" I asked.

"We can't leave him," she said.

"Why not?"

Grandma's lips went into a thin, red line. "We cannot abandon an American cat on foreign soil. What kind of people do you think we are?"

"People who are living in a hotel that doesn't allow cats," I said.

"Look at this beautiful American boy. We can't leave him."

"He could be German."

Moe poked the flub rolling over Grandma's arm. "That's a big fat American cat."

"Not helping," I said.

"See. We can't leave him. They might put him in the pound and he doesn't speak German," said Grandma.

"She has a point," said Moe.

"Does she?" I asked. "The cat doesn't speak German? He's a cat. He doesn't speak anything."

"Mercy," said Grandma. "I'm disappointed in you."

And here we go.

"Abandoning a helpless animal. How could you?"

"I haven't abandoned anyone. He's here, being looked after by Ella."

"What about your Skanky? Would you want Skanky abandoned in a foreign country?" Grandma couldn't have been more dramatic if she'd channeled Meryl Streep.

"Skanky?" Moe asked.

"My cat."

"You named your cat Skanky?"

"I tried to name him something else, but he was, ya know, skanky," I said. "This is off-topic."

"Janine," said Moe, "I know she's your granddaughter, but I don't think I can trust her to make this decision after she decided to name her cat Skanky."

"That's not relevant," I said.

"I think it is," said Grandma. "We're taking him."

"Where?"

"Home. With us."

I threw up my hands. "Hotel. No cats."

"Figure something out," she said. "You're supposed to be good at that."

"We can't just take that cat," I said. "He's not our cat."

Grandma pointed at the table. "You're taking the book, receipts, computers, and cellphones."

For crying out loud.

"Fine. I will call Kimberly and tell her about this cat," I said.

"And tell her we will be bringing her brother's cat home to the United States where he belongs."

"I guess so but not today. He stays here for now."

Grandma deposited Porky Boy on the sofa and smiled. "Alright then. Lunch. Where shall we go for our first meal?"

She bustled out of the apartment with Aaron, pinging him with questions about sausages and dumplings.

"You really need a beer, don't you?" Moe asked.

"You have no idea."

CHAPTER SEVEN

I got my beer and then some. Aaron had directed Moe to some place in the middle of a town. He didn't use Google maps. He just went from memory like some kind of disheveled homing pigeon and before I knew it, I had a ginormous beer in my hand, looking at the modern mixed with old in a brewery restaurant. Grandma was thrilled. Lots of rafters and happy people hoisting beers, eating brown bread and a lot of weird stringy salad. The menu was typical and the place smelled fantastic. I was ready to order anything and everything.

"Mercy, dear," said Grandma. "Do you want to split the Bavarian sausage?"

"For the appetizer? Sure."

"For the lunch," she said.

"Grandma, that's an appetizer. It's like one sausage and a pretzel."

She folded up her menu. "Perfect."

"You want half a sausage for lunch."

"Anything more would be too much, Mercy." She patted her stomach. "I'd get so bloated."

"I have to have more than that," I said.

"Who am I going to split my sausage with then?"

"Don't look at me," said Moe from behind his menu. His admiration of my grandmother only went so far. I didn't bother to look at Aaron. He'd never split anything in his life.

"I'll split it," I said.

"Oh, good. Now we'll be light on our feet." Grandma went back to admiring the brewery and I leaned over to Aaron. "Help me. So hungry."

Aaron nodded and I took Grandma off to the bathroom when the waitress headed our way.

"But we need to order," she complained.

"Aaron is an excellent orderer. He'll handle it."

And he did. He handled the hell out of that order. Our trestle table was covered with Rostbraten, Goulash, various pork dishes, salads, and, let's not forget, Grandma's one white sausage and pretzel.

"Oh, what happened?" exclaimed Grandma. "Didn't you use your German, Aaron?"

"I did," he said, digging in.

"But this is too much food."

"Look, there's your sausage, Grandma." *Small, sad, and lonely with only a pretzel for company.*

"It's huge. I had no idea it would be so large," she said. "Mercy, you have to take half that sausage."

I speared the offending porker and cut it in half. "Consider it done."

Moe and Aaron plowed through the piles of food with a take no prisoners attitude while I tried to be a lady and not look like I was ready to chew the leg off the table. Grandma delicately sliced her half sausage and somehow managed to spend the same amount of time eating almost nothing and proclaiming herself stuffed. But she was having a grand old time. She really could speak German and conversed with the neighboring tables, complimented the waitress, and squirreled away all kinds of useful advice on Christmas markets and castles.

Once the dishes were cleared, she picked up her menu again and said, "Mercy, do you want to split an apple strudel? Claudia says they are freshly made right here by the owner's mother."

Why do we have to split everything?

"Sure," I said.

"Should we ask them to leave off the vanilla ice cream? That will be so rich."

Aaron plucked the menu out of her hands and said, "Apple strudel is eaten with vanilla ice cream."

"It's tradition, Grandma." *Fight that, Janine!*

"Well, if it's tradition," she said. "You boys will have to help us with that strudel."

"Janine, I think you're swell, but I'm ordering chocolate cake," said Moe.

Aaron ignored Grandma's pleas and ordered off-menu. He got Rote Grütze, a kind of warm berry pudding. It came with vanilla ice cream, too. Grandma was so intrigued she tried it and then proclaimed that she'd eaten so much she wouldn't need dinner. Nightmare.

"You should have some of my cake, Janine," said Moe.

No. She'll say she doesn't need breakfast tomorrow.

"I shouldn't," she said.

"Oh, live a little. We're on vacation."

"We're on an investigation," I said.

"Tomato. Tomahto," he said.

"Potato. Patahto," she said.

What's happening?

Then Grandma and Moe sang together, "Let's call the whole thing off."

My phone buzzed and Grandma said, "Moe, you are just so much fun. I will try that cake."

Moe slid the dish over to Grandma and asked, "Who is it?" as I glanced at my screen.

"Novak." I called him back, but then Moe broke into song again, joined by Grandma.

"I'm going to take this outside where I can hear."

Anything to get away from Gershwin. I thought the Germans would frown upon Moe belting it out, but a fab voice came out of that unusual man and before I got outside half the place was singing. I guess everyone knows Gershwin.

I stepped out under the overhang by the door to avoid the continuing drizzle. "Hey, Novak."

"Was that Gershwin?" he asked.

"It was."

"Where are you?"

"Stuttgart," I said.

"I know that. Are you at a musical?"

"I am now."

"What?"

"Nothing. I need some help. Have you got a minute?"

"If you're asking about the plants on Thooft's computer, I put that on the back burner when you said you weren't going until after Christmas," said Novak in his faint Serbian accent.

"Can you get it off the back burner?"

"Sure, but why did you suddenly get on a plane?"

"My dad tried to box me in, but it turns out I'm not square," I said.

"Screw your dad."

"Exactly."

"What do you need?" Novak asked.

I told him about Anton's three old laptops, the two phones, the rumors, and new old receipts.

"Are you cutting Spidermonkey out of this one?"

"Not at all." I loved my hacker, the one that didn't yell and bought me lattes. "He's asleep and you never are."

"True, but he's better at the financial stuff. I can do the computers and phones and get back on those plants."

"What do I do?" I asked. "Just turn 'em on?"

"How old are they?"

"Beats me, but they are heavy and thick."

"You can try to power them up, but they might not boot."

"So..."

"I'll come over."

"Over where?" I asked.

"There. Stuttgart."

"Do you leave Paris?"

"Not often...or ever, but I will in this case," said Novak. "I'm packing."

"What's going on?"

"So suspicious."

"Tommy Watts' daughter, so hell yeah I am. Why are you leaving Paris for me at Christmastime? I'm not even paying you that much."

"My mother's threatening to come see me," he said.

"And that's bad?" I asked.

"I'm not square, either."

"Alrighty then. I'll see you in..."

"Approximately four hours. Hotel?"

I gave him our particulars, which pleased him to no end. Close to the train station.

"What are you going to tell your mother?" I asked.

"That I had a friend in dire need. A female friend."

"That'll do it?"

"She'll be thrilled. I might have to take pictures of us together," said Novak. "For proof."

"She's gonna know it's not true, you and me," I said.

"How?"

"The internet. Me. Everywhere."

"My mother hates technology. She won't go near a computer. Why do you think I love them so very much?"

"You have issues, my friend," I said.

"I'm not the only one."

"Is your mother also stylish?" I asked, thinking of his garish biking attire.

"Hanging up now," said Novak. "Call Spidermonkey."

We hung up and I looked in the brewery window. Still singing. What in the holy hell? I went out to the Mercedes and found the receipts. Then I texted pictures of them to Spidermonkey. By the time, I'd done that, my phone was ringing.

"That was quick," I said.

"Or you were slow," said Spidermonkey.

"I thought you were sleeping."

"It's eight-thirty."

"Is it? I'm so tired. Wicked jet lag," I said. "So you got the receipts?"

I heard him rustle around and a chair creak. "I did. Where'd you find them?"

I told him about Anton's apartment and he started typing like mad. "I've got the ATM. Business area of the town, but there are apartments over the shops. He might've met the blackmailer in a café. I don't see any other charges on his accounts in Weil der Stadt on those days, but I'll go back and see if I can find something before."

"That's interesting," I said. "Ella McWilliams said Anton was seen meeting kids in cafés next to hotels."

"Mercy, there are hotels everywhere."

"I know, but it was oddly specific. Like someone really saw something and put two and two together but didn't want to name names."

"I've seen zero evidence that Thooft had any interest in kids other than academically. I mean nothing. Not a hint and I looked through everything in Liberty High and in Stuttgart. No one made any allegations of any kind."

"Until he was dead," I said. "Then it got weird."

Spidermonkey sighed. "It's kids. They love drama."

"I've got a feeling. There's something to it."

"Alright. I will dig back into the high school there and see what the chatter is. Do you have a name or names?"

"Ella didn't want to say," I said.

"I'll check out Ella," said Spidermonkey.

The thought made me feel bad. That girl was sad and harassed and we were going to go through her private phone? I didn't like it and said so.

"We do this all the time, Mercy."

"But I know her. She's hurting."

"She'll hurt less when you solve it."

"That's what I thought about Kimberly."

"I see what you mean," said Spidermonkey. "How about I check her Instagram and get her contacts and messages? I'll see who's saying this crap to or about her."

"Alright."

"I won't dig into a fourteen-year-old girl's private thoughts. I could, but I won't."

"That is way less comforting than you think," I said.

"I know, but we're the good guys."

"Sometimes it's hard to tell."

Spidermonkey laughed. "Especially when you've got Moe Licata with you."

"I don't know why that happened," I said.

"Calpurnia put him on you."

"Why? It looks like a stiff wind could blow him over."

"Here's a free heads up. Moe is more than he appears to be."

"I bet. Want to elaborate?"

"I want to work so you solve this, come home, and your father stops calling me," said Spidermonkey.

"Are you serious?" I asked.

"He tried to get me to shut down your phone, cancel your flight from Amsterdam to Stuttgart, and more. He's off his nut about a mile and a half."

"*White Christmas!*" I said happily.

"Now that's my favorite detective," he said. "Go out and do what you do. For the record, I'm glad Moe's with you."

"Weird."

"That's your life."

We hung up and I opened the door to the brewery and strains of "White Christmas" burst out. Un-freaking-believable.

"Mercy, wake up."

"I'm awake," I muttered into my pillow.

Grandma shook me. "You're facedown."

"I'm sniffing my pillow."

"With your eyes closed?"

"It helps with the smelling," I said.

"You're sleeping. We're not supposed to be sleeping," she said. "It was your rule."

"Rules are flexible. Go away."

"Rules are not flexible. That's why they are called rules," she said. "Get up and go to the door."

"Why on Earth would I do that?"

"I told you there's someone at the door."

"When?"

"Just now."

"Tell them to go away," I said, burying my face deeper into the high class down of the best pillow ever. Jetlag was a thing and I was no longer fighting it.

"I tried that and he wouldn't go. Mercy, he is the oddest man I've ever seen," said Grandma.

"Is it Moe?"

"Moe's not odd."

"You need glasses."

She shook me hard and gave my butt a smack. "Get up. This man is insisting on seeing you and he might be crazy."

I rolled over, eyes still closed. "What are the indications of insanity?"

"He's wearing some kind of athletic outfit. Is there skiing near here?"

"Skiing?"

"I think he's going skiing. I've seen those kinds of suits in the Olympics."

"Weird."

"Very and he says he knows you, but he wouldn't tell me his name. He could be a stalker. Maybe you shouldn't go to the door. I'll call security or Moe."

"Don't call Moe. He might shoot him."

"If he's a stalker, I don't care."

I sat up and yawned. "He's not a stalker. He's our hacker out of Paris."

A loud knock resounded through our hotel room and Grandma jumped.

"He sounds angry. I'm calling Moe." She pulled out her phone and I rolled out of bed.

"He probably is angry. How long has he been out there?"

"Ten minutes."

"For crying out loud!"

"You wouldn't wake up," she said. "Don't blame me."

I dashed to the door and looked out the peephole. It was Novak and I can't say I blamed Grandma for not trusting him. He wore a skintight racing suit, a pile of gold chains, and had his usual man bun up on the top of his head. I should've expected it. The only time I'd ever seen Novak, it was in Paris during summer and he'd always been dressed in the most garish biking outfits possible.

He knocked again and I opened the door. "What are you wearing?"

"Clothes," said Novak with a smile. "What took so long?"

"I was sleeping and that is not clothes. My grandma thinks you're insane."

"Don't tell him that!" she yelled behind me.

"Too late!" I waved him in and Novak stalked past me six two, rail-thin, and nothing left to the imagination. He walked directly over to my grandmother and offered a hand. "Novak and you are the grandmother?"

Grandma swallowed and took his hand reluctantly. "Janine Watts. What is your last name?"

"I don't have one." Novak did a spin. "So you think I'm insane?"

"It crossed my mind," she said.

"Good. That's the point. People don't bother you if they think you're crazy."

"Mission accomplished," I said, flopping down on the bed.

"Don't go back to sleep," said Grandma.

"She won't get on the right schedule," said Novak.

"I know. She made me stay awake.

"You slept in the car. Twice," I said.

"That doesn't count."

"It does," I said. "I wish we had a coffee maker."

Grandma spun around. "We must have a coffee maker. Where is it?"

"They don't do that here."

She put her hands on her hips. "That is pure insanity. Worse than that getup you're wearing, Novak. Where can I get coffee?"

"Try the café downstairs," I said.

"Will they give me to-go cups?"

"I doubt it, but real cups are fine."

Grandma reapplied her lipstick and ran a comb through her hair. "Don't say anything important until I get back."

Novak waited until she was gone before he said, "Are we waiting?"

"Not hardly," I said.

"Where are the computers?"

I pointed at a chair with our coats piled up on them and he tossed the coats aside to check out Anton's ancient electronics. He placed each laptop at the foot of the bed in a row and then picked up the phones. "Cords?"

"Try that bag. We didn't know what went to what, so we took the whole mess."

Novak dumped the bag and shook his head. "Why do people keep all their cords?"

"Because we don't know what goes to what and we might need them."

"Ridiculous."

"I don't deny it," I said.

After some searching, he did find all the right ones but then picked up each computer, weighing them in his expert hands, like he was assessing something through osmosis.

"This one might have been cannibalized," he said.

"How can you tell?"

"It's a bit light. I'll have to crack it open if it doesn't power up."

"Did you bring tools for that?"

He raised an eyebrow at me and that was the end of that.

"What would be missing?"

"Power supply is my guess, but I've got spares," he said. "I should be able to get these old guys up and running in an hour or so, barring anything too catastrophic. What else have you got for me?"

"Nothing. Have you got anything on the Incel sites or 4chan?"

Novak stacked up the laptops and phones. "Zeroing in on the location of the hack. It didn't originate in Stuttgart. I can tell you that."

"Really?" I asked.

"You're surprised? I thought we were looking at The Klinefeld Group for this."

"Chuck is. I'm not."

"And why is that?"

"Just a feeling. It's not their style," I said.

Novak undid his bun and shook out an amazing head of hair, nearly waist length and wavy. Women would kill for that hair. "They don't have a problem with murder, but kidnapping's off the table?"

"No, but if they wanted to nab me, they wouldn't send a flipping teacher."

Novak nodded. "I've been thinking about that. The combination of sophistication and amateurism is interesting."

"If you track the hack on Anton's computer to Berlin, I'll believe The Klinefeld Group is involved. Until then I'm sticking close to home. Somebody knew him well enough to get the family secret and this is a guy that was very good at keeping secrets."

Grandma came in with a tray of coffees in elegant glass mugs and scowled at us. "You didn't wait. I can tell."

Novak apologized and was even contrite. I didn't think he did contrite. As a human he was the least interested in other human's impressions of him than anyone I knew. Other than Aaron, but that was only because Aaron was completely unaware that anyone could see him and judge. Novak knew and didn't give a crap.

"You're forgiven, but I want a complete rundown," said Grandma.

"I will give it to you, but Novak has to get on Anton's electronics with a quickness," I said.

Grandma smiled. "You sound just like Ace."

"I can't help it."

"I know." She picked up a latte and asked, "So what's next for us?"

Like I have a plan. Puhlease.

"I'll think of something."

Novak looked at Grandma. "She wings it."

"I don't believe that we came all the way to Germany without some semblance of a plan."

"Believe it," I said.

"I thought Ace was making that up."

"He was not."

She rolled her eyes and gave me a latte. "Well, I want a plan or we're going to the Christmas markets right now."

Novak picked up the stack of electronics and hoofed it out. "Enjoy the Christmas markets."

"Thanks for the confidence," I yelled as the door closed.

"Well?" Grandma asked.

"Er..."

"We can walk right over to the Schlossplatz. It's not far."

The caffeine hit me and I said, "I'll call Natalie."

"Who's Natalie?"

"Chuck's friend from when he was active duty. He called her for me. She's going to get me on the military post so I can talk to people," I said.

"What people?" Grandma asked.

"People people."

There was another knock and she answered the door. I was hoping for Novak as a distraction, but it was Moe and Aaron, raring to go.

"What's the plan?" Moe asked. "We're ready."

"My granddaughter doesn't do plans apparently." Grandma crossed her arms and tapped her foot. I didn't know she was a planner. She always just seemed to go with the flow. Grandad wasn't someone who stuck to a plan, not hers anyway.

"Fats told me, but she said Mercy usually has a direction."

They all looked at me, except Aaron. He was looking at the wall.

"There are chimney cakes on the Schillerplatz," said Aaron.

"Oh, I'd like to try that," said Grandma.

"We can split it," I said sarcastically.

She rubbed her hands together. "Perfect. That's the plan."

"That is not the plan for me," I said. "I'll contact Natalie and meet her. You three Christmas nuts can go to the market."

"I'm not leaving you," said Moe. "Fats would have a fit."

"Like you're scared of Fats."

"Everyone with a brain is scared of my niece. I'm not saying I couldn't bring her down, but it would be tight. She can take a bullet and keep coming."

"I don't know what to do with that," I said. "I'm going to see Natalie, if she's not busy. That's all I know."

Grandma put on a brave face and said, "Then that's what we're doing. Christmas market tomorrow. You should have plenty of clues by then and we can take a break."

"Er..."

"That's the plan," she declared.

New plan. Haha. Good luck fighting this one, Janine.

"Well, if I'm going on post, Natalie will have to sign me in," I said apologetically. "Signing in three people is a hassle. You and Aaron can go to the market. We can meet up later."

"She doesn't have to sign me in," said Grandma, digging in her purse and coming up with an ID. "I brought my retiree ID card."

Crap on a cracker.

"Well, that's still three."

Moe held up an ID card. "Two. I've got mine."

"What the...?" I asked. "You brought a fake military ID. Are you crazy?"

"It's not fake."

He showed it to Grandma, and she said, "Nice photo. I always look drunk."

He took a look at hers and said, "You do. Very drunk."

"Who gave you an ID?" I asked.

"The army," said Moe. "I'm a retiree."

"Since when?" I asked.

"1975."

"How in the world did that happen?"

Moe sat down on the edge of my bed and cracked his knuckles. "Eight years of service. Medically retired. Honorably discharged, before you ask."

Grandma pulled up a chair. "That's how you know Ace. I knew it wasn't just the arrest."

"We go way back, right to Vietnam."

Holy crap!

"You were in Vietnam with Grandad?" I asked.

"Not with him exactly, but we knew each other. He Medevaced me once," said Moe. "Guess what my job was?"

Don't say torture. Don't say torture.

"Do I have to?" I asked.

"EOD?" guessed Grandma.

"Good one, but no bombs for me."

Aaron turned from the wall and looked past Moe's noggin and said, "Sniper."

"Give that man a cigar," said Moe.

"That's better," I said.

"Than what?"

"Stuff." I took a sip of my latte and asked, "How did you end up in the military?"

"My mother had the idea," he said. "She wanted to get me away from bad influences."

The Fibonaccis. Smart lady.

"I guess it didn't work," I said.

"Sure, it did. I was hanging with the O'Reillys. We were friends in high school and they were on the path to no good."

"Oh," said Grandma. "The O'Reillys. A nasty bunch. They were big in drug smuggling and prostitution back in the day."

"Exactly. They were particularly violent and it seemed like someone got knifed every other day. My mother wanted me away from that."

"So she sent you to *Vietnam*," I said.

"Well, I wasn't going to college and my options were limited. Besides, the army could use a guy like me. I had skills, even at seventeen."

Yikes.

"On that note, I'll call Natalie," I said, hoping to change the conversation. Fat chance.

"And you stayed eight years?" asked Grandma.

"Until an ambush in Cambodia did this," he gestured to his hump, "to my back. I spent a year in hospital and then they retired me because they couldn't fix it."

I got out my phone and looked in my purse for Natalie's number. I had it somewhere. Why wasn't I organized like normal people?

"Do you miss it?" Grandma asked. "I think Ace does, but he won't talk about it."

I found the number and got ready to dial, but Moe said something that stopped me. "I do miss it. The army was my family and I didn't want to leave. It was the first time I was myself. Just Moe Licata, not Nuncio Licata's kid or Mateo Licata's grandson. If people were scared of me, it was because of me and my skill, not a reputation that someone else earned." He looked at me and said, "You understand."

I did. I really did. Being Tommy Watts' kid and to a lesser extent Ace Watts' granddaughter was a calling card I didn't want to have. Some cops, criminals, and media had a thing about me. Always comparing my performance and finding it less than satisfactory.

"Yeah, I do," I said.

Grandma frowned and started to ask something, but I quickly dialed.

"This is Natalie," said a woman who picked up immediately.

"Hi. This is Mercy, Chuck's girlfriend," I said, walking out of the hotel room and the chatter about snipers and targeting. Don't want to know about that.

"Oh, my God. I was hoping you'd call," said Natalie.

"Were you?"

"Of course. I haven't seen Chuck in forever. Are you here in Stuttgart? You have to come for dinner. Tonight. Are you busy tonight?"

I glanced back at the door to my room. "Tonight's good. Can I take you out to dinner?"

"I wish, but I've got three boys and it's too late for a sitter. They can't be trusted not to burn down the place. I'll make something. It'll be edible," said Natalie.

"Well, I don't want to insult you, but I've got a chef with me. He will insist on cooking."

"Is it Aaron? Tell me it's Aaron." She was breathless with excitement.

"It's Aaron. How do you—"

"I follow him on Instagram. He's amazing. I can't wait."

"Aaron's on Instagram? Aaron of Kronos?"

"Yes, he's got like six million followers," said Natalie.

Maybe I'm still asleep.

"Aaron cannot have six million followers on Instagram," I said. "He's...Aaron."

Natalie laughed. "I know. Isn't he great?"

"Um..."

"So six. We're on Patch Barracks. Call me when you get to the gate and I'll get your passes. I'm so excited."

She hung up before I could respond and I just stood there in the hall dazed and confused. I avoided Instagram like genital herpes. Everyone on there wanted to sniff my feet or say horrible things about me. I had an account at one point, but it was such a dumpster fire that I had to shut it down and Uncle Morty had to get all the fake accounts in variations of my name taken down. It was a nightmare.

I leaned against the wall and googled Aaron and Instagram. There the little weirdo was stuffing a sausage, making arancini, and stewing intestines for andouillette. He did have six million followers. What in the world?

My phone buzzed, but I couldn't stop staring at an Aaron video. He was making a lasagna, pork fried rice, five Worf burgers, and a layer cake at the same time. It looked superhuman and delicious.

"Hey, Mercy."

I looked up and Moe stood in the doorway. "Your phone is buzzing."

"Did you know Aaron is on Instagram?" I asked.

"Of course. I follow him."

I just stared. Aunt Miriam couldn't figure out how to answer her phone or even turn it on, but Moe Licata was a Vietnam vet and on Instagram. The world made no sense.

Moe came over and took my phone. "Maybe you do need to sleep." He took a look at my messages. "Your father. Your father. Your grandfather. Your father again. Oh, and one we want Mr. McWilliams. Sherri

La Roche will talk to you. She lives on Patch Barracks and he sent her number."

"Thanks," I said.

"Are you okay?"

I shook my head. "Just surprised. It's been a weird day."

"Aren't all your days weird?"

"Yeah, but it still surprises me," I said.

"May I make a suggestion?"

"Go for it."

"Let's hit a Christmas market after Natalie's," he said, blinking his bulging eyes at me. "Janine won't rest until she gets to one."

I gave him a thumbs-up before going back to my bed and sniffing my pillow.

CHAPTER EIGHT

We parked in front of Natalie's building on Patch Barracks and it wasn't at all what I expected. Natalie was a captain, so I thought rank had some privileges, but apparently not. The stairwell housing was basic and charmless with uncovered parking and clusters of barbecues between buildings. Grandma said base housing was the pits and while it wasn't a pit I doubted people were clamoring to live there.

"This looks familiar," said Moe.

Grandma laughed. "The military never changes."

Natalie came over from her car and we got out. She wasn't what I expected either. Chuck described her as tough, so I pictured tough. To me, Fats Licata was tough. Natalie Ratliff was not. The Air Force officer was five feet tall and a hundred pounds soaking wet. She had dark auburn hair, green eyes and a face full of freckles. Natalie was somewhere between an imp and an elf and totally adorable. The tough was hard to get. Maybe she was a sniper, too. Apparently, size wasn't a requirement for that.

"Did I tell you how glad I am to meet you?" she asked.

"Yes, you did."

"Well, I am." Natalie took my arm. "Will you introduce me? I'm so nervous."

"About what?"

"Aaron. I hope he likes my kitchen. I cleaned it. Twice. It's not big. Better than off post, but basic. An electric stove. He probably hates electric. I have an Instant Pot. Does he use those? Am I talking too fast? I do that."

"Breathe," I said. "It's Aaron."

"What if he doesn't like me?" She was serious. Dead serious.

I turned around to look at the man who was causing all the fuss, just to make sure she wasn't thinking of someone else. She wasn't. She was looking right at Aaron with his favorite stonewashed jeans, six inches too long, half his hair sticking up and the other slicked down, possibly with butter, and a Star Trek jacket complete with emblem.

"If he doesn't, you'll never be able to tell," I said.

"What do you mean?"

"Aaron likes food. Do you have food?"

"I have food, but what if it's not the right food? He's gourmet," said Natalie.

"He loves hot dogs and those horrible snowball snack cakes. You're good."

She took a breath and I introduced her to what I could only assume was her cooking idol.

"Aaron, this is Natalie. Natalie, this is Aaron."

"Hi," she said.

"You hungry?" he asked.

"Yes."

"Where's the kitchen?"

That was it. She told him which apartment and he trotted inside without waiting. Natalie dashed after him and I dashed after her.

"Don't panic," I said. "He'll make something great."

"I should show him the lay of the land."

"Don't worry about it. He's a kitchen savant."

When we got up to the second floor, Aaron was already in the kitchen. He had eighteen ingredients on the counter and a kettle on.

"What's he going to make?" Natalie whispered.

"It's a mystery," I said, holding out a bottle. "Let's have wine."

Moe pulled the cork and Natalie told us her husband Luke was deployed at the moment and introduced us to her boys. The older two were stepsons and full of acne and angst. The youngest was the spitting image of Natalie, freckles and all.

"Whoa," said the oldest, Daniel. "You really do look like Marilyn Monroe."

"And you look like a freshman," I said.

Daniel was taken aback. "Why?"

"Can I interview you?"

He looked at his stepmother and she grinned. "I guess you're part of the investigation."

The poor kid started fidgeting with his tee shirt and said, "You mean the stuff with Mr. Thooft? I don't know anything about that. I wasn't in his class or anything."

Natalie sent the other two off to play video games. That got a cheer. Video games before dinner was a serious treat. Moe asked what they had and they named some first-person shooter game, so Moe volunteered to supervise, i.e. kick some video villain butt. Grandma decided to help Aaron and we went into the living room with Daniel who would rather have shot aliens any day of the week.

I told Natalie and Daniel what I was doing and why. The more I talked the more nervous Daniel got. It didn't necessarily mean anything. Kids get nervous. Getting in trouble is so easy and can come out of nowhere.

"Have you heard the rumors?"

"Everybody has, but I don't know if it's true," said Daniel.

"Did you ever hear anything bad about Mr. Thooft before he died?" I asked.

"No, not at all. He was great. Everybody wanted to be in his classes."

"Was he especially close to anyone?"

Daniel pulled back and frowned. "No. I don't know. He was a teacher."

Too pointed.

"I meant, did you see him with anyone in particular, a teacher or a student?"

The boy shrugged.

Natalie put her arm around her son. "Come on. He was a student council sponsor. You saw him every week."

"He was like really tight with the seniors and some juniors. I'm just a freshman. I barely knew him."

"Who's on student council?"

Daniel named some names and Natalie asked, "You don't think some kids are mixed up with this, do you?"

I smiled and said, "I'm following a lead."

"What's the lead?"

"The comment about Mr. Thooft being seen with kids outside school in a café next to hotels."

"Oh, I heard that," said Daniel.

I crossed my fingers and asked, "Who was seen with him?"

"I don't know. People were just saying it."

Dammit.

"Who did you hear saying it, Daniel?" Natalie asked. "Who was spreading the rumor?"

"Everyone was talking about it. They said Mr. Thooft was a freak and on those Incel sites. He was a stalker or something."

I leaned forward and looked into Daniel's eyes. "He wasn't any of those things. He was being blackmailed and I think it might have something to do with those rumors."

"Really? That's weird."

"There's a chance that someone saw someone with Mr. Thooft and I want to know who that was."

"But he was a teacher," said Natalie. "He saw kids all the time."

"But this café thing was unusual or at least someone thought it was. I have to follow up." I looked back at Daniel. "Who did you hear saying it?"

"I don't want to get anyone in trouble," he said.

"You didn't tell me anything." I crossed my heart.

"I heard Sergio Tarantina say it. He's on student council."

Daniel described the student council's emergency meeting that was held right after Anton Thooft was shot. Everyone was in an uproar and trying to decide what to do. A teacher was dead and a moment of silence seemed appropriate, but he was a kidnapper. Before the meeting started when everyone was arriving, Sergio was telling people that he always knew Mr. Thooft was a freak and that he hung out with kids in cafés next to hotels. He made it sound like Anton was going into a hotel with a student, but he didn't name any names, and then the meeting started. After that, the whole school knew and then the 4chan stuff broke on the news. It was crazy after that.

"Sergio talking about the café thing, that was the first time you heard it?" I asked.

"Yeah, but my friend Jordan already knew about it when I tried to tell him and he's not on student council," said Daniel.

"Is Jordan a freshman, too?"

"Sophomore. He was in Mr. Thooft's seminar so he knew him better than me."

"Who told Jordan?" Natalie asked.

Daniel shrugged.

"Can you ask him?" I asked.

He tried to wriggle out of it and I understood. Nobody wants to be the one who pointed the finger.

"It's about who blackmailed Mr. Thooft," I said. "It wasn't his idea to hurt me. I deserve to know who's it was."

Daniel sunk back into the sofa, looking as though he'd like to sink inside the cushions. "Does it matter? He's dead."

"They aren't," I said. "Mr. Thooft died and they're just walking around like they had nothing to do with his death. It's not right. His sister wants to know who did this to him and me."

"The adopted sister?" Natalie asked.

"Yes. She needs to find out. She loved him very much."

Natalie got up and found Daniel's phone, tossing it in his lap. "Call Jordan."

"If Dad were here—"

"He's not here. I'm here. I'm always here." Natalie stood there, hands on hips and I saw the tough. That boy could not take her, even though he outweighed her by fifty pounds. "Call Jordan."

Daniel called and the kid did a pretty good job of casually asking about the rumors. He used me. "My mom knows Mercy Watts." "Do you think Mr. Thooft was really a freak?" That kind of thing. When he got off the phone, he said, "He heard it in pre-calc. Alison Fodor said it before class to her friend, Cameron."

"Who was seen in the café?" I asked.

"She just said it happened."

Natalie eyed her son. "That's not enough. Call him back. Ask again."

"No way. He was getting funny," said Daniel. "I could tell."

"It's fine." I leaned back and looked at the ceiling. So frustrating. It could be nothing. If the plants on Anton's laptop came out of Berlin, I could be eating crab and Chuck wouldn't clean a bathroom, probably ever.

"I hope I'm not barking up the wrong tree," I said.

"Was there anything else?" Natalie asked.

"Just that it was in Sindelfingen," said Daniel.

I sat bolt upright. "What was that?"

"Jordan said that Alison said the café was in Sindelfingen."

Ding. Ding. Ding.

I held up a hand for a high-five. "Daniel, you are my favorite freshman."

He blushed and asked, "Can I take a picture with you?"

"You can take twenty as long as you don't post them until I've solved this."

"Let's not go overboard," Natalie said. "I'll take the pictures to keep them on the down-low."

"My dad loves Double Black Diamond," said Daniel. "Could you sign your cover?"

"Absolutely."

I signed the album cover that Daniel's dad had ordered in vinyl. He was an old-school rock fan. We took pictures and I showed him pictures of Mickey Stix and the gang. Daniel forgot all about high school allegiances and we ate well when Aaron brought out bulgogi, papaya salad, and these sweet little rice cakes made with a sticky syrup.

The boys were hesitant but loved the food. They loved Moe even more. He told them he was a sniper and started teaching them techniques for their games. He slayed apparently and the boys were very impressed.

"I don't know how I feel about this," said Natalie.

"That is a constant theme in my life," I said.

"I don't blame you. That attack just happened and here you are."

"Somebody had to do it and the case is closed for the cops stateside."

"What about the *Polizei*?" she asked.

I picked up another rice cake and said, "A crime committed by an American in America isn't their problem."

"But Thooft was here when he was blackmailed."

"Yes, and there is an open investigation, but nobody cares very much. He was an American that's now dead. They did interview everyone and search. Nothing turned up."

"Where do you go from here?" Natalie asked.

"Sherri La Roche," I said.

"Mrs. La Roche is freaking out," said Daniel. "I think she quit teaching."

"She didn't quit," said Natalie. "She took some sick time until Christmas break. They were close, she and Thooft, and it hit her hard."

"Do you know her well?" I asked.

"Pretty well. We volunteer at the Thrift shop together sometimes. She's a sweetheart."

"Have you talked to her about it?"

Natalie had taken over a casserole so Sherri wouldn't have to cook and described Anton's best friend as shattered and in denial. She said it was a mistake. He didn't do it. Couldn't be him. He'd been murdered. But a few days later, Natalie picked up her dish and Sherri had given in to the truth. The video from the surveillance cameras showing him heading for me and then driving away convinced her. Some jerk posted a picture taken of me while I was still in the trunk and that put the nail in the coffin so to speak. Sherri was close to hysterical and people had been pointing fingers on a local Facebook group. How didn't she know? Was she in on it? Pretty horrible stuff.

"I've heard of no links to her," I said.

"You'd know?" Natalie asked.

"I would. My guys have been all up in Anton's communications. Nothing but normal friend stuff going on or we'd be all over it. I do need to talk to her."

Natalie got up and grabbed a second bottle of wine. "Do you have to? She's...really upset."

"I understand, but she knew him best. I can't ignore that."

"If people find out, they'll think she really did have information. That Incel stuff. People really think he was one."

"They're going to find out," I said. "I won't make it public, but things have a way of coming out. It's just the way it is."

"She's very depressed. My lieutenant lives next door to her. He said they can hear her sobbing through the walls."

"I'll try to be as gentle as I can, but," a flash of anger went through me "I'm the one he knocked out and threw in a trunk. If I can deal, she can, too."

"I...I...I'm so sorry. I forgot who I was talking to." Natalie turned pink and her freckles stood out in sharp contrast.

I leaned back in my chair and threw back my wine.

"She's still recovering from her head injury," said Grandma. "It's been difficult."

"And there's the arm," said Moe. "Mercy gets to talk to whoever she wants."

Natalie nodded. "I completely agree, but you might run into a problem with Sherri."

"What's that?" I asked, feeling my temperature go back down.

"Her husband. Crabby Keith."

"Oh, yeah. Mr. McWilliams mentioned him. He won't let me near her?"

Natalie opened the wine and poured me a generous glug. "I have no idea. He's just crabby and doesn't like people to come over. She wanted to hold a book club at the apartment once and he put a stop to that."

"Dad didn't want you to have your knitting group here," Daniel pointed out.

"He's super crabby when he's on shift," said Marcus, the middle son.

The five-year-old, Tommy, raised his hand. "He's crabby when he has to do the dishes."

"Dad hates dishes," said Daniel.

"He's crabbier when he has to clean," said Marcus.

The boys went on to argue about their father's least favorite things as Natalie watched with surprise. Like most parents, she seemed shocked that the kids knew the score. Mom was surprised that I kept track of how many birthdays and holidays that Dad missed because there was a case, like somehow I didn't notice the empty Dad chair on Christmas morning. I'm not an idiot and neither were her kids.

"I'm getting that your husband might be crabby," I said.

Natalie sighed and took a big gulp of wine. "Aren't they all?"

"Ace isn't crabby," said Grandma. "Of course, I've barely seen him for fifty years, so I'm not sure I'd know."

We looked at Moe, who laughed. "Women as a species decided I'm not the marrying kind."

"What about Chuck?" Natalie asked. "He was never crabby with me, but people change."

"Who's Chuck?" Daniel asked.

"He's Mercy's boyfriend."

"How do you know him?"

"We used to date and were engaged for a while before I met your dad," said Natalie, offhandedly. "So is Chuck crabby?"

Used to date? Engaged?

"Uh...not usually," I said.

"He was crabbier when The Blues were playing. Can't interrupt hockey. Does he still watch hockey?"

My stomach twisted up into a knot. "He's been working a lot."

"Now baseball you can interrupt, but he still watched it. Football was somewhere between the two. It depended on the team. Luke doesn't watch sports over here. We can't get them in real-time."

"Maybe that's why he's crabby," said Daniel.

"Dad needs sports," said Marcus.

"The Watts men don't usually go in for sports," said Grandma.

Moe got himself more wine. “But he’s not really a Watts, is he?”

“He’s not?” Daniel asked.

“He’s adopted,” said Natalie. “Mercy’s uncle adopted him when he married Chuck’s mother.”

“You’re cousins?” Marcus asked. “Gross.”

“We’re not blood-related,” I said. “Chuck’s mom was married to my uncle less than two years. She divorced him and married someone else pretty quick. Watts was Chuck’s third last name and he refused to change it when the next husband came along.”

“At least you were only cousins for a little while,” Moe said.

“Sixteen months,” said Grandma. “I could not stand that woman. I knew she’d divorce Rupert. She divorces everyone.”

“How many marriages is she on now?”

“Five?” Natalie asked me.

Somebody is pretty up to date.

I nodded and she got solemn. “He didn’t tell you about me, did he?”

“No, he did not,” I said.

Grandma sucked her lips and Moe made a grumbling sound like a roll of thunder.

“It wasn’t a big deal,” said Natalie quickly. “We only went out for a while.”

“Through all the sports seasons,” I said. “And got engaged.”

“Well, yes.”

“And he was enlisted and you were an officer, correct?”

“Dude,” said Marcus. “Can you do that?”

Natalie stood up and started clearing the table. Ah, the old mom trick for avoiding things. Start cleaning. “We weren’t in the same chain of command.”

My phone buzzed and it was Chuck. I wanted to bite the screen. The man sent me to his old girlfriend and didn’t tell me. Natalie was in the know and I wasn’t.

“That’s Sherri,” I said. “I’m going over.”

“Right now?” Grandma asked.

“No time like the present.”

“She’s okay?” Natalie asked doubtfully.

I composed a quick message to Sherri and pressed send. I hoped she was ready for a visit because I was in no mood to be put off. "I guess we'll see."

I got up and Moe did, too. "Alright. Here we go."

"Here I go," I said. "You stay here. The boys need more sniper lessons."

The boys loudly concurred.

"I told Fats I'd watch your back," he said. "Don't even try to Fi—"

"We're on an Army installation," I said. "It doesn't get much safer."

Moe went to come around the table. "I'm sticking to the plan."

Grandma grabbed his arm and said, "She's fine, Moe. Let her do her job."

"Janine," he started to say, but she cut him off.

"Aaron's got dessert, don't you Aaron?" she asked.

On cue, Aaron bolted to his feet and trotted into the kitchen.

Moe took the hint and asked, "What is he making?"

"Some kind of fluffy Japanese pancake."

Everyone got distracted by pancakes and I grabbed my coat. Grandma gave me an understanding nod as I bolted out the door. I don't know where I was going, but I was going fast.

Sherri answered me after I had wandered around the housing area for ten minutes. She was polite but not enthusiastic. It took some back and forth to convince her that I didn't blame her and I wasn't coming over to yell. I did want to yell, just not at her. I was trying to talk to a reluctant Sherri and Chuck kept pinging me. I was right on the edge of sending him the middle finger emoji when Sherri gave in and sent directions to her apartment.

Five minutes later, I was in more stairwell housing on the other side of the post and knocking on a door that had an enormous Grinch Christmas wreath. It was adorable and I wondered if it was a kind of warning about the husband within.

The door opened a narrow five inches and a blond woman with

eyes so swollen that she could barely see me through the slits looked out. "Hi."

"I'm Mercy. Is it okay if I ask you some questions?" I asked.

"Okay." She didn't open the door and it was flipping freezing. I didn't know thirty degrees could be so cold.

"Well, I wanted to ask about Anton's demeanor before he flew to the States. Was he nervous? Did he say anything about what he was doing?"

"No."

"Was he particularly close to any students?"

"No."

"Were you aware of any financial issues that he had?"

"No."

This is going well.

"Anton repeatedly took money out of an ATM in Sindelfingen. Were you ever with him when he did that?"

"No."

Breathe. You're not angry. You're a detective, dammit.

"Did he spend much time in Sindelfingen?" I asked.

"No."

"Oh, for God's sake, Sherri!" a man bellowed behind Sherri and she jumped a foot. "Open the damn door and let her in."

"I can't—"

Sherri didn't get a choice. The door was wrenched out of her hand and thrown open to reveal a man so muscular and wide he probably had to turn sideways to get out the door.

"Come in, Miss Watts. Let's get 'er done," he said, waving me past his startled wife. "I'm Keith, by the way."

Keith led me into a living room that was a carbon copy of Natalie's. They even had the same curtains. I sat down and he turned off the TV. Sherri hovered by the door, wringing her hands and sniffing.

"How are you doing, Miss Watts?" Keith asked gruffly. "You look better."

"Still getting headaches, but I'm a lot better. Thanks for asking."

"No problem." Keith looked at his wife.

Sherri took a step back and said, "I don't think I can."

Every muscle in Keith's huge arms tensed. "You have been crying for two goddamn weeks. It didn't happen to you. It happened to her. Stop crying, get in here, and answer her fucking questions."

She shook her head. "I'm upset."

"You're upset? That asshole friend of yours knocked this girl out and threw her in a trunk and she's not fucking crying. She just wants to ask you some questions."

"Dr. Roberts said—"

"Dr. Roberts needs to pull his head out of his ass. You're not the victim. You knew the guy for a year and he was a murderer."

"Anton was not a murderer!"

"Oh, yeah? What do you think they were going to do with her? Take her to Euro Disney and buy her Mickey ears?"

"It's Disneyland Paris!" yelled Sherri.

"That's what you think is important?" Keith jolted to his feet. "I can't do it. I have to...I have to leave." He left, left without a coat and slamming the door so hard I'm surprised it stayed on the hinges.

Sherri and I stared at each other. She didn't move. I didn't move. I knew one thing. I wasn't leaving.

"Can you—"

I cut her off. "No. Just sit down and suck it up. It won't be a nightmare, I promise, and I know nightmares. You can trust me on that."

Sherri came over, keeping as far from me as possible, like I might spit acid at her or something. "What do you want to know?"

"Let me tell you what I know first." I ran down everything I had, putting particular emphasis on Anton being blackmailed and his attempt to forestall the inevitable. I made him sound innocent. He wasn't. At some point, he chose protecting himself over me, but it didn't matter. Sherri needed to hear how much he was a victim, so I told her that and it loosened her tongue. She told me everything about him and I have to admit he sounded pretty great. A fun guy to travel with. Great teacher. Interested in cooking. Anton Thooft was the closest friend Sherri had made in twenty years of military assignments. Her grief was real and I did feel for her. I really did, but I still needed information.

"Were there any students that he was particularly close to?" I asked.

"There were so many he helped with recommendation letters to colleges and with student council, but I never saw anyone as standing out."

"Who did he spend the most time on?"

"That would be the AP Gov students. That's a tough AP and he put in a tremendous amount of time with those kids."

"Did he mention any names repeatedly?"

"You don't really think one of our students was a part of this," she said. "They're kids. The biggest thing on their minds is getting into college."

"I bring it up because of that rumor about Anton meeting a student at a café in Sindelfingen."

Sherri thought the rumor was nuts. The only thing she knew him to do in Sindelfingen was to eat at the Greek restaurant there and occasionally hit the mall. I showed her the ATM he took money out of on my phone and she shook her head. "I've probably been by there. My hair salon is down the street, but I was never with Anton."

"Do you know a student named Sergio Tarantina?" I asked.

"Sure. He's a great kid. He's in my class and I think he was in Anton's AP Gov. I saw him in the study group when they were in the library. Why do you ask?"

"I heard that he was one of the first kids to start talking about the café rumor."

"Really? Anton had no problems with him that I know of."

"Do you know how I can get in touch with Sergio?" I asked.

"You can't," she said. "He's gone."

Crap on a cracker.

"He moved?"

"Oh, no," said Sherri. "He's in Austria skiing with his family. Sometimes people pull their kids out early at Christmas. They're here for a limited time and it's Europe after all. We were supposed to go to Norway next week, but I'm too upset. Keith's not happy. He doesn't understand."

Before I could respond, Keith walked back in, panting and covered in sweat. "I'm sorry. I just had to take a breather."

"By breather do you mean run six miles?" I asked.

"It's how I do," he said with a laugh.

"Keith loves to work out," said Sherri, frowning.

Those two had issues and they weren't all Anton.

"Sherri's been helping me out," I said.

"Good," said Keith.

"What were your impressions of Anton?"

Keith glanced at his wife and then laid it out. "He was weird."

"He was not weird," protested Sherri.

Her husband rolled his eyes. "You didn't notice because he knitted, liked The Real Housewives of whatever, and *loved* museums, but the guy was weird."

The handwringing started again, and she said, "He was not."

Keith went on to describe the Anton that I recognized, a guy that wouldn't answer direct questions and was insanely private.

"Private isn't a bad thing," said Sherri.

"He was hiding things and someone found out."

"I don't think so."

Keith threw up his hands again. "He was hiding his screwed-up family and God knows what else."

"There was nothing else!"

"What about that café thing everyone's talking about?"

Sherri stood up and burst into tears before running out. Keith put his head in his hands. "Sorry. I just keep losing my temper. I didn't like him when he was alive. Now that he's dead, I hate him."

"Why didn't you like him?" I asked. "Most people did. Actually, you're the first person I've met that didn't."

Keith sat back and thought it over. "I'm a simple man. You take care of your family. You protect your country. You tell the truth. That's it. You live your life with those things in mind, things work out."

"So?"

"Anton Thooft was a liar and I've got a problem with a guy who lies to my wife, especially when she adores him."

I had a pretty good idea of where this was going, but I asked, "What did he lie about?"

"Being gay," he said. "He told my little sweetheart in there that it was some huge secret and that nobody knew. He made it out like she was so special that he could tell her. I didn't get the big deal. He was gay. So what?"

"Let me guess," I said. "He told other people, too."

Keith shot a finger at me. "Bingo."

"How many?"

"Two that I know of. Miss Watts, this is a small community. We know each other, especially if you live on post. Word gets around. I heard it from a friend of Anton's that works at the gym. Kelly volunteers at Sister Margaret's food pantry in downtown Stuttgart. Anton volunteered there, too. Anyway, she and Anton were tight. He pulled the same crap with her."

I smiled. "She wasn't very good with the secret."

"It just slipped out. I mentioned that Sherri was going to Greece with Anton last summer for a week. I wasn't thrilled. He was always going places with my wife. Anyway, Kelly just laughed and I guessed that she was in on it. After she confirmed, she swore me to secrecy."

"But Sherri had already told you?"

"She did, but when I told her that Kelly knew she blew it off."

"Who else did you hear it from?"

Keith went on to detail an interaction with a woman named Joanne in something called Outdoor Rec. She was tuning up his skis and they got to talking. Joanne knew Anton and had gone skiing with him several times. Her husband was the jealous type and didn't want her going anymore. Keith told her Anton was gay, thinking that might help out the situation, but she knew. She'd also heard it from a coordinator at the USO.

"That guy had issues," said Keith. "I was so sick of him. Anton this. Anton that. I might not be the greatest husband, but I don't lie about who I am." He spread his meaty arms wide. "This is it."

"It was a pattern with Anton," I said. "I don't really know why he did it."

"Screw that guy."

"I'm with you."

"I bet you are," said Keith. "You know who you should talk to?"

"Hit me," I said.

"One of the school counselors is all up in this Thooft crap."

A sense of calm came over me. Keith was straightforward. It was so refreshing. "Will you intro me?" I asked.

"It's Jackson Hobbes. He's one of my gym partners. I can call him right now."

"You're my favorite person in Germany."

Keith grinned at me. "I'm gonna want to take a picture with you for Instagram."

"Not a problem as long as you hold off on posting until I get a handle on this investigation." I posed with fish lips and he laughed a deep-throated laugh that reminded me of Grandad's Vietnam buddies. Good-humored guys that had seen some stuff and dealt with it the best they could. Sherri might be disappointed with her non-knitting husband, but I sure wasn't.

Keith dialed and then said, "Hobbes. La Roche. Guess who I've got sitting on my sofa right now?"

He waited a second and then laughed. "I wish. No. It's Mercy Watts."

A pause.

"I shit you not," he said. "No, I'm not gonna say that, man. Are you out of your mind?"

A longer pause and then a burst of laughter while I waited, still super relaxed. Keith mixed with wine was a good thing.

"She wants to meet up and ask about that Thooft douchebag," said Keith. "Have you still got all his stuff at the school?"

I raised a brow and he nodded.

"Great. Got time or are you hitting every Christmas market in Bavaria this weekend?"

He waited and then asked me, "Tomorrow at the school at nine?"

I gave him a thumbs-up.

"She'll be there," Keith said and then sighed. "Yeah, she's still crying. I'm hoping Miss Watts can find something out that will shut it down. Thanks."

Keith hung up. "He's going to try to talk to Sherri, but he scares her, so I don't think it'll work."

Oh, no.

"Why does he scare her?" I asked.

"Hobbes is old school. A marine from back in the day. He suffers no fools."

"And he's a high school counselor?"

"Second career and he's good. Students like the no-bullshit approach," he said. "Here's the thing with Hobbes. Don't mess around. You gotta come in hot. Do you understand what I mean?"

"My Grandad was a helicopter pilot in Vietnam. I get it."

"Those guys saw some shit. The stories I've heard will blow your mind. I've seen combat, but that was a totally different animal."

I thought of Grandad's burns and nodded. "He won't talk about it, but it was bad."

"No doubt." He nodded solemnly. "Any other questions for me?"

"Just a couple. Know anything about a kid named Sergio Tarantina?"

He shook his head. "Sherri might've mentioned him. Sounds vaguely familiar. Why?"

I told him about the rumors and he nodded, but said, "Can't help you with that."

"How about Alison? Any mention of that name?"

"I have to tell you Sherri loves her kids and she knows an ass-ton of them. I can't keep them straight," he said. "There are pictures. You want to see those."

"You continue to be my favorite person in Germany," I said.

Keith went into what he called the office and came out with a stack of photos. "Sherri got these prints before it all went down. They're for the yearbook. They were working on picking which one to choose before that asshole ran off and attacked you."

He sat next to me and we went through the stack. Mostly student council and the fall play. Natalie's son Daniel was in the student council photos, looking spindly and goofy compared to the older students. He was kind of adorable in a pimply and not-knowing-what-the-hell-is-going-on way.

"You can't name any of these kids?" I asked.

He shrugged his massive shoulders. "Sorry. I've seen them at functions, but I can't name names. Hobbes will be able to do that."

"Mind if I take some pictures of these?"

"Be my guest," said Keith.

When I was done, I stood up and said, "I have one more question. It's not related to the investigation though."

"How'd I get so massive?" he asked with a laugh.

"You got me," I said. "My boyfriend is trying to put on mass and it's not going well."

"For you or him?"

"Both."

"What's he doing?" Keith asked.

"Working out as much as humanly possible and eating boiled eggs and drinking disgusting shakes," I said.

"How many eggs?"

"A dozen, but he wants to up that."

Keith shook his head. "That'll just give him gas."

"Tell me about it."

He asked to see a picture and I showed him one of Chuck at the beach in Honduras. Hot as hell, but he wasn't bulky.

"Can't be done without steroids," said Keith.

"No?"

"No. He hasn't got the structure for it." He went over and pulled a photo album off a shelf. "This is my dad."

The picture was of a middle-aged dude that could've been Keith, just with less hair and a potbelly.

"My dad wasn't a workout guy. He always just had the muscle. The belly came with it. I gotta work my ass off not to have that belly. The muscle comes easy. Your man is always gonna be cut and slim. That's how it is. I'd kill for that body. If I put on a sweater, I look morbidly obese."

"Can't fight nature," I said.

He cocked his head to the side. "Did you try?"

"I did, but I just looked weird. This is what I look like. Unless I want to go the surgery route, this is it."

"You got to accept who you are and enjoy," said Keith.

"I wish my boyfriend could understand that."

"He will in about six months when all he is is gassy and more cut."

I groaned. "Six months."

He laughed and we went to the door. "Is he worth it?"

"God, I hope so," I said.

"Merry Christmas, Miss Watts."

"Merry Christmas."

I left the apartment building into a clear night. The drizzle had stopped and everything was now bright and beautiful. Christmas lights everywhere that I hadn't noticed before. Trees in windows. It was lovely. It was enough Christmas for me and I walked back to Natalie's apartment with a plan, a real thought-out plan. I know. Shocking.

CHAPTER NINE

I curled up in bed, basking in the quiet after a boiling shower and a bar of chocolate Aaron had donated to my cause before he went off to the Stuttgart Christmas market with Moe and Grandma. It took some doing to get them to leave me, but I did have a plan and I couldn't be moved off it.

The pictures Keith gave me were spread out on the bed and I opened my laptop to Google a map of Sindelfingen. The ATM Anton used was in the center of town not far from the Marktplatz. There were three cafés close by and two had small hotels in the vicinity.

There was a knock on the door, forcing me out of bed. Novak stood in the hall, wearing pink and green striped pajamas and what looked like a shower cap.

I flung open the door and yanked him inside. "What are you doing out there like that?"

"Like what?" Novak asked.

"Like a weirdo. Germans don't wander the halls of hotels like that."

"Do Americans?"

He had me there. Novak wasn't normal in any society.

"No, but we have Walmart, so there's that," I said.

"I've heard about Walmart and I am not that odd."

I poked the shower cap. "Oh, yeah? What's that?"

"I'm doing my hair mask. You don't expect me to dry out just because I'm traveling, do you?" He touched one of my ringlets. "You really need a mask. Your hair isn't happy."

"That is its natural state in Germany." *And Paris, and Honduras, and New Orleans.*

"I thought it was only Paris," he said.

"It's worse there."

He did a circuit around me. "What are you sleeping in? Did you rob a bag lady?"

"It's a tee shirt. Leave me alone." I marched back to the bed and got in while stuffing chocolate in my face. "Do you have something or do you just want to criticize me?"

"I can do both," said Novak.

"Swell."

"I have good news and bad news."

"Bad news first," I said.

"The plants on Anton's laptop originated from a laptop in Berlin," he said.

"Crap."

He pulled out his phone and laid it all out. The plants came from a laptop used in one location, a small library. The user accessed Anton's computer from that location and only that location. Remotely, the user went into the Incel sites and 4chan. The pictures that were found on Anton's computer were downloaded at the library and uploaded from there, too. There was no set pattern to when Anton's computer was accessed. Novak couldn't find the user's IP address anywhere else and he put some associates on it. He concluded that the laptop was purchased for one use only and then trashed when the job was done.

"That's less amateur than I would've thought," I said.

Novak nodded. "I agree. They knew how to do it and cover it up, but they didn't put much effort into the actual plants. It wouldn't have been hard to comment on posts and deep dive into those sickos fantasies, but they kept it surface. In and out."

"They...wanted it to be discovered?" I asked.

"I considered that, but they did bother to go to quite a few sites. I think they just couldn't be bothered or were in a hurry. If I had to guess it was a woman."

I pulled back. "Why?"

"A man would spend more time," he said.

"Because dudes are so detail-oriented? Come on."

"No, because a man would've looked out of curiosity if nothing else."

"Did you?"

He sat down on the bed and stole some of my chocolate. "Yes, I did. I'm not into that stuff, even a little, but I looked out of curiosity."

"Gross," I said.

"Very. I think a woman would be less likely to look at that kind of thing than a man. Like I said, it was very surface."

"Like they didn't want to see it."

"Correct."

"Interesting." I took a bite of super dark chocolate and then said, "I might be off base here, but that sounds less pro and more favor."

Novak smiled. "I think so, too."

"So not The Klinefeld Group?"

"We can't rule them out, but they are nothing if not pros. This did take skill. They knew what they were doing."

"How skilled?" I asked.

"Impossible to tell. Not their best effort." He took a look at my screen and asked, "What's this about? Did you get something?"

I told him about Sergio Tarantina possibly being the origin of the rumor and the girl named Alison.

"Those are the pictures I got," I said.

Novak picked them up and said, "I'll scan them and see what I can find out."

"Are there cameras in Sindelfingen? I wonder if we can see if one of these kids was out and about when Anton was getting his money."

"Might be a bit of a long shot, but we can give that a try," said Novak.

"Did you happen to access the ATM footage?" I crossed my fingers.

"I did, but Anton was always alone."

"Can you go back in?"

He sat back against the pillows. "I can. What are you looking for?"

"Direction. He met someone and handed over the money. It'd be nice to know which way he headed," I said, looking at my screen. "I'm thinking he met them in one of those three cafés. They're close and I can't think of a reason he'd go farther afield since he was on foot."

"Nice. There wasn't a whole lot of street surveillance, but I'll see what I can get."

I had a big chunk of chocolate before I asked my next question.

"Did you find any evidence of inappropriate behavior on Anton's old phones or laptops?" I asked. *Please say no. Please say no.*

"Rest easy on that one," Novak said. "I didn't find anything and those bricks date back fifteen years. Anton Thooft had no sexual interest in kids that I could find."

"Thank God," I said.

Novak raised a brow at me.

"I didn't want to have to tell his sister he was a child molester. Flipping nightmare. This is bad enough."

"That rumor is nothing. Just kids talking."

"Yes, but I still think somebody saw Anton in a café with someone and that someone could be our guy."

"A teenager?"

"Or it could be a coincidence. Anton's there to meet the blackmailer. Kid comes up for a chat with their favorite teacher. It gets seen differently after he attacked me."

"So..."

"The kid might've seen who Anton was meeting. At the very least, they can say which café. I can interview the people working there and Spidermonkey can see about credit card charges."

"Could be your blackmailer brought his laptop and stayed a while," said Novak.

"Wouldn't that be sweet?"

"Very." Novak poked his shower cap and said, "Time to rinse. You seriously need one of these."

"Yeah, yeah." I pushed him off the bed. "I have to call Spidermonkey."

"I'm going." He went for the door. "Do you want info tonight, if I get it?"

"I will kill you if you wake me up," I said.

"I'll take that as a no."

"Do that."

He left and I called Spidermonkey to give the names I had. He'd check out Sergio's finances but doubted a teenager would be using cards much, especially in Germany where cash was often preferred. There was some good news. Spidermonkey had checked out Ella's situation and found out that the rumors about her were purely that, rumors. The young cat sitter had no connection to anything.

I breathed a sigh of relief and hung up just as Grandma lurched in. "We're back!"

"I noticed. How was the Christmas market?"

"Enormous." She tossed her coat toward a chair and missed before flopping down on the bed to take off her boots. "I had the worst drink under the sun."

"You can't be talking about *Glühwein*," I said.

"*Glühwein* is wonderful. We had four kinds. One was apple."

"Nice. What was the bad stuff?"

"*Eierlikör*. I thought it was eggnog, but it was like angry egg schnapps."

"That's pretty much what it is," I said.

"Do you like it?"

"It's too strong and also weird."

"Oh, my God," she said. "I don't want to get up."

I yawned and closed my computer. "Don't."

"We have to do our routine," said Grandma.

"Routine?"

She rolled over and slapped my shoulder. "Have I taught you nothing?"

Um...pretty much.

"What's the routine?" I asked.

"Hello. Our skincare routine."

"Do we have one?"

Grandma looked at me and narrowed her eyes. "Oh, right. It's you."

"That's right. It's me. Mercy Watts. Your granddaughter," I said. "How much egg liquor did you have?"

"Hardly any. I was thinking you were one of the girls." Grandma rolled out of bed and landed with a thump beside it.

"Holy crap!" I ran around the bed and found Grandma lying on some throw pillows, looking startled.

"Do you think I broke a hip? That's how Mabel Grossman did it."

"Are you in horrible pain?" I asked.

She thought about it. "No. I feel fine."

"Could be the liquor talking." I checked her out and got her to her feet. "Don't do that again."

"I didn't do it on purpose." She took my hand and started to drag me to the bathroom.

"What are we doing?" I asked.

"The routine. I taught the girls and now I'll teach you."

The routine was Noxzema. She washed her makeup off with it and then slathered a thick layer of the cold cream on her face.

"Let it sit for a minimum of five minutes, but it's better to do ten. Then we'll put on our creams and serums."

I did as instructed and asked, "So who are the girls? Not Millicent and Myrtle."

"Goodness no. The girls. Sorcha, Bridget, and Jilly."

"You're telling me that the trio uses a four-dollar pot of Noxzema, not some potion made in the Swiss Alps out of goat placenta?"

"They did, but it was sheep placenta," said Grandma.

"I was joking, but that's gross."

"I know, but then I taught them and it's the routine. They have beautiful skin and it's hard considering how fair and sensitive their skin is."

"When did you teach them?" I asked.

"During a trip."

"A trip?"

It turned out Grandma J had been taking trips with the Troublesome Trio for years. It started with a trip to the Grand Canyon for Sorcha's high school graduation and became an annual thing, but the Noxzema was a recent lesson that happened in Key West. My grandmother took three of her four granddaughters on a trip to Key West and I never even knew it happened.

Grandma poked the cream on my face. "See how nice that feels?"

It feels pretty crappy.

"Yeah, the cream is nice." It was, but I barely noticed it. "So where was I?"

"When?"

"During the Key West trip," I said.

"Honduras, I think." She turned on the water and said, "Now wash it off."

I washed it off and tried to think of a way to ask why she never asked me to go anywhere, but nothing came to mind.

"Chuck texted me," she said.

"Swell," I said.

"He thinks you're mad."

"He managed to detect that, did he?" I asked.

Grandma instructed me in her serum application. "He said it wasn't serious between him and Natalie."

"They were engaged and he just sent me there without a clue. It was embarrassing. She obviously knew all about me."

She patted my back and said, "I know. It was a big mistake on his part, and I told him to give you some space, but you should call him."

"Hard pass."

"Why not talk to him? He loves you."

"I get to be mad," I said.

Grandma smiled at me. Her face was remarkably soft and unwrinkled, considering her age. "My girls are feisty."

"Am I one of your girls?"

She lurched out of the bathroom, saying over her shoulder. "Of course, you are."

I followed her out, fully intending to question her on the trip thing, but it was too late. My beautiful grandmother collapsed into bed and began doing sweet little snores almost instantly.

Thwarted, I called my mother, who picked up on the first ring. "Are you okay? How's your head?"

"Fine. Just a little headache. Why do you sound so panicked?" I asked.

"You never call me when you're working on a case," Mom said.

"Yes, I do."

"No, you don't. You're just like Tommy in that. I watch the news or call Fats now if I want information."

Am I a jerk?

"Who are you calling this time?" I asked.

"Grandma J. Why?"

"Did you know Grandma takes trips with the Troublesome Trio?"

"Of course."

I was quiet, and Mom asked, "Are you upset?"

"Well, yeah. Why didn't I get invited?"

Mom thought for a minute, and I did my best not to pummel her with petulant questions.

"You had The Girls and the trio had Janine. That's just the way it was," said Mom. "I never thought much about it. You traveled more than they did and got so much."

"The trio wanted to be invited by The Girls," I said. "They told me."

"Really? I didn't know that."

"Why weren't they?"

"That was down to Uncle George. He didn't want The Girls' help. He was weird about it."

"Why?"

"I don't know. He always had a chip on his shoulder about being self-made as if anyone truly is," Mom said. "So how's the trip going?"

"It's good. I might be getting somewhere. It's hard to tell, but I have a good feeling."

"So...is Grandma trying to split everything?"

"She is. What the heck is that about?"

Mom started laughing and telling me stories about Grandma trying to split everything from a chicken leg to an ice cream sandwich. I laughed so hard I almost forgot to be hurt. Almost.

CHAPTER TEN

Grandma was not getting up. That much was clear. I poked and prodded. I threatened not to do the Noxzema thing, but she could not be moved.

"I'm leaving without you," I said to the pillow over Grandma J's head.

There was a muffled ascent, so I threw on my coat.

"Call me when you wake up," I said on the way out the door.

I doubt that she answered and it didn't matter if she did. I had a meeting and I wasn't going to miss it.

"Where's Janine?" Moe asked.

"Sleeping. Let's go."

"She won't get on the right schedule."

"And she doesn't care." I took off down the hall with Moe and Aaron tight on my heels. I had hoped to book it out without the two of them catching on, but Fats clearly got some of her skills from her uncle. Moe had been in the hall, waiting with arms crossed when I made my move. One step ahead like his niece.

"What's the hurry?" Moe asked.

"Appointment at nine."

"We've got time for coffee and a croissant."

"No, we don't," I said. "Traffic in Stuttgart is terrible."

"Google maps says it's fine."

"We'll see."

And we did see. The traffic was a disaster on the A81 and it took twenty minutes extra. We barely got to the main gate of the post five minutes ahead of schedule. Moe drove up to the gate with a big grin and began chatting with the Pond's gate guard who was, surprisingly, an Irishman.

After a back and forth on German weather and the hideous traffic, I said, "We're going to be late."

The guard waved us through and we drove on a kind of cobblestone road past the PX complex. They had Dunkin' Donuts. I so wanted a donut, but we drove on and Moe confidently found his way past the post hotel where Anton met kids and drove over to the school complex that resembled a low-security prison with all the razor wire around the area. The school was pretty nice and had a large parking lot that had more cars than I expected on a Saturday.

We parked and went for the high school that had a large metal panel for visitor check. I was going to push the button, but Moe marched on by, like a man that never asked permission, which I guess he was.

"They're going to ask for ID," I said, trying to delay. High school hadn't been my favorite thing and my counselor, in particular, was a problem. He was always trying to help me when I never asked and by that, I mean he kept calling my mother in for meetings. He just wanted to see her. I'd grown into being my mother and the last thing I wanted was another Mr. Klemper saying, "Oh, don't you just know how to fill out a sweater." I had a headache and jet lag. I might punch someone. "Maybe we should call Natalie and see if this—"

"We're not calling anybody," said Moe. "What's wrong with you?"

"Flashback."

"Murder?"

"High school."

"Arguably worse," he said. "But this is what you do, so we're doing it."

Before Moe could reach for the door, a man wearing a Semper Fi tee and built like a small refrigerator rushed out, hand extended. "Miss Watts. I'm glad you made it."

Startled, I took the hand of the man who was so short he looked me in the eyes but was also twice as wide. "Mr. Hobbes?"

"Yes. Jackson Hobbes." He looked past me and asked, "These are your bodyguards?"

I introduced Moe and Aaron without really specifying their jobs. Nothing fit them. Bodyguards? Come on.

"Come in," said Hobbes. "We're all set up in the library."

I didn't get a chance to ask what we were set up for and I was keenly aware that I didn't come in hot as Keith told me to. On second thought, I didn't really know how to do that. Fats would've. She came in hot to pretty much everything from hair salons to murderers.

Hobbes led us into the high school and down a hall to a small library where a woman was waiting at a table with coffee and an array of donuts. She stood up with a huge smile. "I hope you're hungry."

"You got us donuts?" I asked.

"You're surprised?" Hobbes asked.

"Well...Keith told me this would go a little differently."

The ex-marine ran a hand over his shaved head and then crossed his arms. I'm not sure how he did it with so much muscle. "What did he say?"

I swallowed and said, "He said to come in hot."

To my surprise, he burst out laughing. "That fucker."

Moe joined in on the laughter and then they began going off about the military and the desire to mess with everyone at every opportunity.

The woman stepped up and any reservations I had melted away. Mr. Klemper wasn't in residence. "Meredith Calhoun. I'm also a counselor here. Hobbes thought I might be helpful to you."

"Thanks for coming on a Saturday," I said before introducing Aaron and Moe.

"Not a problem. After what happened, I decided to stick close to home in case there were any problems."

"Have there been?"

Aaron poured coffee and gave me a donut before heading off into the stacks, looking for cookbooks, I guess. I'd never seen him read anything else.

Meredith watched him go before answering. "I've kept up my counseling through the weekends. I don't usually do that."

"The students are upset?"

"I'd say rattled. The ones with previous issues are having a hard time coping. Mr. Thooft was very popular and the thought that he was someone else on the inside has shocked everyone."

I went on to ask about their impressions of Thooft. Not surprisingly, they were pretty much the same as everyone else. Great teacher. Great with students. No problems.

"Keith didn't like him," said Hobbes.

"Do you know why?" Moe asked.

"Yeah, he told me after he died." Hobbes told us about Anton lying and Meredith was shocked.

"I can't believe people knew," she said.

"He told you?" I asked.

"In confidence."

I told her about Anton's pattern of lying and the counselor herself was rattled. Hobbes questioned the website stuff and I reassured them both that the Incel sites were planted.

"At least that's good," said Hobbes. "What do you want to ask us? We really had no idea he was going to attack you. If you'd have told me he would do something like that, I'd have said you need your head examined."

"Well, he was being blackmailed," said Meredith.

"He was," I said. "Did you see any odd behavior before he left?"

"None at all," said Hobbes. "I wasn't close to the guy, but I think I'd have heard if a kid had an issue."

"The staff had no problems either," said Meredith. "He told me he had a family thing and had to go back to the States to handle it."

"Was he distressed when he told you?"

"A bit, but that was normal. Being overseas, we often feel cut off from what's happening at home. Things can seem worse than they really are."

We talked about the last couple of months before and nothing unusual was happening from their points of view. Anton was the same as always.

"Can you think of any reason why he would go to Sindelfingen to go to this ATM?" I asked, showing them the picture.

Hobbes sat back and frowned. "No. He lived in Waldenbuch and there are ATMs at the credit union and PX here on post." He looked at Meredith and she shrugged.

"Do you know any staff that live in Sindelfingen?"

"Not off the top of my head. People live all over. The community is pretty spread out, but Böblingen and Sindelfingen are popular because they're close."

"Do you think students would be living there?" I asked.

"I'm sure there are." Hobbes picked up a donut and asked, "What are you getting at?"

"There are rumors about Anton and some student at a café."

Meredith threw up her hands. "Oh, that's just silly. Teachers can have coffee with students. There's nothing wrong in that."

"It's a lead," I said, not mentioning that I had a feeling. It wasn't right. It just wasn't. "I heard the rumor may have started with Sergio Tarantina."

The counselors looked at each other in surprise and I waited to see what would bubble up. It took a minute or two, but they both said they found that hard to believe. Sergio was a top student with a full load of AP classes and a champion wrestler. They'd had no problems with him or complaints.

"You don't think he'd lie then?" I asked.

"Who told you he said anything?" Hobbes asked.

"My source wouldn't like to be identified. Let's just say I believe what I was told."

Meredith nodded and got a laptop out of her bag. "Let me look and see if there's something I missed." She got to work and we ate our donuts while she went through Sergio's file.

"All his grades are steady. I can't reveal what they are, of course. No discipline problems. No complaints from teachers or staff or students."

"Can you look at Anton's grade book?" I asked.

"I can," she said. "What are you interested in?"

"Anything weird. A kid going from Ds to As or vice versa."

She looked through with Hobbes leaning over her shoulder. There were a few kids that had grades changed in the second quarter, but they said that wasn't unusual. Some students were lax initially and then got it together to save their grade. Some just got less and less interested as the semester went by. There was nothing dramatic.

"Is there an Alison in any of Anton's classes?"

They looked through and said no.

"How about student council?" I asked.

Meredith shook her head. "No. Sorry. Which Alison are you looking for exactly?"

"I don't know. I just heard an Alison might also have been the origin of the rumor." I slapped my forehead, getting sugar all over myself. "Look at pre-calc classes. She's in a pre-calc class with a kid named Jordan."

"You're very well informed," said Hobbes. "That has to be Jordan Morris. I think we only have one Jordan."

"We do," said Meredith. "Let me see."

She found what she was looking for and then pursed her lips.

"What?" I asked.

"I don't know if I should tell you these things. They're confidential."

"Trust me, they're not."

"What do you mean?"

I downed some coffee and said, "I will find out. If it's on a computer, it can be found."

"Like how you discovered that fake stuff on Anton's?" Hobbes asked.

"Exactly like that and let's face it, anybody can search around on Instagram and find a girl named Alison that goes to this school."

"Hell," said Moe. "Grab a yearbook. It's not rocket surgery."

"My dad says that," I said.

"My dad did, too, and it's not."

Hobbes laughed. "Nothing is."

"Fair enough," said Moe. "But we can go find a yearbook easy enough. That's the point."

Aaron trotted out of the stacks, handed me a yearbook, and trotted right back.

"And there you go," I said, holding it up. "Last year, but she's probably in here."

"About a third of our students leave every year, but you've got a good chance," said Hobbes.

I went through the juniors first and then the sophomores before I found her. Alison Fodor. She was an unremarkable girl in that she had zero clubs, sports, or organizations and only appeared in her class photo. She was pretty with brown hair and a shy smile.

There was another Alison, but she was a freshman and less likely to be in pre-calc sophomore year.

"So tell me about Alison Fodor," I said, picking up another donut.

The counselor sighed.

"Oh, come on. Is she a regular rumor mill or what?"

After a bit of persuasion, they gave it up, not that there was much to say. Alison was shy. She did well in class and neither counselor had any dealings with her other than schedule changes and standardized testing.

"So not a gossip?" I asked.

Meredith shook her head. "I wouldn't think so, but you know kids. They can surprise you."

"No problems with Anton?"

"Not that I know of," said Hobbes.

"Any classes with him."

Meredith bit her lip but then shook her head no.

"I wonder how she knew," said Moe.

I flipped through the yearbook to Sergio's photo. He was outgoing. That was easy to see, even from a picture. Broad smile. Twinkle in the eyes. He had *it* whatever *it* was.

"Do Sergio and Alison have a connection?" I asked. "Dating?"

Both counselors shrugged.

"I can't keep up with their private lives, even if I wanted to," said Meredith. "I don't remember seeing them together."

"They're not really in the same group. He's very popular and she's just quiet and keeps to herself," said Hobbes.

"When did you first hear the rumors?" I asked.

"Colleen Davidson told me," said Hobbes. "She's the pre-calc teacher."

"And what day?"

Hobbes tapped his thick fingers on the table. "I guess it would be the day we found out. It was on the news, your attack I mean, but they weren't naming names. Then, on Monday, our principal had everyone come in early for a meeting and he told us it was Anton. Sherri La Roche was hysterical. I took her home and when I came back, Colleen Davidson told me what she'd heard some students saying. She didn't name the student."

"When was the student council emergency meeting?" I asked.

"How do you know about that?" Meredith asked.

I smiled and she chuckled.

"Alright. Alright. It was at lunch."

"When was the pre-calc? Before that, I assume."

Meredith looked at her computer. "It was. First period."

"So that rumor happened pretty quick." I finished my coffee and threw away my napkin and paper plate.

"Is that important?" Hobbes asked.

"I think so. It looks like Alison is the source," I said. "She said the café was in Sindelfingen. The same as the ATM. I don't think that's a coincidence."

"There are no coincidences in my experience," said Moe.

"Are you a detective?" Meredith asked.

Moe gave her a knowing look and said, "Let's just say I come at it from an experienced point of view."

The counselor drew back, but before they could ask me anything about the weird guy with me, my phone rang.

"You're awake," I said.

Novak snorted. "Of course, I'm awake. I'm working."

"I always think of you as a night owl."

"That's true, but I've got six projects going on and sleep isn't an option. Plus, my mother's threatening to come here."

"Great. I'd love to meet her," I said.

"We're not giving her any ideas. Do you want to hear what I've got or not?"

I wanted to say no just to be contrary, but I couldn't do it. We didn't have any time to waste if I was getting back home before Christmas. "Hit me."

Novak accessed the ATM footage again and found Anton consistently turned west when he left with his money. The Café Goethe was the most likely meeting place in that direction, and Novak confirmed that there was no one with Anton during any of the withdrawals so no gun to the back or anything like that. There was only one other security camera in the vicinity and it had Anton walking by alone every time.

"Can I see the footage?" I asked.

"Sure. It's not exciting. Usual foot traffic."

"Any teenagers?"

"Plenty. Did you find something?"

"Maybe. I just want to see if I can see someone in particular. How about the times of the withdrawals? I never asked about that."

"Various days. Various times," said Novak.

"On the weekends?"

"Yes. Three were on the weekends."

"Break it down for me."

I pulled an old school notebook out of my purse. Dad insisted they came in handy and he was right. He usually was, but I never told him so. It was difficult to bear his knowledge as it was. Novak gave me days and times and they fit a handy pattern. I smiled at the counselors and Moe smiled at me, tapping a knobby finger on one particular date. The old guy didn't miss much.

"When does school let out?" I asked.

"Two forty," said Hobbes. "Why?"

I was going to ask Moe to use his phone to check something, but he was already on it and held the screen up to me. I nodded and took it. A quick look confirmed my memory.

"Anything else on Berlin?" I asked and was rewarded with the counselors' eyebrows jutting up. It was fun being back at school and sitting with counselors that weren't trying to tell me in a polite way that my body was a problem. It wasn't my fault it didn't fit into a uniform neatly. I wasn't going to strap my breasts down as one suggested.

"No library footage. I've got a friend looking at parking garages and an ATM down the street," Novak said. "Spidermonkey sent a report on that Sergio kid."

"Not to me," I said.

"He didn't want to wake you and it was only to say there's nothing. No action financially for the kid or his parents."

"Nothing in Sindelfingen?"

"Charges at the IKEA, but that's it."

"I figured, but thanks."

I hung up and pushed my notebook over to Meredith. "These are the dates of Anton's withdrawals. Can you check and see if there was anything going on on those days?"

"Like what?" Hobbes asked.

"Did he take off any of those days? Skip out on a class for a doctor's appointment? Anything like that."

She shook her head. "I don't have access to his employment records, but I don't remember him taking any sick days. Hobbes?"

"Me either. I think Anton would've come in, even if he was on his last legs. That's why I thought the family thing in the States must've been a big deal. Some teachers take off every chance they get. Leave no sick days on the table, but not Anton. I don't think he took any days."

I took back the notebook and underlined four days before sliding it back to Meredith. "How about these days? Anton took money out an hour earlier."

She looked at the dates and checked the computer. "Oh, of course. Those are Thursdays."

"So?" Moe asked.

"Thursdays are early release days," said Hobbes.

"Well, there you go."

"I don't get it," said Meredith.

"Could he leave school during the day?" I asked. "Lunch? Free period."

"Sure," said Hobbes. "He had a free period on Gold days."

"Hobbes!" exclaimed Meredith.

The old marine leaned back in his chair and it gave out a low groan so that I feared for its structural integrity, but it continued to hold him. "Anton's free period wasn't secret. I knew. You knew. Everyone knew."

"I guess. I just don't want to break any rules."

He cracked knuckles and said, "I'm not breaking anything and if I did, it'd be for a good cause."

"How long would he have had on these Gold days?" Moe asked.

"An hour and a half," said Meredith.

"Plenty of time."

"For what?" Hobbes asked.

"To get the money out of the ATM," I said. "Do you have the schedule available?"

Meredith found the correct page and turned the screen to me. The high school had a block schedule, black and gold days. Some of the days of the ATM withdrawals did match Gold days, but no withdrawals were done at the time of his free period. He only went to Sindelfingen after school, never before or during. There were only three weekend withdrawals and two were in Weil der Stadt. I showed the pattern to the counselors, but they shook their heads.

"I don't understand," Meredith said. "What are you getting at?"

"We think he gave the money to the blackmailer at the times that he went to the ATM, so the blackmailer was available at those times, too. Not during his free period, lunch, etc."

"Do you think it's one of us," said Hobbes. "That's crazy. If it was, why bother to go to Sindelfingen? He could just get the money at the PX and hand it over in the hall."

"It's not a coincidence and Mercy's got a feeling," said Moe.

"A feeling?"

"It means something. They were available an hour early on those Thursdays, but not during his free periods." I turned the computer toward us again. "Look at these days. He got money out on all four teacher workdays, but never did it on a holiday, like Thanksgiving weekend or Veteran's day. Why?"

The counselors were thinking hard and fast, but they couldn't quite get it. Moe did. That calculating geezer smelled exactly what I was cooking.

"Witnesses," he said.

"Huh?" Hobbes said.

"Somebody was around on holidays. They couldn't just traipse off to Sindelfingen because they'd notice," he said.

They nodded and Meredith said, "I don't think it means that it's connected to one of us."

I was pretty sure it was, but I nodded because the dots weren't connecting. I could almost see the picture, but not quite. "Can I see Anton's room?"

Hobbes heaved a sigh of relief. "Of course. We didn't know what to do with his materials."

"Some suggested burning, but that's not right," said Meredith. "It's not our stuff to burn."

"I'll take it," I said. "Kimberly might want it."

"Or she might burn it," said Moe.

"It depends a lot on what we find out." I stood up and waved to Aaron who trotted out of the stacks with a pile of cookbooks and his ever-present notebook. "You hungry?"

"I just ate five donuts," I said. "Try bloated and regretful."

Aaron just blinked and Meredith shifted from foot to foot, trying not to look at the little weirdo, who, if I'm honest, never looked odder than he did right then. Hair sticking up all over. Glasses at a tilt and I'm sorry to say it, but he'd exchanged the Picard jacket for what looked like my mother's old winter coat from about six years ago and he'd tied that around his neck like a sweater.

"Do you mind if he takes the cookbooks with us to Anton's room?" I asked. "He's a chef."

At the word chef, a woman popped her head in. "Did I hear my name?"

"Hey Grace," said Hobbes. "Come in."

The counselor introduced the school's culinary arts teacher, a former executive chef who left a Michelin starred restaurant to teach high school students cooking.

"You don't hear that story very often," I said.

"People thought I was crazy, but they didn't understand the situation. I was working ninety-plus hours a week, depressed, and morbidly obese. I'm happier now."

"I can see that," said Moe. "Do you have a kitchen at the school?"

"I do. It's a pretty sweet setup." She looked to Aaron. "You want to see it?"

Aaron trotted out the door and Grace looked at me.

"That's a yes," I said.

"You're all invited, too."

"We'll just get in the way."

"I can't believe he's here," said Grace. "When I heard, I didn't believe it."

"You know who Aaron is?" I asked.

"Of course, he's an Instagram star." She glanced over her shoulder to the door. "I better go. This building is confusing. He'll get lost."

"Don't worry about that," I said. "If there's a kitchen, he'll find it."

Grace left in search of Aaron, who would undoubtedly be standing in front of her stove and testing the burners or whatever.

"To Anton's room?" Meredith asked.

I said yes and we went through the school, upstairs, and around corners. I had no idea where I was or how to get out. It was a good thing I didn't have to.

"Here it is," said Hobbes and he unlocked the door.

Nobody made a move to go in, so I went first. I have to admit that I got a weird little chill going in Anton's domain. It felt...it felt like someone was there. Let me be clear. The room was completely empty, but it didn't feel that way. I had a pressure in my chest, a pushing, pressing knee on the back kind of feeling.

"Well, that's not great," said Moe, coming in and putting a steadying hand on my arm.

"What?" I whispered.

"The guy's still here." He said it like it should be obvious.

"I know, right," said Meredith. "Nobody wants to come in here. One of the MPs came to search for evidence and had a panic attack."

"The *Polizei* didn't fare much better," said Hobbes. "They are a pretty tight-lipped and methodical bunch, but in here, boy, did they move fast. In and out under ten minutes."

"What did they say?" I asked.

"Not a thing. They just left."

"They didn't take anything?"

"No."

Hobbes looked at Meredith, who said, "Not that I saw."

I started moving around the room and if it hadn't felt so bad it would've been really nice. Anton had taken great pains to decorate with pictures of students, posters, and quotes from the famous and unknown alike. His desk had clearly been shuffled through, but it was obviously neat and organized normally. I went through everything with Moe and found nothing of interest, certainly nothing referring to blackmail or money.

There were some pieces of paper taped to the desk under the blotter and papers, along with pictures of Kimberly and the whole Thooft family. No pictures of them were displayed. Anton was very careful about that. There weren't even any up in his own apartment. I took a picture of the papers and asked the counselors. "Are these sayings new?"

They took a look and said they'd never noticed them before.

"'This too will pass,'" said Hobbes.

"'Breathe in. Breathe out,'" said Meredith. "Sounds like meditations."

I ran a finger over the tape around "I am in control" and said, "They look new. The paper is clean and the tape flat.

"Stress control," said Moe.

"Well, classes can be stressful," said Meredith, but she was wholly unconvincing.

"It wasn't the classes," I said, going to a narrow shelf against the windows. Neatly displayed were four sets of books, two in each pile, one black and one gold. The first set was from five years ago. It had "Forever 5s" embossed on the black cover. Inside was a photo of Anton and a group of students holding up five fingers. There was also a list of names and colleges.

"He called those his brag books," said Meredith, her eyes watering for the first time. "These are the kids that got a five on their AP. He was so proud of them."

I picked up another book, one in gold titled "Fabulous 4s". The students were holding up four fingers but were equally happy.

"They got fours," she said. "Still a huge deal."

I looked through the pictures for Sergio, but he wasn't in the photos from last year. "I didn't take AP Gov. When do they usually take it?"

"Junior or senior year," said Hobbes.

"Did Sergio have any classes with Anton?"

They clammed up and Moe laughed. "Look through the papers, Mercy."

"Spidermonkey probably already knows," I said.

"Spidermonkey?" Meredith asked.

"A friend with a keyboard." I looked around. "Do you have some boxes?"

Hobbes went out and got some. We dismantled Anton's room in ten minutes flat and even considering what the guy had done to me, I kind of felt bad about it. His life's work fit into four cardboard boxes that nobody was going to know what to do with.

"I guess that's it." Hobbes glanced at the door, anxious to get out.

"It is for now." I gave them both my card. "If you think of anything else, please, let me know."

I walked out of Anton's room and the pressure lifted. I could breathe again. Whatever that was, it didn't come along with the boxes, which was a serious relief. I had to put those things in my hotel room. Talk about unpleasant.

Meredith went to get Aaron and we walked out to the car, putting the boxes in the trunk. We shook hands and I closed the trunk.

"Thanks for your help," I said.

"Did it help?" Meredith asked.

"It did, but I have one more question."

They looked apprehensive but nodded.

"Does the Café Goethe mean anything to you?"

Hobbes frowned. "Sounds familiar."

"I think it's in Sindelfingen," said Meredith. "But I've never been there. Why?"

"Because I'm pretty sure that's where Anton met his blackmailer," I said.

"I still don't think that it has anything to do with the school," said Hobbes.

"Me either," said Meredith.

And you would be wrong.

CHAPTER ELEVEN

We drove into downtown Sindelfingen fifteen minutes later in search of a parking space. There were none to be had since it was a Saturday and there was a market with everything from fruit to seafood. We ended up driving down into an underground parking garage that was also nearly full. Moe checked his phone when we emerged up top. "ATM first?"

"Sure," I said, and we walked into the *Altstadt*, chock full of half-timbered buildings and Christmas decorations. The cobblestoned streets were a bit frosty, although there was no snow. It was a lot colder than the day before and everyone was bundled up with the biggest scarves you've ever seen in your life. They were more like small blankets tucked up around the ears. My scarf was so skinny it looked like a joke and I have to admit it wasn't doing much for my neck.

"There it is," said Moe.

"Good," I said. "I need cash."

I documented the ATM, like my photo-obsessed father taught me, and got out a couple hundred euros. Then we followed in Anton's footsteps, past the camera Novak had found and then stopped by a small vendor on a street corner. Moe got a paper cone of roasted chestnuts and shared them with Aaron, who started writing a recipe idea in his notebook as we started walking again.

"I don't know about you," said Moe, taking pictures of the houses with their lights, wreaths, and ribbons, "but this is about the most Christmassy I've ever felt in my life. Fats is going to be pissed."

"Send her pictures. I'm going to," I said.

"Not on your life. I don't poke the bear, even when it's my niece," he said. "We will be saying it was stressful and bland."

"She won't buy that."

"Worth a try."

We passed a particularly beautiful building so covered in slats of wood it was practically paneled and then made it into the square with a fountain. The café was across the square and we headed in past children playing tag and shrieking with delight as they caught one another.

The Café Goethe was toasty warm and about half full. It was more like a coffeeshop than a café with ordering at the counter. Their sign said they baked everything in house and they did have a gorgeous array of sandwiches, breads, and desserts. When I got to the counter, I ordered lattes and Aaron insisted on getting two kinds of fluffy rolled cakes. Then he started writing notes for future cake recipes and I left him to it.

The young woman behind the counter gave me my total, which I didn't quite get except that it was fifteen euros and something cents.

I held up my phone and tried to ask her in German if she'd ever seen Anton in there."

She eyed my face for a second and decided not to comment before looking at the photo of Anton that I'd gotten from Kimberly. "Yes, I have seen this man," she said in perfect English.

"When did you last see him?" I asked.

She pursed her lips and then leaned forward. "A few weeks ago. He was the American who attacked a woman in America."

"Yes, he was," I said. "He attacked me."

She brightened up. "I thought so, but I didn't want to say it. Are you alright?"

"Mostly. Can you tell me anything about him?"

"He was nice and polite. He ordered an Americano and that is all."

"The same every time he came in?"

"Yes, but I'm not always here."

The other woman behind the counter loaded our tray and pushed it over to me. Moe took it and went to a table in the corner.

"Was he with anyone else?" I asked.

"I don't think so. He only bought one coffee," she said.

Another customer came in and I stood aside so they could order. Once they'd left the counter, I asked, "Did you notice him sit down with someone?"

"I didn't, but I wasn't looking. We are always busy."

"Of course. Was there anyone you can remember that was always here at the same time? A teenager perhaps?"

She frowned. "I don't know. Maybe—"

An older woman came out of the back and gave the young woman what for, shaking a finger and the whole deal. I tried to apologize for getting in the way of her work, but my German is weak at best.

"It's okay. It's okay," the young woman said.

"Doesn't look that way," I said.

"She's always mad."

The older woman came back out and started again, but then Aaron wandered over to speak German so fast I could only make out an apology and my name, which is pretty pathetic when I think about it.

When Aaron got done, the older woman shook his hand and apologized herself.

"What's going on?" I asked.

"Your friend is a baker?" asked the young woman. "He doesn't look like one."

"What does he look like?"

She bit her lip and I laughed. Aaron kept talking and the older woman started pointing at the dining area. She wasn't happy and I expected some finger shaking to come in my direction, but then she threw up her hands and crossed her arms.

"Oh," said the young woman. "Marta saw him. The man in your photo."

I held up my phone again and she nodded emphatically. Then the anger started again. I caught a few words like woman and pretty, but that wasn't much help. Then Aaron thanked her and went off to a table without saying a word to me.

"Alrighty then," I said. "Can you help me out because he's not doing it?"

"Marta saw that man meet with a young woman several times. He was too old for her. She didn't think it was good."

"How old?" I asked and she relayed the question to Marta.

"My age."

"Twenty?" I guessed.

She smiled. "Yes, exactly."

"What did she look like?"

Marta described the young woman as blonde, pretty, and, most importantly, American.

"Did he give her anything?" I asked.

She asked Marta, who said that he gave her a paper once.

"A paper? Like a piece of paper?"

"A newspaper."

The money must've been inside.

"Just the one time?" I asked.

Marta said she only saw it that one time, but she said they were busy. I asked if the two of them seemed upset or relaxed. Marta said they barely talked at all. The girl would leave her latte half-finished. One time, she saw Anton reach out to the girl and touch her hand, which she jerked away. Marta took that as a romantic gesture, but given what I knew about him, I thought it was more likely a plea for understanding or forgiveness.

"That is all she remembers," said the young woman.

"Did Marta tell this all to the *Polizei*?" I asked.

The young woman asked and Marta shook her head. The *Polizei* hadn't come in and asked. The young woman had recognized him from the photos on the news and the internet, but she didn't think him having coffee had anything to do with it.

"Was I wrong?" she asked. "Should I have called them?"

"There was no reason to think that at the time," I said.

"But it does have something to do with it?"

"I think so, but I can't be sure yet."

"You are investigating? They said on the news that you are a nurse."

"They weren't wrong. I am a nurse."

"Then why do you investigate crimes?"

"I ask myself that all the time." I wanted to explain it, but there wasn't a straightforward answer to give her. Things happened and you do what you have to do.

I gave her my card and turned back to the dining room. That's when I saw him, standing outside the café and looking in through the window and staring right at me. He was young and thin to the point of being gaunt. No spark of recognition lit up and then our eyes met. Just for a second. But that's all it took and he took off, running full out.

I darted to the door and flung it open.

"Mercy!" yelled Moe, but I was already gone.

"Wait!" I yelled and ran down the street, just catching a glimpse of his red jacket as it disappeared between two market stands. I ran through the warren of sellers and patrons, trying to keep up with my lungs burning. We ended up back on the main drag near the parking garage where there were even more stands. I hoped he would go for a car. That would slow him down, but he passed the garage and barreled through a group of women doing their shopping. Baskets and bags went flying with shouts of "*Scheiße*!"

I jumped over a basket and tripped on a cobblestone, but I didn't go down by some miracle. I chased him up a street lined with small shops and crowded with people. It was a hill, not a big one, but my head was thumping. There was no way I could catch him on my little legs. I collapsed against a building, cursing my dislike of aerobic exercise and Chuck for being right.

"I'll get him!" Moe ran past me and I stared slack-jawed as he darted up the street like a man half his age. Heck, like a man a third his age.

It was a new low. I'd been outrun by a seventy-year-old man with a hump. I didn't think it could get any worse, but, of course, it could, so it did.

The women that the boy had barreled into descended on me, making Marta look good-humored. I tried to say it wasn't my fault, but the only language that came to mind was French and I don't really speak French. My stupid attempts in the wrong language only made them madder and my head hurt more. Where was Aaron when I needed him?

The next thing I knew, a *Polizei* was coming through the crowd of women looking about as friendly as you'd imagine German policeman to look in a dark blue uniform and armed to the teeth. I didn't know you could get that many things on one belt. It must've weighed a ton, but he wasn't slowed down. He asked the women what was going on and I got pointed at repeatedly.

Slowly, the women calmed down and the *Polizei* turned to me, asking in German what happened. At least, I think that's what he said.

Say I'm sorry. In German. You know that. Say that.

"*Je suis désolé*," I said.

Goddammit!

"*Je suis désolé*."

Something is seriously wrong with me.

The *Polizei* tilted his head and I half expected him to snap something off his tool belt and whack me with it, but he said, "I thought you were American."

"I am."

Was that English? I think so.

"I am an American," I said.

Yes. Nailed it.

"I'm sorry. I didn't run into these ladies. I was chasing the person who did."

"Yes, I see. You chased him into them and knocked them over," he said.

"That's...a dark spin on what happened."

"That is not what happened?"

I explained that I had seen the boy and he ran. I chased him to find out who he was. That was all.

"Do you chase people a lot?" he asked.

Lie.

"Not every day," I said.

What is wrong with you?

"I only wanted to find out who he was. I didn't make him run. I don't know why he did."

The *Polizei* hooked his thumbs into his shoulder holster and said something soothing to the ladies. They gave me the stink eye and left with many angry backward glances.

"You should not chase people," he said.

"Is there a rule against it?"

"I will have to check."

"I was joking," I said.

"Don't do that. This is a serious matter."

Is it really?

"I'm sorry. Hey, look, I said it in English."

"Have you been drinking?" he asked.

"I could use some *Glühwein* actually."

He gazed at me in a way that only Germans do, very focused and unblinking. It was disconcerting, but I just stared right back.

"Why did you want to know who he was?" he asked.

This is going to sound so stupid.

"I saw him looking at me through the window of the Café Goethe and I thought he might have some information."

Hey, not so bad.

"That makes no sense," he said.

Wrong again.

I sighed and said, "I'm investigating a crime and I'm trying to get a lead."

"A crime in America?"

"Yes."

He frowned deeply and said, "You think a German did it?"

"The kid wasn't German," I said.

"How do you know?"

"The same way you knew I was an American."

He looked at my skinny scarf and North Face jacket and said, "I think you look like Marilyn Monroe."

"And American."

"Yes."

"Can I go?" I asked.

"No."

"Are you going to arrest me?"

"Are you armed?"

"No."

He eyed my purse, so I obligingly opened it. I should've been armed, but I usually forget. Plus, I had Moe the speedy septuagenarian and he probably had four on him.

"I'm surprised," he said and extended a hand. "Viktor Koch."

"Mercy Watts." I shook his hand and wondered where this was going. My track record wasn't great.

"Why didn't you inform us you were coming?"

"Er...inform you?"

"That you would be coming to our jurisdiction and investigating," said Koch.

"It didn't occur to me," I said truthfully.

"That would be polite."

"I guess so."

"How can I help you?" Koch asked and I stood silent for a moment not sure he was serious. After all, I was impolite and causing problems.

"I will help," he said.

"Alright." I told him about the café and Marta seeing Anton Thooft meeting someone. I thought he might be impressed that I got that far in twenty-four hours, but he just did that stare and listened.

"I would like to be in on the arrest," he said when I finished.

"If there is one, sure."

"Blackmail is illegal."

"I know, and you're welcome to whoever did it," I said. "I just want to know why it happened and who was behind it."

"I will have to inform my command of your presence," Koch said.

"Go for it." I rubbed my forehead and asked, "Can we go back to the café? My head is killing me."

Koch agreed, but when we turned to go, I heard Moe yell, "Mercy! I lost him."

We turned around and there came my geezer bodyguard limping down toward us.

"Who is this?" Koch asked.

I told him who Moe was and to say he didn't believe me was an understatement. But then Moe hobbled up, extended his hand, and confirmed it. "The little bastard got away. Jumped on a bus. I was this close."

Koch eyed Moe's sweaty face and bulging moist eyes and I could see a change in attitude. A kind of respect. I guess Koch figured if Moe was watching me he had to have skills and he wasn't wrong, although Moe hid them pretty damn well.

"What was the bus?" Koch asked, taking out a pad and pen.

"It said Böblingen on it," said Moe and he went on to describe the bus.

Koch wrote it down and I encouraged them to walk and talk. I could see the boy's face in my mind. So clear. His description meant nothing at the moment, but I kept seeing his expression. At first, it was terribly sad, weepy even, and then he saw me. Recognition and then shock. Total shock and he ran.

"What time is it?" I asked, fumbling for my phone in my zipped pocket.

"Eleven fifty," said Koch. "Do you have an appointment?"

"No. I just...I'm trying to remember what time..."

We got back to the café and the young woman behind the counter went pink the second we walked in. I glanced over at Koch, but he was oblivious. Men. I went over and said, "Do you know Officer Koch?"

She blushed harder and began wiping the spotless counter. "I have seen him."

"I'm sorry," I said. "What's your name?"

"Claudia."

"Officer Koch, you should interview Claudia. She and Marta saw Anton here."

He nodded and flipped a page on his notebook before starting to question her in German. I gave Claudia a smile behind Koch's back and beat it back to where Aaron was scraping whipped cream off the last plate.

"Miss me?" I asked.

"Huh?"

"Never mind." I sat down, took some Tylenol, and drank some of my now-cold latte. Yum.

Moe sat down. "Let's have a talk."

"About?" I asked.

"You will not Fike me. Don't even try."

I almost dropped the latte. "You know about Fiking?"

"Everyone knows about Fiking and you will not Fike me," he said. "Got it?"

I said I did and I even crossed my heart, but I didn't mean it. Fiking happened. I couldn't fight it. "Seriously, how did you hear about Fiking?"

"I saw it in action. I almost felt sorry for your father. Michael Fike was a Grade-A jerk and I'm saying that as a human, not as a member of the opposition."

That was an interesting way to put it. The opposition. And Moe was right about my dad's first partner, who hated him and did everything he could to ditch the wet behind the ears Tommy Watts, trying to make him a laughingstock. The term Fiking was born. I'd done a fair bit of it myself.

"Why did Fike hate my dad so much?" I asked.

"He was Ace's son and great things were expected. Your father has a way about him. He knew he would be a great cop and detective, even with nothing to base it on. It irritated people."

"Sounds like my dad," I said.

Moe groaned and rubbed his leg. "I should've listened to Fats. Don't tell her I said that."

"What did she tell you?"

"To wear gym clothes, but I'm not an animal. I'm not walking around Germany looking like some gauche American in Under Amour. It's embarrassing."

"I definitely wouldn't tell her that."

Fats Licata only wore workout gear. It was going to be a problem for her wedding and we hadn't found a solution yet. Uncle Moe didn't look like he owned workout gear. But he was pretty natty for an old guy and I had to admit he fit in, more than me and Aaron anyway. We never fit in anywhere.

"I won't. But I should've listened and worn sneakers." He held up a pointy-toed lace-up in camel. "These are terrible for a chase."

"Imagine that," I said.

"Hey, you couldn't get him and you're young enough to be my granddaughter," said Moe.

"I don't deny it."

"Don't beat yourself up. Fats says you have other skills." He said it like he doubted it was true.

"Thanks a bunch."

"Why'd you ask about the time?"

"I think that kid was standing there right at the exact time Anton met that girl here, but I have to check," I said.

"I thought that was after school," said Moe.

"Except one Saturday." I texted Novak for the time of that one Saturday withdrawal. He came back almost instantly with eleven twenty-five.

"Dead on," I said. "We got here at about what? Eleven fifteen?"

"Thereabouts," said Moe, nodding. "You think he was doing a kind of vigil?"

I thought about the kid, his sadness and the tightness on the lines of his narrow face. "I think he was visiting the scene of the crime."

CHAPTER TWELVE

Getting back to the hotel took a lot longer than I expected, two hours longer to be exact. Koch insisted on taking us to his station for a formal interview, which wouldn't have been so bad if we hadn't sat in the waiting room for an hour. It was the quietest police station I'd ever been in and that includes tiny St. Sebastian.

The station looked like it was built in 1820 and had hard plastic chairs to sit on in a partitioned-off area. At one point, I dared to put my feet up on a chair and an officer that was walking by somehow saw me through the partially frosted glass. He stopped, put down his load of files, and came back to tell me to take my feet down. He was pretty pissed and I wasn't thrilled, either. The orange seats looked to have been installed in the seventies and I'd have to use a blowtorch to harm them but whatever.

Eventually, Koch's boss Tomas Nachtnebel made time to see me and it went about how I figured it would. He said I was in their jurisdiction, blah blah blah, no authority, blah blah blah, case dead in the water, blah blah blah. I told him what I had. He dismissed it. It was a lot like the States actually, except more rule-oriented. That guy took a look at me and decided I wasn't going to get anywhere. Not the first time that's happened, but it was the first time when I was jet-lagged and having a lingering headache. I was less accommodating, I admit. Moe didn't have a word to say and Aaron never does. Nachtnebel did the majority of the talking. Although he liked to hear himself talk, it also appeared to irritate him.

"This is an American crime, Miss Watts," he said.

"I agree," I said.

"Then you will go home and deal with it there."

"I will." *Eventually*.

"Good." Nachtnebel gave me a dismissive wave and Koch walked us out to the car.

"Your boss is a dipstick," I said as I opened my door.

A smile flickered across Koch's face before being firmly replaced by his usual stern expression.

"He doesn't like cases being messy," he said.

"How's that working out for him?"

"Well. He's made rank quickly."

"Alright then," I said. "I'll be on my way."

Koch frowned. "You will?"

"To the hotel." I laughed. "You know who I am. You really think I'm leaving? I've got solid leads."

"I've got another," he said.

I cocked my head to the side and said, "Do tell?"

"I love your accent."

"Really? I don't."

He laughed and said, "I'm still in your loop?"

"You are, just keep that guy off me and we're all good," I said.

"No problem. Nachtnebel's off to Solden on Monday. Skiing."

"Perfect. What have you got?"

Koch told me the bus the kid got on was 768 to Böblingen. The bus driver let him off at the *Mineraltherme*. Koch figured he was either catching another bus to the US garrison or heading for Goldberg train station. There were cameras at each stop, so he took a look at the cameras at Goldberg and spotted a teenager with a red coat buying a ticket. He couldn't access the ticket kiosk, but he did see the kid get on the S1.

"Where does the S1 go?" I asked.

"It has a lot of stops. He could've gotten off anywhere."

"Does it go to Weil der Stadt by chance."

That made him pause for a moment and then he asked, "Why do you ask that?"

I told him about Anton's Saturday withdrawals in Weil Der Stadt and he paused again.

"I'm not going to ask how you got that information. It is not in our investigation," said Koch.

"And I'm not going to ask if you're allowed to just look at train station footage whenever you want," I said.

"We understand each other."

"I think we do." I gave him my card and got in.

Moe drove us out of the parking lot, breaking about five traffic rules and since it was Germany it was probably more like eleven.

"What is your problem?"

"Nachtnebel treated you like a cupcake," Moe said through gritted teeth. "I wanted to pop him in his smug face."

"Oh, well, I'm used to it," I said.

"You shouldn't be. That jackass has got nothing. You'll track this down in under the week we have."

"I hope so."

He gripped the steering wheel, staring over the top edge with grim determination. The Sindelfingen cops hadn't paid any attention to Moe Licata. I only hoped they wouldn't live to regret it.

I like to think I don't get surprised *that* much anymore, but what I walked in to find in my hotel room surprised the heck out of me. Novak was there with a face covered in Noxzema, three laptops on the desk, and a keyboard in his lap. Grandma J was standing behind him braiding his hair into cornrows with a shower cap on her head.

"What in the world are you doing?" I asked as I dropped one of Anton's boxes on the bed.

"Occupying myself until you got back," said Grandma J. "Novak wanted to try out cornrows."

"And Noxzema," he said.

"How's that working out?" I asked.

"Love it."

"Since when do you know how to do cornrows?"

"Jilly went through a phase during her volleyball years and I learned," said Grandma.

"I don't remember that," I said.

"I'm not surprised. You're very busy. Always were."

I started pulling the AP books out of the box and said, "I'm not that busy."

"Do you remember Jilly wearing cornrows for three volleyball seasons in a row?" she asked.

I didn't remember Jilly playing volleyball, but I wasn't saying that. "No."

"I rest my case. So what did you find out?"

I gave her a quick rundown and then checked out Novak's screens. There was some pretty questionable material on there. "You're not worried about Grandma seeing that?"

"I'm not wearing my readers," she said. "I can't see a thing."

"Well there you go," I said. "What is that? A boat?"

"Human trafficking ring bringing girls in from Morocco," said Novak casually. "Nice reward involved."

"I assume that's why they do it."

"That's why I'm tracking. The girl on the left is a runaway from a prominent family. Her father offered 10,000 euro for her safe return."

"What about the other girls?" I asked.

"A bonus save."

I checked out all the screens, two of which had multiple panes open and were confusing, to say the least. "You don't mind me looking?"

"You can't make head or tails," said Novak.

"Insulting but true," I said. "What's going to happen?"

"Spanish authorities are at Malaga waiting, so is the father." He pressed a button and another window popped open showing a plethora of cops and a distressed father waiting in a white room overlooking the ocean.

"Are you too busy or can I see that footage from the street camera?" I asked.

"No problem." He brought up the camera footage, but the kid I'd seen wasn't on there. Several women that could've been twenty walked by, but there wasn't anything to mark them as our person of interest.

Novak clicked a few more keys and brought up more footage. "This might be more helpful."

There I was, looking flipping enormous in my stupid puffer jacket, but I digress. The camera caught me running after the boy on the street cam and another ATM got us behind some guy taking out money.

"Can you roll that back?" I asked.

He did and I said, "Freeze it."

We got a somewhat blurry side view of the kid full out sprinting. No front view, unfortunately, but he hopefully would be recognizable to someone who knew him well.

"Do you want me to do some calculations?" Novak asked.

"Er...sure," I said. "What would those be of?"

"I can get his height."

"Do it."

After some clicking and measuring and some comparing to structures and other people, Novak declared our suspect to be six feet tall give or take a fourth an inch.

"He got on the S1 in Böblingen. Can you get that camera?"

"I can, but I'll have to get through their security. It'll take some time."

"How about the ticket kiosk?" I asked.

"That, too," said Novak. "The Germans are very tight on their train security with the terrorist threat. I'll have to work it pretty hard.

"But you can get in?" Grandma asked.

"Of course."

"But...if you can, the terrorists can." She stopped cornrowing and bit her lip.

"Yes," said Novak. "Lucky for us, they are generally not patient nor geniuses. It will take time and work. The systems to actually mess with the trains, tracks and whatnot, are a whole other level of difficult. This is much easier."

"I think I feel better."

"You should, but not much," he said.

"Not helping," I said.

"You didn't hire a liar."

I checked my phone to see if Spidermonkey was up, but he'd been silent so far. "Do you have anything on Alison Fodor or Sergio Tarantina yet?"

"I do, and I think you'll like it."

Novak had managed to work on my normal teens along with his trafficked ones. Sergio lived in Stuttgart West with his parents and three sisters. He was currently in Austria skiing. Novak got into his laptop and Sergio had been reading everything he could find on Anton and going to some Incel sites to have a look around. Most importantly though, he was hooking up with Alison Fodor. They weren't dating though and barely communicated. They saw each other at some unnamed lake and at parties. There was only one text between them that could be relevant for us. Sergio and Alison saw each other the Sunday after Anton nabbed me. The counselors sounded like Anton being the kidnapper came as a surprise on Monday morning, but both Sergio and Alison already knew it was him. Sergio sent one text on Sunday night just before midnight.

"Why won't you tell me who it was?"

Alison didn't answer. He texted her twice more since then about innocuous things, but she didn't answer those either.

"It sounds like Alison told her best friend Cameron at school on Monday morning and Sergio on Sunday," I said. "What else have you got on Alison?"

Novak smiled and pressed a key. A map appeared on his right screen. Sindelfingen.

"Holy crap. She lives four blocks from the café," I said.

"I thought you'd like that."

"Did she text the name to anyone?"

He shook his head, causing Grandma to squawk and tug on his hair.

"Cameron Little knows the name," he said. "The texts between the two of them implies that. They've agreed not to tell anyone because they don't want to get the person in trouble. Looks like Alison regrets telling Sergio. She says she told him to keep it a secret, which he didn't do. She's pissed."

"Nothing in particular about the person at all?" I asked.

"No, but she knows them personally. I can show you the texts, but I think it's someone in the high school."

"Do you have a recent photo of Alison?" I asked. "Full body?"

"What are you thinking?" Grandma asked as she tied off a braid.

"It could be Alison," I said. "She could be the blonde in the café with Anton and doesn't want to admit it."

"You saw her picture. You think she could be mistaken for twenty?"

"I was all the time."

"That can't be true," said Grandma and I decided not to expand on it, but I got mistaken for eighteen at twelve. At fifteen, I got businessmen asking for my number while I was wearing my school uniform. You'd think that plaid would be a dead giveaway, but it wasn't. A womanly body changes everything no matter how young the face. I got told great costume in August. I blame Brittney Spears.

Novak typed for a few seconds and then Alison's mother's Facebook account opened. He brought up a picture taken in Venice over Thanksgiving. Alison had changed her hair. She was blonde now, but I just didn't see the twenty in her. Also, older people tend to see others as younger than they are, not older.

"It's not her," I said.

"Good," said Grandma. "I don't want it to be her."

"You're such a grandma."

"Guilty as charged." She smiled and started another braid.

Moe knocked and brought in the two other boxes, dumping them on the bed and making a growling sound that was reminiscent of Fats, and I suddenly missed my giant bodyguard. Moe never ate toothpicks. Never. Not once.

"I have half a mind to go back and tell that cop to drop dead and rot," he said.

"Where have you been and why did it make you madder?" I asked.

"I was walking it off."

"Didn't work."

"No."

"What happened?" Grandma asked and Moe went into a tirade about cops and treating me like a cupcake. I kicked off my boots and curled up on the bed with the yearbook, half-listening. I could see that kid's face looking through the window at me so clearly, but in the yearbook everyone looked the same. He was kinda generic and the photos were black and white. I could see how witnesses got confused during a lineup and started looking for nervousness or familiar clothes. I switched to the other photos that Anton had, Sherri's student council photos, and the AP books. He wasn't in any of them. I was pretty sure on that, so I went back to the yearbook. It was last year's book, so much could change in a year for kids.

Moe came over and sat down. "You know we might be totally off base on that kid. Marta didn't see Thooft with a boy."

"I know. I just can't shake this feeling. He's a part of this."

"Instincts. I understand," said Moe.

"Is Alison here?" I asked Novak. "In Stuttgart, I mean."

He shook his head, getting another squawk out of Grandma. "She's in Amsterdam. These military people do not stay put. Before you ask, the friend Cameron, is in the process of moving back to the States. Her family is in Ramstein to catch something called the rotator."

"Crap on a cracker," I said. "I guess I could call Alison."

"She's pretty guarded," said Novak. "You'd do better in person."

Grandma grinned at me. "Are we going to Amsterdam?"

"No. We don't have time for that. There has to be a better way," I said.

Moe went to Novak's side. "Have you got a printer?"

"I do. What are you thinking?" he asked.

"Can you print that kid's photo from the video?"

"Sure." He pointed at a bag on the floor. "Get it out and we'll do it."

Moe set up the printer and I went through the yearbook again. The school had about 600 kids and he might not even be in there. Hobbes said a third move every year. That was a lot of newbies.

"Let's print Alison, too," I said.

"Ooh, where are we going?" Grandma asked.

"Back to the café," I said. "But you're not."

Her lower lip poked out and she was adorable despite the shower cap. "Why not? I'm part of this investigation."

"You've got goop on your head."

"That's easily fixed and you need a translator," she said. "Aaron saved your bacon today."

"And he can do it again," I said.

Moe cleared his throat. "Actually, Aaron went to the spa."

"I'll get him."

"It's a naked spa."

"Never mind." I pointed at Novak's head. "What about that? You can't leave him half done. He'll look ridiculous."

Novak looked up at me with his face full of Noxzema and then swept an arm over his skintight ski getup. "As if that's something I'm concerned with."

"Alright, Grandma. Rinse your hair. It's back to Sindelfingen."

"Are you going to tell that cop you're coming?" she asked.

"I'll tell him after."

"What happens if his boss catches us?"

Nothing good.

CHAPTER THIRTEEN

"Oh, I love this town," said Grandma. "It's a lovely town."

Moe and Grandma walked ahead of me, arms linked in no particular hurry. Sindelfingen was even more crowded and people were rushing around laden with boxes and bags. Moe was right. It was super Christmassy and I'd have been smiling, if we weren't immediately disobeying the *Polizei*. Koch's charmless boss wanted to be told when we came back so someone official could be with us. Pass. First, I didn't want some cop leaning over my shoulder the whole time making sure I could add two and two, and second, people were less likely to pony up some info if they were.

The Saturday market was starting to close up, but Grandma dragged us through there, asking questions a mile a minute in her phenomenal German and once she got going, there was no stopping her. She bought a handy basket for shopping: flowers, oranges—we needed the Vitamin C—two Christmas ornaments, potpourri, and a hat for Grandad.

"Don't you think Ace will love this scarf?" She held up a wide scarf in a green plaid.

"I've never seen Grandad wear a scarf," I said.

"That's because he doesn't have this one. I'm getting it."

I tried to be patient. I really did, but there's only so much shopping I can take when I'm not the one doing it. "Fine. I'll go to the café and you two keep buying."

I tried to dart off, but Moe's wrinkly old hand snatched me back. "Oh, no you don't."

"Come on. Claudia and Marta might leave or we might get caught by Koch. You just know he's lurking around."

"He's on our side."

"Maybe, but I'm not taking any chances."

Grandma tucked the scarf into her basket and said, "I'm done. So there."

"Okay. Great. Let's go." I started across the square and heard behind me, "Oh, look, chocolate-covered strawberries. Let's split one."

I spun around and marched back. "No splitting anything until we do our interviews."

"Fine. Fine," she said. "Were you always this bossy?"

"No."

"Fats says yes," said Moe.

"Swell. Come on." I got on the other side of Grandma and forced her through the crowd to the café that was filled to the gills. We got in line and Grandma started talking about what we could split. She saw a sandwich in the window and thought it was so big we should do thirds.

I'm going to lose weight on vacation.

"I'll have my own sandwich," I said.

"You don't want all that. You'll get gas."

A man in front of us chuckled and I cursed the German school system that made just about everyone under forty learn at least some English. He snapped a picture with his phone over his shoulder. Awesome. My nose was red and running, so it was sure to go right to Instagram with hashtag gassy.

"Mercy was the gassiest little girl I ever saw," said Grandma. "My goodness did she toot."

"She looks gassy," Moe said with a chuckle. "How about burping? Did she burp a lot?"

"You're fired," I said.

"You can't fire me, gassy girl," he said.

I blew my nose and the guy ahead caught me mid-blow. That would be a good one. It seemed like Germans ought to have some law about taking pictures of people they didn't know. I ducked the next time he tried, but I'm pretty sure he got a bad action shot with my mouth open or something.

We finally got in the shop and Claudia recognized us, but not in a good way. She kept looking past us and tried to go in the back, but Marta wouldn't let her. Grandma got to the counter and ordered the sandwich cut in thirds, which confused Claudia, but Marta totally understood. Then we got lattes and two pieces of cake. I was excited, until I realized that Moe got one and we were sharing the other.

Grandma paid and I put the picture of the boy on the counter next to the little money dish. Claudia took a look and ignored it. She just took the money.

"Claudia, do you recognize that kid?" I asked. "Has he been in here?"

"The *Polizei* said I'm to talk to them about the investigation, not you."

"Koch said that?" I asked.

"No, the other one."

"Older guy? Crabby? Thinks I'm a cupcake?"

"Huh? This is English that I didn't learn," said Claudia.

"It just means he thinks I'm a fluffy, useless woman," I said.

She nodded and turned to the next customer.

Dammit.

"Just tell me," I said.

"I can't," she replied and went to cut a hunk off a huge loaf of brown bread.

Marta rang up another customer, gave me a hard look, and then headed into the back. I pushed the cakes and sandwich into Moe's hands. "Find a table and get our coffees."

"Wait what?" he asked and I got to see his eyes bulge more. Not a pretty sight.

"Come on, Grandma." I grabbed her arm to drag her around the end of the counter.

"What are we doing? We can't go back here."

"Watch us."

"This is wrong," she said.

I pushed her through the swinging door and said, "This is investigating."

"I don't like it."

"Bummer," I said. "You're my translator."

Grandma straightened up. "Oh, yes. I am. Let's do it. You just surprised me."

We went through the oven area where two bakers stopped shoving brown bread in an oven and yelled.

Grandma said something about Marta and was pretty aggressive about it. They backed off and pointed to a back door. We went through and found Marta smoking a cigarette in the alley behind the shop. She picked a bit of tobacco off her lip and eyed us before saying, "Show me the picture."

"You speak English," I said.

She shook her head. "Hardly at all. I was not a good student."

"Could've fooled me."

She smiled and I showed her Alison's photo and she shook her head. "No. I haven't seen her."

"How about him?" I handed her the boy's photo. She took a drag and then tapped it. "This is the one you chase earlier."

"Yes. Do you recognize him?"

She nodded. "It's a little blurry, but yes. He comes quite often, but not in the last couple of days."

"An American?"

"Yes, of course. Look at that coat. I recognize the coat."

Take that, Koch.

"Have you ever seen him with the man I asked about before?" I held up Anton's picture on my phone.

She shook her head. "No. The boy was always alone."

"How often do you usually see him?"

Marta took a long drag and then tapped the cigarette against her lower lip. "Every other day. Very often but less lately."

I crossed my fingers. "When did it change?"

"Oh, a couple of weeks now."

Grandma and I exchanged a look. A couple of weeks ago Anton left for the States.

"Did you ever see him talk to the blonde woman you saw the man with?" I asked.

"No."

"Was he there at the same time?"

She tapped her lip again. "I think so...yes." Then she frowned. "He was there the same time a lot."

"Every time?" I asked.

"I couldn't say," said Marta.

I got out Alison Fodor's picture and showed her. "How about her?"

"Another American?"

"Yes."

"I'm sorry. She is a little familiar, but I don't think she comes to us a lot."

"You haven't seen her with that man, the boy, or the blonde?" I asked.

Marta took the boy's photo back and shook her head. "No. The boy was always alone. I remember thinking it was sad that he had no friends to come to the café with. Children these days are too much with the computers and games. Not enough of the social."

"Did he have a computer with him?" I asked.

"Yes. Always with a computer. We have the free Wi-Fi."

I made a fist and said, "Yes. That is perfect."

"This is helpful?"

"Absolutely fantastic."

Marta took out another cigarette and lit it before finishing the first. I waited. She had something to say and I wanted to hear it. At least, I thought I did.

"You know the officer? Koch," she said.

"I wouldn't say I know him. He saved me from a crowd of angry shoppers and basically threatened to arrest me."

"But he didn't."

"No."

"He likes you," she said.

Where is this going?

"Koch wants to make an arrest. He thinks I can help him do that," I said.

She nodded. "You will be calling him?"

"Yes. I promised to keep him in the loop."

"I have helped you with this investigation you are doing?"

Here it comes. What'll it be? Fix a ticket? DBD autographs?

"You have helped," said Grandma. "What can we do for you?"

For crying out loud! She could ask for anything. Blood. Fingernails. It's happened before.

Marta looked at me and I nodded. What else could I do?

"Speak to him about Claudia," she said.

"What did she do?" I asked.

"You saw that she is...interested in him, but he does not see her. I've tried, but he is oblivious."

"Oh," said Grandma. "That's lovely. So nice of you to help."

"I am her mother and he is the only one that she has looked at."

Can't say no to Mom.

"I'll see what I can do," I said.

Grandma patted Marta's arm. "We will take care of it. Mercy knows how to get attention."

"We don't want him noticing me."

She waved that away. "No problem. We can do it."

"Since when am I a matchmaker?" I asked.

"Well, I am." Grandma went on to tell us about fifteen marriages she'd arranged, including Uncle George and Aunt Christine. They were all still married. She had a perfect record. Her one failure was Uncle Rupert. He refused to meet with Grandma's pick and married Chuck's mother instead. She was still pissed about that.

Marta leaned in, bringing her cloud of cigarette smoke with her. Gag.

"How will you do it?"

"Well," said Grandma in true scheming matchmaker style. "We'll be in Esslingen tonight at the market."

"We will?" I asked.

"Shush."

"We're here to invest—"

"If you don't be quiet, I'll tell your mother about the time you pretended to have cramps to get out of school to go see Radiohead."

"I don't like Radiohead. That must've been Jilly," I said.

"Nevertheless."

"Not nevertheless. Details are important."

Grandma looked at me and channeled Aunt Miriam. The stink eye was so hard I felt it in my kidneys. "We will help. That's what we do."

I turned to Marta. "So we will be in Esslingen tonight."

"I will make sure Claudia is there, too."

The ladies hatched a romantic plan that included me luring Koch to the medieval Christmas market in Esslingen wherever that was. How I was going to do that was unclear, but God help me if I didn't pull it off.

"We're all set," said Grandma and she gave Marta my number and hers.

"Thank you," said Marta. "They will be perfect together, if only he would see her."

"I'll take your word for it," I said.

"Mothers know," said Grandma.

Whatever.

We went back inside, leaving Marta polluting herself in the alley. Claudia was still behind the counter and looking seriously worried. "Is everything fine?"

"Yes. Your mother is very nice and helpful."

A wrinkle formed between Claudia's eyes, but she nodded. We left her and went to find Moe. He'd gotten a table in the far corner and the plates were empty. No sandwich. No cakes.

"You pig," Grandma said. "You ate everything?"

Moe put his nose so far in the air I could see the hairs, a whole lot of hairs. "I certainly did not. There were some bums that needed a break. I shared. It's Christmas."

Oh, come on.

"What a sweetheart you are," said Grandma. "I'll get some more."

Seriously?

"I'll be right back. Same thing?" she asked.

I plopped down in my chair and asked, "Why not?"

Grandma got in line and I glared at Moe. "You big fat liar."

"She's happy. That's what's important."

"Is it? I'm starving."

"You ate five donuts this morning," he said. "You'll survive."

He had a point, but I wasn't happy. I still wasn't happy when Grandma came back with the one sandwich cut into thirds and Moe, the bastard, ate one section *and* one whole piece of cake. I got half a piece of cake and one-third a sandwich. I ended up hungrier than when we sat down.

Grandma, of course, was stuffed and moaned about it as we left the café. She was so distracting I wasn't paying attention to our surroundings. Big mistake.

"Watts!"

There past a vegetable stand was Nachtnebel, holding an apple with a face the same color. He charged for us. The vegetable guy chased him, yelling about euro. Grandma elbowed me and said, "Run."

"What?"

"Run." With that, my prim grandmother clutched her heart and called out something in German. I think it was about blackness coming over her, but I didn't have time to process it. Moe grabbed my arm and we darted behind a flower seller's truck. He was packing up, so it was a huge mess and a minefield. We jumped over buckets of roses and juked around large Christmas table arrangements. Moe was moving. The tennis shoes he'd put on might've looked stupid, but the geezer could corner.

We sprinted behind a butcher's truck and Moe yanked me to a stop. "We lost him."

I peeked around the edge of a truck to see the *Polizei* double back to Grandma, who was prostrate on the cobblestones. He wasn't happy about it, but the onlookers were pointing and demanding his attention. He knelt by her side and she threw an arm over her eyes and let out a groan. Who knew that the woman who was reluctant to go to my dad's retirement ceremony because she might have to say a word or two could be such a ham?

Moe smiled and squeezed my arm. "Where has she been all my life?"

"Married to my grandad," I said.

He pointed a finger at me and made a circular motion. "A tiny insignificant detail."

"Why does that sound familiar?"

"*Love Actually*," Moe said. "It's my favorite Christmas movie."

"Are you serious?" I asked.

"What did you think it was?"

"*Die Hard*."

"That's a good one, but I'm a romantic," he said. "I bet *Love Actually* is Janine's favorite, too."

I crossed my arms. "It is not."

"You're lying."

Dammit.

CHAPTER FOURTEEN

We left Grandma J in Sindelfingen. Once upon a time, I would've worried about her but not anymore. She could handle herself and the *Polizei*. She'd probably fix their skin issues, put them on diets, and intro them to their future spouses before she was done. They deserved it and I deserved a break and a snack, but I wasn't going to get either.

Moe and I headed for our rooms in the hotel, only to find Koch leaning on the wall outside mine.

Oh god damn. Thirty minutes. That's all I get.

"That took a while," he said.

"We don't have sirens," I said.

"You should have a bell around your neck to warn bystanders."

"I don't know what you mean."

"Disaster follows you and Nachtnebel isn't happy," said Koch.

I batted my eyes and put a fluttery hand on my chest. "Why is that?"

He snorted, choking back a laugh. "Your grandmother is in the hospital."

"You don't say," I said.

"She convinced half of downtown Sindelfingen that she was having an attack of the heart"—he referred to a notebook—"gout and also herpes. All at the same time. The paramedics were so confused they took her in."

"I love that woman," said Moe.

"Stop it!" I said.

"Too late."

"Someone will have to go get her," said Koch. "Nachtnebel doesn't realize who she is yet and I'd like to keep this connection secret."

"I'll do it," said Moe a little too fast.

"Nope. Forget it. I'm going," I said. Time alone with Grandma J was not a good idea, even if it was with the weirdest looking mobster of all time.

Koch tucked away his notebook. "Neither of you can go. You're both very...recognizable."

My room door opened and Novak stepped out. I had hoped he'd have fixed himself up a bit, but no such luck. Half his head was in cornrows. The other half lay in silky waves to his waist. He had Grandma's red readers perched on his nose for some reason and wore an even more garish ski outfit with a Hello Kitty fanny pack.

"I'll go," he said, and Koch was stunned into silence, so that was nice.

"You don't know what we're talking about," I said.

"Janine's in the hospital with fake everything and this guy's boss is lurking around, trying to catch your scent," he said. "How's that?"

"I guess you do know." I looked behind him. "How thin is that door?"

"Janine called me." He held out his hand. "Keys."

Moe reluctantly handed over the keys to the Mercedes and Novak took off. I didn't even have a chance to catch him up on what we'd found out.

Koch watched him go and then said, "Do you work with anyone normal?"

"Watch it, buddy," said Moe.

"My apologies, but you must admit this crew of hers is...unusual."

"We get the job done."

"Some of my people are normal," I said.

"Name one," said Koch.

Moe eyed me expectantly.

I've got nothing. Absolutely nothing.

"Carolina," said Moe.

"Ha! My mother. So there," I said.

"I've seen pictures of your mother. That lady isn't normal."

"Incredible, isn't she?" Moe smoothed his odd brindle hair. "What a looker. Puts Mercy to shame really."

"Hey!" I said. "I'm standing right here."

"Carolina's got something. That's all I'm saying."

"Swell. Great." I went for my door. "Can I go or would you two like to harass me some more."

"I'm just saying you have no normal people with you," said Koch. "It's an observation."

"It's your opinion."

"Mercy!" called out a woman. "There you are."

Right on time to prove Koch's point, Isolda Bled sashayed down the long hall toward us, and boy did she fill it up. Isolda was one of those people that was impossible to ignore, like Big Steve Warnock she commanded attention wherever she went. For one thing she was the tallest female Bled at nearly six feet. She had broad shoulders and big hands. Her eyes were the Bled pale blue, but the rest of her must've come from her father and nobody knew who that was.

Isolda originally had ash-blonde hair, but it was now white and like her cousins, Millicent and Myrtle, she liked to have it up in a swooping style of coils and curves. My dad called her handsome, but I thought she was beautiful. My opinion was probably more about her personality than her actual features, but I, like so many others, was blind where Isolda was concerned. I loved her. I didn't know anyone who didn't.

"Wow," said Moe.

Koch said something in German under his breath. I think it was along the lines of "who the hell is that?"

Isolda's smile grew wider as she got to us. She pulled off her long black gloves and tucked them inside the pocket of her floor-length mink coat before taking me by the shoulders and giving me kisses on both cheeks. "My dear, I have been looking all over for you."

"Did you call?" I asked.

"Where's the fun in that?" Isolda turned her spotlight on Moe and held out a hand. "Moe Licata, I presume."

Momentarily stunned, Moe just stood there until I elbowed him.

"Yes, yes, I'm Moe." He took her hand gingerly like he hadn't ever seen one before, but then she pulled him in for a hug.

"I'm so pleased to meet you," she said. "Janine can't stop raving. We're going to have fun." Then she turned to Koch, whose mouth was open. If Claudia could've seen him at that moment, she'd have been less sure of her attraction.

"Trouble with the *Polizei* so soon," she said. "Dear me, Mercy, you do stir up a hornet's nest whenever possible."

"Who?" whispered Koch.

"Of course," she said, holding out her hand. "I'm sorry. I'm Isolda Bled, daughter of Imelda and a kind of step-godmother to Mercy."

"Viktor Koch." He took her hand much the way Moe had and said, "You're a Bled as in Bled Beer?"

"Yes, that is the family business. I'm on the board, but I'm not a brewer. I can brew. We all can, but I don't as a general rule."

"You're...part of Mercy's investigation?"

"No, no. I'm here to visit, say hello, and see the sights," said Isolda.

I saw my opening and took it. "We're going to Esslingen tonight. There's a rocking Christmas market there."

"What fun," said Isolda and she looked at Koch as I knew she would. "Are you joining us? If you're not arresting our Mercy, that is. I understand if you have to. You wouldn't be the first."

"What the...?" I exclaimed.

"He may as well know what he's getting into," she said. "You are a Watts."

"I am guilty of that, it's true, but he's not arresting me," I said. "But he should come tonight."

Koch was slack-jawed again. "Come to what?"

"Esslingen," I said. "We're going to the market and you should come."

"But...you and I...it's official business," he said.

I wrinkled my nose. "It's more like unofficial business."

"Hold on."

"I'll keep my promise," I said. "But I don't have much to share at the moment. Tonight, there will be plenty."

"At the market?" Koch asked. "Why there?"

"Because that's where I'll be and I'll have the information."

"Can't you just tell me now?"

"I don't have it now," I said. "Where should we meet you? Do you have a spot in mind?"

Koch stuttered for a moment and then said, "There's a giant Christmas pyramid in the main square. We can meet there."

"Perfect," said Isolda. "I look forward to knowing you better."

Stunned, Koch nodded and left, wandering down the hall a bit like he'd had a few too many.

"So," Isolda leaned over to me, "what are we up to with him?"

"How did you know?" Moe asked.

She smiled and hooked an arm through his. "Mercy would never speak of an outing in front of someone she didn't intend to invite. We didn't raise her that way. So she must have a particular reason for having the *Polizei* there."

"You know her well," said Moe.

"I do."

Isolda looked at me and I said, "We're paying back a favor by hooking him up with a woman named Claudia. She likes him and he doesn't know she's alive."

"Romantic intrigue and on my first night in Stuttgart. I knew this would be worth the trip. What do you say? Let's go to the hotel café. I'm starving, and since you're with Janine, you must be, too."

I burst out laughing and hugged her. She enveloped me in her warm, soft fur and then soothed my hair. "My favorite girl. Nice to see you. Let's eat."

"You go ahead," I said. "I have stuff to do."

"You must eat. Janine has put the kibosh on that. I can tell."

"She likes to split things."

"I know," said Isolda. "It's odd, but we love her anyway. What can I have sent up for you?"

"Anything but seafood."

"Hot chocolate?"

"You're the best ever."

"I try." Isolda took Moe with her. I don't think he quite knew what was happening, but he was extremely pleased about it. I ducked into my room, kicked off my boots, and collapsed on the bed amid Anton's papers, books, and boxes. I had to call Spidermonkey, but I was so tired, I decided to close my eyes for just a minute. It was a long minute.

The knocking on my door was persistent, but my will to ignore it was stronger. Whatever they were selling, I didn't want it. But then my phone started buzzing and you can't fight on two fronts, not for long anyway, and expect a good outcome so I rolled over and stumbled to the door, wiping the drool off my chin.

A room service guy was in the hall and his face said he had to give me the food or else. A Bled had ordered it and people tended to freak out about such things.

"Sorry," I said. "I was sleeping."

He blew out a breath and rolled in the cart. It had so much food on it. Thank God for Isolda. I tipped him well to make up for the stress and answered my phone the second he was out the door.

"What's up?" I asked Spidermonkey.

"I was getting worried. First, Janine and then you don't answer."

"Grandma's fine."

"They don't want to release her."

"Huh?"

"The doctor's think she's got an arrhythmia."

I yawned. "She does. It's under control."

"Well, they are insisting on checking her out fully," said Spidermonkey.

"Fine with me. Second opinions are a good thing."

"You're not worried?"

"She's on meds, fit, and otherwise healthy," I said.

"Is she taking them?" he asked.

"I assume so."

"You probably need to check."

"Alright, you old worrywart. I will do that," I said, rolling my eyes. "What have you got for me?"

Spidermonkey got quiet and that was never a good sign, but I was patient and just listened while I uncovered my cloches. Isolda knew me better than I thought. I got eggs benedict, crepes stuffed with quark and strawberries, and a large slab of quiche.

"So about the money," he said finally.

"Uh-huh." My mouth was full and I didn't care. Quark, my beloved cheese that really isn't cheese, I love you.

"Are you alright?"

"Eating."

"I'll just go ahead," said Spidermonkey.

I could tell he didn't want to and I should've been concerned, but there was hollandaise and no grandma trying to split it. Heaven.

Spidermonkey took Alison Fodor and Sergio Tarantina's families back to the studs just in case they had something to do with the blackmail, but they were clean. Well, maybe not clean. Alison's mom was sleeping with a gate guard and Sergio's dad had a gambling problem that his wife wasn't aware of yet, but they hadn't done anything to Anton. The Café Goethe didn't take credit cards other than for large party orders and there was nothing suspicious there. Spidermonkey had a mind like a mole. Once he went down a hole, he just kept digging. I loved that about him. He went through both counselors lives. Hobbes and Meredith were clean. No extra money and they appeared to be genuinely nice people.

Then he moved on to Sindelfingen and Weil der Stadt, checking everyone connected with the school that lived in the communities. It was a good amount of people and it took him most of the night, but no one renting houses in those two towns had come into money.

"You got into everyone's banks?" I asked.

"There aren't that many banks that Americans use for their

German needs. N26, Volksbank, the credit union on post. Pretty easy really."

"I'll never get used to this."

"It's for a good cause," he said.

"Because it's you."

"True, but let's not dwell on it."

"Oh."

"What?"

"You've really got bad news," I said. "I'm going to eat all this quiche."

He did have bad news and I did eat the entire slab. I regretted it, but I still did it. Spidermonkey kept pretty good tabs on me and so did my Uncle Morty when he was well. They'd both been alerted to someone tracking me. Uncle Morty wasn't supposed to be working, but he'd snuck into his office when his beloved Nikki was out shopping. He discovered someone hacked the airline—super easy apparently—and got our itinerary. It did take them twenty-six hours to find our hotel because my credit cards are so heavily guarded. They only found out by hacking Petra at the Bled travel office. She'd logged into her work accounts from her personal computer at home. A big no-no. They were able to log in using her computer and get my hotel and rental information.

We did confuse them with the Mercedes rental. They had to go through all the rentals that day until Moe's name caught their notice. They tried to break into his accounts, but he was as well-guarded as I was. The Fibonaccis don't play, but apparently, Mercedes does. Our car had a handy-dandy tracking system installed called Mercedes Connect. They got ahold of our movements up until Sindelfingen when Spidermonkey caught on and cut the feed.

"I can't go anywhere anymore," I said.

"You never could, Mercy," he said. "Morty was just handling it for you."

"I'll have to thank him."

"You should."

"What else?" I asked.

"You'll probably get a call from the rental agency. They'll notice the car is offline and want to check on the situation," he said.

"They're tracking me, too?"

"No, but the Connect service is for emergency calls. They want you to have it for safety."

I poured some coffee and went back to my crepes. "Kind of a double-edged sword, isn't it?"

"For you, yes," he said.

"I'm afraid to ask, but what else?"

"They've been trying to get into your phone and computer through the hotel server, but I've blocked that," he said.

"For crying out loud," I said. "Leave me alone people."

"I'm afraid that isn't going to happen. Since you went on the move, attempts on your mother have doubled as well as The Girls."

"So it's The Klinefeld Group, not some creepy bottom feeder of 4chan?"

"Yes, it's them," said Spidermonkey. "They obviously think you're onto something."

"Like them and Anton. I'm going to lose that bet," I said.

"Bet?"

"Chuck and I bet about whether it was The Klinefeld Group that sent Anton. I said no. He said yes. I'm screwed."

"Well, this might make you feel better," he said.

"Do tell."

Spidermonkey had worked his way backwards through the attempts and they weren't local. They were sophisticated enough to bounce their work around the world through various IPs, but he narrowed it down to the Berlin area.

"No movement on the attempts?" I asked, feeling a bit better. "Not coming this way?"

"Not so far, but it's not like they only have one person working for them."

"Does Novak know about all this?"

"He does and interestingly, they don't appear to know about him. No attempts on him whatsoever."

"Do they know he exists?" I asked.

"If you're in our world you know Novak exists, but they haven't connected him to you, which surprises me after Paris," said Spidermonkey. "I think if they had boots on the ground here, they'd know he's with you."

"Me, too, but maybe they just didn't put the effort in."

"That doesn't sound like them."

"I guess not." I poured a fresh cup of coffee and suppressed a burp before lying back on my pillows. "I know you've been up all night, but I did get something today. I was going to ask Novak to do it, but he's at the hospital."

"What is it?" Spidermonkey's voice got tight.

"You okay?"

"I'm just worried. I had hoped this trip would escape The Klinefeld Group's notice."

"Sorry," I said.

"Don't apologize for something that isn't your doing. What did you find out?"

I told him about the boy being there during Anton's meetings with the blonde and gave him the Wi-Fi password to make it easier.

"You're sweet," he said.

"I thought it would be helpful," I said with a laugh. "It could've taken you a whole ten seconds to get CaféGoetheFrühstück."

He chuckled as he typed like mad. "That is a tough one."

"I thought so."

"I'm in," said Spidermonkey. "Anything else?"

"Who bought the tickets?"

He was typing at lightning speed and didn't slow down as he asked, "What tickets?"

"We were in first class over here?" I asked. "Who did that?"

"Isolda Bled. It was kosher. I checked. I didn't know that you knew her," said Spidermonkey.

"I thought it might be her. Who put Moe in our group?"

"That would be me."

"Without asking me?" I asked.

He chuckled and his typing slowed slightly. "It came from the

Fibonaccis. Calpurnia herself called. Am I going to say no to that woman? Not a chance."

"You could've warned me."

"What would you have done?"

"Changed my tickets. Escape somehow," I said.

"And you'd have failed because the Fibonaccis don't."

I sighed because it wasn't only the Fibonaccis. If Spidermonkey was in on it, I had no hope of going it alone. I wasn't ever going to go it alone and I'd like to have tried it at least once to see if I could.

"Mercy, Moe is good. Don't leave his side for a second when you're out of that hotel."

"What about in the hotel?" I asked. "Someone could get in here. It's not Leavenworth."

"I've got a friend monitoring their security and it's pretty good. If someone comes in and asks about you, we'll know. Use your peephole and always keep the bolt locked when you're in. That can't be breached with a swipe."

"That's good, I guess." I was feeling less and less secure the more he said I was.

"I'm serious about sticking to Moe," said Spidermonkey. "Control your instinct to Fike him. Don't say anything. We both know you love to break free. Just don't."

"You think it's The Klinefeld Group," I said.

He abruptly stopped typing. "I don't know if they ordered it, but they are connected. I have no doubts about that."

"Swell."

"It is what it is." He started up again and said, "Let me call you back. We've got a lot of Wi-Fi users in the café and looks like the entire building taps in. This will take some sorting."

"Thanks."

"You're welcome."

He hung up and I opened my computer, feeling a little weird about it. Someone was out there butting their head up against Spidermonkey's wall. If you bang on something long enough there was bound to be a crack.

I pushed the food away and sat down on the bed to go through

Anton's photos again. All those young faces, happy and hopeful. They were the very opposite of the boy at the café, but he was connected. He had to be, but something wasn't right. Something about his pain, that guilt. Why feel it? He wasn't at the table with Anton. But he knew the woman. He must or else where did the guilt come from?

One of Anton's boxes contained different sets of papers, graded and ungraded, from his different classes. The boy looked about seventeen, so I put aside the freshman government class and went with the higher levels. Separating the boys from the girls I ended up with two sets of possibilities, but I kept going back to the AP Gov pile. That look on the boy's face. It wasn't a casual relationship. He knew Anton well. That said AP. Anton was close to those kids.

I came up with a list of twelve names and then started going through the boxes again for some hint of who the blonde was. Anton knew women. He liked women. Marta said twenty, but the woman could be as old as twenty-five or thirty. Age could be well hidden with makeup and clothes.

"Another teacher? Parents would be too old. Someone he knew but wasn't friends with." I drifted off to sleep to have dreams of Anton's hooded face, but now it wasn't coming at me in the dream. He was silent, unable to move. Trapped.

CHAPTER FIFTEEN

"Mercy!"

I jumped and knocked two of Anton's boxes on the floor. "What happened?"

Grandma marched over to the bed. "You can't be sleeping. You have to get on the right time zone."

I yawned and stretched. "It's fine. Just a nap."

"How long have you been sleeping?"

I glanced at the clock. Four hours. Holy crap. "Not long. Where have you been?"

"The hospital. Germans are very thorough," she said. "I got the works."

"Good and what's the verdict?"

Grandma ignored me and took a look at my plates. "Did you eat all of this?"

"It's not that much." It was. I ate all the quiche and half of the eggs benedict and crepes. I would've eaten the rest, but I couldn't force it down my gullet.

"Your poor stomach. You'll have indigestion."

"I don't," I said.

"You will."

"I won't."

Grandma couldn't be persuaded to believe that my stomach that was regularly fed by Aaron, who thought small portions an insult, could handle that much food. She marched into the bathroom and came out with a glass of water and a packet of Alka-Seltzer. "Here drink this."

"I don't—"

"Mercy, we have things to do. Sorcha, Bridget, and Jilly listen to me. Why don't you?"

"They don't listen to you," I said. "They don't listen to anyone."

She fixed a beady eye on me and I plopped the tablets in the glass. Alka-Seltzer and Noxzema. I was losing track of what year it was. 1965? What was next? Tang and pimento loaf?

"Good," she said. "Now we have to get going. I called Marta and Claudia. They will meet us before we meet Koch. What's your plan?"

To get this glass of fizzy weird down.

"Er...nothing," I said.

"What are you going to say to Koch to get him to notice Claudia?"

"You're the matchmaker. You tell me."

I drank my Alka-Seltzer and Grandma cooked up a plot to throw Claudia and Koch together. I've got to say, it wasn't half bad and I sort of felt for Koch. Grandma was thinking a June wedding and I could see it. Grandma had done her homework. They did have things in common. Hiking, skiing, and dog rescues just for starters. According to Grandma, and I don't know how she found this out, Koch thought he was too young to marry. Grandma and Marta thought otherwise. He was twenty-five and ready because they decided he was. He wanted to make rank and Grandma had all kinds of research saying married people rose faster than single ones. Koch wouldn't know what hit him.

"How come you never tried to matchmake me?" I asked and then burped. I did feel better, but I wasn't going to tell her that.

"You're going to marry Chuck." She applied fresh lipstick and a dab of blush to her cheeks.

"I mean before we were dating."

She got out a different lipstick and handed it to me. "Try that. I think the pink gloss will look very nice with your new hat."

"I didn't buy a hat," I said.

She pulled out a poofball hat with two poofballs instead of just one. It was adorable and pink with metallic green thread through it. "Put this on."

I did and she was right. The hat and the lipstick were good. Not too Marilyn. I generally avoided lipstick because it always accentuated what I didn't want accentuated. "Nice," I said, and she gave me a little blush.

"Are you going to answer the question?" I asked.

"You were always going to marry Chuck," she said.

"I hated him."

She gave me my coat and opened the Mauser's box. Like a true Watts, she cleared the chamber, checked out the two clips I had, chose one, and slapped it in. "Here. You need this on you at all times."

"Who have you been talking to?"

"Moe," she said. "Do you have your panic button?"

I showed it to her and pulled my pepper spray out of the luggage. "Happy?"

"If you stay with Moe, I'll be happy," she said.

"What did he tell you?"

"That someone is trying to track you. After what happened to Carolina and you, I'm taking no chances." Grandma got out her own pepper spray and a rape whistle. "I'll be right with you, too."

"I can handle myself," I said.

"Of course." The expression on Grandma's face said, nope, but she'd never say it. She was too polite. "Do you have enough tissues?"

"Huh?"

Grandma rolled her eyes. "A grown woman should have tissues in her purse."

"Um...why?" I asked.

"In case someone needs a tissue." She got three little packs out of her carryon and made me put them in my purse. I guess there was going to be a lot of sneezing. No wonder moms have such big purses. "All set?"

"I guess. Let's get Moe and the other two."

"Who?"

"Novak and Aaron."

"They're not coming," she said.

"Seriously? Does Aaron know there will be food in Esslingen?" I asked.

"I assume so, but you can tell him yourself. Novak said they would be in Conference Room C."

"Weird."

"I'm sure it's normal for them," she said and with that marched out the door.

We found Conference Room C, but the door was locked.

"Are you sure about this?" I asked.

Grandma knocked. "Of course, I'm sure."

A second later, the door was unlocked and one of Novak's brown eyes peered out at us. "Oh, it's you. Come in."

I don't know what I was expecting in that conference room, but it wasn't what I got. It was a medium-sized room with a large oval table that was completely covered in a map with mountains, trees, and fortresses. Tiny little figures were clustered in different areas. On one side of the room was a kind of buffet. There were five computers set up along with external hard drives.

"What in the world is going on?" I asked.

"I'm working," said Novak.

"Are you? Which figure am I?" I picked up a tiny guy. "The one with the flaming sword or the one that's half scorpion?"

"Don't touch that." Novak gently took the figure away from me and placed it back on the table. "They're very delicate."

"Is this Warhammer?" Grandma asked. "Looks like you've got the Imperial Guard and who's this other army?

I stared at her. "Who are you?"

"Oh, right. Da Orkz," she said. "It flew right out of my head."

Novak threw up his arms and did a double fist pump. "I knew you were cool."

"Well, don't get too excited. I only know because my dear friend Kathleen's husband, Ralph, plays with their grandsons. It's taken over their entire basement."

"Still impressive," said Novak.

"Where did you get all this stuff?" I asked.

"I brought it. Aaron's into it and I thought we could have a game."

I didn't even know what to say. I thought I knew nerdy, but this was bringing it to a whole new level. "Alright. Did you get anything for me?"

"Spidermonkey sent me the Wi-Fi data he collected and we split it." Novak waved me over to the computers. "Ignore those three on the end. These two have your stuff on it."

One screen had some sort of YouTube video up with a creepy figure that might've been Native American if it were alive. The other screen had the Instagram of a guy named Ethan. "What am I looking at?"

"We've narrowed it down to five possibilities for your guy. Ethan is an American that goes to the café to do homework and look at porn."

"Novak!" Grandma exclaimed.

"It's a fact, Janine," he said, totally deadpan. "You can see he bears a resemblance to the photo we have."

I leaned in and got a good look. "It's not him"

"You're sure?"

"Pretty sure. Why?"

"He was there on several of the days Anton was there," said Novak.

"But not all?" I asked.

"No one we found was there on all the days." He showed me three more guys all seventeen or eighteen. They all had been in the café at least forty percent of the days that Anton had been there.

None of them was my guy, but they were so similar, if they'd been in a lineup it would've been hella hard to decide who was who. I was starting to doubt my memory as it was.

"What about this other screen? What's that about?"

"That's a strong contender. Spidermonkey says it's him, but I'm not sure. He was in the café less than the others about thirty-seven percent of the days. His visits go back months and he's still coming. The sessions are longer than the others, two or three hours. Most of the others are there two at the most."

"Show him to me," I said.

"That's the thing," he said. "I can't."

Novak explained that the computer was fairly old and was only used in the café. There was no home Wi-Fi on it. Nothing. The guy came into the café, connected to the Wi-Fi there and did his thing.

"What about files and social media?" I asked.

"Nada. If he connects again, I can get in there and poke around, but he's dark right now."

"How do you know he's not doing social media and other stuff?" Grandma asked.

"The IP address is only reaching out to SCP and SCP related material," said Novak. "He is American. Everything is in English."

I sat down in front of that screen. "What's an SCP?"

"Stands for Special Containment Procedures."

"I don't like the sound of that," said Grandma.

"Actually, it's very cool."

Novak explained that SCP was a kind of collective fiction project. Anyone could join in and add to the wiki. There were videos produced about the different stories. They were usually Sci-Fi or horror. Novak typed a website into the other computer and it was a simple website, but I have to admit super intriguing. One section was called "Not all Gods Decompose" and under the title, it said the SCP was not contained.

"So he's reading these...stories?" I asked.

"And writing them. He's very prolific when he works. Not slow. High typing speed. He probably plans when he's not online."

Grandma stood behind me and said, "I don't understand what this is."

"Have you ever seen the show *Warehouse 13*?" Novak asked.

"I loved that show."

"The stories are kind of like that. Some object is magical, usually dangerous to humans, and has to be contained. The stories are about trying to contain them."

"That is fun," she said.

"Why does Spidermonkey think this is our guy?"

"He was there on the one Saturday, but no other Saturday," said Spidermonkey. "He thinks that's too much of a coincidence."

"Sounds reasonable," I said. "You can't get anything else on his computer?"

"It was purchased in 2008 by James Edgewood in Los Angeles at a Costco. Edgewood was sixty-five and he's now dead."

"How did it end up in Germany?" Grandma asked.

"Probably given away or sold on eBay. It could've passed through several hands before it got here. If he shows up at the café, I'll get in and we'll know more," said Novak.

"Until then?" she asked.

"Mercy will investigate. Figure it out," he said. "I just give information. She's the one who uses it."

I clicked play on the SCP video and text started rolling on the left side while a man's voice that reminded me of a news anchor's read what it said. Basically, it was about some creatures that resembled humans that ran around and attacked people.

"He's watched this one?" I asked.

"Several times and he's added to the wiki."

"Can you send me everything he's watched or added to in the last two months?" I asked. "I'm just looking for a list."

"Sure." He leaned over and chose a different video. "Look at this one."

Grandma tugged at my sleeve. "We have to go. We'll be late."

Novak straightened up and said, "I'll send you everything."

I hated to leave, but I couldn't think of a way out, so I said goodbye and we went to Esslingen to make a match and have *Glühwein*. I totally needed *Glühwein*.

Esslingen could've been better, but I really don't know how. We'd stepped through a portal into a place that only had smiling faces, medieval buildings decked out in lights and bowers of evergreen, people wearing armor, and booths selling everything to make you merry at Christmas.

It was hard to keep up with Grandma and her basket, but Moe somehow managed it. The town was packed and the *Glühwein* was flowing. Grandma got in a line. I wasn't sure what she was going for, but she came back with two pretty mugs.

"Here," she said. "We can keep them and take them home if we want."

"I know," I said, pointing to the sign. "It's called the Pfand."

She wasn't really listening; her eyes darted around and glistened with excitement. "If you don't want to keep it, they give you some money back. Isn't that smart?"

"Brilliant," said Moe. His eyes were glistening, too, but he was only looking at my grandmother.

"Do you want to keep it?" she asked.

"Yes," he said.

"What was that?"

I elbowed him and he grinned. "Mercy wants to keep her mug. It's adorable."

It was adorable with a pretty painting of medieval Esslingen on the side, and I did want to keep it, but I'd have ditched Moe quick if I could.

"I have to go back to the Stuttgart market," she said. "I didn't know we could keep them."

"I'll take you," said Moe, looking as though he'd take her anywhere. Forget about Fiking, I might very well get ditched if Grandma made the slightest move in that direction.

"We'll see," I said. "You probably need to eat."

I led her over to a stand selling wild boar goulash and predictably she had to split it with Moe, which thrilled him to no end. Then we went through the stands, buying ornaments and a hat for Aunt Tenne and lavender soaps for my mom. Moe followed the smell of sausages roasting on huge grates hung by chains over wood fires and got one to share with Grandma.

"It's too much," she said.

"Live a little, Janine," he said. "Mustard?"

She said yes and he grabbed one of the bottles that were swinging upside-down from the rafters of the hut and squeezed on a liberal amount. They ate their sausage and I went up on my tiptoes. "We have to find the pyramid."

"I know where it is," said Moe.

When they finished, Grandma checked her phone. "Isolda is coming, but she got held up."

"Let's find Claudia and Marta," I said.

It was hard to get through the crowd when Moe kept stopping to take pictures of the people in period dress, everything from knights to peasants to wenches were in Esslingen.

"This is better than Stuttgart," Grandma said. "Oh, there they are. What in the world is that thing?" She pointed up at a kind of wooden sculpture looming over the market.

"That's the pyramid," said Moe. "There were some little ones in Stuttgart."

"I don't remember that."

He laughed. "I'm not surprised."

Claudia and Marta stood next to the pyramid, which wasn't really a pyramid the way we think of one. It was four stories in wood and each story had a different Christmas theme with characters and candles. At the top were windmill blades like a flat crown. Myrtle and Millicent had a real pyramid that I picked out in Nuremberg on one of our trips. When you lit the candles, the blades turned from the rising heat. It fascinated me as a child and I couldn't wait to light it every year.

Marta saw us and waved. Grandma grabbed my arm and said, "Don't forget our plan."

"You mean your plan," I said.

"Whatever," she said with a boozy smile. A little *Glühwein* went a long way with my grandmother.

"Claudia," I said. "So nice to see you."

Claudia was confused, but she went with it, not that she had any choice. Grandma cornered her and grabbed me. "Mercy, give an update on our progress. It's only right since she's essential to our work."

"Essential?" Claudia asked.

"Absolutely," I said, feeling a little boozy myself. "You are part of the investigation, a crucial part."

"I am?"

"You have to know all the particulars in case that Nachtnebel comes around," I said. "You don't want to look like you're holding out on him."

"No, of course not," said Claudia.

"I will get more *Glühwein*," said Marta.

"I'll go, too," said Grandma.

"Not for me," said Claudia.

Marta acted like she didn't hear her daughter and they melted into the crowd. I turned to Claudia and did what I never did. I told her what I had, even though I'd have liked to have kept it close to the vest.

"I know about SCPs," she said. "My brother watches them."

"Excellent. Tell me what you know. It's a huge help."

Claudia knew quite a bit and the trip wasn't a waste of time at all. Her brother was a talker and Claudia told me that SCP stories tended to fit into some loose categories, Safe, Euclid, Keter, Thaumiel, and Apollyon. Basically, the easiest to contain anomalies were in Safe all the way up to the most dangerous in Apollyon that were a constant threat to human life. Claudia's favorite was some Play-Doh soldiers that could form into just about anything but were harmless because their ammunition was also Play-Doh.

"So you watch these things?" I asked.

"Sometimes, but not the hardcore ones. They'll give you nightmares. Do you know which one the boy was watching?" she asked.

"I will."

"Pay attention to that. It says a lot about him if he only likes the scariest stuff, I mean," said Claudia. "I met someone a while ago and he liked the most violent of the SCPs. He wasn't very nice."

"Good to know."

Grandma and Marta came back with multiple mugs, smiling Cheshire Cat smiles. What a couple of old schemers.

"*Mutti*," complained Claudia. "I said no. I have to drive."

"We are having fun. Don't be so serious. We will take the train home."

"Our car is here."

Marta pushed the mug into her daughter's hands and Claudia was more confused than ever. She sipped her *Glühwein* and told me more about SCPs. I was getting a decent picture of our guy, if it was him.

"He's a creative then," I said.

"Oh, yes. Certainly," she said. "He might be a writer. You could find him that way."

I nodded. "Yes, through the high school. The counselors might know. Brilliant, Claudia."

She gave me a shy smile and that's when I spotted Viktor Koch coming into the square between a hut selling *Lángos*, a fried flatbread covered in cheese, and another selling *Spätzle*. He cleaned up well and was wearing a typically European black wool jacket, a red scarf, and a fedora tilted at just the right angle. Marta would be pleased.

"Oh, my God," I said. "You won't believe who's here."

"Is it him?" Claudia spun around, looking for the boy.

"The *Polizei* that's helping us." I waved frantically. "I was hoping he'd come."

Claudia shrunk back as if she could melt into the wood of the nearest hut. "Why is he here?"

"I asked him to come. He's so nice to help us, even when his boss isn't happy with me. Viktor!"

Koch came over, predictably oblivious to Claudia's distress, and focused on me. "Do you have news?"

"I do and even more than I came with," I said. "Claudia has been a huge help."

"Claudia?" he asked.

I turned and Claudia had gotten herself five feet away. Marta was barely retaining her motherly urge to kick her daughter over to the handsome officer. Since she looked like she might do a runner, I took Koch's arm and we cornered her against the hut.

"Claudia. Viktor. Viktor. Claudia," I said happily.

"Oh yes," he said. "You work at the Café Goethe."

She nodded and was mute.

"Viktor is the *Polizei* that interviewed you, remember?" I asked.

Another nod. This was going to be harder than I thought.

"Okay. Here's what's happening." I told him about the boy and gave him a copy of the picture we had.

"How did you get this?" he asked.

"Do you really want to know?"

"No."

"Good answer." I told him about the Wi-Fi access and narrowing it down to a few people being in the café at the right time.

"It's illegal to access Wi-Fi networks other than your own," he said.

"Imagine that," I said. "It's a good thing you don't know anything about those kinds of activities."

"Is this how you solve crimes?" Koch asked. "By doing illegal activities?"

"How many leads did you have before I showed up? None? That's what I thought," I said. "Now a café with a Wi-Fi password of CaféGoetheFrühstück is hardly worried about security. Half their building is poaching it. More than half actually."

He gave me that hard German look I was so familiar with from my days of traveling with The Girls. They got it quite a lot when someone didn't want to give them entrance to a library or archives. It didn't stop them and it didn't stop me.

"So do you want to give me the stink eye or do you want to learn about SCPs?"

"I...uh...what?"

"SCPs," I said. "We've got a solid lead and Claudia knows all about it."

He looked at Claudia. She was terrified and I sighed.

"Claudia, please explain SCPs," I said. "They're kinda a sci-fi thing, right?"

"Oh, sci-fi," said Koch. "I love sci-fi."

"Really?" Claudia asked.

Thank you, God. I appreciate it. 'Cause I have to pee.

"Tell him about the Play-Doh," I said. "And the types. Our guy could be a psycho."

"Well," she said quietly, "there are different levels. SCP stands for—"

"I'm going to find a bathroom. Be right back." I left them bent over Claudia's phone and went to the matchmakers.

"Very good," said Marta. "I knew it would be right."

"He's into sci-fi," I said.

"Claudia reads that."

"Another thing in common."

"Who has something in common?" Isolda swept in, wearing a different fur with a matching hat and carrying two baskets full of wrapped presents.

"Our scheme is working," said Grandma and she pointed to Koch and Claudia.

"You are a genius, Janine," said Isolda.

"Has anyone seen a sign for bathrooms?" I asked.

"Yes," said Isolda. "This way."

Isolda hooked arms with Grandma and said, "So how mad are you at Ace? A six or a seven?"

"I give it an eight point two," said Grandma.

"Ooh that beats the great unretirement of 1995."

"Consider it compound interest."

I glanced over at Moe who was scanning the crowd for threats and smiling a tiny bit like the Grinch when he was plotting to ruin Christmas. I took his arm and said, "No."

"I don't know to what you refer," said Moe.

"Uh-huh. Sure."

"Hurry. We're going to lose them."

We weren't going to lose them. Our progress to a much-needed toilet was snail-like. We stopped at a stage performance with musicians playing what I assumed were medieval instruments, including some weird guitar thing that had strings, keys like a piano, and a crank on the end. It sounded like the music from *The Last of the Mohicans*, one of my mom's favorite comfort movies. We watched it three times when she was in rehab.

I had to push Isolda and Grandma to get them moving because just giving me directions wasn't going to do it. We had to stay together. They thought I'd get lost. I would, but I was willing to risk it for a toilet, a hole in the ground, or a flipping bush. Things were reaching critical mass.

Isolda led us to the medieval town wall and pointed up an alley to a sort of trailer toilet set up. I dashed up and handed the lady manning the pay to pee table a euro. Paying for toilets was one of those things that was hard to get used to, but I'd long since learned to have change at all times.

"All better?" Grandma asked when I came out.

"Yes. Thank you," I said. "Where to now?"

"The Kinder area," said Isolda. "I love the Kinder."

She and Grandma headed through an arch in the wall and we entered the children's delight. There were merry-go-rounds that were half modern and half medieval with wooden buckets for the kids to sit in, a Ferris wheel all in wood and run by a guy with a crank, a petting zoo, and more food. Grandma decided to split a waffle with Isolda and they waited in line while Moe and I hung back to watch the Kinder walk by dressed like they were in twenty below blizzard weather when it was actually not that bad out at about forty-two degrees. In Germany, it wasn't unusual to see parkas and puffer coats in sixty-degree weather.

Marta jogged up and hugged me. "They are still talking. I could not get a word in."

"Congratulations," I said.

"Where is Janine? I must tell her."

"Waiting for waffles."

Marta joined them in line, joyfully telling the ladies about the success. I could practically see the thoughts of grandchildren spinning around in her head.

Moe did a quick turnaround to check the passing crowd and then said, "Did you know that Isolda doesn't know who her father is?"

"Of course, it's kind of a family mystery," I said.

"I thought that kind of thing only happened to the lower classes, not people like the Bleds."

"The Bleds are people, just like everyone else."

Moe looked at Isolda with her furs and dangling diamond earrings. "No, they aren't."

"How did you find out?" I asked. "Did she tell you?"

"She's not ashamed," he said with admiration. "She was very upfront about it."

"Why in the world did it come up? She's never mentioned it to me and I've known her my whole life."

"Well," Moe marked a pair of men coming through the crowd that looked a little out of place and watched them until they'd passed through without a glance in my direction and then continued, "it's why she's here in Germany, so she told me."

"What's Germany got to do with it?" I asked.

"She thinks he's German."

It took me a second to process that. I'd never heard anyone in the family give any hints as to who Isolda's father might be. As far as I knew, The Girls had no clues to who he was and they weren't particularly concerned and neither was anyone else. I couldn't blame them. Isolda's mother's mysterious pregnancy had happened so long ago and she wouldn't say a thing about the father, which wasn't surprising considering her mental state.

Imelda was mentally ill her whole life. She was diagnosed with everything from garden variety insanity to schizophrenia to female hysteria. It sounded to me like she had bipolar disorder from the frantic elation and deep sadness The Girls described. Imelda was in and out of mental hospitals, but the Bleds refused the harsh treatments the doctors wanted to do, like a lobotomy and hydrotherapy. The Girls still got mad when they talked about it. One doctor thought immersing Imelda in ice water for hours would shock her into normalcy. When he wouldn't leave Imelda's father alone on the subject, he ended up chasing him out of the office with a cane. It made the papers.

In the end, the Bleds decided to keep Imelda at home instead of institutionalizing her. She went from house to house, family member to family member, only in the hospital when absolutely necessary. She was at the Bled Mansion being looked after by The Girls' mother Florence when in 1943 Imelda disappeared. She always had a companion with her, a woman named Rose, but there was a flu epidemic going around that winter. Myrtle and Millicent got it and were terribly sick, so was Florence, and most of the staff, including Rose, who ended up in the hospital.

During the sickness, Imelda Bled walked out the front door and disappeared for three months. The family did everything they could to find her, but the police and private detectives found no trace of her, until she had what the family described as an episode in New York City where she ended up at Bellevue Psychiatric Hospital and was recognized. She had Isolda seven months later and was by all accounts a wonderful mother when she was stable. The family decided Nicolai and Florence would take responsibility for raising Isolda and she lived in the Bled Mansion, even when Imelda was in another house. It wasn't an ideal solution, but I don't know what else they could have done.

"He can't be German," I said.

"Why not?" Moe asked.

"It happened in 1943. We were at war. There weren't a whole lot of free-range Germans running around."

"She sounds pretty sure and it's not like the cops had a clue about what happened to her mother," said Moe. "They were useless and caused trouble instead of finding Imelda."

"Isolda told you that?" I asked.

"I already knew."

"How? Nobody talks about Imelda's disappearance anymore. The family barely does."

"I got briefed when Fats did," he said.

"What in the world are you talking about?" I asked.

"Families have long memories. Calpurnia and Cosmo thought there might be an issue when they put Fats on you."

I'm so freaking confused.

"You mean my dad might have an issue?"

"We knew he would. Tommy Watts was always going to have a problem with us," said Moe. "But then he didn't. Go figure. What did you do to handle that?"

"Nothing. He just never did anything," I said.

"He knows."

"I know he knows, but he just got over it."

Moe's eyes left the crowd to look at me. "Since when does Tommy Watts get over anything?"

"Good point, but I still don't get it. Calpurnia briefed you on Imelda Bled because my dad might freak out about Fats bodyguarding me?" I asked.

"Of course not," Moe said. "She was concerned about how your godmothers might react and she wanted Fats to have a response if they did."

"Millicent and Myrtle? Why would they care?"

"Because the Fibonaccis were accused of kidnapping Imelda."

"Are you serious?" I asked. "Why would the Fibonaccis kidnap a mentally ill woman in broad daylight in the middle of a flu epidemic?"

"They wouldn't, but the cops had nothing else. They figured it was a ransom-type situation and we might have knowledge of who did it, even if we didn't do it ourselves."

"That sounds like a stretch," I said.

Grandma got her waffle and pointed at a sign for the petting zoo. The ladies took off and we followed much slower.

"When the cops have nothing, they go fishing," said Moe. "My grandfather got pulled in three times and smacked around pretty good. He wasn't the only one. They yanked in the O'Reilly gang. To be fair, kidnapping was more their style. They used to grab up working girls from other cities and put them to work downtown."

"That's fairly horrible," I said. "But was there a ransom note or something?"

"As a matter of fact, there was," he said. "Some dingus mailed one to the brewery, trying for a quick score. Grandpa used to talk about that. The cops yanking people off the streets, trying to find that idiot."

"They just picked up random people?"

"It was the good old days. Cops could do what they wanted. Grandpa came home with a broken nose and cigarette burns. He was seventeen."

"Oh, my God."

"Yeah, well, he gave as good as he got. He beat the crap out of two of those cops a year later. Put them in intensive care. No charges. Cops knew when to step back."

"It sounds like the Wild West," I said.

"There was a missing Bled and the papers kept saying it might happen again to the little girls."

"Millicent and Myrtle?"

"That was the fear. Let's just say the cops were motivated to get something and they didn't care how. Grandpa thought it was all BS.

You know the Bleds got a history of topping themselves and that Imelda, we knew she was nuts. Everyone knew. They just didn't say it because it was the Bleds."

"The Fibonaccis thought Imelda killed herself?" I asked.

"Sure. It made sense, but the cops were all over the kidnapping idea. The way I heard it, they had people on every Bled house, sleeping in the hallways, trying to catch someone doing something. Hey, is that how your family met them?"

My head was spinning. The Watts were cops forever. One of us could've been on that investigation. "No...Grandad met them during an investigation. There was a break-in at the mansion."

"You don't sound so sure," said Moe.

"I'm sure that's how Grandad met them," I said.

"But he might not be the first?"

"Maybe not. I never asked about earlier investigations. I didn't really know there were any," I said. "What happened with the ransom note?"

"Delivery driver for the brewery," said Moe. "Nothing to do with it."

"I bet it didn't go well for that guy," I said.

"It did not."

Isolda waved me over with a big smile and I nodded before asking, "She really thinks her father is German?"

"She's convinced, but she didn't say why. Maybe her mother told her something." He took my arm and we walked over to the petting zoo.

"Aren't they adorable?" Grandma was scratching a donkey, who was trying to get the waffle.

"Adorable," I said.

"Are you alright, Mercy?" Isolda asked.

"I'm fine. I just...need some more *Glühwein*."

Grandma grabbed my hand. "There's a white one we haven't tried."

We went through the rest of the Kinder area and back into the main market where we admired jugglers and performers with ribbons swirling around them. We did get the white *Glühwein* and one with schnapps and one with rum. Grandma and Isolda got pretty tipsy. They wanted to stay, but when Grandma decided to give *Eierlikör* another try, it was time to go.

It was a good thing Marta stayed with us, she knew the way back to the pyramid, where we found Koch and Claudia at a barrel table drinking *Glühwein* and talking a mile a minute.

Grandma exchanged cheek kisses with Marta. "Merry Christmas."

"Yes, it will be very happy and thank you," said Marta and then she turned to me. "If you need anything else for your case, come to me. I will help."

I thanked her and she went to join her daughter and Koch. Neither of them looked thrilled to have the mother at the table, which was the best sign of all.

"I will leave you now," said Isolda.

"No, no," said Grandma. "We aren't leaving you."

"I have a driver." She made a quick call. "He will meet me by the church. St. Dionys."

"It's on our way to the parking garage," said Moe. "We will walk you."

He pointed the teetering ladies in the right direction and they walked off ahead.

"Tomorrow," said Isolda over her shoulder. "Dinner."

I ran to catch up. "What was that?"

"I'd like to take you all to dinner tomorrow night," said Isolda.

"Great. Wonderful," said Grandma.

"Well, I am on a case," I said. "I might be—"

"Nonsense," said Grandma. "Isolda wants to talk to you about something."

"Do you?" I asked Isolda.

The elegant lady in mink and diamonds burped and then giggled. "I do and I have to hurry."

"Why?" I asked.

"You might solve your case and go home." She bumped into a building then Grandma got the giggles.

We let them go ahead and Moe squeezed my arm. "She's going to hire you."

"To do what?"

"Find her father."

"Ah, crap. Talk about a cold case," I said.

Moe scanned the waning crowd and said, "She must have something and a little bird told me that you have an interest in that German charity."

"The Klinefeld Group couldn't have anything to do with it," I said. "That's to do with Stella Bled Lawrence and The Bled Collection."

"Fats said it goes back to WWII and Imelda disappeared in 1943."

Crap on a cracker!

CHAPTER SIXTEEN

Back at the hotel after running around the lobby and telling everyone who'd listen and some who wouldn't how much she loved Germany, my grandmother, the formerly quiet and contained Janine, stumbled into our hotel room, bumped into the walls twice, and then started stripping in the middle of the room.

"Maybe you want to do that in the bathroom," I suggested.

"We're all girls here," she slurred and then looked around. "Aren't we?"

I picked up her coat and hung it up. "Yes, it's just you and me."

"Where's Moe?"

"His room or playing Warhammer. I have no idea."

"You should make sure he's okay," said Grandma. "He had a bit to drink."

"No, he didn't," I said. "He was driving."

"He had *Punsch*."

"That was *Kinderpunsch*. No alcohol."

Grandma threw up her arms. "I liked it."

"You liked everything," I said.

She gave me boozy smile. "I did. I do. This is a great trip."

"It's pretty okay."

"You are pretty," she said. "I've always said you're pretty."

Grandma stumbled and fell on the bed. I inwardly groaned and took off her boots. "Okay. Now get under the covers and let's go to sleep."

"We can't go to sleep in this stuff," she said.

"What stuff?"

Grandma rolled out of bed and flung the last of her clothes on the floor. Then she peeled off a layer of shapewear to reveal another layer of shapewear.

"How much spandex are you wearing?" I asked.

"You have to double up to get smoothing," she slurred. "Have I taught you nothing?"

"We've already covered this." I helped her out of the last layer and pulled her nightgown over her head. "Get in bed."

"No, no. We have to do something..."

"No, we don't. Go to sleep."

"Skincare. You can't skip skincare." Grandma rolled out of bed again and lurched toward the bathroom.

"Let's don't and say we did," I said.

She came back and grabbed me. Skincare was happening. Sleep was not.

"Okay. Fine, but I want to ask you something."

"Ask me anything," said Grandma as she bounced off the door to the room and used the momentum to get in the bathroom. It was quite impressive actually.

I watched as she pulled off her fake eyelashes and flung them on the counter. "I don't think I need those. Do you think I need those?"

"I don't." The eyelashes went into their case and I said, "So Moe told me that when Fats was—"

Grandma spun around. "That rascal! I told him not to say anything."

"Well, it's not a big deal," I said.

"It certainly was and I want credit." She started smearing on her Noxzema. "Are you not..."

"What?" I asked.

"Giving me credit."

"Well, it's not really anything to do with you," I said. "I mean, you might know, so I was going to ask when our family—"

"Our family. That's just what I said. Holier than thou. *Psst.*" Grandma spit on the mirror and I just stared.

"What are we talking about?"

"Our *bad* family," she said.

"Who's bad?" I asked.

"Well, not my family. We were always law-abiding citizens." She shoved the Noxzema into my hands and groped around for her toothbrush.

"And the...Watts aren't? Since when? We've been cops forever."

"Not forever and that's what I told them."

Grandma went on to say that the Watts weren't always cops. We started in St. Louis as criminals. Like real criminals. My ancestors were part of that O'Reilly gang and she used the word thugs several times. Thugs!

"That can't be true," I said.

"Yes, it is. Your great-great-grandfather was a thug," she said and slammed on the faucet.

"No, he wasn't. He was a cop. You named my dad after him."

"Not Thomas. His father."

"Well, that would be my great-great-great-grandfather," I said.

"Don't get technical with me, young lady."

Oh, no. She's pulling out the young lady.

"Sorry, but I don't know what this has got to do with Moe and—"

"That's how you got to keep Fats," Grandma said. "I told that grandfather of yours—"

"Your husband," I said.

"That's the one. I told him and that father of yours that I would tell reporters that the Watts were criminals the next time they show up and you know those media piranhas will be back. They always come back and I'd tell them. Think of the coverage. Negative publicity." She waved her arms around. "Negative publicity. Oh no."

"That's why Dad never said anything about Fats and the Fibonaccis?" I asked.

"Yes. 'Don't be taking that bodyguard away from my girl. I will kick your ass,' I said. That's what I said."

"Go, Grandma. Thanks."

She gave me a smeary Noxzema kiss on the cheek. "And there you go."

"That's not actually what I was asking about," I said.

"What else is there?" She picked up a comb. "Do your hair."

This was new, but I started combing under Grandma's stern direction. There's a right way to comb. Who knew?

"Let's get back to the Bleds. Grandad met them when he was working on a case, a break-in at the mansion?"

"That's right." She screwed up her mouth. "I don't feel so good."

"Why don't you wash that stuff off and lie down?"

"We're not done. Get me an Altoid. They settle my stomach."

I got her a mint and found her sitting on the toilet, filing her nails.

"Here you go," I said. "So did you know the Bleds before that break-in?"

"How in the world would I know the Bleds?" She slipped off the toilet and landed in a heap next to the tub. "Oops. I'm not supposed to be down here. Help me up, Mercy."

"Just stay until you want to rinse your face off."

"Three more minutes," she said like we were timing ourselves.

I sat down on the toilet and said, "Okay. I meant did the Watts know the Bleds before that break-in? Moe said there were lots of cops on Imelda's kidnapping and that they were practically camping at the mansion. Great-Grandpa could've been there."

"Ace's father? He was in the war."

"Was he already? In 1943?"

She yawned and said, "He was in Europe."

"We didn't get to Europe until D-day in 1944," I said.

"Well, he wasn't in D-day. I know that." She held out a hand. "Time to rinse."

I helped her up and we rinsed. Well, she rinsed and I kept her from falling.

"Why are you asking about Elijah?" Grandma asked.

"Elijah?"

"Great-Grandpa's name was Elijah. You know that."

"I forgot. Everyone calls him Great-Grandpa and nobody was named after him," I said.

"You were going to be, but you were a girl," she said. "Rinse your face."

"Are you okay?"

She burped and said, "Fine. So fine. I love *Glühwein*. Did I tell you that?"

"You did." I rinsed and said, "So you never heard Elijah talk about the Bleds?"

"Goodness no. He did go to the mansion once though."

A zing went through me. Was this it? Could Elijah be Josiah Bled's son? Was that how we were Bleds? I couldn't do the math. When was he born?

"When did he go?" I asked my voice so tight and strange I thought she'd notice, but she was checking her crow's feet in the mirror. It was a wonder she could find them.

"With Ace, of course. After he was on that case," she said. "Hand me that stuff in the clear jar, dear."

I gave it to her and asked, "Why did he take Great-Grandpa?"

"Oh, I don't know. They invited him."

They wanted to see him.

"Why would they do that?" I asked.

"Oh, Mercy, I don't know."

I'd aggravated her, but I couldn't let go. It was rare to get my family talking and it was too good a chance. "Why do you think they liked Grandad so much? They helped his career and everything."

She finished her skincare and ordered me to do mine. "Who knows why? I wondered myself, but people click. It's chemistry. They fell in love with your grandad and then your parents."

"Leo was on that case," I said. "He's a charming guy. I wonder why it wasn't him?"

"People have favorites, like parents. Parents have favorites." She lurched toward the bathroom door and I hurried up behind to make sure she got through.

"Parents aren't supposed to have favorites," I said.

"You're your mother's favorite."

"I'm her only child. It's not a stiff competition."

She stopped walking a foot from the bed. "I forgot my neck cream."

So close.

"You can skip that," I said.

"I'll get turkey neck. I don't want turkey neck."

And back to the bathroom we went. She dapped on the cream and then made me do it. "Only child is no guarantee," she said.

"Oh, right. I'm not my dad's favorite," I said.

"Well, Chuck looked up to him from the time he was adopted by my son who wouldn't listen to me," she said, "and you were a pain in the butt from day one. Pain in the butt."

"Thanks, Grandma." I followed her out of the bathroom again.

"It's not a bad thing. I was quite proud that you told that son of mine to stick it."

"I did not."

"You did. You didn't want to be a cop and you made no bones about it. Most children would," she waved her arms around, "pretend to make the old man happy. Not you."

"He still made me learn it all."

I pulled back the covers and she sat down on the edge of the bed to take off her jewelry. "He *made* you. Chuck wanted to learn. That's why he's the favorite."

"That's fair."

"You know Elijah wasn't the favorite, either, and he was an only child, too." She laid down and I covered her up. "He told me."

Stands to reason if he wasn't Thomas' kid.

"What did he say?" I asked as I lay down.

"He loved his father, but he was nothing like him," said Grandma. "Have you seen the pictures of Thomas and Elijah?"

"Probably."

"He was a huge man, tough and proud," she said.

"You knew him?" I asked.

"He died before I met Ace, but there were plenty of stories."

"What was Elijah like?" I whispered. It was like a vault had been opened and I was so afraid it would close again.

"Such a gentle man. Sweet. He loved the opera and poetry. Can you imagine that? A Watts loving the opera? His father was a bare-knuckle boxer in his youth."

It makes sense if Elijah wasn't a Watts at all.

"How did he end up a cop?" I asked.

"Some people want to please their parents." Grandma chuckled. "He didn't go far. Just a regular street cop, but two thousand people came to his funeral. Two thousand. He was loved in the neighborhoods he patrolled and he worked almost fifty years altogether in uniform. Died on the job. Heart attack."

I didn't know what to say. Elijah was extraordinary in his own way and no one had mentioned it. I felt terrible that he was just another Watts cop in my mind before that. I assumed he was as driven and nutty as Grandad and my dad, but Elijah was something else entirely.

"Did he take after his mother?" I asked.

"Oh, no. I met her and she was a force. Tall and red-haired with a temper. Elijah was so proud of her." Grandma closed her eyes. "He adored his mother. He talked about her until the day he died."

I whispered, "What did he say?"

"She nursed people through the Spanish flu in the wards downtown. She wasn't afraid. She wasn't afraid of anything. She started a pie-making business during the Great Depression and fed people from the proceeds. Oh, Elijah was so proud of her."

Her voice faded away and I resisted the urge to poke her. There were plenty of Christmas markets around. Maybe with a little more *Glühwein* lubrication I could get some more information. Grandma might not know what she knew. They were just strange little family quirks like Elijah not resembling his father, but they meant a lot to me.

"Aren't you going to ask me who my favorite is?" Grandma said quietly.

"I thought you were asleep."

"I am a little," she said. "I've never told anyone who it is."

"The favorite?" I asked.

"Yes."

"Is it my dad?"

"No," she spat out. "You must be joking. Tommy was a nightmare. Always crying and once he could walk, he kept escaping from the house. I thought he would get killed in the road."

"So not my dad," I said.

"He was so difficult. Everything was a problem. Always messing with things. When he was ten he took apart our brand-new TV set to see how it worked. You know what, it never worked again. I thought Ace would wring his neck or mine. He was so mad. And a perfectionist. If Tommy didn't get a perfect grade at school, he would throw a fit. I had a nervous breakdown when he was in the third grade. I had to take pills for the stress."

"Holy crap." *Does Grandma hate my dad?*

"Holy crap is right. I almost wished the social services had taken him away."

Wait what?

"Social services almost took my dad? Why?"

"Tommy wouldn't eat. The doctor thought I was starving him because he was so thin. It wasn't my fault. The boy wasn't interested in food. He was interested in driving me crazy."

"What happened? How'd you get to keep him?"

Grandma blew out a breath and I thought she'd gone to sleep, but she came back with a vengeance. "Well, I thought maybe his father could do some good and I tried to get him to come down to the doctor, but there was a case and you know when there's a case nothing else matters."

"Don't tell me. Grandad didn't go?"

"He did go, but I had to call his lieutenant and tell him that the St. Louis police forces' best detective was about to have his kid taken away for neglect and how's that going to look?"

"Then he made Grandad go?"

"He did and the doctor took one look at Ace and his skinny butt and said never mind."

"Thank goodness for that lieutenant," I said.

"He was a flaming racist. I hated him, but he did have his uses," said Grandma. "He grabbed my butt at a picnic one time and Ace said

I had to just avoid him instead of beating the crap out of him. The seventies was a terrible time for women."

I'm learning so many things I didn't want to know.

"So..." *I'm afraid to ask but here goes.* "Who is your favorite?"

"Kevin."

"Who is Kevin?"

"Our neighbor's son. He was the nicest most polite boy. I just love Kevin. We still go to coffee every other week."

"Kevin Oliphant, the Children's Hospital volunteer director?"

"Isn't he lovely? Such a nice young man."

I decided not to ask what was wrong with my uncles. She would tell me and I didn't want to know. I definitely wasn't going to ask who her favorite grandchild was. It wasn't me. I didn't even know about Noxzema until a day ago.

"Grandma?" I whispered.

"Uh-huh?"

"What was Elijah's mother's name?"

"Gladys."

I made a face. "That's unfortunate."

"It wasn't her real name," said Grandma, her voice barely a whisper. "She wanted to be American."

Ding. Ding. Ding.

"What was her real name?" I asked.

"Giséle."

"Grandma...was Giséle French?"

"Yes."

A faint snore came from Grandma's side of the bed, but I was wide awake. It was Elijah. He was the Bled.

CHAPTER SEVENTEEN

Grandma threw back the curtains, turned the TV to BBC International, and flipped on the lights about seven hours before I was remotely interested in being awake.

I pulled a pillow over my head and said, "What the hell are you doing?"

"Language, Mercy, please," said Grandma. "Now get up and get going."

"It's like two-thirty in the morning."

"It's six o'clock in the morning."

Grandma's pillow joined mine until she yanked it off.

"Hey!"

"We're leaving in a half hour. No time to shower, but you don't need to. Nobody will be smelling you," she said.

"I don't smell." *Do I?*

"That's right. Up and at 'em. We'll get breakfast afterward."

"After what?" I asked, rolling over and searching for the remote. I so didn't need to hear dreadful news on some political strife or an earthquake. "Rubble Hill. Isolda told me about it and we're going to hike it to see the sunrise." Grandma pinned a brooch on her sweater and looked at me expectantly.

"Are you still drunk?" I asked.

"Don't be silly. I'm Irish."

"What's that got to do with it?"

"I took an Emergen-C last night while you were asleep. I'm right as rain," she said, frowning at me. "I should've given you some. You're very pale."

"I didn't sleep well."

"How come? Last night was wonderful. I can't remember when I had such a good time."

I had nightmares about having a kid like my dad and going freaking crazy.

"I was talking to Spidermonkey," I said. "I am on a case, remember?"

"Oh, that."

"Yes, that." *And so many other things.*

She tossed a pair of jeans at me. "The hike will clear your head."

"Never going to happen," I said.

"I'm going to brush my teeth and when I come out. I want you dressed," Grandma said.

"Good luck with that." I found the remote, turned off the bad news, and checked my phone. Spidermonkey hadn't come back with anything new since I'd gone to sleep. Disappointing, but expected. I had been working long into the night like I'd told Grandma, but it wasn't on our case. Spidermonkey and I were going through the new lead she'd given me. Gladys Watts was really Giséle. Spidermonkey was absolutely stunned that that hadn't turned up. He had no idea that she was French either. Gladys Watts had an American birth certificate. She was supposed to have been born in Iowa to American parents. Spidermonkey hadn't had any reason to question her documentation and had taken it at face value. Everything added up until I threw France into the works. Grandma didn't give me a last name, so all he had to go on was Giséle and the timeline.

"You really think Elias the Odd was Elijah's father?" Spidermonkey asked.

"Definitely," I said. "No doubts."

"The numbers don't line up. Elias disappeared in October 1910.

Thomas Watts married Gladys in December 1910 and Elijah was born in September 1911."

"They got a fake birth certificate for Giséle. They could get one for Elijah," I said.

The two of us combed through ships manifests looking for a Giséle. I'd begun to think it was impossible when Spidermonkey found a Giséle Donadieu on a ship out of Marseille on November 1, 1910. She took a fast steamer and made it to New York in two weeks. He could find no trace of her after that. Giséle Donadieu disappeared from history. She never made it on a census and had no death certificate.

"What about Gladys?" I asked. "Can you find anything on her so-called parents?"

"There's nothing, not in Iowa anyway, but it's possible I just don't know where to look. Don't get too excited."

"Too late. I've got a feeling and I got it the second Grandma said Gladys wasn't her real name. I knew she'd be French. I just knew."

"But you thought it might be Josiah Bled until you heard Elijah's birthdate," he said.

"I did. I mean come on. Josiah was a ladies' man. It would track for him to have sired a child out of wedlock. Even The Girls think there's probably at least one or two of his offspring running around somewhere."

"Really?"

"Of course, but with Giséle coming from France and the name. It's Elias."

"The name?" Spidermonkey asked.

"Elijah. It's out of character for our family. We get pretty boring names. Thomas, George. So I looked it up. Elias and Elijah are basically the same name. Two different versions of it."

"That *is* a bit of a coincidence."

"We're not Watts at all. I know it," I said.

"What's your theory?"

"Giséle is the prostitute that supposedly broke Elias' heart."

"That's a rough take on your ancestor," said Spidermonkey.

"I'm not saying it's true. People can be pretty harsh. Throughout history women like Josephine Bonaparte, for instance, have been called prostitutes without any proof just because they had power or made someone mad. I'm just saying it's Giséle. She obviously had some kind of relationship with Elias and he wasn't called Elias the Odd for nothing. As Moe recently pointed out, the Bleds are known for suicides. He could've just been clinically depressed and his friends blamed her."

"Naming her as a prostitute is a pretty bad indictment."

"It's a weapon, calling her that. It made her nothing. Hey, you said something about her name. What was that?"

"Donadieu. They often gave orphans that last name."

"How did people feel about orphans?" I asked. "Not great. You had no family. No status."

Spidermonkey began typing. "I'll look into the name in France and see if I can find where she came from."

"Elias was a Bled. An orphan wouldn't have been good enough and who knows what was going on. Grandma said Gladys was smart, a nurse, and started a business. She had a temper. Maybe she caused trouble for Elias' friends, cutting off his generous ways."

"She had skills," said Spidermonkey thoughtfully.

"And initiative," I said. "I don't see the prostitute thing."

"You never know. A female orphan didn't have a lot of choices back then."

"She did have money to buy a second-class ticket on a steamer. That wasn't cheap," I said.

"What do you think happened?" Spidermonkey asked.

"I think Elias killed himself for whatever reason and Giséle found herself pregnant, so she went to St. Louis for help," I said.

"But they didn't help her," he said softly.

"The prostitute that caused Elias' suicide turns up pregnant at the family doorstep? No way. Elias' mother was Brina Bled. She was a force to be reckoned with. She'd never have believed that baby was Elias'. Giséle's lucky she didn't have her shot."

"That's a good point."

"What is?"

"I'll look for an arrest record for Giséle," he said. "But I'm not convinced that Thomas Watts would do everything you say he did. He was a cop. He had a standing in the community. If there was a hint of scandal, it would've ruined his career."

"All the more reason to turn Giséle into Gladys," I said.

"And raise another man's son?"

"They never had any other kids. Maybe he was infertile."

"Would he know that?" Spidermonkey asked.

"He was no spring chicken at the time he married Gladys, was he?"

Spidermonkey typed and then said, "He was forty-five."

"It's not like there were condoms and birth control pills at the time. Maybe he noticed he never got anyone pregnant and figured it out."

"Funny he never married before Gladys."

"Are we sure he didn't?" I asked.

"Nothing popped up, but I'll take a look," he said and hung up.

Hours later, he didn't have anything new and now that I was awake, my mind was buzzing. We were so close. I texted Spidermonkey asking if he had anything on an arrest for Giséle or an earlier marriage for Thomas as Grandma walked out of the bathroom and put her hands on her hips.

"What did I say?"

"Go to sleep Mercy. You're exhausted," I said with a grin.

"Hilarious."

"I thought so."

"Get up." She checked her watch. "Moe will be here any minute."

"He can take you," I said. "I'm fine here."

She shook her head. "We can't leave you unguarded."

"I'm not going anywhere."

"Oh, really. I know you lie about things like that," said my grandmother, doing a masterful impression of Aunt Miriam's stink eye.

I crossed my heart. "I swear, I won't go anywhere. I probably won't get out of bed."

"I can't do it. I promised your mother I'd watch you," she said.

"Look, I've got things to do and I can do them right here," I said.

"Like what?"

I reminded her about the SCP research that Novak had sent me.

That alone would take me hours. He'd sent me a ton of links and times, not to mention the kid's own writings.

"And what will all that stuff tell you?" Grandma asked.

"I won't know until I look," I said.

Grandma paced around the room, wringing her hands, torn over the decision. "Why are you so difficult? You are just like your—"

Oh, it's coming back to you now.

"What?" I asked innocently.

"I had a dream that I was talking about...did we talk about your father last night?" A pink tinge came up under Grandma's makeup and that was quite a feat. She was not light-handed with the foundation.

"I forget."

The pink got darker. "What did I say?"

"Don't worry about it," I said.

"Did I happen to mention the name..."

"Kevin," I offered.

Grandma dropped into a chair and put her head in her hands. "I can't believe I told you that."

I picked up the room service menu and said, "It's not a huge surprise considering."

She looked up. "Considering what?"

"That as a third-grader, my dad had you on drugs."

"Oh, my God."

"It's fine. I should've known he was a total pain from day one. Grandad told me about his freak out over the SATs," I said.

"That was a nightmare. I thought we might have to commit him. He was that crazy over his score and it was a great score." She buried her head again. "I do love them, all of them."

"I know."

"I couldn't understand it. I was normal. My whole family was normal and I got three weirdos. Three. What are the odds?"

"Pretty good apparently," I said, thinking of the Bleds.

"Between the shoplifting and the fires and the crying teachers, it's a wonder I wasn't committed," said Grandma.

So this is getting worse.

"My dad stole stuff? My dad. Mr. Law and Order."

"Goodness no. That was George. He went through a shoplifting phase and Rupert burned down the garage."

That's where I get it.

"They're all right now," I said.

"I guess."

"What do you mean, you guess? They're law-abiding citizens with jobs and stuff," I said.

Grandma jolted to her feet. "You can't tell anyone about Kevin."

She sounded like she was having an affair or something.

"Believe me, I won't."

"I love all my boys." She came and sat down next to me. "I really really do."

"I believe you," I said.

"Why? I told you that Kevin was my favorite and he's not even mine."

"Because they had a happy childhood. You might've been miserable, but they had a great time."

She wiped her eyes. "They always knew how to have fun, but I'm a bad mother."

"Look, Grandma, you didn't kill them or beat them, did you?"

"I thought about smacking your father with a wooden spoon," she confessed.

"But you didn't. I call that love. So you like Kevin best. I like him best, too. Everybody does. Kevin is awesome."

She threw her arms around me and hugged me tight. "If you promise not to tell anyone, I will leave you here."

"I'm not blackmailing you, Grandma," I said.

"Is it a deal?"

"Sure. I'll stay in bed and you go flipping hiking at the crack of dawn. Sold."

There was a knock on the door and she wiped her cheeks before getting it. Aaron trotted in with a mug and a teapot. Moe was right behind him, looking like I felt.

"I'm ready," he said in a hoarse whisper.

"Mercy's staying here," said Grandma.

"How'd she manage that?"

She slapped his arm. "Oh, you. Let's go. It's going to be beautiful."

Grandma grabbed her coat and dashed out.

"Seriously," said Moe. "How'd you do it? I hate hiking. It's for hippies and nature nuts."

I shrugged. "I'm the granddaughter."

"Life isn't fair."

"Granted."

Moe bowed his head and walked out to unwillingly hike and Aaron poured me a thick hot chocolate.

"You always know," I said, taking a sip. "Wow. Love the orange blossom essence."

"You noticed," he said.

"You've improved my palate immensely," I said. "Is Novak up yet?"

"He was."

"Was?"

Aaron topped off my mug and said, "We just finished."

"You were playing Warhammer all night?" I asked.

"Yeah. You hungry?" He was looking in the direction of the room service menu.

"No. I order you to go to bed," I said.

"You're hungry."

"Not anymore. I've got hot chocolate. You go to bed."

The little weirdo didn't leave and he didn't try to feed me. Something was up.

"If you're not going to bed," I said. "What are you doing?"

"Planning a menu."

"For what?"

"The culinary class at the high school. I'm going to teach tomorrow."

I sat up. "That is so cool."

Aaron went up on his tiptoes. "Want to come?"

"Do I have to cook?"

"You can eat."

I grinned at him. "I'll be there."

Aaron turned around and trotted out.

Enough about that, I guess.

I sank back into bed and picked up my laptop. It was true. I did have work to do. Novak had sent a ton of SCP material. Everything from the last two months, which was wise. I needed to get a view of the boy before Anton's troubles began, but it was so much material. Hours and hours of videos and I didn't even know how much original work he'd done. It was a crap ton though.

I took a sip of heavenly hot chocolate and got started. No time like the present.

Two hours later, I had a headache and a pretty good idea of who I was dealing with. Neither was a good thing. The boy, whoever he was, was in big trouble. I'm no expert in child psych, but I was pretty damn worried about him.

Before the blackmailing began, the boy's interest in the SCPs was fairly normal. He was into it but not overboard. First, he watched mainly Safe and Euclid videos and wrote on those storylines, too. During the blackmailing, his interest gradually left the Safe zone altogether. He moved into only Keter and then to the more bloody and frightening stuff. I seriously wished I hadn't read some of those stories. Stephen King had nothing on those guys for horror.

I tracked the boy's mood as he spiraled down into darkness, never coming back into the Safe or Euclid zones by the time of my kidnapping. After Anton's death, he started looking at some SCPs regularly that he'd only touched on before.

One called "What comes after" depressed the hell out of me. The boy read it multiple times a week. I don't know how he could stand it. The afterlife was the worst thing that could possibly happen to you. Total nightmare.

Another one wasn't as scary, but what the boy did with it worried me. The story was about a musical score that compelled the people that saw it to finish the piece. They would go insane and finish with their own blood and eventually commit suicide. The boy started writing new stories about how the SCP escaped. In one, a high school student who saw it was slowly killing himself by draining all his blood.

Another had a family working on the piece together and dying one by one.

In the last two weeks, the boy looked at nothing that wasn't incredibly bloody or about dying a hideous death. All the light SCPs were totally gone. He didn't look at any thread where the object was contained, except for the musical score one, and he changed that to fit his dark mood.

I tried calling Novak, but he wasn't answering. I had to do something. But what? I didn't have a name and the picture wasn't great.

Hobbes.

"I hope you're not in church," I said as I dialed the counselor.

He was not in church because he wasn't awake or thrilled with me.

"I'm so sorry. I just had to call."

"Did you? Really." He was slurring and sounding a whole lot like Grandma.

"Are you drunk?" I asked.

"I might be if I was awake, but I'm not," said Hobbes. "Call me later. I'll be awake later."

"I think you have a suicidal student."

"Son of a bitch. I'm awake."

I explained the situation and the counselor calmed down.

"You don't know it's one of our kids," he said.

"He's an American, about seventeen," I said. "It's a safe bet."

"There is an international school in Degerloch."

"Does it matter if he's yours or not?"

Hobbes cleared his throat and said, "No, a kid in trouble is a kid in trouble, but I don't know what I can do about it. You don't have a name."

"I'll send you the picture. You might recognize him," I said.

"Where did you get this picture?"

"Let's leave that alone, shall we?"

"Jesus, you are trouble," said Hobbes. "Go ahead and send it."

I sent the picture and a few minutes later, Hobbes called me back. "Sorry. That picture's so grainy. It could be one of a dozen kids I know and I only have a segment of the population last names L through P. I sent it to Meredith. She's got F through K, but it's still a no."

"Would you tell me if you did recognize him?" I asked.

He paused and thought it over. "I would, but I wouldn't tell you who he was."

I named the boys on the list I'd made from Anton's AP papers. "Could it be one of them? Are any of those boys writers?"

"Not that I know of," he said.

"Can you ask around? See if anyone recognizes him?"

"I still can't tell you anything."

"You know what? I don't care. I just want you to find him," I said.

"It's that bad?" Hobbes asked and I could tell the fog of drink was lifting.

"Yes, it is. I have an instinct about things and I'm usually right."

"The famous Watts intuition?"

"That's it," I said. "Something isn't right with this kid. He needs help and quick."

"Beyond the mental stuff...do you think he played a part in your kidnapping? We don't have a troubled youth population, not like big cities. Crime with our kids is practically nonexistent."

"He knows something, Hobbes," I said. "And it's tearing him up."

He sighed and said, "I'm up. I'll gather the troops and see if we can come up with something."

"Thanks."

"Thank you."

I hung up and ordered breakfast. Hopefully, Aaron wouldn't be too peeved since I was going to his class. While I waited, I took a shower, doing all the little beauty things Grandma taught me. She had a lot of potions and stuff, so it took a while, and when I got out my breakfast was at the door with a very tired Novak clutching a huge mug of coffee.

I took my tray and Novak slipped in to collapse on the bed.

"What are you doing up?" I asked.

"You called."

"I left a message."

"What did you want?" He spoke into the pillow and I could barely make it out.

"Well, a conscious hacker might be nice," I said.

"I'm up."

"Could've fooled me."

Novak flipped over and I asked, "What is going on? You wouldn't get up for me."

"My mother."

"What about her?" I asked. "Oh. Is she still coming for Christmas?"

"She's there."

"Where?"

"In Paris." He ran his hands through his half-cornrowed hair that looked...not great.

I put my tray on the bed and took off the cloche to smell the heavenly scent of more eggs benedict. "Well, if you've got to go home, I get it. I never expected you to come here in the first place."

"She's cleaning," said Novak. "She called five times this morning and she's cleaning my apartment."

I'd seen Novak's apartment and she didn't have much to do. He was a neat freak.

"I'm surprised you let her in," I said.

"I didn't. She sandbagged one of my associates and he let her in."

"Mom's impressive."

He bared his teeth. "Yes."

"So what if she cleans? You like clean."

"The entry area. She's cleaning my cover."

"Oh," I said. "Well, that's fantastic. I think I saw hepatitis on the floor."

"It's not fantastic. Do you know how long it took me to get it to the perfect amount of crack house until no one wanted to come in?"

"I do not and I think you're crazy," I said. "Hey. How about we get to work on my case? I've got a swell lead."

"Will it get you to the kid and your blonde perp within a short amount of time so that this flipping interlude will be over?" Novak asked.

"Yes!"

"Not interested."

"What in the hell? I'm paying you."

Novak flipped back half a head of hair. "Not enough." He looked a little sleazy and sweaty and I got worried. Usually, I could spot a man with a jonesing for me a mile away, but this came out of nowhere. He was recommended. Spidermonkey wouldn't let him within a mile of me if he was a problem. I stepped away from the bed.

"I think you should go now," I said, picking up my panic button.

Novak's eyes went back and forth between my eyes and the button a couple of times and then he burst out laughing. "Don't flatter yourself."

"It's not a compliment to me that you look creepy," I said.

"I look exhausted." Once he got himself under control, he went into the bathroom, Noxzema'd his face, and offered me a deal. A pretty good deal as it turned out.

"You want me to lie to your mother and say we're a couple?" I asked. "And she'll leave you alone for another year if I do?"

"I'll do all your snooping for free," he said.

"She'll figure it out. I'm the sort of person that people know."

"My mother is not an internet person. She doesn't know you."

"I don't like to lie," I said.

He laughed again. "Since when? It's practically your hobby."

"It is not." I forked my poached eggs and glared at him.

Novak calmed down and got serious. "This is a lot of money and you're splitting some of the cost with the client right?"

"I am."

"Think of the savings. You'll make a nice profit on this one."

"It's mean, making her think she's got a hope of grandchildren at Christmas," I said.

He drew back. "She has more than a hope of grandchildren. She's got sixteen already. My brothers are all married."

"Oh, well making her think you have a woman."

"I have women."

My doubts must've shown on my face because he said, "You don't believe me."

"I do not," I said.

Novak went on to show me several very attractive women in various locations around Paris. He was in the photos and they did appear to be genuine.

"So just show her those and she'll go home," I said.

"I don't want her to see my real women."

I threw up my hands. "Fine. But I'm not talking to her. Just pictures."

"Now?"

We took a bunch of pictures in bed, cuddled up because it was more convincing and then he had a long conversation with his mother while I was supposedly in the shower. She was happy. He was happy. I felt dirty but profitable.

Novak flopped back on the bed and said, "Not bad for a morning's work. She's going to see my brother in Madrid. He's not raising his daughters right."

"Poor guy," I said. "What about you? She hasn't seen you."

"She really just wanted to force a call and do some shopping."

"Whatever. Ready for what I've got?"

I showed Novak all my research and he was mildly impressed, which was pretty good for me. He went and got three laptops and set up on the desk again while I ate.

"What's the priority?" he asked. "Sindelfingen?"

"Weil der Stadt," I said. "I think it started there."

"Good. Less Americans live there."

He got to work and I got into my mom's Ancestry account. She uses the same password for everything so it wasn't exactly a challenge. From Mom's account, I was able to see Grandma's. She'd done a lot of work on the family tree. Most of her research was to do with her own line, but she had the Watts stuff in there, too. Grandma was quite thorough in the tree making. She'd loaded pictures and there were tons of branches and these little leaf hint things connecting our family to other families. I looked at the pictures going back slowly. I wanted to see each face and compare. First, my dad and then Grandad and then there he was, Elijah Watts. Of course, I'd seen that very picture proudly displayed on the mantle at my grandparents' house, but I never paid it much mind. It was just one face in a sea of faces. But this was a face that ought to have stuck out. It was not a Watts' face.

The photo was from WWII. Great-Grandpa sat in a foxhole cooking something in an ammo box. Every time I'd looked at that photo before it was the chunky concoction in the non-too-clean container that I focused on, not the heart-shaped face of a slender man with pale eyes. Elijah was smiling, despite the fact that he was filthy with matted hair and what could've been blood on one of his hands. It was a great face. The face of a man you'd like to know.

Novak came over and stole some of my coffee. "Who's that?"

"My great-grandfather Elijah," I said.

"Kind of old for war, isn't he?"

"He was thirty-three in 1944."

"That is old," he said. "Did he get drafted?"

I clicked on some connected documents and found Elijah's enlistment papers. "He volunteered," I said.

"That's unusual. The older men usually had families and didn't go."

"He wasn't married yet. Grandad was born after the war."

"That explains it." Novak went back to his search and I returned to Elijah's picture. There was a weapon lying on a small backpack. The Mauser. My heart went out to my ancestor in a way it never had before. It was his weapon. I knew that, of course. But now it was our weapon.

I clicked the link for Elijah's parents and another picture came up, also familiar. It was Dad's namesake, Thomas, in his uniform and he was, also, not a Watts as I knew them. He wasn't thin, far from, with big meaty hands and powerful shoulders. Thomas did have a certain twinkle in his eye, like he knew a joke that he was itching to tell. That could be my dad, but nothing else of Thomas was in any of my uncles or cousins or Grandad, for that matter. You'd think the big nose and lantern jaw would've shown up somewhere, but it hadn't.

Next, I hovered my cursor over Gladys' name and held my breath. I'd seen her face. Of course, I had. But now I was really going to see it. I clicked and she appeared. My family appeared. The Watts I knew. Gladys or Giséle was thin, tall, and pretty. She was holding a fat baby as though he might break apart in her grasp. The photo was black and white, so I had to take Grandma's word for it that she was the origin of the Watts red hair. I clicked through a couple of photos and found the wedding picture. She didn't appear pregnant, but the Edwardian dress and bouquet would've hidden that easily. It was a great photo and her face, something about her face...Gladys was smiling, but her eyes weren't. Her jaw was clenched and I bet she had a death grip on those flowers, but was that fair? Old wedding photos from other eras were rarely the huge smiley things of today. Thomas didn't look anything but stalwart and dignified.

I went back to the photo with my great-great-grandmother holding Elijah and that was Gladys. She might be a nervous mother but there was none of that tightness. Her smile was genuine and sweet.

"I know you," I said.

"What was that?" Novak asked.

"I've seen her before."

"Who?"

"My great-great-grandmother Gladys," I said.

He didn't stop typing and was doing it at a speed that boggled the mind. "Your family has photos, don't they?"

"Yes, but I don't know. I've seen her somewhere else."

"Where?"

"No clue. She's just so familiar. That smile."

"You're just remembering other photos," he said. "Don't get worked up over it. Look at something else and then it will come to you."

"Is that what you do?" I asked.

Novak turned around and said, "I do. Sometimes my algorithm isn't working or a firewall will not fall and I just have to turn to something else. Then it works. My brain needs a break."

"My brain is busy. It doesn't like breaks."

"Then it needs them all the more." Novak turned back and typed even faster than before. None of my hackers from Uncle Morty to Spidermonkey ever worked in front of me before. They were very secretive about their methods and even their identity. Novak wasn't Novak. I knew that much. Whether that whole mother thing was real was up for debate. Him hiding his home and office inside a crack house told me he'd do the oddest things to hide who he was, but right then I had a full view of his screens. Nothing was hidden. I'd like to say I could make heads or tails of it, but massive amounts of data was crossing his screens. I caught little things like internet providers, but the rest was a mystery my brain could never solve. He probably knew that and figured I was safe. Kinda insulting but accurate.

I turned back to my computer and something I could understand. Grandma had conveniently attached Elijah's birth certificate. Even though the certificate was pretty faded and the handwriting wasn't the greatest, but I could make out the attending physician Dr. Walter Ames.

Finding the doctor's information was shockingly easy because he died seven months later of dementia at the age of seventy-seven.

"Thomas, you wily bastard," I said.

"Did you get what you need?" Novak asked.

"Some of it."

"Fun isn't it?"

"It actually is," I said, and I clicked back to Thomas' records. He knew that doctor well enough to get him to fill out a fake birth certificate and it was fake. No way a seventy-seven-year-old guy with dementia was attending births. Dr. Ames wasn't a relative, so there was one other way he'd know him. "No, it can't be that easy."

Novak chuckled and I stared at my screen. Dr. Walter Ames was the doctor on Thomas' birth certificate. It was that easy. He went to who he knew. The marriage record was standard and nothing looked off about it. I had no reason to think it didn't happen when it supposedly did. Since the whole snooping around thing was fun, I looked for an arrest record for Giséle Donadieu, but she didn't exist, so I joined Mom to the international version of Ancestry and rooted around there. That was much more difficult. Gladys' age on the marriage certificate said twenty-two and I assumed that to be in the neighborhood of the truth, but I couldn't find any Giséle's that fit the bill with Donadieu as a last name. The ones that were the right age didn't appear to have left France.

"Are you ready?" Novak asked.

"Depends," I said.

"I've got five families in Weil der Stadt with boys between the ages of fourteen and twenty."

"That kid was not fourteen."

"For the sake of being thorough, I included him. Kids can fool you."

"Alright," I said. "But he's not."

Novak waved me over and I pulled up a chair. "Of the five families, two have kids checking out SCPs regularly and one is active on the wiki."

"Can I see them?" I asked.

He pulled up two photos from Facebook. They were white kids, average height, and fairly thin, but I shook my head. "I don't think so."

"Look again." He blew up the photos.

The boys fit the bill, but I wasn't feeling it. No spark of recognition. "It's not either of them."

"That was my instinct, too, but you know how eyewitnesses get it wrong."

I leaned back and crossed my arms. "You're right. It happens all the time. Can you check and see if any of the candidates read SCP-012?"

"Good idea." He began typing again and then said, "Or perhaps not. They all looked at it and viewed the various videos. It's a pretty basic one."

"Alright. Who had Anton in school?" I asked.

Novak chuckled. "All but one, the fourteen-year-old."

"Dammit."

"I know, but keep thinking."

"AP Gov?"

"Three out of the four," he said.

"Any emails to Anton?"

"A few about grades and test dates," said Novak. "Nothing personal."

"Do you have any good news?"

He shrugged and cracked his knuckles. "We're narrowing things down."

"So no," I said. "Can you show me all the faces?"

"Sure, but you won't like it."

I didn't like it. I didn't like it a lot. All five of those guys were practically the same guy. Sure the twenty-year-old was more mature than the fourteen-year-old, but the faces, I couldn't pick one out. I'd looked at so many photos in the yearbook and in Anton's photos, they were all blending. Was I looking for the face in the window or for one that was familiar from one of the photos?

"Anybody jumping out?" Novak asked.

I pointed at the twenty-year-old, but I didn't know why. I didn't think it was him.

"I figured."

"Why?"

"Check the expression. He's unhappy. This was taken on vacation in Madrid. That's a guy who didn't want to pose. I picked it because it was the only photo that was dead on and close. Check this one."

Novak brought up another photo and I instantly said, "It's not him."

He laughed. "Because he's smiling, right?"

I groaned and put my head in my head. "We need something else."

"I can move on to Sindelfingen and check those families."

"Hold on." I went back to my computer and clicked through one of the stories our kid had written. Then I checked another one. "Is there anyone who didn't look at SCPs at all? I mean never."

"Ah, yes." He typed for a minute. "I've got two."

"Great. Are you in their computers?"

"I can be," he said. "What am I looking for?"

"Google searches for Gurkh Kukri," I said.

Novak looked back at me. "I checked for visits to suicide sites and there was no activity."

"Not for that. Our SCP guy used that knife in his stories about the musical score and in another story, too. He was very detailed about it, talking about the carved handle and etched blade. Either he had one or—"

"He googled it." He typed for a few minutes and then smiled back at me. "Got him."

CHAPTER EIGHTEEN

While Novak searched through the life and times of Jake Purcell, a very depressed seventeen-year-old junior at the high school, I got dressed and slapped on some of Grandma's makeup in a vain attempt to hide the ginormous bags under my eyes. I don't think they'd ever been that big before. They were practically luggage.

I yawned my way back to the bed and my phone buzzed. Grandma sent me a slew of hiking photos and then some of the lovely and leisurely breakfast she was having. I didn't want to think it was romantic, but it kinda was. Two old folks hanging out in a café off the Marienplatz and looking at Christmas decorations. I couldn't remember the last time Grandad did something like that with her. Heck, he didn't do things like that period. A two-hour breakfast with a man that didn't eat? Not going to happen. Moe might be super-weird looking, but he was a lot more fun. I considered warning Grandad, but I doubted he would've been bothered. To say he trusted my grandmother was the understatement of the year. She did love him and he had the Watts charm in spades, but I was starting to wonder if that was enough.

I asked her when they were coming back and she said that they were heading back in a few minutes. She needed a nap. I said that we had a good lead and she only responded with, "Nap."

"Turns out it's nap time," I said to the back of Novak's head.

"Yes, it is." Novak yawned. "I'm finished."

"What do we have?" I asked.

"Everything but the finances. That's Spidermonkey's department."

He opened up a window and showed me Jake Purcell's life, at least the online portion. It was a family of three. Mother, sister, and Jake. Dad was killed in Afghanistan in 2010 and Mom was active duty Army. They'd been stationed in Stuttgart for three years. Jake wasn't a social media guy. He had Instagram but didn't post. Mostly, he used it to communicate with other gamers. He was big into world-building games, not first-person shooters, I'm happy to say. Grades were good. No sports or clubs. No discipline issues at school. He saw a therapist for depression and anxiety and was medicated. Novak could get those records, but he hadn't yet.

I got a funny feeling as Novak talked. The Purcells sounded pretty average, but Jake was involved in Anton's situation. I was sure of that and he hadn't gone to the MPs or the school counselors about it. There had to be a reason for that.

"Show me the sister," I said.

"I was wondering when you'd get to that." He pushed a button and a family picture came up. The three Purcells together next to a canal in Amsterdam. "Before you ask, she's twenty."

"And blonde," I said.

"Very."

"College age. Is she here?"

He smiled. "She is. Working at Pizza Hut on post and going to college online."

"I never considered that the blonde might be his sister," I said quietly.

"Why would you? That German said they were never together."

"Could be a coincidence."

"Could be, but I doubt it," he said. "I'll tell you this. She's not a hacker. Minimal interest in computers. She didn't put the 4chan stuff on Anton's laptop. And there's zero communication with him."

"Was she in his class?"

"She was AP Gov. She got a four."

I went back to Anton's AP books and looked at Madison Purcell's smiling face in the photo from two years ago. Would that girl blackmail her teacher? Why? And more importantly how would she ever have known about Kimberly and the adoption thing?

"What is Madison into?" I asked.

"Typical girl stuff. Clothes. Makeup. Kittens. Clubbing."

"Kittens?"

"She likes cats. She follows Fat Cats of Instagram, for instance."

I flopped back on the bed. "This is ridiculous."

"If you want my opinion," said Novak. "It's her."

"We're saying a twenty-year-old pizza maker who loves kittens and makeup set up a blackmailing scheme, got Anton Thooft to kidnap me, and hired a private jet to bring me to Germany?"

"That is what we're saying." He stood up and stretched. "Spidermonkey might find a financial motive."

"Like what? She gambled away her eight bucks an hour and thought 'hey kidnapping, that's the ticket.'"

Novak chuckled and started packing up his stuff. "I don't do motives. If you want me to find something, I find it."

"What about that jet?" I asked. "How in the world did she swing that?"

"Nobody booked it and Spidermonkey said nobody paid for it."

"But it still came to Missouri to get me?"

"It did," he said. "My money is on a favor."

I sat up. "A favor to that girl? She wears H&M clothes and way too much highlighter."

We looked back at the remaining open screen where Madison smiled with her brother and mother. An innocent, happy face. I couldn't square it with what happened to me.

"When was that taken?" I asked.

"August. Right before school started."

"Jake looks good. Not so thin."

"I noticed that. He's lost weight," said Novak as he closed the screen. "I sent you the photos taken over the last few months, but there weren't many."

My phone dinged and Grandma said they were pulling into the parking lot.

"Don't park," I texted and grabbed my hat and coat. "We're leaving."

"Do not leave that room," texted Grandma with an angry emoji.

"Novak will walk me out."

She gave me a thumbs-up and Novak agreed to be my watchdog in exchange for being allowed to sleep for a very long time as if I could stop him.

We walked out of the hotel and the Mercedes was parking. Moe and Grandma were getting out and I waved and said, "Oh no, you don't. We're going to Sindelfingen."

"I'm not," said Grandma. "I'm sleeping. That hill was bigger than advertised."

Moe followed her and I cut him off. "Where are you going?"

"Also to sleep. I hiked for the first time since the Army and I did not miss it."

"Hand over the keys then," I said. "We've got a lead."

"Don't you dare, Moe," said Grandma.

"Why are we going to Sindelfingen?" Moe asked.

"I've got a photo that I want Marta to see," I said.

"Flipping text it. I'm exhausted."

"So am I and I would, but she's not answering."

"She's asleep like any normal person would be after a night of partying," said Moe.

I turned him around and pushed him toward the car. "She's working. She said so last night."

"Oh, goddamn."

"I know, I know, but this is how we roll." I turned around to say goodbye to Novak and Grandma, but they were already through the door. It didn't hit them. "It's just you and me, Moe. I think Aaron's sleeping."

"Lucky him." Moe got in and I followed.

He pulled out of the parking lot and I said, "We've identified the kid."

"That's not as exciting as you think." He gave out a jaw-cracking yawn and I mean that. I heard his jaw crack.

"We're close," I said.

"Not to a nap."

"I noticed you had plenty of energy to have a long breakfast with my grandmother."

"That's different. Janine and I have fun."

"Don't get used to it," I said.

He only smiled in return and my worry got a tad bit worse.

It was sunny and quiet in Sindelfingen. The remnants of Saturday's market were completely gone and all the shops were closed. We scored street parking and found the café to be once again packed. The line was out the door and people were even sitting at the outdoor tables with blankets, smiling over cups of coffee and plates of rolled cakes. I wanted coffee and cake but sitting outside was a no-go.

We waited in line for ten minutes, during which Moe started talking about the various pillows of his life. His favorite feather pillow. A weird one made of hard foam. His helmet pillow in Vietnam. He slept pretty well on that helmet, but I think that was pure exhaustion from trying to not get killed while killing other people.

"We're in," he said as we stepped over the threshold. "I was right on the edge."

"Of what?"

"Leaving."

I snorted and he grumbled.

Marta spotted us and waved with a tired but absolutely joyful smile.

"What would you like, Mercy? Moe?" she asked.

"Double espresso with an Americano chaser," said Moe.

"Latte and some of that raspberry kuchen," I said as I got out my phone.

"It's got alcohol in it," said Marta.

"So much the better." I smiled and we shuffled down to the cash register.

Marta leaned over the counter. "A table is opening at the back."

Moe didn't wait. He was off like a shot, leaving me to pay. It was only fair. The whole trip was my idea.

Marta rang me up and the other woman behind the counter got the coffee. "So..." I asked. "How was the setup? Did they figure it out?"

"Not at all. They think they are working on the case." Marta handed me my change.

"Oh, no. Not a love connection?"

She smiled. "I went home and Claudia came in at three in the morning."

"I call that a success."

Marta crossed her fingers. "Can I get you anything else?"

The people behind me were restless, so I said, "Can you come to the table for a second? We've got a lead."

She nodded and turned to the next in line. Moe looked comatose when I got to the table and was listing to the side so much that several of the other patrons were looking pretty worried. I'm not sure how he stayed upright at that angle, but his eyes were open if a bit glazed.

I poked him and said, "You're freaking people out."

"I do that."

"Try not to look like you're having a stroke," I said.

"Like you'd know," Moe said.

"I would, in fact, up close and personal."

Moe's eyes flew open wide and he straightened up. "I'm sorry. I forgot about your mother."

"It's not only her. I'm a nurse."

"Now you're a detective," he said, taking his coffee.

"It's not permanent."

Suddenly, he threw up his hands and said, "Nothing's permanent!"

I pushed down his hands. "Are *you* having a stroke? Be quiet."

"It's *Moonstruck*. Haven't you seen *Moonstruck*?"

"I've been busy." I drank my latte and forked my super tender cake.

"It's Janine's favorite," he said. "We're going to watch it together tonight after dinner with Isolda."

"Tell me it's not a romantic comedy."

"It's a great romantic comedy about Italians, and there's no criminal elements before you ask."

"I wasn't going to ask, but you know I'm now watching that movie with you two," I said.

Moe threw back his first espresso and laughed. "I figured."

"I'm going to call Fats about this."

"And say what? Her odd uncle found a friend? She's going to do something? I don't think so."

You know you're odd?

"She'll tell you to back off," I said, although I wasn't sure. Fats Licata was full of surprises, not all of them good.

"You hold onto that hope. Janine and I are friends. Deal with it."

I was about to retort when Marta came up and sat at our third chair. "You have found the boy?"

"We have." I showed her Jake's picture and she clasped her hands together.

"You did it. I do not know how, but it is impressive."

"Thanks. I've got another photo for you." I switched Jake's photo to one of his sister Madison. "Do you recognize this person?"

Her eyes went wide and she pulled back. "That's her. That's the woman who met the teacher. How did you find her?"

"She's the boy's sister," I said.

"You don't say," said Moe. "A little family conspiracy."

"I get the feeling the boy wasn't all in. The problem is that we don't have a motive and really anything other than it was them."

"You will tell Viktor?" Marta asked.

I steepled my fingers over my coffee. "I figured Claudia could do that."

She smiled. "I've always liked Americans. I have to go. We are very busy."

Moe took my phone and looked at the picture of Madison Purcell and said, "I don't think so."

"You heard Marta," I said. "She was meeting Anton on the right dates. Her brother was here, too. It's them."

He put down my phone and tapped the photo. "She didn't put this thing together."

"Because she's a girl and young and pretty?"

Moe threw back his espresso and raised a wiry brow over a very moist, bulging eye. "Trust me. I know a thing or two about putting together operations."

"Oh, I bet you do," I said.

"From my time in the Army."

"Naturally."

"That girl may have done it. She may have wanted it to happen, but she didn't put it together," he said.

The more I thought about it, the more I agreed. For one thing, she wasn't a computer person. Neither was her brother. "Give me one good reason," I said just for the sake of argument.

"She's pretty and young and a girl."

"I will smack you."

Moe threw back his head and laughed. The whole café jumped with the burst of noise and then settled back down to look at the two uncouth Americans with distaste.

"You should see your face." Moe wiped his eyes with a napkin. "Oh, that was rich."

"I can't tell if you believe it or not," I said.

He shook his head and leaned over to another table that was listening intently while pretending not to. "She thinks I don't think women are capable of high crimes and misdemeanors. My boss is a woman and she directed me to work for this curvy little cupcake."

"Don't call me a cupcake," I said, thinking about the Mauser in my purse.

Moe ignored me. "My niece is the biggest badass you ever saw in your life. She could snap you in half and use you to pick her teeth and she would if it were required. Do I think a pretty young woman could pull off a complicated crime? Yes, I do. I don't think *that* young woman could."

"Why not?" asked a man who was dressed in a three-piece suit with alligator shoes on a Sunday morning because we were in Germany.

"Because she works at Pizza Hut."

"Oh, yes," he said. "A girl that works at Pizza Hut could not do the crime you are alluding to. I've been to a Pizza Hut in California. Criminals might work there, but they aren't good ones."

"I tend to agree," I said.

The elegant man and his equally elegant friend got up to take their cups to the front. She leaned over to me and said, "I love your look. Are you that detective?"

"I am," I said.

"Autograph?"

I gave her an autograph and the whole café was looking again.

"Let's get out of here," I said, standing up myself.

"But my Americano," Moe protested.

"Throw it back old man. The cupcake is on the move."

He laughed, joined by a couple of tables, and we were out of there.

"I thought I couldn't call you a cupcake," Moe said.

"You can't. I can," I said.

"Women are confusing."

"Like men aren't."

"Where to?" Moe asked as he tied a scarf around his neck.

"Weil der Stadt. Let's go check out our not-so-mastermind."

He rubbed his hands together and got a twinkle in his eye. "Roger that."

It didn't take us long to get to the little town of Weil der Stadt and was it pretty. Nestled in a valley with an intact city wall and a plethora of half-timbered houses, it was just the sort of town Grandma wanted to see and I felt a little guilty for seeing it without her.

"Well, every town's nicer than the last," said Moe. "Did you see that tower? I half expected someone to shoot arrows at us."

I looked up from texting Spidermonkey, who wasn't up yet. "It feels homey to me," I said. "My parents' house is a Tudor."

"But not German like this."

"No, not like this. Nothing's like this."

As if to make the point, a few fat flakes started coming down. After we drove around the town and then down a cobble-stoned lane past houses decorated with lights and evergreen boughs over the doors, there was a light covering of snow because it wasn't charming enough.

Moe oohed and aahed over the Christmas pyramids in the windows and these beautiful arched candle holders carved out of wood depicting Christmas scenes. I didn't have one and I needed it. Everyone needed a Schwibbogen. That's what they're called. I'm not kidding.

"I think we should park here," he said, finding a spot.

"You just want to walk in the snow," I said.

"It's an experience. When you get to my age, you want as many as you can get."

"Let's do it."

We got out and walked through the streets to find the main square with a huge Christmas tree and a statue of a pretty chill guy with a super pointy beard and a globe under one arm.

"That's Johannes Kepler," said Moe.

"Wow," I said.

"Don't be obnoxious. He was a mathematician and astronomer. Look there's a museum."

Regretting this big time.

"Oh, it's closed," said Moe. "We'll have to come back."

That'll happen.

"We're on a case," I said.

"We have time," he said.

"Let's find the Purcell house." I steered him away from the statue and museum to wander down the hilly cobbled streets and finding a charming new sight around every bend. In one little square, we discovered a fountain filled with black metal sculptures celebrating *Fasching*, the celebration before Lent. Moe couldn't get enough of the witches and trolls and took at least a hundred pictures. I'd been to a couple of *Fasching* parades in Stuttgart and they were an experience with wild costumes designed to scare winter away. Young women got chased around by trolls and monsters to be marked up with colorful grease pens, tossed onto the parade floats, and have hay or confetti dumped over their heads. Children were rewarded for their costumes with loads of candy and the bands were fantastic. Think Mardi Gras without the drunks.

After I managed to drag Moe away, we found the Purcell house down a side street and across from a small bakery that happily wasn't packed. We went in and I got Moe another espresso against my better judgment. Then it was just waiting to see if anyone came out. The lights were all on and they'd been home earlier. The street was parked up, but all the streets were. It was impossible to know which cars were theirs. They didn't have a driveway.

"There's an Italian grocery store in this town." Moe looked up from his phone, his eyes gleaming with anticipation.

"Closed."

"It might be open."

"Closed on Sunday. Everything is closed on Sunday."

"I keep forgetting it's Sunday," he said. "I could've used some Italian wine and some prosciutto. Another reason to come back."

I looked at him in consternation.

"What?" he asked.

"You are a different kind of Licata. Fats never stopped for food."

"She didn't get that from me. Her mother is a problem. She was always on Fats about her weight."

"Really? She doesn't have an ounce of fat on her," I said.

"That's why," said Moe. "How long are we going to wait?"

"As long as it takes."

"Who taught you this crap technique?"

"My dad and it's not crap. It's surveillance."

Moe tapped his empty cup on the table. "This espresso was terrible and I need a nap. I say we pound on the door and ask why the hell that girl decided to get you killed."

"That's a hard no," I said. "I want more information before I have a confrontation. When Spidermonkey wakes up, he'll scour their financials."

Moe groaned.

"You can leave me here. There are buses."

"Not a chance in hell. I don't think that girl masterminded that disaster of a kidnapping, but you're a sitting duck over here."

"Hardly. I've got my Mauser."

"In your handbag."

"Where else should I have it?"

He eyed me and said, "Shoulder holster."

"Never. That would put attention where I don't want it."

"There's no avoiding that, cupcake," he said with a grin.

I crossed my arms. "I noticed you didn't like that other guy treating me like a cupcake."

"He treated you like a cupcake," Moe said. "I'm calling you one. It's an affectionate nickname."

"I will get Fats to kill you."

He laughed and looked back at the Purcell house. Then my phone buzzed and it was Novak, who wasn't as good a sleeper as he wanted.

"Did the German confirm?" he asked.

"Yep. It's them."

"The house is quiet?"

"How did you know where we are?" I asked.

"Are you kidding? You've got a tracking device around your neck," said Novak.

"That's not good," I said.

"It's fine. Let me see what's going on in there," he said. "Here we go. Mom is on Pinterest. Madison is writing a paper on self-harm, ironically enough. And the kid is playing a video game."

"Not all that helpful. Has either Jake or Madison looked into me?" I asked. "Do they know I'm here?"

"They both googled you after it happened," he said. "Looks like they were checking on your condition. Then there was some interest in St. Seb and the case there, but nothing since."

"Well, that's good," I said. "Do they follow Aaron on Instagram?"

Novak chuckled. "Not a chance. No food whatsoever." He paused and then said, "This is interesting. We've got another phone."

"Oh, yeah?"

"A burner."

"Sweet," I said. "Whose is it?"

Novak typed for a few minutes and then said, "It hasn't been on the home Wi-Fi in five months.

"That's a long time."

"It was super active for about two weeks and then went dark. I'm tracing the provider now, but it's encrypted."

"Beyond Madison's capabilities?"

"She has no capabilities," he said. "Looks like it's definitely Madison's phone. It was used when Jake was in school and the mom was at work."

"When was it first used?" I asked.

"June sixth. This is going to take a while," said Novak.

"You're in Madison's regular phone, right?"

"Sure. What do you want to know?"

I drummed my fingers on the table and Moe watched me silently. I thought he'd have his two cents like Fats always did, but he wasn't a bulldozer like his niece. "Give me the best friend. Boyfriend. Somebody I can interview."

Novak messed around for a minute or two and came back with, "Bad news is that Madison's high school friends either moved or went to college back in the States."

"But she has a boyfriend," I said.

"She doesn't. She's told several of the friends that, but the contact is sporadic."

"Is there good news?"

"She's friends with people at work. Not close as she was with the high school friends, but they go out and do things occasionally."

"Name?"

"MacKenzie Saperstein at Pizza Hut is the closest. Olivia Jones is in there, but not as much. She works at Burger King."

"Can you send me their addresses and whatnot?" I asked.

"On it."

Moe tapped the table hard. "She's on the move."

"Got to go," I said to Novak and hung up.

Madison got an ice scraper out of the trunk of an old Kia and we stood to leave.

"We'll never catch her," I said.

"Why not?" Moe asked, leading me to the door.

"We have to get to the car."

"It's half a block away."

"Really?" I asked.

"Fats said you had no sense of direction, but I thought she was exaggerating." He opened the door for me and we walked past Madison angrily scraping ice and snow off her windshield.

"That'll take a minute," said Moe. "Ours is clean."

Once we turned the corner, we broke out in a jog and jumped into our car in record time. Moe drove back to the Purcell house slowly like he was afraid of the ice and we got there just as she finished clearing the back window. Moe put on his blinker to park and Madison waved at us before she jumped in to pull out of the only parking spot on the block.

"What's the plan?" I asked. "She's seen us."

Moe snorted. "She hasn't *seen* us. We're just a car wanting a spot. White Mercedes are a dime a dozen around here. I've seen six just while we were walking around."

He waited until Madison turned a corner before he took off after her.

"They weren't the same make," I said.

"You think she knows?"

"I did."

Moe grinned at me, showing off a golden bicuspid on his left side and I had a *Home Alone* flashback. "You aren't normal."

"Thanks," I said.

"I meant it as a compliment."

We caught up with Madison, keeping back a few car lengths with a Smart car between us. We needn't have bothered. She wasn't paying any attention. Her head was bopping around to music I assume, either that or she had a spastic condition and shouldn't have been driving. That head was really moving.

"See," said Moe. "She's clueless."

"It seems that way, but she has a burner phone," I said.

"Who doesn't?"

"Me," I said.

"Yeah, well, everyone else that doesn't have a cadre of hackers on the payroll does."

"I guarantee you that the average twenty-year-old girl doesn't." I told him the burner history and he nodded sagely. "I told you. Someone else is in charge. He gave her a burner and she screwed it up until he caught it."

"What are you talking about?" I asked.

"You don't use the home Wi-Fi for a burner phone," said Moe. "Anyone with access to the router could see that it was on there and get nosy."

"He knew she was doing it somehow and shut it down?"

"I would. Whoever gave it to her was monitoring the data. He's smart enough to do that."

I sat back and watched Madison's head bouncing around. "But not smart enough to make the plants on Anton's laptop convincing."

"They were convincing to the cops. That's what he was going for." Moe grinned at me again. Very Harry Lime. "He didn't bargain on you and the sister questioning it. He's no genius. If he thought about it, he would've worked hard."

"Yeah?"

"He sent somebody to nab Tommy Watts' daughter. It doesn't take a lot of brainpower to know a little surface work isn't going to do it."

"Dad wouldn't let it go or Fats or Leo," I said.

"Or Chuck or your grandad or flipping Calpurnia. This moron came after someone with friends. He's not a thinker."

"That's why I don't think it's The Klinefeld Group. He gives her an encrypted burner, sets this whole thing up with a private plane but uses a teacher to grab me."

"He's all over the place. That's why you'll find him."

I nodded, but I wasn't feeling particularly confident. I didn't say it, but I was feeling more and more like our non-genius had connections of his own. If he was part of The Klinefeld Group, they could easily mask him with a new identity. He could head off to Argentina as other psychos had done before.

"Are we going to Böblingen?" I asked.

"That's my read," said Moe.

"Work?"

"Probably."

"You sound disappointed," I said.

"I was hoping she was going to visit her felonious friend," said Moe.

I laughed. "You're hanging with me now, not the Fibonaccis. It's not going to be that easy."

"I like easy," he said with another grin.

"Get used to disappointment."

Moe left the highway and we followed Madison to the post gate. We didn't even have a car between us anymore, but she never glanced in the rearview once. I was watching.

The gate guard checked Moe's ID and my pass quickly, so we stayed right on Madison's tail, following her to the packed parking lot in front of the PX complex.

"Wow," I said. "Everybody and their mother's brother is here."

"It's Sunday. Where else are you going to go if you need cat litter and a bottle of wine?"

"Good point."

We parked about as far from the doors as possible, but we weren't in a rush. Madison was obviously going to work. Moe and I headed in without our subject in sight. That would've driven Dad insane. He taught me to always have eyes on, but sometimes you can just relax. I'd learned that much on my own.

Moe slapped on his VFW hat. I'm not going to say what he called it because...gross. He couldn't stop grinning about it though.

"I bet you wouldn't say that with my grandmother around," I said.

"That is absolutely right. I'd never say that in front of a lady," said Moe, nodding to some soldiers in uniform who definitely had respect for the hat.

"Hey," I said. "What about me?"

"You're not a lady. You're Mercy."

"I'm insulted."

"So be it. You can't tell me you're the same as Janine or your mother," said Moe as we went into the building.

"What about Fats?" I asked.

"That's more like it."

I can see it, but it still sucks.

"I'm liking you less."

"No, you're not." Moe stopped in front of a vendor with a Goufrais chocolate display.

"Would you like some samples?" the vendor asked.

"I'll take two and give them both to my pretty friend if that's alright with you," said Moe.

"Of course, sir." The vendor held out a tray with little chocolates shaped like tiny bundt cakes and I took two.

"Oh, my God," I said. "Those are amazing."

"I'll take three bags," said Moe.

"All for Grandma?" I asked.

"For you, Fats, and Janine. You and Fats might not be ladies, but chocolate is always appropriate."

I considered saying something snide, but I had luscious chocolate and Moe was less offensive through that lens.

He paid and I wandered through the tables crowding the wide passage to the food court. It was packed with families eating burgers, fried chicken, and cheesesteaks. I didn't really get it, but I guess it was a taste of home kind of thing. I stopped next to the drink dispensers and kept an eye on the Pizza Hut storefront through the crowd. Each of the fast-food joints was mini, even smaller than the typical mall food court places, but they seemed to keep pace with demand. I was grateful for the noise and crowd. I'd worried about being recognized, even with my hat pulled low, but nobody noticed me.

Moe joined me and then said, "I'm going into Starbucks. I need another espresso."

"Do you though?" I asked. "We're on the job here."

"You've got it covered and it's not like somebody's going to grab you up next to a table of toddlers."

"Well—"

Moe was off and I leaned on the wall, watching and pretending to look at my phone. Eventually, Madison came out to the Pizza Hut cash register, wearing a uniform that wasn't as clean as it should've been and exchanged words with a guy who wasn't happy to see her. She chatted and helped get the customer's food, while he rang up the order, but there was definitely a cold shoulder going on. Madison didn't seem to notice or maybe she just didn't care.

After the order, she took over the register and said something to him, but he didn't reply before taking off his cap and going in the back. Madison shrugged at the customer at the register and gave them a huge smile.

I texted Moe that I had a co-worker going off shift and headed out the doors into the swirling snow. There might be a back way out of the complex and I didn't want to miss him for lack of trying. But I was lucky, the guy came out the front doors and turned right toward a side parking lot.

I chased him through the incoming customers to an ancient Jeep that didn't seem roadworthy and yelled, "Excuse me!"

He didn't turn around until I slid on the ice and banged my cast on his hood.

"What the—"

"Sorry. Sorry," I said. "I slipped."

"Oh," he said. "Are you alright?"

"Fine. I just wondered if I could talk to you for a second."

He opened his car door and said, "No, thanks. I'm good."

I hated to do it, but that guy was not looking receptive, so I whipped off my hat and did the old fluff the hair and bat the eyes. "Can I please ask you some questions?"

He glanced back at me through the falling snow and I saw the double-take and then the confusion I'd seen so many times before. The who-exactly-am-I seeing look.

I stuck out a hand and said, "Mercy Watts. I'm doing an investigation and I'd like your help if you're willing."

He was frozen. I'd seen that, too. Nothing to do but continue. Marilyn was a double-edged sword sometimes.

"So I saw that you work at Pizza Hut."

Nothing.

"And you work with Madison Purcell," I said.

That woke him up. The deer in the headlights look vanished, replaced quickly with a scowl. "Yeah, I work with her."

"Great. Would you mind talking to me for a few minutes? I won't take up very much of your time." I was using the Marilyn voice. You know, a little breathless and ditzy. He liked it. I can always tell.

"Um...sure. You're really her?" He was blushing now. A flipping great start. Couldn't have asked for better.

"I am and I'm on a case," I said. "How well do you know Madison?"

"Not at all. She's super stuck up," he said. "Is this about that teacher that tried to kill you?"

I smiled and said, "You got it."

"And you think Madison had something to do with it?"

Still breathless, I said, "Oh, no. It's just background."

"Okay. What do you want to know?"

I stuck out my hand again. "Your name is?"

"Gareth." He took my hand like it was on fire and dropped it immediately.

I asked Gareth the basic questions and saw Moe watching us from beside the garden center wall. He let me go on alone without interrupting and I appreciated that, but I wasn't getting a lot. Gareth had worked with Maddison since he graduated from high school and he wasn't a fan.

"So," I said, "you don't like her at all. How come?"

"Like I said, super stuck up. I'm not good enough for her, you know?"

Good enough for what? Oh!

I took a leap and asked, "Why did she say no?"

"To what?"

"When you asked her out?"

He blushed furiously and asked, "How did you know?"

"She kinda seems like the type to say no to everyone," I said to soothe his pride.

"Not everyone," said Gareth with hurt plain in his voice.

"Who got in there?"

"Some old guy."

Score!

"But she's only twenty," I said aghast.

Gareth warmed up to the subject and said, "I know. I asked her out and she acted like I shit on her shoe. But she'll go out with some old dude just 'cause he's got money. I'm not some loser. I'm going to school full-time. Pre-law."

"I get it," I said. "Tell me. Who's this old guy? Does her mom know?"

"She didn't tell her mom. That's for sure. I only know because I heard her talking to MacKenzie."

Gareth described a conversation with no particulars to my great disappointment. The girls referred to whoever Madison was with as Mr. Big and there was talk of a trip to Paris and Prague. Dinners and some clothes Mr. Big bought Madison.

"How do you know he was old?" I asked.

"Nobody in college is going to be taking a girl to Paris for the weekend and staying in some swanky hotel."

"Isn't travel pretty normal over here?"

"Sure, but it's like this. I went to Amsterdam last weekend with a bunch of people. We stayed in a hostel. Madison wasn't going to hostels or cheap hotels."

"How do you know?" I asked. "Did she name the hotel?"

Gareth sneered. "No, but it was in St. Germain. That's not super cheap. I stayed in a hostel last year and it only cost eighty-five bucks for three nights, but you're not in the tourist area. Madison was bragging about how the hotel had a Nespresso in the room. Total tourist thing."

I laughed. "I know, right. Europeans don't care about coffee in the room."

"It's weird. Sometimes you get a kettle and tea though.

"That doesn't do it for me," I said. "It sounds like MacKenzie was impressed with the trips."

"It's not hard to impress MacKenzie," he said. "Don't get me wrong. She's sweet but doesn't get out much, ya know?"

"Is she around today?"

"No, she took some days off. I think her family went to Copenhagen."

"Nice."

"Copenhagen rocks. The pastry is rad."

We yakked about pastry for a minute and then I asked for MacKenzie's info. He had her phone number because sometimes he had to call her for work stuff. She lived in Dettenhausen, but he didn't have an address, not that I needed him for that.

"She has another friend, Olivia Jones," I said. "Do you know her?"

"Not really. She works at Burger King, but I've never talked to her." He gave me a sly look and I knew what was coming. "Can I take a picture with you? Nobody's going to believe that you interviewed me if I don't have evidence."

"I totally get it, but I want a favor in return."

He shuffled his feet and said, "What?"

"Hold off on posting anything with me in it."

"Why?"

"I'd rather stay on the downlow as much as possible." I took some selfies with my phone and promised to send them to him if he stayed quiet about our interview for a couple days.

"You'll know if I don't?" Gareth asked.

"I will."

He grinned at me. "That's kinda cool."

"A few more questions?"

"Sure. My Instagram is going to blow up."

"Has Madison's mood changed recently?" I asked.

Gareth thought about it and said, "I don't know. She's pretty fake. Always smiling no matter what."

"What about after my attack and Mr. Thooft's death?"

"Oh, yeah, but everybody was upset. A flipping teacher turns out to be a freak. It was crazy."

"But Madison, in particular, was she upset when it happened?"

He shrugged. "I don't know. She was off that weekend. Pissed me off, too. She was already off on Sunday and then she called in sick on Saturday. I had to cover."

"Do you think it was because she was upset about Mr. Thooft?" I asked. "She was in his class."

Gareth shivered as a wind kicked up and blew snow in our faces. "I've gotta go. I told my mom I'd go to the commissary and it's going to be packed."

"Just a second. I swear," I said. "Do you think it was about Mr. Thooft?"

He got in his Jeep and the old engine rumbled to life. I stepped in the way of the door closing and Gareth's shoulder's slumped. "No. She was probably at her other job."

That's new.

"What's her other job?"

"She does inspections for housing," said Gareth, cranking the heat.

"Two jobs and going to school," I said. "That's ambitious."

"It's greedy."

"You wanted that job?"

"No way. But for months, she was begging for shifts and I was getting shorted on hours." He reached for the door handle. "I gotta go."

"I'll give you a hundred euro if you tell me everything you know about Madison's shifts," I said.

"Dude. Really?"

I took out a hundred euro and held it up. "Really."

Gareth told me every detail he could think of and he had a good memory when properly motivated. He didn't know when Madison started dating the old guy, but Paris was in July. He remembered because it was boiling hot and she bragged how the hotel had air conditioning. Gareth thought it was idiotic to go to Paris in July. He was pretty sure there was a trip to Prague in August, also stupid in his opinion, but he didn't remember what weekend she asked off for.

"When did she start asking for extra shifts?" I asked.

"Like September. She was kinda acting weird. MacKenzie said something about how she needed money, like it was a family thing or something. She got all the extra shifts. We were going to hire another person, but then she begged our boss just to let her do the shifts."

"And she's still doing that?"

"Hell, no. She quit that in like November and Eric, that's our boss, had to hire somebody quick. All the sudden she didn't need money anymore," said Gareth.

There was a windfall named me.

"How did that go over?" I asked.

"I got a bunch of shifts until the new guy started. Now she's at it again."

"At what?"

"Asking for shifts. It's not so bad because everyone wants to travel, but after Christmas it's gonna suck. I'm so sick of her crap. I told her if you need money that bad you shouldn't be buying purses and shit."

She was rolling in Anton's cash.

"Expensive purses?" I asked.

"Yeah. They sell them in the PX. She got one of the big ones. MacKenzie was all about it and then Madison tried to sell it to her for like three hundred bucks. It was freaking used."

"Did MacKenzie buy it?" I asked.

"She doesn't have money for that. She took a gap year to work so she can pay for college. She's going to Notre Dame on a big scholarship, but her dad's a master sergeant so they're not exactly rolling in it."

"Did Madison ever talk about Mr. Thooft? Ever?"

Gareth frowned and then said, "You know, I don't think she did. Mackenzie was so upset. She really liked Mr. Thooft. She's still upset, but I don't think Madison said much." Gareth's phone buzzed and he took a look. "Shit. That's my mom. I gotta go."

I gave him the euro and my card. "If you think of anything else, please call me."

Gareth started to close the door and then stopped. "You think Madison had something to do with Mr. Thooft doing that to you, don't you?"

"I think she's in trouble, but I don't know what kind yet," I said.

"You'd think that old guy could've given her the money if she was having a problem. She said he was loaded. I wonder if she asked him."

"That is a very good question."

Gareth smiled and closed the door. He drove off in the increasing snowstorm and I made my way back up to Moe.

"Got yourself a good one, eh?" he asked.

"I did, but I'm freezing my feet off."

"Starbucks?"

"Absolutely."

We hurried inside and found a table in a secluded corner. Moe got me a hot chocolate that was nothing like Aaron's, but it was hot and that was the most important thing. I told Moe what Gareth had to say and he got dark. It was unexpected.

"What?" I asked as I sipped the hot chocolate.

"It was money."

"Looks like it."

"You're not upset?" Moe asked.

"I haven't really thought about it," I said. "Money seems reasonable. I mean, other than sex that's the main motive for kidnappings. What did you think it was?"

"Something to do with The Bled Collection. You know things."

"That's what Chuck thinks, but there was a ton of activity after I was in St. Sebastian the first time. The Klinefeld Group was trying to get through my firewalls, my mom's, The Girls'."

"So?"

"So they could've made a play then. They were convinced I found something out," I said.

"Did you?"

I thought about my great-grandparents' effects from their plane crash that lead us to the liquor cabinet that ended up leading us nowhere.

"Sort of. But I don't have what they want," I said.

"Did you have it?" he asked.

"Nope, and I still don't know exactly what they're after."

"Round and round."

"It keeps going, but whatever they want is important enough to keep after since WWII. Going out on a limb here, but I'm guessing that if I found it, it would be big news. Nothing happened so..."

"So they don't think you have it...yet."

"That's my take."

Moe nodded. "I hate the money angle."

"Why particularly?" I asked.

"We don't do that kind of business. We never have. It offends Calpurnia, so it offends me," said the aging mobster.

"Your world fascinates me."

"You and everyone else," he said with a small smile. "But it's a lot more corporate than you think."

"I'll take your word for it."

"That's best." He finished his latest espresso and asked, "What now?"

"Call Novak and then Hobbes," I said.

"How about I call Novak and you call Hobbes," said Moe.

"Deal."

We left the PX while still on our phones. Madison was behind the counter at Pizza Hut and I took a second to look at her face. Gareth said she was all smiles no matter what and he was right. She was all smiles. You'd never know her life had gone to shit and I was pretty sure it had in a huge way.

CHAPTER NINETEEN

Moe pulled into a small parking lot and we lucked into a parking space that was both angled and inconvenient to get into and out of.

"This better be the place because the parking is the pits," grumbled Moe.

I pointed at a plain grey building that I admit didn't look like it housed a restaurant. "There's the sign."

"It says motor sports or something."

"Under that sign. Hello. Indian restaurant."

Moe shut off the car and said, "Why did it have to be Indian? We could've found some good Italian."

"Because Hobbes wanted Indian and he's helping us out." I got out and practically dragged my elderly bodyguard toward the stairs.

"We're helping him out," said Moe. "He had no clue that one of his kids is a criminal."

"I don't know that Jake is, but we're buying lunch."

"Indian gives me issues."

"We'll see," I said.

"Yes, you will," said Moe, and he opened the door to what looked a bit like the inside of a small mall. "Wrong place. Just the sports place. Dagnabbit."

"Alright, Yosemite Sam. See the rickshaw," I said. "I think we're on to something."

We turned to the restaurant entrance and Moe said, "It was Elmer Fudd."

"Are you sure?"

He muttered under his breath ala Yosemite Sam until we found Hobbes sitting at a table with drinks and a plate with the biggest slab of naan bread I'd ever seen. The counselor jumped up and shook our hands. "Glad you could come. I'm really a face-to-face kind of guy. You just can't get a read on the phone."

We sat down and Moe asked, "A read on what?"

"How serious it is? We take the mental health of our students very seriously," said Hobbes. "I ordered mango lassis for you and you can't come here and not order naan. It's practically a law."

"No complaints here." I tore off a piece and it should be a law. Best naan ever.

Moe took a sip of the mango lassi. "I hope this doesn't put me on the toilet for a day and a half."

"You're safe," said Hobbes. "So, Mercy, you said you had more information."

"I do. Are you ready?" I asked because the counselor was so tense I could see the corded muscles on his forearms through his long sleeve tee. Fats would've been impressed.

"You don't have a name?"

"I have two names." I told him that Madison and Jake Purcell were our targets and, leaving out exactly how I got the information, I told him why we were completely sure that it was them.

The waiter came with menus and Moe grumbled until I ordered mild butter chicken for him and vowed to find some German Pepto-Bismol if required. The waiter gave me a look and I returned an apologetic smile.

Please don't spit in my food.

I ordered dal and more naan and then Hobbes ordered something that sounded like it might blow off the top of his head, but he said he liked his food serious. The waiter nodded, unconvinced, and left us alone.

"I think you're wrong," said Hobbes.

"Then you'd be wrong," said Moe. "This cupcake knows her business."

"What did I say about the cupcake thing?" I asked.

"What did I say about Indian food and my intestines? It seems we both don't listen."

I groaned and looked at Hobbes. "Why do you think I'm wrong?"

"Madison and Jake are both mine. I have the Ps. They're good kids. No problems at all. Good grades. Teachers like them."

"Did Anton like them?" I asked.

Hobbes twitched and there it was. He knew something. He didn't want to, but he did.

"Well?"

"I don't know about Madison. She was in his AP class and did well."

"She got a 4. I know," I said. "What about tutoring? Did she do that?"

He frowned. "Probably. The ones that are serious do, but that doesn't make *her* special."

Her.

"So why was Jake special?" I asked and Moe made an approving noise in the back of his throat that sounded a lot like Pickpocket about to get a treat.

"I didn't say he was," said Hobbes, avoiding my eyes.

"The kid is suicidal over this, so it stands to reason," I said.

"I read that stuff you were talking about. It doesn't mean anything necessarily."

I sat back and picked up my lassi. Hobbes had sweat on his brow, just a light sheen, but it was definitely there. "Nobody's blaming you."

"Me? How could I have known about any of this?"

"You couldn't, but you did notice something was going on, didn't you?"

Hobbes beat around about sixteen bushes, but he finally came out with it. Jake Purcell was a good kid, but perhaps not a typical one. He had few friends and rarely spoke. Several teachers had tried reaching out, and his mother had been in several times seeking guidance, but Jake wasn't interested in help. Hobbes thought that he was probably on the autism spectrum, but Jake had never been tested. Anton had him in his government class and the two had clicked. Jake ate lunch in his room every day, whether he was leading a tutoring session for the AP students or not. They often took walks after school and Anton got him involved with the yearbook staff since he had an eye for design and graphics.

"Do you think..." Hobbes choked up and I got it.

"No, nothing like that," I said quickly.

"Oh, you think Thooft was a sicko," said Moe.

Hobbes took a deep breath and asked, "Was he?"

"I've seen zero evidence that Anton was anything but a stellar teacher. Put your mind at rest on that score."

"Can I ask you something?" The wide marine looked oddly uncomfortable.

"Sure," I said.

"Why do you call Thooft Anton? I mean, after what he did...it seems familiar and almost kind."

"He was a person and he wasn't the instigator of this nightmare. I suspect he would've avoided it if he thought he could," I said.

Hobbes nodded. "Remarkably understanding."

"Oh, I don't understand," I said, "and I'm still pretty upset."

"Sympathy for the devil."

"I hadn't thought about it that way, but I guess so."

The waiter brought our food and through the steam, I saw Hobbes relax a little but not completely.

"What else?" I asked.

He scooped up a fiery curry with some naan and said, "Nothing else."

"Oh, come on. I saw your face when I said Jake's name. What else?"

Through bites of curry, Hobbes revealed that he'd seen a change in Jake in the time since Anton's death. He stopped going to yearbook and once he found him standing in the bathroom during lunch. Just standing there. Waiting. He couldn't be persuaded to come out and as far as Hobbes could tell, he didn't eat. He was waiting for lunch to be over so he could go back to class. When Hobbes tried to talk to him, Jake flat out refused to say a word.

"I didn't think he was suicidal," he said. "I still don't know that he is."

"Put it together," said Moe. "Thooft and the kid were close and it looks like the sister had something to do with Thooft getting killed. I'd be depressed."

Hobbes dropped his spoon and bowed his head. "I don't know what to do. You got this information, I assume, illegally, so I'm not supposed to know it. I've asked Meredith and some others about worrying signs from our students and they haven't seen anything."

"No concerns with Jake Purcell?" I asked.

"He came up with Melissa, his AP Lang teacher."

"She's worried?"

"Actually, no, but Jake was the only one she could think of that was particularly close. He's been withdrawn, but he always is. She was going to talk to him tomorrow and see how he's doing."

"That's a plan."

"Is it enough?" Hobbes asked. "I wish I could drive over to their house and just knock on the door, but I can't do that. Mrs. Purcell wouldn't believe me anyway."

"Why not?" Moe asked. "You're a school counselor."

"She's protective of her kids. Her husband got killed in 2010. Did you know that?"

"I did," I said. "How protective is she?"

"I suggested having Jake tested and it didn't go over well. She worries about him fitting in, but she doesn't want anything to actually be wrong. It's just the three of them. They are very close. Madison didn't go back to the States for school because she thought her mom needed her."

"Did she?"

Hobbes went back to his curry. "I don't know. She seems okay. I've seen a lot of crazy parents. I thought she was one of the good ones. Shows up for conferences. Listens. I just...you really think Madison did this to you?"

"I'm positive she had a hand in it, but I'm starting to think someone else was pulling the strings," I said.

Hobbes' spoon stopped halfway to his mouth. "Why do you say that?"

I told him about the burner phone and Madison's lack of computer skills, the expensive purse and then trying to sell it. The mysterious older boyfriend came up and those trips she supposedly took to Paris and Prague.

"Who told you all that?" Hobbes asked.

"A co-worker." I wasn't willing to give out a name. Gareth had been a huge help and while Hobbes was great, I had no illusions about him keeping silent.

"You believe her?" he asked, assuming it was a girl.

"My source is solid. What's your feeling about Madison?"

"I don't see it. She was never a flashy girl, very conservative in her clothes. Some girls have to show as much as possible. Not Madison. She had lots of friends and was in student council."

"Was Anton part of it then?"

"Sure, he was. Kids loved him." Hobbes swallowed hard. "He spent a lot of time working with them. A lot. I can't believe Madison Purcell would blackmail him. How would she even have anything to blackmail him with?"

"We haven't figured that out yet. What about friends or boyfriends?"

"Lots of friends. She hung out with Lily Bruns a lot, but she PCS'd even before graduation so she's not around. Almost everyone from her class would be gone, with our rotation kids are extremely lucky if they get four years in the same high school, most have two and sometimes three."

"Nightmare," I said. "I was in the same school my whole life."

"The military is a different world."

"Amen to that," said Moe as he scraped the bottom of his butter chicken dish. "What about boyfriends?"

"Let me think. I know she had one senior year. There were the usual promposals. I think she got one." He got out his phone and started checking photos. "We do a kind of collage for prom. I have some pictures in my cloud."

I finished my dal in the time it took for him to find the pictures from Madison's senior prom. I had to eat fast because Moe was eyeing it. So much for not liking Indian food.

"Got it," said Hobbes. "Ethan Elbert. He wasn't one of mine. Let me call Jackie. She'll know."

I paid the bill while Hobbes talked it over with Jackie. He had to reassure her that he wasn't worried about Ethan Elbert's mental health before he got back to us.

"Alright. Ethan and Madison went to prom together. Jackie was Ethan's counselor and she thinks they went out for a while. Six months or so, probably until Ethan went off to school in the States. You'll like this. The Elberts are still here and Jackie ran into Ethan's mom at the PX recently. He flew home yesterday for Christmas break."

I sat up straight. "You think they'd still be in the area? Everyone seems to travel."

"I'd put money on it. The kid'll be jet-lagged, but you shouldn't wait around if you want to talk to him."

"Don't worry about that. Do you have a phone number?"

"Jackie sent it. They live in Schönaich. Jackie will call them if you think it will help. She's down for getting to the bottom of this."

I asked him to have Jackie call for an introduction and he did. Jackie came back five minutes later and said the family was home and pretty excited to meet me. The mom was a huge DBD fan so that boded well.

We stood up and Hobbes reached out to me. "I've been thinking. I will go over to the Purcells. I don't give a crap about the legal stuff. If you think that Jake might..."

We walked out of the restaurant and I said, "He was gaming earlier and his mother was home. I'm not super concerned at the moment."

Hobbes didn't look convinced and there was every chance the big guy might run over there and blow the whole thing before I had a chance to figure out what was going on with Madison. I didn't want that, but I didn't want Jake doing anything rash, either.

"Let me call my guy and we'll see what's up?"

He grimaced. "You can do that? Just see what the Purcells are doing right now?"

"Well, not see, but we can find out what they're up to online." I called Novak real quick and to my surprise he was awake and working. He took a quick look. Mom was still home, looking at houses on a realtor site and Jake was still on the same game. The kid had stamina. I couldn't have played that stuff for more than an hour.

"He's fine and his mother is home," I said.

"That's no guarantee," said Hobbes.

"No, it's not."

We stopped at our car and the counselor opened my door for me. "If it were you, what would you do?"

"It kinda is me," I said with a smile. "I'm the one that told you to worry."

He chuckled. "I'm losing it. It's been a rough few weeks."

"Tell me about it." Hobbes reddened and I quickly said, "I'm fine. I wasn't trying to point anything out. As for Jake, you were right. You can charge over there and tell his mother. It might do some good or it might trigger him if he knows someone is working on his family. You getting private information would reveal that. He might panic."

"I didn't think of that," he said. "This situation is a nightmare."

"We're going to figure it out and get something concrete on Madison and whoever gave her that burner. When we have the information, we can deal with his involvement and hopefully have a better idea of where he's at. But you'll have to have patience."

The big man sighed. "Not my forte."

Mine either.

The Elbert family lived in a townhouse in the small and not terribly picturesque town of Schönaich. Don't get me wrong, it was a fine town but no Weil der Stadt. I missed the walls and turrets, but you can't have everything. Hobbes said they had a great Thai place and that went a long way.

Mrs. Elbert didn't let any grass grow and was waiting in the cold for us with a huge smile on her face. “I could not believe it when Jackie called. I thought she was pulling my leg. I really did.”

“Thank you for seeing us,” I said.

“I have to give you a hug. I just have to.” She pulled me into a warm embrace and the smell of White Linen and cookies enveloped me. It was like being hugged by Aunt Tenne. Delia Elbert didn’t look anything like my aunt, but she had the same kind spirit and generosity and I felt a little bit of the weight come off my shoulders just by being in her presence.

She released me and hugged Moe as well. He received the affection but kept a beady eye on our surroundings, an empty street with no moving cars.

“I heard you’re a huge DBD fan,” I said.

“I am. I’ve been to fifteen concerts,” she said. “Call me Delia by the way.”

A college-age boy appeared at her shoulders and asked, “Are you going to let them in, Mom, or do they get to freeze to death?”

That could’ve sounded snarky or complaining, but not the way Ethan Elbert said it. He had his mother’s warmth and it was easy to feel, even at a distance.

“Oh, my gosh,” said Delia. “Come in. Come in. Where is my brain?”

“Baking,” said Ethan and an alarm went off.

“The cookies!” Delia rushed off and Ethan shook his head in amusement as he led us into a small but well-decorated living room. There was a fire blazing in the fireplace and a fat beagle curled up on a cushion in front of it, enjoying the heat and snoring.

“Can I get you something to drink?” Ethan asked. “My dad made eggnog.”

Moe got a funny look on his face and blurted out, “Bathroom?”

“Are you okay?” Ethan asked.

“Indian food.”

Ethan directed him to the bathroom and Moe sprinted out. I was totally going to hear about that for a while.

I accepted some eggnog sans alcohol and sat down on the sofa. Ethan sat opposite me and rolled his cup between his palms. “Mrs.

Bostick said you wanted to interview me about Mr. Thooft. I don't think I know anything about what happened."

"It's not really about Mr. Thooft directly," I said. "I understand you know Madison Purcell pretty well. I wanted to ask you about her."

The rolling stopped but not in a bad way. Ethan's mouth opened slightly and I could tell his mind was jumping all around trying to figure out why in the hell I was asking about Madison.

Delia hustled in with a red face from the oven and sank into an easy chair with a sigh of relief. "I've been baking since six this morning and I am worn out. What are we talking about?"

"Madison," said Ethan.

Delia had much the same reaction as her son. "Madison Madison?"

"Yeah."

"I don't even know when you saw her last."

Ethan thought for a second and said, "Last summer a bunch of us went downtown to party a couple of times."

"When was that?" I asked. "Early summer?"

"May, I think. I was just back from school."

"Oh, I remember that," said Delia. "You went out two weekends and then you started work. You didn't go out much after that."

"I work at the commissary during the summers," said Ethan. "It's kind of exhausting, but I still do stuff, just not as much."

"Did you see Madison after those weekends?" I asked.

"No. She kinda fell out."

"Why was that?"

Ethan glanced at his mother, who frowned in response. "I don't care, honey. Whatever it is, go ahead and tell her."

Her son fought the battle all kids fight. Parents say they won't get mad, but we know the truth. Angry is always on the table.

"Ethan," I said, "I probably already know. I'm looking for confirmation and I'm thinking your mom can be trusted not to call Madison's mother and spill it."

Delia crossed her heart. "I promise I won't."

Ethan wasn't totally convinced, but he spilled it anyway. Rumor had it that Madison had hooked up with an older guy. After those two weekends of partying at clubs down on Theodor-Heuss-Straße,

Madison pretty much disappeared from their group. Although she was included in group chats for planning some nights and a trip to Amsterdam, she stopped responding after saying she was dating somebody and was busy. She did tell people things individually when she saw them in person and Ethan described it as bragging and his cheery disposition darkened slightly.

"Oh, honey," said Delia. "I'm sorry."

"It's nothing, Mom. I didn't want to get back with her or anything. It was just kinda obnoxious. Like that guy was so much better than us or something."

"What did she say to you?" I asked.

"Nothing direct. She'd hint that he was super important and rich, but she wouldn't say what his job was, like it was a big secret."

Interesting.

Delia's frown grew deeper. "Do you think he was married?"

"Probably," said Ethan. "We didn't get to meet him or anything. She called him Mr. Big. I don't even know his real name. It was so freaking lame."

"Mr. Big like in *Sex in the City*?" Delia asked.

Ethan shrugged. "Beats me. She was so weird we took her off the group chat."

"Did you see her with anyone outside of your group at those clubs?" I asked.

He took a sip of eggnog, leaving a tiny milk mustache and said, "There was a guy at the clubs. He was talking to Madison."

"What did he look like?"

"Old, like thirty."

Delia laughed. "Thirty isn't old."

"It is when you're nineteen, Mom. Would you want Ava to go out with some thirty-year-old that wears suits to clubs like an asshole?"

"Ethan!"

"Sorry, Mom. But that's what he looked like. He had a freaking tie on at two in the morning. Who does that?"

"A good suit?" I asked. "Tailored well?"

"Dude, I have no idea. My dad wears a uniform. He doesn't even have a regular suit."

"Did he seem rich?" I asked. "What's your first thought on that? The very first one."

"No," said Ethan and he looked surprised at his own answer.

"Why?" Delia asked. "He had that suit."

"I don't know. It was just weird to dress like that."

Moe came back in with much dignity like nothing had happened and said, "He was trying to impress. A suit when no one's wearing a suit."

"But he had the suit," said Delia. "Lots of people don't."

"If you've got money, you don't have to prove it like that," said Moe. "You might have an expensive watch on or high-dollar shoes, but you'd fit the situation."

Ethan nodded. "I guess that's it. He didn't fit."

"Did you see him more than once?" I asked.

"Yeah, he was there both weekends. I think Madison arranged it, but seriously I never got near the guy. She would go off and then we'd see her with him. We could tell she didn't want us around. Not cool."

"Did he have the suit on the second time?"

"He did. I guess the idiot didn't notice how weird it was the first time," said Ethan.

"What did he look like?" I asked.

"Oh, man. It was a club all dark and flashing lights. He was just a guy in a suit."

"Taller than Madison?"

"Definitely." Ethan described a man with a conservative haircut, dark hair, and white. Madison was five eight and never wore heels because she thought she was too tall and the guy was looking down at her. Delia was five eight, too, and using her and Ethan's comparative heights, we guessed Madison's guy at six one.

"You know, I totally forgot, but Alexis asked Madison about that guy at the club," said Ethan.

"Alexis Jackson?" Delia asked.

"Yeah, she was curious if he was the boyfriend because you know, he was weird, but she said no. I'm sorry. I should've remembered that before."

"Do you think she'd lie?" I asked.

"Maybe. Alexis thought he was old."

"Alexis is pretty harsh sometimes," said Delia. "If you look fat you better be prepared to hear that you are."

I laughed. "So a straight shooter."

"Some would say rude."

"Mom, Alexis isn't rude. She's just honest."

"There's such a thing as too honest," said Delia.

"Whatever, Mom," said Ethan.

I finished my eggnog. I usually wasn't a fan, but it was really good. "Are you still in touch with Alexis?"

"Sure. She's cool."

"Can you call her?"

"I don't know if she's back yet, but I can try," said Ethan and he got up to get his phone.

Delia refilled our cups and offered some fresh-baked Russian teacakes. "How is this helping you with Mr. Thooft?"

"We think the boyfriend might've been behind the blackmail that got Anton to attack me," I said, fudging the truth a little, but I didn't want Delia riled up. Moms were nothing if not unpredictable. I didn't think she'd rush off to call people about Madison if she thought she was unwitting. A major part of the scheme was another matter altogether.

"He would have to be some kind of career criminal, wouldn't he?" Delia asked.

"One would think so," I said. "But I don't think they are in contact anymore."

She sat back and took a breath. "Well, that's good anyway. Madison was a sweet girl. I can't imagine she would've done anything to hurt Mr. Thooft. She and Ethan were in AP Gov together." She leaned forward and in a hushed voice said, "I heard that the stuff on his computer was fake. Is that true?"

"It is."

"Thank God. Everyone I know was asking their kids if he did anything to them. What a mess."

"What did the kids say?" I asked.

"Nothing. My friends that had kids in his classes had only good things to say. There's a ton of grief, but they don't feel like they can grieve."

"His family feels much the same way."

"And his sister hired you," said Delia. "That's extraordinary."

"She's extraordinary," I said.

"And you're both doing okay?"

"As well as can be expected. If I can find out who blackmailed Anton, it will go a long way to helping his sister get over it."

Delia nodded. "I imagine it will help you both. Maybe you don't want to hear this, considering, but Mr. Thooft was great. I liked him instantly. Whatever they had on him must've been absolutely devastating because he was not evil. Nothing can convince me of that."

"I think you're right, but they found his currency and used it."

Ethan walked back in, still on the phone. "I get it. Uh-huh. Later."

"Is Alexis here?" Delia asked. "She can come over if you want."

"She's at the airport, waiting for her luggage. Her plane got delayed in Chicago and she missed her flight in Atlanta, so she's frigging exhausted. I told her I'd call her back if you needed something else."

I itched to get on the phone with Alexis, but you can't have it all and as it turned out Ethan got enough. Alexis confirmed that Madison said her boyfriend was not the guy from the club, but Alexis thought she was lying because she wouldn't give the names of either of the men.

"Did she give a reason for that?" I asked.

"Alexis said she acted like he was famous."

"Which one was famous?"

"Both, I guess. It's total bullshit."

"Ethan!"

"Jeez, Mom, I know, but it is. Like Madison Purcell met two famous dudes at the same time and they both liked her? Give me a break."

Delia sighed. "What is going on with that girl? Why not tell the truth? You all have known each other forever."

Very good question.

"Did Alexis say anything else?" I asked.

Ethan flopped back down in his chair. "Oh, yeah. Get this.

Madison stopped talking to Alexis because she said Alexis was jealous and just trying to ruin what she had."

"That doesn't sound like Madison," said Delia.

"I know, but that's what she said," said Ethan. "Alexis thinks that Madison totally made him up. She's not that hot. I mean come on. Alexis is probably right. He doesn't exist."

"He exists," I said.

"Are you sure? Because if you're going with what Madison's saying forget it."

"I've got independent information. Tell me about Madison. What was she like before all this happened?"

Ethan and Delia described a sweet girl, eager to please, and very close to her mother and brother. Ethan did think she was lying about the boyfriend as least in some way, but he didn't think she was a liar before that guy came on the scene. It appeared that those two weekends in May changed Madison Purcell's life and to some extent her personality but why remained a mystery.

"Was she gullible?" Moe asked after he polished off a glass of eggnog.

"She's not stupid," said Ethan, just a bit offended.

"Not stupid," I said. "Innocent. Trusting."

"Oh, yeah. Definitely. Madison was super sweet about stuff. You could tell her anything and she'd totally believe you. She's not stupid though. She just likes people and believes them. It wasn't even fun to prank her because you know she'd fall for anything."

"You weren't pranking Madison, were you?" Delia asked. "That's not nice.

"God, Mom, I just said we didn't because she'd fall for it. Everyone knew that."

Everyone knew.

"How did everyone know that about Madison?" I asked.

Ethan shrugged. "I don't know. You just can tell. She was super sweet."

"How well do you know her brother?"

That took him back and the confusion set in. "Her little brother?"

"Yes. Jake," I said.

"I met him, I guess," said Ethan. "But he's way younger. We never talked or anything. Madison said he was really shy."

"Nothing else?"

"Like what?" Delia asked.

"Any information can help," I said.

"Sorry. I never met him. We took pictures of Ethan and Madison for the prom and at graduation, but I don't remember seeing her brother."

"He was there," said Ethan. "But he just kinda stayed in the background. I think he was really smart and not friendly like Madison. Well, like she used to be anyway."

I couldn't think of anything else so I gave Delia my card and took a bunch of pictures after extracting a promise not to post for twenty-four hours because it might get back to Madison and cause a problem for the investigation.

"Alexis knows you were asking about Madison," said Ethan. "She's probably going to tell people."

"Is she going to tell Madison?"

"No way. They aren't friends anymore. None of us are friends with her anymore."

Ethan agreed to call Alexis and ask her to keep my interview quiet, but it was going to get out at some point. With Novak and Spidermonkey keeping tabs on Madison, I'd know the minute she knew. Still, later was better.

I thanked them both and wished them a Merry Christmas before going out in the cold again. Moe opened my door and I got in feeling so tense my shoulders were up around my ears.

Moe got in and radiated something that's hard to define. Not anger but it was in the neighborhood. "You will not tell your grandmother about the Indian food. Understand?"

Because I like to live dangerously, I asked, "Or else what?"

The old sniper turned in his seat and gave me a look that sent an icy lightning bolt down my spine.

"Never mind."

"Smart girl," he said.

"I feel a little nauseated now. Thanks."

"That's the feeling of knowing where you're at."

"Scared shitless of my own bodyguard?"

He started the car and said, "You know who I am. That's good. Let's hope our quarry does, too."

"Doubtful, but okay," I said.

"Bad news for them. Now you could call the friend from Pizza Hut and see what she knows."

"No," I said, swallowing some bile. "They're too close. MacKenzie will tell Madison immediately."

"You've got to do something. We don't have much time left and we've got to get that cat to a vet."

I put my head back and closed my eyes. Anton's cat. I totally forgot.

"I just have to chill for a minute," I said.

"I'll put on some music. AFN isn't bad."

I got out my phone as we left Schönaich and said, "I've got the best band for just smoothing things out." I connected my phone and chose a song. It went for a couple of minutes.

"Not bad," said Moe. "Who is it?"

"Rainbow Kitten Surprise."

"Was there booze in your eggnog?"

"That's the name of the band."

"It is not," he said.

"It is."

"Damn millennials."

"What does that mean?"

"Everything has to be ironic."

"It's not ironic," I said.

"That name has man buns and grandpa sweaters written all over it."

You're not wrong, but I will never admit it.

"Whatever."

We drove through Böblingen and merged onto the highway. "Tell me you played this for Fats. I bet you said that name and she punched somebody."

"She drives and picks the music," I said.

"So that head-banging rap?"

"The baby likes country."
"The baby is a grub with no ears," he said. "Answer your phone."
"Do I have to?" I asked. "I just want to listen and forget."
"You can, but you'll regret it," said Moe.
Damned if he wasn't right.

CHAPTER TWENTY

Moe smacked my leg and I reluctantly opened my eyes to see the dashboard. Rainbow Kitten Surprise totally knocked me out.

"Look alive," he said. "We've got a possible issue."

"With?"

He made a sharp turn without braking and I scrambled for the door handle to keep from flinging into him. "Hey!"

"Look."

I sat up as we sped into our hotel's parking lot.

"Oh, no!"

The parking lot was filled with *Polizei* and an ambulance. I grabbed the door release, but it was automatically locked. "Let me out. Let me out."

"Calm down. I'll park."

"Don't park. Stop." I looked at my phone. Grandma. It was Grandma that called. "Stop now."

"You don't know it's her," said Moe through gritted teeth.

"She called."

He slammed on the brakes and threw the car into park. "Don't—"

I was already out and running into the lobby. There were two

Polizei behind the front desk and I startled the hell out of them by yelling in French, "*Qu'est qui s'est passé?*"

Why is it always French?

"*Fraulein*—"

I ran, bypassing the elevator and going straight for the stairs. Moe was behind me yelling, but I couldn't stop. It was her. I knew it was her.

Up three flights and I burst through the stairwell door to find the hall filled with more *Polizei* and EMTs in their orange outfits bending over a person lying on the hall floor.

"*Qu'est qui s'est passé?*"

Dammit.

A *Polizei* moved to stop me, but I pushed past him to see Novak on the floor. I'm ashamed to say I felt a split second of relief to see my hacker there instead of my grandmother. Then I saw the blood and the relief vanished. The *Polizei* were talking to me, but it was just irritating noise. The EMT lifted Novak's head off a bloody towel and placed a large pad underneath. Novak took the EMT's hand and his eyes fluttered. I went for our room's door, but the *Polizei* grabbed me. I struggled with him and a lot of radios erupted into frantic chatter. I was a problem.

"Mercy." Grandma stood in the doorway with wet eyes and clasped hands. She opened her arms to me and I dashed around Novak's feet to get to her. People were trying to stop me, but it made no difference. I got to her. I was always going to get to her.

"What are you doing?" Grandma asked as I ran my hands over her, looking for a wound, like I had in the alley with my mother. This time I found nothing, except for a shaking body and red eyes.

"You're okay." I threw my arms around her and we shook together.

"Hello," said Novak. "Someone is wounded and it's me."

I looked down, wiping my eyes. "What happened?"

One of the *Polizei* got between us and gently asked Grandma who I was or at least that's what it sounded like. I wasn't paying much attention, too busy trying to see around him at Novak. His eyes were open and he responded to commands. He had on a cervical collar, wasn't happy about it, and kept trying to take it off. I darted around the *Polizei* and said, "Stop that. Let them do their work."

The EMT blew out a breath. "Yes, please. I must keep you still for transport to the hospital."

"I'm not going to the hospital." Novak's voice was funny. He had a tremor in his hands and his eyes were darting around until they settled on me. "She's a nurse. She'll watch me."

"You have to be assessed," I said.

"No."

The EMT looked at me and said in perfect, accentless English, "He has a head injury and he must go to the hospital for a scan."

"No," said Novak.

I squatted by his side and took his hand. "How's he looking? Any slurring? How are the pupils?"

"He must go in," said the EMT.

"No," said Novak.

"How bad is it?" I asked.

The EMT was reluctant to tell me because he was right. Novak had taken a bad blow to the back of the head. He'd been knocked unconscious for at least a couple of minutes and had bled a tremendous amount. That was normal for a head wound, but he needed stitches. Something between eight and ten. Novak was staunchly saying no. He wasn't going to the hospital and it was starting to sound a bit like a phobia.

"You can do it," he said.

"I'd like to know where you think I've been keeping my CAT scan," I said.

"You can do the stitches."

"I'm not a suture tech. It would be ugly." I should've known he wouldn't care about that. The man was wearing a ski suit in orange and lime green with pink high-heeled cowboy boots. I was starting to think he was color blind. There were fashion choices, but that couldn't be called fashion. I don't care who you are.

"Fine. Do it," he said. "I will not go to the hospital."

Grandma bent over and said, "Yes, you will."

"Janine, no."

"I called your mother."

He passed out. I'm not kidding. Out cold.

The EMT checked his vitals and said, "He must hate his mother."

"Quick," said Grandma. "Get him on a gurney."

The *Polizei* and the EMTs sprang into action and got the groggy Novak on a gurney before he came to, strapped down and everything.

"What? What happened?" he asked.

"You passed out again," I said. "You're going to the hospital."

He struggled against the straps. "No. No."

"It's fine. I'll be with you the whole time."

Moe stepped up and said, "No, you won't. You and Janine will stay here. Neither of you are getting out of my sight again."

"I can't," Novak cried out. "I can't."

He started to hyperventilate and I heard the EMTs start mentioning sedatives.

"No," I said. "We can't do this. This is worse than the head injury."

"It is not."

"He can choose, can't he?" I asked.

The *Polizei* looked iffy on that, but there was a hotel manager standing by, wringing his hands. "Do you have a house doctor?"

He stepped up and said, "Yes, but he comes for the illnesses."

"Call him, please." I squeezed Novak's hand. "A doctor's alright?"

He shuddered and then nodded. The *Polizei* and the EMTs discussed and decided Novak would have to wave their responsibility for his medical situation and the in-house doctor was called.

The doctor, who was so old that he might just have served in WWII, showed up and as old doctors often do, he poo-pood the whole going to the hospital thing. I half expected him to say we could just rub some dirt on it as Grandad would've said.

He took off the collar, proclaimed Novak's neck good enough, and then walked back into the room to inject some lidocaine and stitched his head. The *Polizei* left Grandma with him and insisted I leave for an interview.

"I don't know what I can tell you," I said. "I wasn't here."

"Where were you?" he asked.

"In Schönaich having eggnog with an American family."

He eyeballed me pretty hard, but I wasn't impressed. "Why were you there?"

"What has that got to do with Novak falling in the bathroom?"

"He didn't fall," said Moe. "Am I right?"

Novak didn't fall. He was in our room, hanging out with Grandma and working. They were going to do pedicures. I thought that might sound weird to the *Polizei*, but he took that in stride. Novak had gone to the bathroom and was coming out when someone was at the door. There were a couple of tries at getting in and Novak thought it was me. Then the door flew open and he was face to face with a man in dark clothing and a brimmed hat pulled low. Novak yelled and the man shoved him. He flew backward and hit his head on the sink. Grandma had seen the whole thing and screamed so loud that half the floor heard her. The man turned tail and ran. Nobody knew where he went and the interviews didn't have a better description than Grandma.

The doctor finished and came out with a prescription for some kind of liquid painkiller and was gone before I could ask any questions. The EMTs left right after, but the *Polizei* weren't going anywhere. They just kept asking me questions. It was clear they knew I'd been interviewed in Sindelfingen, but they never referred to it. They just kept asking why I was in Schönaich, like I was up to something nefarious and I wished they'd just get to the point. I was about to say just that when Grandma appeared in the doorway behind my main interrogator and made a stretching motion with her hands. Then she closed the door and he looked back.

"What is going on in there?" he asked.

"I have no idea," I said. "Pedicures maybe."

"I saw all that equipment."

One of Dad's more useful lessons was don't offer information if you don't absolutely have to. No filling in blanks. Zippo. Say nothing. Sometimes I forgot, but I didn't that time. I just looked at him.

"I could take the equipment," he said finally.

"On what grounds?" Moe knew the lessons, having learned on the other side.

"He may be doing something illegal." The *Polizei* eyeballed me again and I waited patiently and silently.

"We know you are investigating the Thooft situation," he said.

Finally. Took you long enough.

"I am."

"What do you have to say about that?"

"Nothing."

"Why not?"

"Client confidentiality," I said.

"Who is your client?"

I didn't think that could hurt, so I said, "Thooft's sister. She's anxious to know what caused her brother to act so out of character."

"Perhaps it wasn't out of character," he said.

"Perhaps."

A muscle in his jaw twitched and I have to admit I enjoyed irritating him. He was irritating me.

"Do you have information for me?" I asked.

He drew back and puffed up in indignation. "We do not give information to Americans who have no business getting in the way of our investigation."

"So you are investigating."

He sputtered and Moe smiled. The *Polizei* tried to get invited back into our room, but it was a no-go. I don't know what they were doing in there, but he wasn't going to see it.

"Anything else?" I asked.

"When do you plan on leaving?"

I surprised him with, "As soon as possible."

"Really?" he asked.

"Absolutely."

I'm not sure he believed me, but he left with a warning about not getting into any more trouble as if I'd broken into my room and damaged Novak.

Whatever dude. Hit the bricks.

Once the *Polizei* were on the elevator, we went inside to find Novak at the desk, typing like mad with Grandma holding ice wrapped in a towel to the back of his head.

"What the hell do you think you're doing?" I asked.

"Mercy!"

"Sorry, but seriously he has a head injury. Don't make me regret getting him out of going to the hospital."

"Almost there," said Novak.

"Where?" Moe asked.

"Got it." Novak snapped his fingers and then bent over. "I think I'm going to vomit."

I grabbed a trash can, but he didn't vomit. I got him on the bed, facedown so there wouldn't be any pressure on his stitches and I took a look. The old guy did a swell job. Better than I could've done for sure.

"What is going on?" I asked. "Why did I have to keep talking to the cops?"

"Tell her, Janine," muttered Novak.

Grandma went to one of the laptops and pushed a key. The screen filled up with six video feeds off the hotel security system. "We had to get it before the *Polizei* took it off the server."

I sat down. "Sweet. What have we got?"

Grandma, showing expertise I didn't know she had, got us through the parking lot camera all the way through to the elevator camera on our floor. A well-built man in dark clothing and a heavy high-collared black coat with a fedora pulled down low appeared in the parking lot, walking purposefully through the lot looking for something and when he didn't find it, he headed to the front entrance. He didn't have a car himself and came from the general direction of the main train station.

Once he was inside, the front desk camera showed him neatly avoiding the front desk clerks who were swamped with check-ins. On the elevator, he kept his head down and away from the corner camera and got off to march down to our door, where he pulled out a key card and swiped it without hesitation. The first time he did it too fast, showed some irritation, and then tried again. He went inside for about five seconds. Seriously, five seconds and then came running out. That time he went to the stairs that I'd come up. He ran down, skipping stairs, got himself together on the main floor, and then walked through the lobby, returning the way he came. The video ran through until it showed me running in, completely panicked.

"Can you back it up to the point where he's at our door?" I asked.

Grandma backed it up. "What are you looking for?"

I touched the screen at the top of the guy's head and then went to our door, opened it and stood in the same spot. "I'm five four. What's he?"

Moe went back and forth between me and the screen. "Six foot. Six one."

"Yeah," said Novak. "He was about my height. Maybe a little shorter."

"That fits," I said.

"With what?"

I told them what we got from Ethan Elbert and had Grandma go back to the elevator video. It was the closest image we had. The unknown subject, as Dad would've called him, took great pains to hide his face. A little too great, bending his head so far that he revealed his neck between his scarf and hat. We got a decent view of the back of his neck and part of the side. It wasn't much, but he was dark-haired, clean-shaven, and it was not the neck of an older man. By that, I mean, he was younger than forty for sure. No wrinkles. No thickening of the skin. It was young, firm, and healthy. Ethan may have considered that guy to be old, but I'd have guessed from his walk and style that he was about thirty.

"He's our guy," said Moe.

"I think so," I said. "But..."

"Not a pro."

Grandma looked hard at the elevator video frozen as he pushed the button for our floor with a gloved hand. "How in the world can you tell? He had a key card."

"Easy," said Novak. "Universal cards can be had on the web."

"That's not good," she said.

"You have to know where to look and he did."

I sat down next to Novak's prone body. "But he didn't know anything else. It couldn't be The Klinefeld Group that sent him. He did this on his own."

"How do you figure that?" Grandma asked.

"Because they don't go in knowing half the information and unprepared."

"But you think they killed Lester at the mansion."

"Exactly," said Moe. "They found someone in the house and they killed him. They didn't have a problem with that. This dipstick freaked and ran away."

"The Klinefeld Group would've surveilled the hotel," said Novak, "since I blocked access to internal security and Wi-Fi. They'd have known that the Mercedes being gone was only an indicator. A pro would've known that Mercy and Moe left you here, Janine."

Grandma's voice got tight. "Maybe he was okay with that. Maybe he was going to hurt me."

"No. He was shocked. I took him completely by surprise."

"Did you get a look at his face?" I asked.

"Not really. You saw the video. It was seconds."

"How about an impression?"

Novak took a breath and closed his eyes. "White, handsome."

"Did you see his eyes?"

"Dark, but I don't know the color," he said before opening his own eyes again. "Sorry. It was so fast. I could never pick him out."

"I didn't think you could," I said. "But the handsome is interesting."

"Just a feeling. An instant impression."

"Those are generally right."

"Are they?" Grandma asked.

"Usually and then people talk themselves out of it." I leaned back on the pillows and yawned.

Grandma went and got her purse. "Okay. Let's go."

"Where?" Moe asked.

"To the pharmacy. Novak needs his painkiller."

"Don't bother," Novak said. "I'm out of here."

"I don't think so," I said. "I'm watching you like a hawk for at least twenty-four hours."

Novak got on all fours and then sat back beside me. "I appreciate that, but I have to go. The *Polizei* aren't stupid. They'll be back and they'll have a warrant for my computers."

"How?" Grandma asked.

He raised his palms. "Somehow. It will happen. I have to leave. Tomorrow morning at the latest."

"I agree," said Moe. "I've seen that look before. The cops are thinking. We can't give them a chance to bully their way in."

Crap on a cracker.

"Didn't you give them your name?" I asked. "They can track you back to Paris."

"I gave them *a* name and I'm not going back to Paris, not until you're done," said Novak.

"Why not, if the name is a cover?"

"My mother is there," he said, crossing his arms.

"But we got rid of her," I said.

Novak glared at Grandma, who defiantly glared right back.

I threw up my hands. "Oh, give me a break. She didn't really call your mother."

Grandma bit her lip.

"How in the world? I couldn't call her. I don't even know his real name."

She put her nose in the air. "I haven't been married to Ace Watts for fifty years for nothing. I saw him punch his code into his phone. When he was laid out with the medics, I called you, but you didn't answer, so I did what any decent mother and grandmother would do. I called his mother."

"I will never forgive you," said Novak.

"Deal with it," she said. "She knows and is waiting on me to call her with an update."

"I changed my code, evil woman."

Grandma rolled her eyes. "She gave me her number. Who do you think I am? I'm a mother, not some rank amateur."

I've unleashed the Kraken and it's Grandma.

"You still can't leave," I said. "Call her and tell her that. Or she can come get him."

"I will harm you," said Novak.

Grandma smacked his foot. "Go see your mother."

"No."

"She loves you."

"That's not the selling point you think it is," he said.

"Well, you're not leaving until tomorrow anyway," I said.

Novak closed his eyes. "You can put me on a train immediately. There's a direct to Gare de l'Est."

"Not until the morning," said Grandma. "You're stuck, but I'm sure Mercy will think of something to keep the *Polizei* off our backs."

Everyone looked at me and I asked, "Will I?"

"You must know someone," said Moe.

I did know someone, sort of, but I wasn't sure I wanted to call him or even if the number he gave me was still good. The name Sean Connery was still in my phone. I'd never even considered calling that number for help from the French spy Thyraud, and maybe I didn't have to.

"What are you thinking?" Novak asked.

"I'm thinking we have a mutual friend with connections in government," I said.

"Really?" Moe asked. "Who?"

"Sean Connery."

"What on Earth are you talking about?" Grandma asked.

Novak smiled. "We do indeed. I should've thought of it myself."

"I blame the concussion," I said. "You'll call?"

"If you help me back to my room."

Grandma came over and offered her arm to help Novak up. "I will stay with you tonight."

"You are not spending the night in a hotel room with some weirdo." I glanced at Novak, "No offense."

"None taken. It's accurate." He looked at Moe who held up his hands.

"I sleep alone," said Moe.

"That's a sad commentary on your life, my friend," said Novak.

"Don't I know it, but it's still not happening."

I stood up. "Fine. I will do it, if you promise not to work or game all night. I have got to sleep."

Grandma shook her head and said, "You are not spending the night in a hotel room with some weirdo." She glanced at Novak, "No offense."

"Still none taken," said Novak. "Aaron will do it. He doesn't mind gaming."

"Aaron!" I ran to the door and Novak yelled, "I've got his second keycard!"

I dashed back and grabbed the card.

I forgot Aaron! I forgot Aaron!

I ran down the hall and overshot Aaron's door in my panic and doubled back to swipe the card without knocking. Probably not the best idea with anyone else, but it was Aaron and he wouldn't care.

I ran in, gasping, to find my little pudgy partner asleep on the bed, fully clothed, I'm happy to say. I caught my breath and bent over the foot of the bed. I didn't really think he'd been a target of anything, but who knows. Stuff happens. There were multiple sirens going for a long time, not to mention a bunch of people in the hall. How did he not notice that? He could've been dead or having a stroke for all I knew.

"Thank God," I gasped.

One eye opened behind the glasses he still wore and Aaron said, "You hungry?"

"I need hot chocolate."

He jumped up so fast he was a blur and went for the door in socks, leaving his key card on the desk.

"Hold on." I grabbed his arm and gave him a hug. Aaron just stood there and let me do it. He didn't hug back. I thought that he was probably thinking about chocolate and cream and marshmallows, but for once, he wasn't.

"Is Janine okay?" he asked, and I hugged him harder. So hard he might've regretted the question.

"She's upset. We all are."

"Everyone?"

"Well, probably not Moe." I told him what happened and Novak's injury.

"I'll stay with him," he offered without hesitation.

"That's perfect. Thanks."

"We can play Warhammer."

"Obviously," I said. "Don't forget your keycard."

Aaron grabbed his card and was out the door in a flash. I don't know where he was going, but he didn't put on shoes, so it must've been in the hotel. On second thought, Aaron would never let a little thing like footwear get between him and making food. He could be going anywhere.

I went back to my room to find Novak on the phone with his distraught mom, who was threatening to come to Stuttgart to take care of her baby. That's what Grandma said she said. It turns out Grandma could speak French.

"Do you know any other languages?" I asked.

"I took Latin."

"Not so useful."

"Well, I thought I was going to be a nurse and the nuns told me it would be good for understanding medical things."

"You wanted to be a nurse?" I asked. "I didn't know that. What happened?"

"I met your grandfather and I got married instead." Grandma didn't sound bitter, more like resigned.

"You couldn't do both?" Moe asked to his credit.

"We were military and moved. I couldn't stay in school long enough and then I got pregnant so that was that. I got a job with the phone company near post and that worked out well with all the moving. I have a nice little retirement, so it's all right."

I sat down next to her. "There are so many things I didn't know."

"That goes for all of us," said Grandma. "But it's not too late. I'm still here."

"I have some ideas about things."

Moe laughed and Grandma said, "You always did. That's why you're my favorite."

My mouth fell open.

"Ask me anything, my dear," said Grandma. "I will answer."

I was about to do just that when my phone buzzed and Moe picked it up. "Spidermonkey."

"Don't answer it," I said.

"We know how that works out."

My questions would have to wait, but some answers were heading my way.

CHAPTER TWENTY-ONE

I kicked off my shoes and climbed on the bed before I called Spidermonkey back. I wanted to be comfortable. Sometimes you just know you need to be.

Grandma and Moe helped Novak to his feet as he argued with his mother and they left me alone to see what ten texts and three calls were about. I'd missed a lot during the excitement and Spidermonkey was sure to tell me off with good reason.

"Sorry," I said by way of an opening.

"You should be," said Spidermonkey. "I was about to call the *Polizei* and report you missing."

"Don't do that. They're not my biggest fans."

"What did you do?"

"I was me and stuff happened around me." I told him about the break-in attempt and the typing started, more frantic than usual. "It's fine. We're all fine."

"I want that footage," he said.

"Novak will send it."

"I never thought The Klinefeld Group would make a play for you. Novak said the attempts to break his firewall were steady and still coming from Berlin. I should've known they'd send someone."

"They might have someone here, but it's not that guy." I explained why and my favorite hacker calmed down.

"I almost had a heart attack," he said. "How is your grandmother? It must've been a huge shock."

"She's calmer now, but it was."

"Are you going to tell your parents?"

"You must be joking," I said. "So did you get the Purcell's financials?"

"I did," said Spidermonkey. "Hold on to your hat."

"Got my hat. We're all good. Lay it on me."

He paused for effect and then said, "Nothing."

"What the...?"

"I know. No unusual activity in any of the accounts. Zippo. Nada."

"How is that possible?" I asked. "Madison was taking that money from Anton. I know she was."

"I believe you," he said.

"Well, what's she doing with it? Putting it under the mattress?"

He chuckled. "I wouldn't be surprised. Her accounts are on USAA and they are all together with her mother's and her brother's. If Lisa Purcell opens her account, she can see everything. She's co-signer on all the kids' stuff."

"Interesting," I said. "I took my parents off my accounts the day after I turned eighteen."

"You were always rebellious that way, not that I blame you," said Spidermonkey. "Your father is a bit intrusive."

"Ya think?"

"Still is. Morty's all over your accounts."

"I know. I've accepted it."

"What other choice do you have?" he asked.

"None. Obviously," I said. "I guess Madison and Jake don't have those issues."

"Not that I've seen. Very close and open."

"Not that open." I gave him a rundown on what Ethan Elbert had to say and Hobbes as well. "You never saw anything about an older boyfriend, so I doubt the mom knows."

"When did Madison have that burner on the Wi-Fi?" Spidermonkey asked.

"June sixth. Why?"

"I didn't look back that far for communications with the mother. Did Novak?"

"He didn't mention it. He just said you were doing the money."

"I am and there's nothing there," he said. "She could've handed it off to the boyfriend."

"That's a solid bet," I said. "Maybe he's blackmailing Madison."

Spidermonkey kept typing furiously. "With what? The girl was completely normal until this all came up."

"She couldn't be. A normal girl doesn't just start blackmailing people out of the blue."

"It wasn't out of the blue," he said softly. "She met a man and he changed her."

"Gimme a break. How weak is she?"

"You say that because you aren't the gentle type."

Am I being insulted?

"Oh, no?"

Spidermonkey told me a story about his daughter, the one that ended up being a physicist. She met a guy in sophomore year that had her shunning the family and doing pot at record levels. Before Spidermonkey and his wife Loretta knew it, she was off the rails. The guy had convinced her that he was the one that loved her and knew her. Her family was crap and her future could only be good by listening to him.

"What happened?" I asked. "You said she finished her degree and has a family. Not with him, I hope."

"No, he's long gone," he said. "I'm not without skills and connections, as you well know."

"I can't wait to hear this," I said. "My dad could take notes from you."

"He could. From what my daughter did say about Horatio, yes that was his name, I surmised that his money wasn't family money and that he was likely dealing drugs. This was during the crack epidemic, you see, and it was a big deal. A few well-placed calls, a tip here and there and Horatio ended up getting his upscale apartment raided. He went to prison and that was the end of Horatio. Good riddance."

"To bad rubbish as my grandma would say. But..."

"What's bothering you?" Spidermonkey asked.

"They haven't fallen out. The family is strong. There's love. I'm sure of it."

He thought about it and said, "Yes, I see your point. But what's another reason she could've done this, if not love?"

"Maybe it was love. We just don't know where it was directed yet," I said. "Do you have everything from Novak? All the phone stuff?"

"I have everything he has," said Spidermonkey. "My money is still on Madison's Horatio. That money is going somewhere and she wanted it for a reason."

A reason...

My brain lit up and I grabbed my laptop to look at the money, all the sums Anton had taken out.

"Mercy?"

"Hold on." I looked at everything, the crime scene photos, me in the trunk, Anton dead on the ground, the plane, the plants on Anton's computer, all of it, and then I looked at her. Madison Purcell. That twenty-year-old sat in a café and took money from a teacher. A teacher, for God's sake. It's not like they're loaded and she got small amounts.

"She bought that one purse," I said.

"Yes?"

"It was a treat."

Spidermonkey stopped typing. "So? She took her teacher's money and bought herself a purse. Despicable, but so what?"

"Madison could do that. She had control of that money. I've been thinking of this as one thing. One crime."

"It is," he said. "A conspiracy to kidnap you."

"That's a big crime and *that* is not Madison. She's twenty years old. Her big idea is treating herself to buy a purse. Kidnapping me is not purse money."

"I agree. So...the second crime is the small sums?"

"Yes. That's Madison's speed. What does she make at Pizza Hut?"

He started typing. "Ten twenty-five an hour."

"A hundred euro *would* seem like a lot to her. That was her idea. I bet *Horatio* doesn't even know about it," I said.

"Madison has to know about the big payday. She's the point of contact," said Spidermonkey. "But he's the cause of all of this. I know it."

"I agree, but let's leave him alone for now. We don't know him. We know her," I said. "She's the way in."

"Okay. So both crimes are about money, big and small."

"Madison is getting it every which way she can. If it was just greed, why not spend a bunch of it? The PX has all kinds of stuff. I saw signs for Lancôme and Michael Kors boots. She could've had a spending spree."

"Maybe she did and the co-worker only knew about the purse," he said. "There's a mall in Sindelfingen and a luxury mall out in Metzingen. I checked when you mentioned the purse. It's got Prada, Hugo Boss, the works."

"I don't think so. Madison wouldn't brag about the purse and stay silent about everything else. It was her treat. The thing she gave herself and then..."

"She tried to sell it to her friend," Spidermonkey said slowly.

"After the deal with Anton went bad. She needed the money and not for her Horatio. For herself. She was desperate for hours at work and suddenly she wasn't."

"When they hatched the plan to nab you, she didn't need them, but now she's asking again. What in the world could she need money for? She lives at home," he said.

"College money?" I asked.

"I checked that. Madison and Jake have college funds. They got them after their father died. The mom funded them with the life insurance."

Hold the phone.

"How much life insurance was there?"

"Let's see," said Spidermonkey. "SGLI in 2010. 400,000."

"I assume that's not in Lisa's savings account," I said. "Where'd it go?"

He typed away and then said, "She got the payout a few months after the father's death. It did sit in the savings account for about two years. She didn't touch it."

"Grief. Makes sense," I said. "Then what?"

"She took out fifty grand for each of the kids and put it in 529 plans for them. Not inventive, but she made solid choices for the funds invested. They made money. Madison has been dipping in every semester to pay for tuition and books. She's living at home and the school's online so it's not super expensive. She'll get through with no debt. Jake's account is just sitting there. No withdrawals."

"Everything is where it's supposed to be for the college money, so where's the rest?" I asked.

I held my breath while Spidermonkey worked. This was it. I just knew. Madison needed money. What for? College was all good. I'd seen her. Not a drug addict, unless she was hiding it super well. She looked healthy and fit. It was Mom. She needed it. Something about retirement coming up. The retirement money for enlisted couldn't be a golden parachute, but still blackmail? What was up?

"Lisa Purcell took the money out in the form of a cashier's check in 2012," said Spidermonkey.

"Holy crap. The whole 300 thousand?"

"All of it. I didn't see this before, but to be fair, I wasn't looking at Mom hard."

"What in the world did she do?" I asked.

"Nothing dramatic. She opened a brokerage account with a firm in Colorado Springs. She gets emails from them occasionally, but she's not interested. She doesn't open them. Probably doesn't want to think about that money and how she got it."

"Is it still there?"

"Working on it. The brokerage is tight. I'm going to have to be at this for a while," said Spidermonkey. "But I can tell you she hasn't opened an email from them in years. If I had to guess, she set it and forgot it."

"Can you read the emails?" I asked.

"Sure, but they just say she should try new account structuring, shift her funds into different areas, or look into their retirement plans. They're just mass emails. Nothing on Lisa's account in particular."

"Check Madison's computer," I said.

Spidermonkey paused and said, "You think she took it?"

"She needs money for something. I'll bet the farm that account is empty."

"Why?" he whispered as he worked.

"Just tell me it's gone and then we'll find out," I said.

"Madison has the account on her computer."

Wait for it.

"It's gone," he said with pain in his voice, dripping, angry fatherly pain. "She took it all."

CHAPTER TWENTY-TWO

Spidermonkey and I worked for the next two hours. By the time we were done, I was depressed and exhausted. Grandma was crying. That money was gone and Lisa Purcell had no idea. Her husband had lost his life serving his country and his own daughter had stolen what he left his family. Grandma couldn't stand it. Vietnam came back for her. She lost friends over there. Grandad had in large numbers. Thinking about the sacrifice brought her to her knees. Moe, too, truth be told. The old sniper didn't cry, but he looked like he might be ready to take up his old profession again.

Even Aaron's hot chocolate didn't soothe them and it was a masterpiece. That's saying something when it comes to Aaron. Everything he does is exceptional. I wanted to cancel our dinner with Isolda, but Grandma insisted. She put on lipstick and a new dress she bought just for our trip. Moe pulled out all the stops, wearing a three-piece suit and a tie. He looked like he stepped out of the 1930s and even with the hump and eyes, he was almost handsome in a grizzled sort of way.

I, on the other hand, didn't have a suit, dress, or lipstick on. Moe thought I looked like I was going camping. If you know me, you know how unlikely that would be. I camp only under duress. My dad's stinky old Army tent scarred me for life.

"I do not," I said. "This is just regular clothes."

Grandma pursed her lips. "We're going to a Bled restaurant."

I sighed. "And what is a Bled restaurant?"

"Fancy. Isolda promised a treat and you know what she's like."

"I do. She wears fur to the grocery store and shops at Goodwill," I said.

Grandma sucked in a breath. "Oh, she does not."

"I've been to Goodwill with Isolda. We bought end tables circa 1960 and she refinished them."

"Those funky ones in the Soulard apartment?" Grandma asked.

"The very ones. Fifty bucks for the pair."

Moe snugged up his tie and asked, "Why would Isolda Bled buy things at the Goodwill?"

"She likes it. You find cool stuff there," I said. "She bought the end tables and donated five thousand dollars at the same time."

"Now that sounds like Isolda, but the restaurant will be fancy," said Grandma.

"She bought me lunch the same day. Tacos out of a trunk. You never know with Isolda," I said.

"How were the tacos?" Moe asked.

"Delish."

"Please, put something nice on," pleaded Grandma. "We could end up at a Michelin-starred restaurant and you're wearing old hiking boots and a stained sweater."

I'm not going to lie, I was wearing a stained sweater, but that's only because Grandma spilled stuff on it while she was drunk. The boots were for warmth, not hiking. I don't hike, either.

"I'm going to come clean," I said. "I don't have anything nice."

"You have a dress. Wear that."

"No dress."

"How can you not have a dress? You have to prepare for different occasions," she said.

I held out my foot. "I prepared for cold and chasing people."

"Have I taught you nothing?"

"You keep asking that. The answer is the same."

Grandma put the stink eye on me and said, "What's the answer?"

"Careful," muttered Moe under his breath.

"That you did teach me," I said. "I don't learn."

She grumbled and went over to the small wardrobe, flinging it open. "Where are your clothes?"

"Suitcase."

"They'll be all wrinkled."

"Not a huge concern for me," I said.

"Have I taught—"

"Give it up, Janine," said Moe. "She's hopeless."

"Thanks," I said.

Grandma grabbed my suitcase and riffled through it until she came up with the other sweater I brought, super wrinkled but stain-free. Then she did the extraordinary. She got out a tiny steamer and steamed my sweater.

"Put that on and no complaining," she said. "I will pick out jewelry and you will wear it."

"It's like I've got a little angry butler," I said.

"Don't push me."

I took the sweater. "Not pushing. Getting dressed."

I went into the bathroom, changed sweaters, and put on deodorant. Probably should've done that before, but I was on a case. I forgot things.

Before I could do anything else, Grandma banged on the door and then barged in to apply makeup to me against my will.

"Are you this way with the Troublesome Trio?" I asked.

"You shouldn't call them that," she said as she selected a gloss to put over my lipstick.

"You do. Everyone does."

"Still."

"What does that mean?" I asked.

She gave me the once over and said, "You need mascara and shadow."

"It makes me look more like Marilyn."

"Oh, please. I'm not buying that. You're just lazy."

You are not wrong.

"Fine. Mascara it is." I did as instructed and Grandma was as good at makeup as Fats and that is saying something. But she even topped my bodyguard by pulling out a curling iron. It was not a good thing.

When she finished, I sighed. "Oh, come on. Really?"

"What?" Grandma clasped her hands under her chin. "You are stunning."

"Can you see me?"

"I always see you." She put her purse in the crook of her arm and said, "Let's go."

I followed her out and Moe said, "Hot damn. Too bad you don't have the dress."

"What dress?" I asked.

"The one from The Seven Year Itch. You are the spitting image."

"Swell." I grabbed my poofball hat and Grandma said, "Don't even think about it."

"People will stare."

"Let them. This is who you are." She tossed the hat on the bed.

"But I don't want to be this."

Moe herded me toward the door. "We will be late. Let's go, ladies."

I made a move for the hat, but he blocked me and I had to go out looking like Marilyn in full makeup or possibly worse, a drag queen. I was getting that more and more. There were stares. Oh, yes, there were. And pictures. So much for being on the down-low during an investigation.

Moe got us into the car without incident and I have to admit his hawkish behavior probably kept a few people in the lobby at bay so that was something. Not enough, but something.

"So where are we going?" I asked.

"Back to Waldenbuch," said Moe. "Isolda texted me."

"You look happy," said Grandma.

"We're having Italian. My gut can rest easy."

Please don't ask.

"Has your stomach been bothering you?" Grandma asked.

Here we go.

"Has it?" Moe regaled us with stories of his gut, notably leaving out our lunch. Instead, we went all the way back to Vietnam. Apparently, you can have diarrhea for an entire year and survive. I didn't want to know the details, but I got them.

Then they started in on various old people issues. Reading glasses. Glaucoma. Bursitis. Forgetting why they went into a room. Moe sometimes forgot why he was packing a gun and had the beginnings of cataracts. By the time we got to Waldenbuch, I was questioning my safety and that of others. On the other hand, he didn't need a map to get to the tiny town and knew exactly where to park. I just hoped he didn't have cause to draw the gun he forgot he had.

"Oh, this is charming," said Grandma, looking up at a half-timbered building just off the town's square. The little osteria was blazing with light and the scent of baking pizza and roasting meat filled the air.

Isolda stepped out of the front door and waved at us. The fur was gone, replaced by a red satin trench that was just about the coolest coat I'd ever seen.

I followed Grandma and Moe and watched as they exchanged hugs. Moe was in there, easily accepted by Isolda. If she had any reservations because of the Fibonacci accusations about her mother's disappearance, I couldn't tell.

"Where on Earth did you get this delicious coat?" Grandma asked.

"Copenhagen in a vintage shop. It was fantastic. We have to go." Isolda turned to me and we exchanged cheek kisses. "My dear, you look exhausted." Then she paused and looked us over. "You all do. Has something happened with your case?"

"It has and Isolda, it's just the worst thing," said Grandma, getting teary again.

"Our table is waiting. Let's go up and talk it over." Isolda led the way into a little ground-floor shop with wine and olive oil for sale. Moe got distracted and we had to pull him away from the displays of aged balsamic vinegar. He had a lot of opinions on the proper aging of vinegar, but we got him upstairs into a little dining room with just about ten tables, most of which were full. Our table was in the corner and the owner hustled out to greet us and offer wine from her home region in Southern Italy. She spoke German, but Moe answered in Italian and they started a lively conversation about Italy and wine and oil and food in general. Soon, everyone in the restaurant was talking to us. There were questions about me, I'm sorry to say. Pretty sure someone asked if I was a man and that didn't help my mood, but mostly it was the usual before Christmas joy.

I joined in as much as possible, picking a wine and snacking on the wonderful amuse-bouche that came out. I don't know what was in the soft cheese that came with some crunchy fried dough, but I could've just eaten that alone and been happy. Well, maybe not happy. I couldn't get my mind off Madison and what she'd done. Spidermonkey had worked through Madison transferring the money out of her mother's investment account to an account she'd got at the credit union on post. It sat there until everything cleared. Then she opened a wallet on a bitcoin exchange and started buying bitcoin. It was more convoluted than it sounds. She went through several exchanges and somehow all of the investment was gone. It looked like it was lost in a dramatic downswing in the market, but there wasn't a downswing on the day it happened. In short, Madison Purcell lost her father's insurance money gambling on bitcoin, except she shouldn't have lost. Spidermonkey was looking to see if it went to another exchange in a more volatile market or if she went into a different crypto and lost it there. Something like Ethereum was high on my hacker's list and once Novak was feeling a little better, he got into the act and started working as he played Warhammer with Aaron. They were sure they'd figure it out, but I already had a feeling about that bitcoin thing. Something wasn't right. Madison didn't know about that stuff. She didn't make those decisions.

Moe and Grandma ran down the whole case for Isolda once the restaurant settled down to their respective dinners and she became as somber as I felt.

"Can you get it back?" she asked.

"I don't see how," I said. "She lost it all. We're just trying to figure out how."

Moe cracked his knuckles and said, "That boyfriend of hers is behind it. He got her to do it and then cooked up the plan to kidnap Mercy to make up the loss."

Isolda's eyes went wide and she reached for my hand. "Do you really think so?"

"The dates line up. The money was lost and then Madison started asking for more hours at work. She started blackmailing Anton and stopped the extra work."

"She thought a payday was coming in," said Isolda. "Do you think that she would've given the money back to her mother?"

"I don't know," I said. "I haven't thought about it."

"She did try to sell her purse," said Grandma.

"Maybe she needed to give the money to the boyfriend," said Moe.

"There's no way of knowing until we ask her," I said.

The three of them got bright-eyed.

"When will you do that?" Isolda asked.

I took a big drink of an excellent primitivo and said, "When we know where the money went. I want all that info before I confront her."

"Tomorrow?" Grandma asked reluctantly.

"Probably. Depending on how much Novak can work. He's got a bit of a headache and I didn't want him working at all, but he's a dog with a bone. He can't let go until he's got the answer."

"My kind of guy," said Moe. "But let's talk about something else. Mercy needs a different puzzle to think about."

"Do I though?" I asked.

He shot me a look and I clammed up.

"So Isolda, I'm fascinated by the research you're doing," he said.

Oh, that puzzle. On board.

"I had no idea that you thought your father was German," I said.

"Well, it's something I haven't wanted to talk about," said Isolda. "But I'm getting up there now and it's time to know the truth if it can be known."

"Who told you he was German?" Moe asked.

"My mother did. She was dying and..." Isolda's voice got thick and throaty.

Grandma gave her a hug and said, "You don't have to talk about it if you don't want to."

Isolda took a breath and a good slug of wine before smiling. "I want to. It's just that you're the first people I've discussed it with."

"Really?" I asked. "What about The Girls? You could tell them."

"Oh, my dear, they have such guilt about it I've never wanted to make them feel worse."

"Why would they?" Moe asked. "It's not their fault."

"Of course not, but Nicolai and Florence always blamed themselves for my mother's disappearance. They never got over it, especially Florence. She felt she'd let the family down and my mother, in particular. It's ridiculous, but that's how she felt."

"Why is it ridiculous?" I asked, garnering a sharp look from Grandma. "I'm not accusing Florence of neglect or anything, but ridiculous is a strong word."

Isolda smiled at me and squeezed my hand. "Because Florence wasn't at fault. My mother wasn't kidnapped. She wasn't lost or confused. She knew exactly what she was doing. Almost everyone at the mansion was sick, my mother saw her chance and she took it. In her words, she escaped."

Imelda lay on her deathbed in the Bled Mansion when she made her confession. It happened in my bedroom in my bed. Information I totally could've done without. I hope they changed the mattress. That's not a lot better, but I'm going to say it is.

Isolda thought her mother was in a coma. She had been for several days and the doctors didn't expect her to last the night and she didn't. But Imelda did wake up to everyone's surprise at eight in the evening and told everyone but her daughter to leave the room. They did and that's when in a hoarse whisper she told Isolda what she'd done.

It was love, she said, and regretted nothing, least of all Isolda, her beloved only child. She claimed to have met a German prisoner of war and they had fallen madly in love, emphasis on the madly part, in my opinion. We were at war, for crying out loud. But that didn't matter to Imelda. Her beloved was perfect and beautiful. He thought the same of her. That's what she said anyway.

I didn't know that there were German prisoners of war in Missouri, but apparently there were several camps and one of them was at Jefferson Barracks, where her beloved was imprisoned. Isolda asked how they met and her mother said that he was a bricklayer and mason and the camp was fairly loose about the prisoners, allowing them to work. Some helped farmers and others were living on riverboats and repairing the levees. He had been doing that for a time before being sent to Jefferson Barracks where he was put on a detail, tuckpointing the brick buildings and shoring up foundations. Later, he was sort of rented out with other POWs to work on businesses around St. Louis. Imelda didn't say which ones, but Isolda assumed that the Bled Brewery was on the list.

The two lovers met as often as possible and wrote almost every day. Imelda's caretaker Rose was in on it. She mailed and received letters for Imelda. Rose didn't know that her charge planned on running off. They had cooked up a plan and when Imelda saw the flu showing up in the house, she sent a letter for him to escape, which he did. Then on the day that Rose got ill, she simply walked out the door while everyone was busy. He was waiting for her on the corner next to the gatehouse and off they went.

Imelda told her daughter it was the best time of her life. They traveled around the country, seeing the Grand Canyon and San Francisco, but it couldn't last and Imelda always knew that. She would have a downturn eventually and she did. It happened in New York City and it was bad. She'd found out she was pregnant and that might have been the trigger. Imelda knew her illness well enough to know that certain things set her off. Pregnancy would fit the bill with the excitement and stress of being on the run. To make matters worse, someone had heard them talking at their hotel and they realized he was German. He'd been careful the whole time to let Imelda do the talking in public, but the cops were alerted and came looking for him.

Imelda tearfully told of their parting. She had to go home and be cared for. He said he would try to get back to Germany to help his family. He left minutes before the authorities arrived. Imelda convinced them that she didn't know any Germans. How could she? It was ridiculous. They were persuaded to believe her even though she was currently in a mental ward because they didn't know she was pregnant at the time. She didn't reveal that until she was back in St. Louis safe and sound and she never told anyone until the night of her death what really happened.

"Why not?" Grandma asked. "He was long gone. They weren't going to catch him."

"Yes, but the war was intensifying. Having an affair with a German would've been a scandal for the family and Florence already felt bad enough."

"And there was you," said Moe. "She made you a Bled, not a child of a Nazi."

Isolda nodded. "My mother suffered greatly with her illness. I saw it all my life, but she was a kind, thoughtful person. She thought it through. She protected me."

I'd stayed quiet throughout her story and it was plausible, I guess. Imelda did disappear. She did turn up pregnant. It happened.

"What did they do for money?" Grandma asked.

Isolda shook her head and chuckled, "Well, my mother took quite a bit with her. She'd been saving up her pin money and she wasn't a prisoner. Some of the newspapers acted like she was, but she did go out shopping and dancing. She was very pretty with those blue eyes and lovely legs. When she went to restaurants, she said men always wanted to buy her dinner or a drink. She'd ask for money from her trust and got it, but she didn't spend it. She had it hidden under her bed, taped to the headboard."

"She was a thinker," said Moe.

Isolda teared up again. "She was and such fun when she was well."

"How did you end up here?" Grandma asked. "Do you have a lead?"

"I do. I got all the POW records and I started going through them, cross-referencing with the men who were on the prisoner boats and by occupation. There were 400 men at Jefferson Barracks and a few did escape, only to be brought back later. Some were gone for months before being recaptured."

"All of them were recaptured?" Moe asked.

"Yes and when the war was over they were returned to Germany."

"Imelda never heard from him again?" Grandma asked.

"No. She never did. She told me she thought he probably did get back to Germany and died during the war. She didn't think anything but death could keep him from her."

We sat in silence for a moment and the owner brought our food. I got a wild boar goulash with wonderful house-made pasta. I lost myself in it for a while and then found a way to ask the question that had been percolating in the back of my mind. "What was his name?"

"Oh," said Isolda. "Didn't I say?"

"No, you didn't."

"It was Jens."

I set down my fork. "But that wasn't his real name."

Isolda's mouth dropped open and then she said, "How did you know that?"

I told her about The Klinefeld Group's odd use of the name Jens Waldemar Hoff as a kind of cover for different men through different generations.

"Does your father know about this?" Grandma asked.

"Mom does."

Her pretty face darkened. "Then that's the way we'll keep it."

"Excellent," I said. "So, Isolda, what reason did he give for not using his real name?"

Isolda reached down and picked up her purse, a big one, the kind moms liked to carry so they can have an arsenal of crap with them at all times. In her case, it was an arsenal of information. She pulled out a fat file folder and laid it on the table. "He said it was to protect her in case they were caught. She could say she didn't know who he was."

"And she couldn't put them on his trail if he got away," said Moe.

"That's not the way she thought about it, but I suppose so," said Isolda. "Do you think that my father might have been someone from that group? The same group that sued The Girls over the collection?"

"It could be a coincidence," I said.

"But you don't think so."

"Coincidences aren't big with me. What's with the file?"

"I was going to hire you to find him," said Isolda. "Get a professional on the job. I knew you would keep it quiet."

Moe turned to Grandma and said, "Pay up."

"Oh, for heaven's sake, you greedy buzzard." Grandma slapped twenty euro in his palm. Being super gracious, Moe kissed the bill, snapped it straight a couple of times, and then put it in his wallet.

"Thank you very much," he said. "Nice doing business with you."

"You can still hire me," I said. "I'll do my best."

She handed me the folder. "This is everything I have, but now I'm wondering if it's worthless. He might not have been a prisoner at all."

"Fats told me about this group," said Moe. "I didn't know it went that far back though."

"Neither did I, but there were some break-ins in the 1940s that I think were them," I said.

Isolda shook her head and then ordered another bottle of wine. "I knew about them, of course, but I didn't know how bad it was until Lester was killed. To think my father..."

Grandma sniffed and said, "I hate to say this, Isolda, but maybe he was pulling her leg on the German thing."

"No. I'm sure she was right. Positive, in fact," said Isolda.

"How?" I asked.

"I had my DNA done. I'm half German. Whatever he lied about he didn't lie about that."

DNA. Yes. Thank you.

"Did you do it privately?" I asked. *Please say no.*

"I did an Ancestry kit on a whim and lo and behold sixty-two percent German," she said.

Ancestry. Sweet.

"Sixty-two?" Moe asked.

"I have some German from several ancestors on the Bled side," said Isolda.

"Can I have the folder?" I asked.

"Certainly." She handed it over and I opened it to see a list of German prisoners of war.

"Do you have anything on your mother's disappearance?"

She reached in the purse and came out with another folder, not as fat but good-sized. "I do. I've got all the news coverage. Honestly, I didn't realize what big deal it was until I saw the headlines. There were articles in the New York Times and the San Francisco Bee."

"There was a big reward," said Moe.

"How did you know?" Isolda asked.

"My grandpa got pulled in over it."

"No!"

Moe smiled. "He had associations."

"The Fibonaccis?"

"You got it."

The two old folks looked at each other and then smiled.

"Looks like we have a history we didn't even know about," said Isolda. "I'm sorry about your grandfather."

"He was a rough customer so he was okay."

They started talking about the kidnapping, or rather the escape as Imelda put it, and I went through the second file. Plenty of newsprint and lots of photos of the pretty Imelda. She looked a lot like Stella, although not quite as delicate looking as the spy, but they both had the Bled eyes, high cheekbones, and small pouty mouths.

Moe leaned over and gave out a whistle. "What a looker."

"Too bad I didn't take after her in the looks department," said Isolda.

"You do," I said. "You've got the eyes."

"I do, but the rest is him, whoever he is."

"He was a big guy," said Moe.

She nodded. "Over six foot and very strong, but she said he was very gentle with her. Mercy?"

I looked up from the newsprint. "Yes?"

"I think it was real. He might've connected with my mother to get entrance to the Bled Mansion, but something else happened when he did. I'd like to know why he never came back."

Probably not the reason you think.

"I'll see what I can do," I said. "Tiny's heading the new DNA stuff for my dad. He's got a head for it and he'll be a big help."

"Oh, your cousin. I forgot he's working on that. The Girls told me. They called it reverse-engineering the bloodlines for all those adopted babies."

"That's a great way to start," I said. "Did you get matches in Ancestry?"

"I don't know. I just got the profile before we came," said Isolda. "There could be matches. It's so exciting."

We went back to eating and then ordered dessert. Tiramisu. It had to happen. Isolda insisted on a dessert wine and also cappuccinos. The three of them talked about the DNA and family history. Midnight trips to Steak-n-Shake and skating at Steinberg. Drive-in movies and sledding on Art Hill. They hadn't known each other growing up, but it seemed like they had been within arm's length their whole lives.

I went through everything Isolda had on her mother's disappearance and the German POWs, although that was probably a no-go. Then I circled back around. I'd seen something. Familiar. A face. I smiled.

There you are. Just where I knew you'd be.

"Isolda?" I asked.

She set down her coffee cup and wiped tears from her eyes from all the laughter. "Yes, dear."

I turned the news story from the Post-Dispatch around and pointed at the face of a police officer standing guard in front of the Bled Mansion. "Do you recognize him?"

She looked and then got out her reading glasses, red with lots of bling. "Let me see. No, I don't think so. Who is he?"

"Grandma?" I gave the paper to her and she borrowed Isolda's glasses.

"Would you look at that," she said. "It's Elijah. You were right, Mercy. Look at that."

"Who is it?" Isolda asked, and I watched her closely in case she tried to fudge the truth, but I got nothing off her but curiosity.

"Elijah Watts," said Grandma. "Ace's father."

"Of course, it is." She threw up her hands. "I should've recognized him."

"You knew him?" I asked.

"Well, yes," said Isolda. "Ace's father was lovely."

"How did you know him?" Grandma asked. "From this? The kidnapping."

"Florence talked about him. The wonderful policeman who was so kind when it was all happening. Elijah Watts. He came to guard the house in case someone came for The Girls and he was so nice, they requested he stay until the whole thing was over." She wrinkled her nose. "Some of the other policemen weren't so kind because my mother was ill. They thought she killed herself and they wanted to stop looking. Elijah was a great favorite."

The first favorite.

"And you knew that was Ace's dad?" I asked.

"Well, yes. Shouldn't I have?" she asked.

"Not really," said Grandma. "I just never heard anything about him knowing the Bleds."

"The way Florence and The Girls told it he was very gentle and quiet. I don't think he would've talked about the family out of turn," said Isolda.

"You're right about that," said Grandma. "He would've considered it bragging."

"What about when Grandad got to know the Bleds?" I asked. "What did he think about that?"

"Oh, I don't know. He didn't say anything about it to me. Ace might not have told him."

"Elijah knew all about it," said Isolda.

"What do you mean?"

"He came to the mansion with Ace."

Grandma sat back stunned. "Really? Why?"

"I don't know. I came home after they'd left and Millicent mentioned it. Remember, we had a couple of break-ins and Ace worked those. I think Elijah came by for old time's sake."

And that's not all.

An hour and a half later, Grandma and I were curled up in bed with Moe in the armchair with *Moonstruck* started on the TV. Novak had downloaded the movie for us and Grandma was all excited to show it to me.

"Why are you so interested in Elijah all the sudden?" she asked, surprising me. I'd begun to think she wasn't paying much attention to what I was asking.

"My life is all wrapped up with the Bleds. I want to know where it began."

"I guess it was with Elijah. I never knew that, but it makes sense that he would've been wonderful at such a terrible time. I told you how beloved he was."

For more than one reason.

"You did."

"I'll have to ask Ace about it," she said.

"Shush," said Moe. "It's starting."

We shushed and it was starting.

CHAPTER TWENTY-THREE

The Stuttgart Hauptbahnhof was frigid the next morning and I couldn't get inside fast enough. Unfortunately, Novak was no hurry. I think he'd been planning on ditching his train to Paris and going somewhere else, anywhere else than to his waiting mother, who planned to be in Gare de l'Est to pick him up.

"Why are you walking so fast?" he asked as he crept through the impressive main hall of the station with its 1930s architecture intact. He kept trying to divert to McDonald's or a pretzel seller or the enormous Christmas tree set up in the center of the hall. Novak acted like he'd never seen a Christmas tree before. Give me a break.

"Your train leaves in ten minutes," I said. "If you wouldn't have been so slow before we wouldn't have to rush now."

"I didn't need such an early train," he said.

"Yes, you do and so do we," said Grandma. "Aaron's culinary class is second period at the high school and this is the only direct."

"You could've dropped me off."

"Fat chance." I got behind him and steered him out the door to the platforms where it was significantly colder. "You're trying to get on the wrong train."

"Wrong is relative," said Novak.

"Not in this case," said Grandma. "I promised your mother."

"*You* promised."

Grandma took his arm. "Mother to mother. It's a done deal. Now stop your whining."

"I'm not whining."

"He said in a whine," I said. "Let's see you're on track—"

"Seven," Novak said.

Nice try.

"Thirteen," I said. "They changed it."

He muttered something in what I presumed was Serbian and we frog-marched him down to the correct track.

"Here we go. First class," said Grandma. "You'll be well looked after."

Novak made a great show of hugging us and I had to smile at his last desperate try. He didn't know my grandmother. Granted, I didn't know her that well either, but I was getting the picture.

Janine Watts pushed Novak, the six two hacker, onboard and followed him right on.

Startled, Novak said, "You don't have to—"

"Hush up. I wasn't born yesterday." Grandma steered him left into his car and I could hear the bickering as they put his luggage on the rack.

Moe laughed. "That woman. He's no match."

"He really thought he could go in one door and get out another without us noticing," I said.

We walked down to look in the windows to see Grandma physically push Novak into a seat, buttonhole a porter, and give him a good talking to about his passenger's condition. The chances for escape were nil. "He was going to give it the old college try."

"He doesn't know us Watts at all," I said.

"Especially, since you're not Watts," said Moe.

I gave him the side-eye and asked, "What are you talking about?"

"All that stuff about Elijah Watts and the mansion last night. Who knew who? When did they know who? Janine hasn't figured it out yet, but she will. She's sharp and it won't take long."

I watched Grandma tip the porter, kiss the top of Novak's head, and hustle toward the exit as the warning buzzer went off. "I'm interested in family history. That's all."

"Fats told me about the Bled stuff."

Dammit.

"She had no right to tell you anything," I said.

Moe took my arm and kept his eyes searching the crowd. "I needed to know all the information. You're more than you appear, so the threats are too."

"Don't say anything to Grandma."

"I won't, but you'll have to."

Grandma stepped off the train a second ahead of the final warning and the doors started to close. A portly man came running down the platform and banged on the door as it locked tight. He cursed in French and banged on it in frustration.

"Too late, my man," said Moe under his breath.

"So irritating to miss the fast one," said Grandma.

The man kept yelling as the train jolted and started moving. I turned my gaze back to Novak's window. His corn-rowed head was still in place, not looking at us, but with a jolt, I realized someone else was. A man was standing up and leaning over the next row of seats, looking straight at me. Our eyes met and he jerked back. The train moved him away out of the station and I was running alongside. Me and the old guy. He was still banging on the side. I was trying to look in that window. Dark hair. Handsome. Tall. Well-dressed. Gone.

Moe caught up to me. "What on Earth are you doing?"

"He was on the train." I bent over panting.

"Who?"

"Him. The one that pushed Novak."

Moe looked back at the disappearing last car and said, "How do you know that?"

"He was looking out at me. He saw me. It was him."

Grandma came up and Moe told her what I said. "But Mercy, you don't know what he looks like. It could've been a fan or God help us a stalker."

"No. I saw the way he looked at me. He was shocked in a bad way, afraid and angry. I know that look. It was him."

"Son of a..." Moe trailed off. "He got away."

"Novak's on that train with him," said Grandma, frantically reaching for her phone.

"It's fine," I said. "It was never about Novak. He was going for an empty room to search for what we know."

"Still. We have to tell him," said Moe.

I called Novak and told him who his traveling companion was. He said it was almost worth the trip.

"Can you see him?" I asked.

"No. He's left the car," said Novak.

"Naturally. It can't be easy."

"Oh, it's easy. I've got money and Janine made friends with the porter. I will get it done."

"Pictures would be ideal," I said.

"How about a name?"

"I assume that will be fake."

"He's not a genius," said Novak. "You never know."

We hung up and I shivered.

Grandma took my arm and snugged me up to her side. "Are you upset?"

"I think I'm shocked."

"Well, he can't get off that train," said Moe. "No stops."

I nodded. "We'll need a tail in Gare de l'Est."

"Come on," she said. "We have three and a half hours to arrange it. Novak has friends. It will get done."

"I hope he doesn't try to do it," said Moe.

"That man is not the action type," I said. "Besides, his mom will be there."

"Thank goodness for that," said Grandma. "Let's get out of here. Aaron is waiting. I hope they didn't make him move."

The *Polizei* hadn't made Aaron move out of the drop off spot, but they were trying. If I had to guess, his oddity worked in our favor. They'd talk and he'd act like he didn't know what was going on. He might get arrested on suspicion of being on mind-altering substances, but they wouldn't get him to move.

"Here we go," said Moe. "Better hurry."

A *Polizei* moved to the driver's side of the Mercedes and reached for the door. Grandma sprang into action. She dashed over, talking a mile a minute about Aaron and parking and the trains and who knows what all.

The *Polizei* ended up holding his hands up against the barrage from a little old lady and eventually started smiling. Aaron got a pass and the *Polizei* opened my door for me.

"*Merci. Salut*," I said, beaming a smile at him and I got a surprised look in return as he recognized me or at least recognized Marilyn. Grandma had had her way with my makeup again. I was quickly learning not to fight it. Or...

"Was that French again?" I asked Moe as he got in the back with me.

"What do you think?"

"For crying out loud. I need an MRI or something."

"You're fine," he said. "He didn't even notice. Too busy looking."

"That's the good shock. Not like the guy on the train. Totally different," I said.

"I believe you." He checked his watch. "Will Spidermonkey be awake?"

"Maybe, if he's on a roll with the financial trail."

Grandma turned in her seat and said, "Call him. He'd want to know about that man on the train."

I was reluctant to wake up my elderly hacker, but Grandma was right. Spidermonkey would want to know. I called and he answered on the first ring.

"Great minds think alike," he said.

"In this case, a great mind and a so-so one," I said. "What's up, Oh Mighty One?"

Spidermonkey chuckled and then got somber in a flash. "I got through it all. Well, almost all of it."

"And?"

"She was robbed."

"We know that," I said.

"No. Madison was robbed," he said.

I sat back and pulled off the poofball hat Grandma had allowed me to wear under duress. "How? What? Who robbed her?"

"I should've seen it instantly, but it looked legit."

Spidermonkey explained that one of the massive issues with cyber currency was that it was cyber, which sounds kinda stupid, but there's no physical building you can go to about your money. It's all online. You can follow a solid recommendation for a company, a good reputable company, and end up on an imposter site. Madison clicked a bad link, deposited her money, and it was gone. Stolen.

The fake site gave stats for her account for a few days and then claimed a sudden drop in the market made her investment worthless. Madison had sent frantic emails about the money and got automated responses saying that there was a warning before she made her investment that nothing was guaranteed.

"She was pretty hysterical," he said.

"I bet. Excuse me while I fail to weep for her," I said.

"You might find this interesting. In her third email, she says 'This was my mom's money for retirement. Please help me figure out what to do.'"

"Her mom's money that she stole."

"It is, but it got me thinking," said Spidermonkey.

"It's got me thinking she's a piece of crap," I said.

Moe muttered, "No doubt."

"Hear me out. I got to wondering where she got this site. Madison isn't exactly a savvy investor. Her mother did everything with the 529 plan. I can't find that Madison did anything with it. Lisa took the money out to pay the tuition and books. Madison never even went in and checked the amount or funds allocation."

"So?"

"So where'd that girl get this bitcoin idea in the first place?"

"The boyfriend," I said. "Has to be."

"That's my thought. Handsome, successful older man says invest here. He tells her she'll make a mint so she steals her mother's money and does it."

I balled up my hat and unclenched my jaw. "Did she research sites at all?"

Spidermonkey made an approving noise, the kind I loved getting. "I wondered that, too, and the answer is no. She didn't look at any other sites. She went straight to the imposter site. He gave it to her." Spidermonkey explained that the legit site had normal spelling in the URL and the fake one had slang. Think Litcoin instead of Litecoin. That kind of thing. I could totally see how it happened and how he covered himself. If she happened to catch on that it wasn't a legit site by some miracle, he could easily say it was a mistake. He said the right name. She misheard. It wasn't his fault she did it wrong."

"I can't believe it. The boyfriend stole Lisa's money from Madison," I said. "Hello, karma."

"Yes, but I have a feeling it's not that simple."

"You think she's an innocent little flower that got taken advantage of?" I asked. "Oh, come on. She went through some hoops to get that money. It wasn't an accident."

"There's more to the story," said Spidermonkey. "I get feelings, too."

"Granted, but in the end there's no excuse and when the money was gone she blackmailed Anton," I said.

"I know that, but I think the boyfriend was the driving force. It comes back to him."

"More to the story? Puhlease. You old softy."

"Speaking of more to the story," he said. "Can you talk?"

I glanced at Grandma chatting away to Aaron about menu planning and getting an explanation of what mochi is. I guess the kids would be making mochi.

"I think so," I said as Grandma inquired about the right kind of rice for mochi. I knew from experience with Aaron this wouldn't be a short conversation nor a simple one.

"I got a chance to look into those records you were interested in," said Spidermonkey.

"You have been busy."

Moe raised an eyebrow at me and I gave him a hold on look.

"You nailed it. Giséle Donadieu was arrested in November 1910."

I couldn't believe it. Too crazy. I was right. "How in the world did you find that out? It's not like it's online."

"There was a newspaper article on said arrest."

"There was a whole article on it? What did she do? Break down the door or something?" I asked.

"She returned several times to each of the Bled houses trying to get them to talk to her. She was refused and they finally called the cops," said Spidermonkey.

"What did they charge her with? Tell me it wasn't anything to do with prostitution."

"It wasn't. The charge was harassment. The article said she wanted a job at the brewery and was denied."

"That's not so bad," I said. "She didn't go to jail, did she?"

"There were no articles after the fact and the original was just a little paragraph. It would never have made the paper if it hadn't been for the Bled involvement."

"So we don't know what happened?"

"Of course, we do," he said with a laugh. "Don't you know me at all?"

"I take it back," I said. "But how did you figure it out?"

"Pretty sure the charges were dropped."

"Why? Harassing the Bleds had to be a thing," I said.

"Since she married the arresting officer a few weeks later, I'm sure she got off easy."

"No way."

"I figured that was how she met Thomas, but I didn't think it would be that easy."

"Kind of romantic in a way," I said. "And they lived happily ever after."

"It looks that way."

Grandma turned in her seat. "What's romantic?"

"How Madison's boyfriend turned on the charm," I said. "She didn't stand a chance."

She ground a fist in her palm. "Just wait till we get ahold of him."

"Very threatening, Janine," said Moe with a smile and I have to admit she was pretty adorable when she said it, not a bit threatening.

"I was trained in weaponry. I'm a crack shot."

"You are a woman after my own heart."

"You're such a naughty boy, Moe Licata," said Grandma.

"Getting nauseous," I said. "Aaron food. What are we having?"

Aaron started in on choices of pork for sausage. Not scintillating to me, but Grandma was literally taking notes. God knows why. There wasn't going to be a quiz after.

"Are you still there?" Spidermonkey asked.

"Yeah, just having a bit of an issue with the old folks," I said.

"Who are you calling old folks?" Moe asked.

"You were in Vietnam for crying out loud. You're no spring chicken."

He wasn't impressed with my logic, but I got a laugh out of Spidermonkey.

"Anything else for me?" I asked.

"Thomas was married once before and as you suggested I think he was infertile. Twelve years married. No kids. Her name was Mary and died when she got hit by a streetcar."

"Well, that's terrible."

"It was and it happened five years before Giséle turned up on the scene," said Spidermonkey. "I think he and that beautiful young French woman came to an arrangement."

"That sounds bad," I said. "Like she had to do it."

"There weren't a lot of options for ladies in her predicament, but I prefer to think it worked out for both of them. He got a son and she got status that no out of wedlock mother would've gotten. From how Elijah turned out, it was a happy life. Thomas certainly didn't control Gladys with her going into business and doing charity work. I read her as independent."

"I hope you're right. Anything on the...um...background?" I didn't want to say anything about France in case Grandma suddenly dialed in.

"So far, a dead end. Her passage says Paris as does her paperwork at Ellis Island, but I'm not seeing anything with the right particulars in Paris."

"There's no hurry on this stuff," I said.

He yawned and then said, "I almost forgot. Your timeline is getting tight."

"Tell me about it. I saw the Instagram posts. My mom was all over that stuff." Quite a few posts had come out of my look the night before. Some complimentary. Some not so much. So I wore a baggy sweater. Get over it.

"There's nothing from Gareth. The boy stayed true to his word."

"I will reward him," I said. "Anything else?"

"None of the posts have made it to the high school that I've seen, but other people are now discussing why you're in Stuttgart."

"I'd think that would be obvious."

"It is and it's started to spread with the usual theories and conspiracy theories. Watch yourself and get it done quick."

"Roger that," I said.

"All military already," said Spidermonkey.

"Moe taught me."

"Roger that."

The driveway up to the school complex was packed. Just getting on post took forever with the busses and people coming to work. The line to get into the parking lot stretched all the way under an overpass and into the regular part of the post. It was the second to last day before Christmas break and cars appeared to be full of party supplies, projects, and more than a few stressed out kids. The military kids had a different school schedule so they weren't having finals, at least. But it took me back and not in a good way. Christmas parties in my younger years weren't always the greatest.

My dad never showed up, of course. Mom tried to come, but you'd be surprised how many cases Big Steve had going in the run-up to the holidays and since she was his paralegal she had a hard time escaping the pile of motions and briefs on her to-do list. I'd like to say I had no shows when it came to parties. That would've been preferable to Uncle Morty showing up with what he called dog barf dip and looking disturbingly like the serial killer BTK. Sometimes The Girls came and that was wonderful, but not always possible. I got Isolda once and that was the best year ever. We got gourmet cupcakes, sparkling apple cider, and tales of the world. Isolda was once peed on by a Moroccan man who decided that urinating out of his kitchen window was appropriate. She was full of stories like that and we laughed for two hours. Uncle Morty smelled like musty old pizza, talked about bloody crime scenes, and basically spent the time doing the school party version of get off my lawn. It was not awesome.

I totally felt for the kids with glum expressions trudging into the elementary school with their mothers in tow, waving and chatting everyone up. My mom was the one that the dads showed up to get a gander at and that was almost worse than smelly Uncle Morty. People got mad at me. I couldn't help what my mother looked like. That was just her face. I had no idea at the time that I would have the same problem on steroids. Mom was at least demure. Demure wasn't an option for me. Nature and circumstance conspired against me in that regard and that day was no different.

Grandma insisted that I "look nice," which meant I looked like me with no hat as concealment. When we got out of the car, people pointed. Not ideal, and I hustled for the school much the way my mother had, eyes down. Making eye contact would encourage actual contact. That wasn't good in a world with cell phones everywhere and the less people knew about my presence the better in terms of Jake. Spidermonkey had provided his bus schedule. He'd be arriving after us and still showed no signs that he knew I was in the area thankfully. His lack of social contacts was helpful in that context and sad in every other. Still, someone could mention seeing me and it was making me nervous.

"Hey!" yelled Moe. "Where are you going?"

I grimaced and turned around to find him at the popped trunk offloading his weaponry. I dashed back and dumped my purse with the Mauser inside. "I totally forgot."

"Good catch," said Grandma, beaming at Moe. "Very smart. We don't want to cause any issues."

"There's an issue." Moe pointed at Aaron, who was heading for the high school as fast as his little legs could carry him. We had to run to catch up and slipped in the door with the students to get visitor badges from the school secretary. She tried to give directions to the culinary class, but Aaron was already out the door. Grandma chased after him, smiling and saying hello to all the students.

"I'm actually supposed to be meeting with the counselors," I said.

"Really?" she asked and then lowered her voice to a whisper that wasn't a bit effective since the office was filled with kids and parents asking questions but with one ear on us. "About Mr. Thooft?"

"In a manner of speaking," I lied, "I'm supposed to pick up some more belongings for his sister."

"Didn't you already clean out his room?"

"I guess there's something else."

She wasn't convinced but gave me directions. Moe and I made a beeline to the counselors' offices and were surprised to find the little waiting area packed.

"Miss Watts," said Principal Newsome, "it's a pleasure to meet you. Donut?"

"Don't mind if I do," I said, picking a glazed raised. "We didn't have time for breakfast."

"Sir?" he asked Moe, holding out the box, but he declined.

"Shall we sit down?"

Hobbes said nothing, but there was a big vein throbbing in his neck and Meredith kept licking her lips. The other two counselors just looked slightly confused and curious.

"Sure," I said, and he went to put up a sign saying counseling was closed for the time being and locked the door.

We sat in the waiting area and everyone looked at me. I looked at the principal until he shifted in his seat and reluctantly began. "Do you have information on one of our students that we should know about?"

"I do. Has Hobbes filled you in on what I've been doing?" I asked.

"He has, but I'd like to know where you got the information."

"Confidential."

"Not illegal, I hope."

Hugely.

"Confidential."

"So you think Jake Purcell is in trouble?" asked Meredith.

"I know he is and it's about to get worse," I said. "He's involved in what happened to me. I suspect as a witness, not as a participant given his increasing depression, but I could be wrong. Did Hobbes fill you in on the SCPs?"

The principal wasn't convinced it was the indicator I thought it was, but he was going to take it seriously. I told them about Jake being present at the blackmailing by his sister in the café and the mood got a whole lot more serious.

"Why would Madison Purcell do that to Anton or you for that matter?" Jackie, Ethan Elbert's counselor, asked.

I told them about the money and where we thought it went. The group went silent until Hobbes got out his laptop. "Jake has English and calc this morning."

"Is he there?" I asked. "In class, I mean."

Hobbes checked and said Jake had been marked as present. I breathed a sigh of relief that everyone noticed, but nobody commented on.

I suggest we pull him in at lunch," said Hobbes.

"I agree," said Meredith. "I'm really worried. He's a sweet kid and we have to get ahead of this."

"You're already behind," said Moe.

"What do you mean?" Principal Newsome asked, bristling.

"Jake Purcell is already in a hole. He's not getting ready to fall in."

Newsome nodded and poured us all a second cup of coffee. "We've never dealt with something like this before." He looked at me, his high forehead wrinkling. "Will the FBI be involved? These are international crimes."

"Yes," I said. "But keeping Jake safe is my priority right now. We have the location of Madison's accomplice and bringing Madison in for questioning won't be too much of an issue as long as she's surprised."

"We won't tell her," said Hobbes. "How are you going to do it? Go to her house?"

"I'd say bring in Jake's mom at lunch and ask that Madison come as well. Once they're all three here, you can separate Madison from her mother and Jake. I'd like a word with Madison to see what I can get, but then it's all you."

"Us?" Meredith asked.

"Well, the MPs and the *Polizei*. I'm just a PI. Info gathering is my thing. I'll probably be able to get Madison to admit it. If not, I'll ask her mother to check her accounts in front of her. If that doesn't break the dam, we'll know that Madison has more of a criminal turn of mind than I'm thinking right now."

"Couldn't she be innocent?" Jackie asked.

"She is not innocent. She stole the money and set up Anton. She knew what she was doing," I said. "The question is why and where the money is now."

"Can you find it?" Hobbes asked.

"If we—"

My phone buzzed and Novak had texted, "We got him."

I stood up and said, "I have to take this."

Hobbes told me to take his office and I dashed in there, dialing as I went.

Novak answered on the first ring and said, "Bastard was in the bathroom."

"Seriously? This whole time?"

"Yep. That's what took so long. My friend, Frederic the porter, went looking and searched the entire train to no avail. Another porter said a bathroom had been occupied for thirty minutes."

"So either somebody has a serious problem or..."

"They're hiding," said Novak. "This happens a lot apparently. People sneak on without a ticket or steal something and hide out."

"It's been over an hour," I said. "Where was he the rest of the time?"

"He's smarter than I thought. He moved from toilet to toilet for the first half hour, but then he couldn't move because the other ones were constantly occupied so he hung out."

"Did you get a picture?"

"Frederic got several and even better, a name," said Novak.

"Sweet. Lay it on me."

"Our guy is Sebastian Nadelbaum and he used his own credit card to book his ticket."

"A real credit card?" I asked.

"Like I said not a genius. It appears to be legit and the booking site had all his information. I've got a friend working on it. We should have everything within say an hour."

"Christmas came early."

"It did indeed," said Novak. "Do you want a picture?"

"Oh, so very much," I said.

He sent me a couple of shots, front and side views, and Nadelbaum was as Ethan Elbert described him, tall, handsome, about thirty, and well-dressed. In the case of the train, he didn't look out of place like he did in the club. Nadelbaum was appropriate and I looked closely at his face. Yes, I could see how Madison could fall for him easily. He was just the right amount of handsome, not over the top. His nose was a little bulbous. Shadows on the dark eyes and the jawline wasn't perfect. It was believable. Madison might be on the young side, but she was in his league.

"Do you recognize him from the hotel?" I asked.

"He's familiar but nothing more," said Novak. "He's got the right look for sure."

"Are you doubting that he's our guy?"

He chuckled a little. "Not a bit. He saw you and me and hid in bathrooms for an hour. It's him."

"Can you get a reception committee for him in Gare de l'Est?"

"Already arranged. The train will be covered."

"What's he doing now?" I asked.

"Sitting in his seat. Frederic insisted. He's four rows behind me."

"He might try the bathroom thing at the station."

"Frederic will have them searched. It will not work out for him," said Novak with a yawn.

"How are you feeling?" I asked.

"Better now that we've got him. I'm going to enjoy introducing him to my mother."

"Oh, yeah?"

"She kicks."

We both hung up laughing and I came out of Hobbes' office to find everyone literally on the edge of their seats.

"What happened?" they asked in chorus.

"Anybody recognize the name Sebastian Nadelbaum?" I asked and they shook their heads.

"A German, I assume," said Newsome.

"Looks like it." I showed them Nadelbaum's picture and nobody had seen him before.

"He looks too old for Madison," said Meredith. "I can't imagine her mother was happy."

"I doubt she knew the particulars," I said. "But we'll find out."

Hobbes ran his hands over his head and said, "I can't believe this. Madison and Jake. I don't know what I'm going to say to their mother."

"Let's just get them here," said Meredith. "You should call her."

He typed something into his laptop and took a breath. "Alright, lady. This is when your life turns to shit." He dialed his phone, stood up, and went into his office.

"That is not going to be a good time," said Jackie. "So glad it's not me."

"I second that," said Meredith. "The depressed ones scare the crap out of me. I never know what's going to happen."

"You haven't had any suicides, have you?" Moe asked.

"No, but with the kids, they're so impulsive. I worry all the time. They just take action when they should stop and think."

Hobbes came out. "Well, that was easier than I thought."

"What did she say?" Newsome asked.

"She's been worried. Jake's not sleeping or eating. He won't talk to her. She was thinking of calling me for help, but I beat her to it. I'd say she's relieved."

That won't last long.

"What about Madison?" I asked.

"She's calling her, but she thinks she's probably still asleep," said Hobbes. "Oh, and she didn't want to wait until lunch. She's taking the duty bus over from Patch. She should make it for second period."

"What do you think?" Newsome asked me.

"It's fine, but I better tell Aaron that I'm not going to be front and center for the chef show."

A huge smile replaced Newsome's frown. "I have to admit I'd never heard of your friend but then Chef showed me his YouTube channel and I was hooked. That guy's amazing."

"He is," I said, standing up.

"Our Culinary 2 students are thrilled to have him. They will be in a competition this spring and Aaron's going to give them a lot of confidence."

I never thought of Aaron as giving confidence. I wasn't even sure if he was confident, just incredibly focused on food or Dungeons and Dragons or whatever he was doing.

"I hope so. If nothing else, he'll probably give them ideas. He's chock full of them," I said.

"He barely talks in the videos," said Meredith.

I laughed and it felt good, a tiny bit of stress disappearing from my chest. Aaron had that effect on me. "He barely talks in real life, except about hot dogs and gaming."

"Hot dogs?"

"He's passionate about hot dogs."

"Why?"

"Beats me," I said.

Newsome shook my hand and didn't release it for a moment but not in a creepy way. "I should've said right off how sorry I am for what happened to you."

"Thanks. I appreciate that."

He patted my hand and said, "Thanks for bringing Aaron with you. The whole school is buzzing about him. It's a nice distraction."

"I didn't bring Aaron. He just comes with me," I said. "But I'll tell him how happy you all are."

"Too bad he doesn't have time for Culinary 1," said Jackie. "They're missing out."

"Oh, no," said Hobbes. "Jake is in Culinary 1. I'm glad he's not in there."

"I thought Chef was thinking about inviting the first years to a tasting at lunch?" Meredith asked.

"Was she? I didn't know that," said Jackie. "We should check with her."

"We'll already have Jake in here with us, so it's okay," said Hobbes.

"Actually, I'm not sure he'd go anyway. He's been so shut down. I'd be shocked if he knew who Aaron was."

The thought of Jake put the heavy right back in my chest and I excused myself to go to Culinary. Moe trailed me out, his forehead furrowed. "I hope the meeting with the mother goes well."

"I'm not sure there is a way for it to go well," I said.

"But there's a way for it to go very bad."

"Aren't you just a bowl of sunshine?"

"I've seen men crack up. It's not pretty."

There's wasn't a good response to that, so I just walked with my bodyguard through the halls, getting lost twice, until we ended up at the culinary class. I'm not sure how we passed it, but once we got turned back around we could see through a door into a classroom where Grandma was sitting at a desk talking up a storm with five girls who were excitedly pointing at pictures in magazines and at their phones.

I walked in and said, "So what's all the excitement about?"

Half the class was in there and I got blasted with questions with everything from cosmetic surgery to Chuck. That's right. They knew about the hot boyfriend. Gen Z doesn't have much of a filter and they asked all kinds of things I didn't expect before we got to food. It was a bit of a battle, to be honest.

"Are you excited about cooking with Aaron?" I asked.

Another furious blast of questions came at me and it was all I could do not to duck. Seriously, I'm not kidding.

"Does he ever talk a lot?"

"Why does he smell like hot dogs?"

"Did you ever go out? Because that would be weird."

Yes, it would.

"Does he make mochi for you like all the time?"

"Can Aaron make those hand-pulled noodles like they do them in Asia?"

"Would he do that today?"

"I want to learn that. It's so crazy."

"Can you ask him? He'll do it if you ask."

I looked at Grandma and she said, "They're excited. It's not often you have a celebrity chef in the house."

"Aaron's a celebrity chef?" I asked.

That caused an eruption of epic proportions. Didn't I know who my friend was? Apparently not, but in my defense it was freaking Aaron. He never talked about himself, even when I asked. I was lucky to know he had sisters. Who they were remained a mystery.

I held up my hands. "I will ask him about the noodle thing."

"Now?" asked a girl named Madison. There seemed to be an inordinate amount of Madisons in Gen Z.

"Sure. Now, do you want to do it or just get a demo."

"Do you think he really knows how?" one of the two boys asked. "I heard it takes years to master."

"It's Aaron, so I would guess he does." I turned around, looking for the kitchen.

One of the two Madisons in the room came over and said, "You can go through that door there right into the kitchen prep area or go out in the hall and go in the other door to the pantry area."

"Prep area it is." I vamoosed as fast as possible before they asked about cheese making or my favorite mascara. They'd proven to be interested and unfocused at the same time.

I walked through the door into a kitchen that surprised me. Tons of stainless steel, very industrial, and well-appointed. I wished I'd had culinary in high school. Home economics on an ancient Sunbeam stove just didn't compare.

And there was my little partner holding court, if you want to call it that, at a giant island. One half was stove and the other prep. About ten students were chopping veggies and three were working at the burners, whisking, tasting, and salting in a concert of creativity. Aaron was talking and it made my eyes mist. Compliments, directions, and criticism came quietly and often all in the same breath.

"Aaron," said a girl, bending over a stockpot. "I think it needs something."

He leaned over and sniffed. After a second, and without tasting, he said, "Saffron. Mercy?"

"I'll get it," I said automatically as I did when we were cooking in my apartment or the mansion or Kronos. I use the term *we* loosely by any standard. My knife skills were decent, but how you could sniff a need for saffron was beyond me.

Aaron looked up because I hadn't moved, his glasses steamed, and I did an about-face to go toward where one of the Madisons had said the pantry was. I didn't get far. Only to the edge of the island where the dicing and slicing was fast and a little bit worrying. There were so many young fingers and a lot of sharp flashing steel.

He saw me first, a boy in the doorway, his arms filled with stacks of bowls, each stuffed full of produce, spices, and tools. I felt his eyes before mine left the bowls with spices. I'd been wondering if there was saffron in there. I never found out because I looked up to ask and the face from the café's window stared at me with much the same expression as it had then. I didn't move. I was afraid to. His face was so pained. So tight in its struggle that even breathing seemed a dangerous thing to do.

Jake Purcell's eyes slid to the left. There was a counter with piles of bowls, cutting boards, and multiple knives caked with veg and bloody bits of meat.

"Don't," I whispered, and it was a mistake.

He dropped his burden in a spectacular crash and darted out of sight. It happened so fast I wasn't sure that he didn't grab a knife as he spun around. He could've. There were plenty to choose from.

"Moe!" I screamed as I ran through the mess to the other door and slid into the hall on rolling peppercorns and shards of glass. I banged my cast on the door jamb and pain jolted up my arm.

Moe came running as I slipped around. "What? What?"

"Jake!" I pointed down the hall at the boy running toward the office.

Moe took off. I cleared the debris as Grandma yelled, "Mercy!" But I was gone, running down that long empty hall, hoping to God someone would stop him and if they did, no one got hurt in the attempt.

But no one turned up, Jake banged out of the front bank of doors, sprinting with long legs. Neither of us could match him and when we burst out of the doors, we found the quad area between the schools empty.

"Where'd he go?" I asked. "Did you see?"

Moe grabbed my arm. "He turned right. Parking lot."

We ran for the lot that was completely filled and devoid of people. The area was fenced in with the extra measure of razor wire on top. Jake couldn't go running off into the woods or something. He must've run toward the road.

I ran for it, looking through the rows of cars with Moe panting beside me.

There was a sturdy guardrail at the edge of the lot and I slammed into it to lean over and look for Jake running under the overpass, but he wasn't there. He was fast, but not that fast. He couldn't have cleared the parking lot that quickly. Of course, he couldn't.

"He's...still here," I said to Moe, who nodded.

We started to work our way through the cars to see where he was hiding when an engine roared to life. A newish Volvo station wagon backed out of a spot and was jammed into drive. Jake floored it to race down the row of cars.

"Come on!" Moe was at our car and backed out before I got there.

I threw myself in and he hit the gas. "Don't have an accident!"

"Do you want to catch him or not?"

"Yes!"

"Buckle up!"

We left tire marks at the end of the parking lot and raced under the overpass.

"There he is!"

The Volvo narrowly missed a minivan and made a wide turn, bumping up on the sidewalk next to the bowling alley.

"Where the hell is he going?" I asked.

"The other gate," said Moe.

"There's another gate?"

Moe did a better turn than Jake and we saw him barreling down a short stretch, bypassing cars coming toward us and rolling up on the sidewalk to pass others on our side. He was getting through. It didn't seem like he could, but somehow he did and we were right behind.

"They'll stop him at the gate, ri—" I screamed as Jake sideswiped a car and nearly hit a woman on the sidewalk.

"No," said Moe. "They won't."

They didn't. We raced past a small commissary and over a little hump in the road. Jake had taken the sharp left turn at too great a speed. The guards dove for cover and were on the cobbles. Jake took out a pillar of the tent structure that was erected over the small gate and hit a second car that was coming in. The structure groaned and began to topple forward toward us.

"Go!" I yelled. "We'll lose him."

Moe got us under the falling tent and to the main road so fast I didn't blink. Jake had left a trail of destruction behind him, sideswiping a car that had been turning into the gate and a fender bender in the other direction. Moe drove us around the mess and yelling drivers to get behind the Volvo that was gaining speed.

"I have to call someone," I yelled. "Who do I call? Who do I call?"

"You're asking me?" asked Moe. "I've never called the authorities in my life. *I'm* the reason people call the authorities."

"Not helpful!"

"Driving!"

"MPs or *Polizei*? MPs or *Polizei*?"

"Koch!"

I patted myself down. No purse, but my phone was wedged in the seat under my butt. "Where is the damn traffic? There's always traffic!"

"Clear today," said Moe as we merged onto the A81 without incident and started working through the lanes and cars with a brisk efficiency I recognized.

"Did you learn from my dad?" I asked.

Moe smiled, his bulging eyes trained on the road. "He learned from me. You gotta get fast to catch Moe Licata."

"Did he?"

"Close, but no banana."

That was a good description of the Volvo. We couldn't quite get to him. The boy could drive. I called Koch. The *Polizei* could cut him off. They were known for efficiency.

"Hallo," said Koch in a breezy way that I was about to banish.

"We're chasing Jake Purcell!"

"Mercy?"

"Who else would call you about chasing people?"

Koch stammered and then asked what was happening. I told him, using as few words as possible. Not enough as it turned out.

"Who is Jake Purcell?"

"The kid from the café. He's suicidal. I think he is. I don't know."

"*Scheiße*!"

"I know. Send somebody. We're on the A81," I said.

"Let him go!"

"I can't let him go. He might have a knife or hurt himself."

"You'll have an accident!" Koch yelled.

Moe shook his head. "We're not having an accident and the kid is doing okay."

"We're okay," I said. "And Jake isn't doing badly."

"Where's he going?" Koch asked.

"How the hell should I know?"

"Why did he run?"

"He saw me at the high school," I said.

"And he ran? What did you do?"

I felt like throwing the phone out the window for all the help Koch was being. "I frigging stood there and he ran. Send somebody to slow him down."

"I'm coming," said Koch.

"Where are you?"

"Stuttgart Süd."

"Is that close?"

"Close enough." A car engine roared to life and Koch yelled to someone, "Get in!"

"Mercy," said Moe. "He's slowing down."

I told Koch and he asked where we were.

"Passing Vaihingen," I said.

"He's going to exit," said Koch. "Probably at the university."

"How do you know?"

"There's an easy access overpass."

I went ice cold and turned to Moe. "He's getting off at the University so he can jump off the overpass."

"No," said Moe and he put on speed.

"I'm coming," said Koch and he hung up.

I dropped the phone and gripped the dash. "Maybe this is the wrong thing? He's terrified."

"We're committed," said Moe. "And he was already terrified."

Please help us.

The Volvo exited right where Koch said it would, but there was some traffic that Jake couldn't get around. We were one car behind bumper-to-bumper with a BMW that wasn't too happy with us. Cars were passing on the overpass. The cars in front of Jake weren't moving.

"He's going to run for it," I said.

"Wait!" yelled Moe, but I was out, running up the ramp. Jake was out of the Volvo before I cleared the BMW. He got to the half-moon of pavement above the highway and grabbed the railing.

I stopped where the curve began and touched the railing with the fingers sticking out of my cast. I needed it to steady myself, but I couldn't get a grip while I hoped to God inspiration would strike and I would find the words to make a seventeen-year-old boy not jump off a bridge.

Horns were honking. People were yelling. Traffic came to a stop under the overpass. Drivers got out, waving and shouting to Jake as he sobbed so hard his body was quaking with the spasms. He didn't look at me, but he knew I was there. I could feel it and somehow I think that gave him pause. Me. My presence. Maybe it was just another person being on the bridge, but I didn't think so.

"Please don't," I said. In the end, the words just came with no thought or planning at all. I was guided. By whom, I couldn't say.

"You don't know," said Jake without looking at me and the wind kicked up, making the loose legs of his jeans flap around his thin legs. We were both shaking. I couldn't tell if it was cold or the fright, but I almost thought I would be pitched off that bridge right along with Jake should he choose to go.

"It wasn't your fault," I said.

He put a foot on the lowest rung of the guard rail and swung the other leg over. “It was.”

“I forgive you!”

Jake stopped mid-movement and looked at me, his face full of surprise and denial. “You can’t.”

“I certainly can, Jake,” I said, wanting to edge closer but knowing it was a bad idea. “Don’t forget I was the one in that trunk, so I get to choose, don’t I?”

He swallowed hard and I watched the Adam’s apple in his throat bob up and down. It made him look so delicate, so fragile. “Why?” he asked.

“Why do I forgive?”

“Yeah.”

Several *Polizei* arrived from the direction of the university and stopped, cutting off all cars and getting out to approach us. I held out a hand and to my surprise, they froze.

“Because I know what really happened now. It’s bigger than me or you or even Madison. Much bigger,” I said.

“I don’t know what you’re talking about,” said Jake and he shifted his weight forward, just an inch, but it was enough to send my heart rate through the roof.

“Let me tell you then. I just found it all out and I will tell you everything I know,” I said. “I won’t lie or hold anything back.”

“I already know,” he said, and a fresh wave of tears coursed down his face.

“You don’t. You couldn’t, unless you’ve got serious hacking skills. Do you?”

Jake came back an inch and I could see the officers beyond him take a breath and say something in their walkies.

“You have a hacker?”

“Several, actually, and they found out things even Madison doesn’t know,” I said. “Let me tell you about it.”

“Tell me now.”

Crap on a cracker.

“The money wasn’t lost. It was stolen.” Because I had to say something, I said, “We can get it back.”

“Mr. Thooft is still dead,” said Jake.

Did we have to go there?

"Kimberly will forgive you," I said.

"Who?"

"Anton's sister. She wants to know everything and only you can tell her. Surely you can do that for her. She's such a nice person."

"Mr. Thooft was a nice person," said Jake with renewed sobbing.

"It wasn't your fault, but you can still tell her you're sorry," I said. "That's important. You're sorry for what happened to me, aren't you?"

He nodded but couldn't speak.

"You should tell her and your mom."

Jake jolted forward at the mention of his mother and tipped forward. A blast of screams came up from below us. "I can't."

He was going. It was happening.

"Death can't make amends. Only life can do that," I said.

"I can't tell her." He went up on the ball of his foot and was so precarious a stiff wind could've taken him over.

"I'll do it. I'll tell her and make her understand. Then we'll get the money back." I wasn't sure about the money, but at that point, I would've said just about anything.

"Madison said it was gone. My mom's retirement. Everything our dad left us."

"It's not and we know who has it."

Jake focused back on me. "Who?"

"Madison's boyfriend. He used her and stole that money. His name is Sebastian Nadelbaum and he's on a train to Paris right now. We're going to catch him. Please come down and help us."

Just for a second, I thought he was going to go anyway, but then Jake Purcell made the other choice and swung his leg back over the railing. A cheer went up and I ran over wrapping my arms around his thin, shaking body.

"Thank God. Thank God," I said.

"Why do you care?" Jake whispered.

"I couldn't live with it."

He hugged me back and softly said, "I don't know if I can. It's my fault about Mr. Thooft. I told my sister his secret. I did it and now he's dead."

CHAPTER TWENTY-FOUR

It's been my experience that after things are slow, like watching a boy decide whether or not to kill himself, things get really really fast. The *Polizei* were all over us. Yelling and blankets. Traffic and high winds. It was all a rush, blurred beyond belief. Later, I would remember what happened in a fuzzy unreal way, like I dreamt it instead of living through it.

Thank goodness for Moe. I never thought I'd say that, but the old mobster might not call the cops, but he sure knew how to handle them when they showed up. There was talk of arrests and hospitals, but Moe masterfully delayed until Koch showed up on the scene, then he began explaining, saying I was known to the Sindelfingen department. He made it sound like I was authorized to do something and Moe was, too. This was a suicide and we don't arrest people for stopping suicides. The bosses that came onto the scene weren't convinced, but somehow Jake and I got moved into a squad car to watch the conversation in the relative warmth.

I kept my arms around him and I thought he would protest at some point, but he didn't.

"I don't want to go to the hospital," he said.

"You won't," I said.

"You can stop it?"

"I think something will, not necessarily me."

"Was all that stuff you said true?" Jake asked.

"Absolutely." I told him what we'd uncovered and then asked, "Did you meet Nadelbaum?"

Jake shook his head. "I saw him pick her up after she met Mr. Thooft in the café."

"Did that make you suspicious?" I asked. "That you never met him."

"Kinda. Madison said he was a secret because he was older, but he's an asshole. I knew that pretty quick. Madison loved him though."

"When was the last time she saw him?"

"I don't know. Weeks ago. He stopped answering her texts and phone calls. He just disappeared." Jake wiped his tears away and his voice got stronger. "I knew he was a dick. Do you really think he took the money?"

"I'm certain of it," I said. "Tell me what happened."

Jake and I watched the *Polizei* talk to Moe and Koch and then start to clear the traffic as Jake spilled his version of what happened. He was a typical boy and not paying close attention to what was going on around him until it was too late. He was aware that Madison had gotten a boyfriend, but only because his mom was making a big deal out of not meeting him. Madison started lying about the trips to Paris and Prague, saying she was going with friends but then confiding to Jake that it was really the boyfriend who was taking her and paying for everything. She was very impressed with the money and talked about that a lot.

At some point during the summer, Madison started talking about bitcoin and how they could make a ton of money in the market. Mr. Big as she called him was teaching her all about how to invest and she told Jake they should take their college money and put it into bitcoin. Jake said he hadn't really been listening to her up until that point. She liked to talk and he let her, usually while he was gaming or whatever, but when she started talking about taking the college savings out he perked up quick.

"What did you tell her?" I asked.

"I said no freaking way was she doing that," said Jake. "That was all I had for college and I'm not going to risk it like some moron."

"What did she say?"

Jake pursed his lips and said, "She got kinda funny about it. I don't know. It made me nervous, so I told her that if she didn't give it up, I'd tell Mom."

"And that worked?" I asked.

"I thought so. I told her I had the passwords to our accounts and she better not do anything. She just laughed and told me I was right. We couldn't risk the college money." Jake's eyes filled again and said, "I never thought she'd take Mom's money. I mean, Jesus, who does that?"

"I'm sure it was Nadelbaum's idea," I said. "When did you find out?"

"Not until it was all over. I mean, all over all over. Mr. Thooft died and she was hysterical. I couldn't believe it. I freaked. I didn't know what she was doing."

"How did you end up at the café when she was there with Anton?"

Jake took a breath. "I'm so stupid. Madison said she'd get me a computer for SCPs. She knew I wanted to check them out, but Mom blocked the sites on our router, using a firewall. Somebody at work told her they were a bad influence or something."

"So you had to go to the café?"

"Yeah. First, it was at home in Weil der Stadt, but then Madison said that people might see me, so I had to go to Sindelfingen. I didn't really care. I just wanted to work on my stories."

"You never saw Anton there?"

"I wasn't paying attention at first, but then I did see the two of them at a table. I asked her what was going on, but she just said he was helping with her college classes. He did stuff like that." Jake got choked up and said, "He was really nice. I believed her."

"Why do you think she wanted you there?" I asked.

He shrugged. "I don't know. I saw her point at me one time and Mr. Thooft looked upset, but when I asked her, she blew it off."

Outside the squad car, the scene had calmed down. Our cars had been moved to a side street and traffic resumed. The tense discussions had died down, too, but in a way that made me nervous. Jake and I looked out and saw what looked like a very senior cop turn red in the face, stick a finger in Koch's chest, and then do an aboutface to march back to a black Mercedes.

"What do you think is happening?" Jake asked with a quaver in his voice.

"I wish I knew," I said.

"I'm going to get arrested. They should arrest me. I totally freaked out."

"You did, but I think the only harm done was to some cars."

"I hope so. I didn't want to hurt anyone. I just...I saw you and I thought that Mom's going to find out about everything. Madison's a freaking thief and a kind of murderer and what am I going to do. I should've stopped her."

"It wasn't your fault," I said. "Hold on. Here we go."

Koch left Moe haggling with another *Polizei*, trying to get his license and passport back, and came over to our squad car with an expression that was a mixture of confusion and relief. He opened the door and said, "Come on. Let's get you out of here."

"Where are we going?" Jake asked, his voice tremulous.

"Back to the Army post."

We got out and I asked, "What's going on? That was a lot of arguing."

"Yes, it was," said Koch.

"But you're not arresting me or Jake or Moe?"

"We're not. You're free to go."

Jake and I looked at each other. Now I know you shouldn't look a gift horse in the mouth and all that, but sometimes the begged question just has to be answered. "Why not? I don't know how many laws we broke, but it has to be a lot."

"It was, but it came from up high," said Koch. "You're free to go. I'm going to escort you back to the US military and they get to decide what to do with you three. It's out of our hands."

"Really?" I asked.

"Who do you know?"

My mind was a blank and I know it showed because the certain stiffness in Koch's face relaxed. "Somebody put in a word and you get to leave without charges or any problems of any kind. With us anyway."

"Well," I said. "I don't get it, but alright."

"I wish I knew how you pulled it off," said Koch.

"Me, too."

He chuckled and shook his head. "You are trouble and you don't even know what's going on."

"I have some clue but not a lot. Did Moe tell you what we found out?" I asked.

"He did, and I'm not sure what to do with the information since you didn't get it from any legal channel."

"Ah, there's the rub," I said, folding up our blankets and putting them in the squad car.

Moe hurried over and said, "Let's hit the bricks before they change their minds."

"They won't," said Koch, "because they can't."

"Let's not push it." Moe shook Koch's hand. "You're a good man, and I hope this doesn't reflect badly on you."

"You know, I don't think it will. It might actually help me."

"Why? I mean, they know that you know me and I'm not looking so good," I said.

"You are looking connected," said Koch. "And so am I. That doesn't hurt."

We said goodbye and walked down a couple of side streets to get in the Mercedes.

"What about my mom's car?" Jake asked.

"You banged it up pretty good and it was leaking fluids. They're towing it." Moe gave him a card for the towing company.

"I wish I hadn't driven today. Nothing would've happened if I didn't drive."

"The world turns on the small choices," I said, twisting in my seat to look at Jake sitting in the backseat. His eyes were big and scared. "I will explain it to her. She will understand."

"She won't understand about Madison," he said. "I don't."

"What happened to Anton is beyond me, too, but we'll figure it out."

Moe waited for Koch to get to us in his car and I smiled to see who was in the passenger seat. Claudia waved at me. Something good had come out of all this and I held onto that.

We got turned around and entered A81 going the other direction. Traffic, of course, was now backed up on both sides of the road. It couldn't have been that way when we needed it. Oh, no. Of course not.

I turned on my seat heater and got comfortable as we snailed it toward Böblingen.

"Don't forget to send those photos to the Pizza Hut kid," said Moe. "He did you a solid."

I'd totally forgotten about the very helpful Gareth and quickly sent him a thank you with the selfies we took. He was surprised that I meant what I said and was very happy. At least someone was.

That done, I took a breath and said, "Since we have time, Jake..."

"Yeah?" The boy sounded like I was about to hit him on the nose with a newspaper and I smiled over my shoulder at him quickly for reassurance.

"How did you know Anton's secret?" I asked.

"Oh, that," he said with a bit of pride and plenty of regret. "I'm a science guy."

"You lost me, kid," said Moe as we exited A81 toward Waldenbuch and Böblingen. We didn't have long before we reached the post and once we were there, I'd have lost my chance to interview Jake. The Army and his mother would take over.

I twisted around and said, "We'll be there soon. Tell me quick."

Jake pushed back in the seat and clasped his hands in his lap.

"You're not in trouble, but I probably won't get to interview you again before I go to get that douchebag Nadelbaum."

He gave me a hint of a smile and Moe slowed way down. Like his niece, he knew what to do without being asked.

"I want to be a bioengineer or geneticist," said Jake. "I take all the science classes and I always get As."

"I know," I said.

His hands relaxed. "You do?"

"Everyone knows how smart you are."

"Not that smart," his voice filled with pain again.

"Some things aren't about smart. They're about betrayal. Don't get lost in the sauce," I said and that got a smile. "So science showed you his secret?"

Science had and I marveled at how easily Jake Purcell had uncovered a secret that Anton's own family and those around them had missed, but love is like that, I guess. It blinds you to the obvious. Jake didn't love Kimberly or know her at all, so he could see her, but he couldn't see his sister and what she was doing.

It was all about the face Jake told me. Anton had pictures of his family on his desk, the ones I'd found under the blotter. Jake had found them when he was cleaning the room. Anton gave extra credit for cleaning up and Jake always did all the extra credit in case he didn't get his A the regular way. He was very thorough, he assured me. Nobody else really was. He Lysoled the desk and there they were. Jake recognized at once that it was odd that the pictures weren't framed or pinned to a board like the other teachers' family photos. In science, you look for patterns or things that are missing that shouldn't be missing.

"Like a detective," I said, and his smile grew. Science. He was comfortable again.

Jake came back to those pictures over and over again, looking for the reason they were there. He and Anton were close. They talked every day and Jake considered him a friend, so he'd heard all about Kimberly and her wonderful voice. He knew about the love in the family that was supposed to be so close so why were they under the blotter?

After closer examination, Kimberly's face told him that she didn't match. Jake knew about genetics. There should've been some commonality between the siblings but there just wasn't any. He took pictures of the pictures and studied them at home on his computer, analyzing the bone structure, height, and coloring. He knew Kimberly wasn't a blonde right away. Her skin tone wasn't right for it and so the boy concluded that Kimberly was either adopted or Anton's mom had had an affair. Jake wasn't bothered by either conclusion. He just wanted to know if he was right and he worked on Anton until he figured it out or at least he thought he had. He concluded that adoption wasn't shameful and an affair was, so it was an affair. Through many conversations Anton got the picture that his favorite student knew the secret, even though Jake never came out and said it.

We stopped at the last light before the post and Moe asked, "He wasn't mad?"

"He was kinda freaked at first, but then he was okay. He told me once that it was nice to be known when you've never been known before," said Jake. "But I never knew the real truth that his mom had traded his brother for Kimberly. That's crazy."

"How long ago did you figure it out?" I asked.

"About a year ago." Jake's voice got quieter. "I told Madison about it. I thought I was so smart. I didn't know she'd hurt him with it."

"Do you think that's what she did?" I asked. "She threatened to tell people about Kimberly?"

Jake didn't answer and we arrived at the gate with Koch right behind us. I got out my pass, expecting to be turned away, troublemaker that I was, but the guard didn't say anything. He checked the IDs and my pass and waved us through.

I turned around to wave at Koch. Claudia waved back happily and kissed Koch's cheek before they did a U-turn and went back the way they came. On the other side of the gate was a military police car. An MP stood beside it and signaled for us to follow him. We did and drove slowly through the post that was exactly the way it was before. I don't know why I expected it to be different, but I did.

"Did she tell you that she threatened Anton with the truth?" Moe asked.

"Yeah, but I didn't really believe her," said Jake. "I mean, I think she did that, but it was like she knew something else, too."

"Any idea what?" I asked.

"She wouldn't tell me." Jake came up between the front seats. "She thought she was going to get a bunch of money for kidnapping you. Did you know that?"

"I figured," I said. "What did she say when I got away and Anton died?"

"She was totally freaking out. I don't think she thought anything bad would happen."

"She had Mercy thrown in a trunk so she could be sold," hissed Moe.

"I know. I don't understand it. She was crying about Mr. Thooft and she was crying about the money and just crying all the time. That's when she told me and I knew it was my fault for telling her Mr. Thooft's secret. She couldn't have done it without me." Jake touched my hand. "I'm so sorry."

"I forgive you," I said. "I really do."

"Do you think he would forgive me?"

"From what Kimberly has told me, Anton would."

He squeezed my hand. "Why do you call him Anton and not asshole or something? He hurt you pretty bad."

"When I started investigating he became a real person and a victim, too," I said.

"Do you forgive him?"

"I'm working on it."

We walked into the MP station and the first person we saw was Hobbes. The big marine was pacing back and forth in front of the front desk, looking like a grenade with a pin about to be pulled.

"Hey," I said.

He looked up, saw Jake, and ran over to grab the boy up, smothering him in that great big chest. "Thank God. Thank God."

"You really care?" Jake asked.

"My man, I care so much I'm about to go crazy," said Hobbes and he looked over Jake as if he expected to find an arrow sticking out of his back or something. "You're okay? I mean physically."

"Yeah," said Jake shyly.

"Were you really going to do it?" Hobbes asked bluntly.

The boy didn't hesitate. "I think so. I was planning it before I saw her and then it all exploded."

I admired the honesty, naked and right out there as much as it hurt to see a kid say that.

Hobbes hugged him again and asked, "Is that why you had the car? You don't usually drive."

"I was going to Obi for rope."

"Jesus, you can talk to me. I'm here for you."

"The last teacher I talked to got killed," Jake said simply.

"That's not your fault," said Hobbes.

"It kinda is, but I didn't mean it to happen. Is my mom here?"

Lisa Purcell was there. The MPs and Hobbes had told her what they knew, which wasn't much. Jake was safe and that was the most important thing.

An MP interrupted and said that they were working on the accidents that Jake caused and he had to surrender his license. He did and kind of seemed relieved about it. Less ability to get rope, I guess.

"He needs serious counseling," I said.

"I'm a licensed therapist," said Hobbes, turning to Jake. "You can tell me anything and I won't say a word."

"I already told her everything," said Jake.

"Do you feel better?"

"I think so. What did Madison say?"

Madison had said nothing. She was in the wind as my dad would say. Gone and not responding to calls or texts. The *Polizei* were looking for her in case she was looking for an overpass herself, but I didn't think that was her goal. She was probably looking for Sebastian Nadelbaum, the cause of everything and the only port in the storm she helped to create.

"Are you ready to see your mom?" Hobbes asked.

Jake moved closer to me and said, "Yeah. How mad is she?"

"Scared more than mad."

"Did you tell her what you know?" I asked.

"I gave her the broad strokes, but she didn't believe me," said Hobbes.

"Of course, she didn't," said Jake. "Madison's her favorite. She'll think it's my fault."

I took his arm. "She won't when she knows the truth."

Jake got glum and then said, "Okay. Let's go."

The MP held up his hand. "CID are here."

Jake's eyes went wide. "Why are they here? I thought I was just losing my license?"

"What's CID?" I asked.

"Criminal Investigation Division," said Hobbes. "Don't worry. They had to come. There were crimes committed."

"Not by me," said Jake and his voice got tight.

I put my arm around him. "No, not by you. I will handle it."

"Yeah?"

"Promise."

Just then a pair of men wearing blue windbreakers with badges printed on them came through the doors. Every federal law enforcement branch seemed to have those jackets. The government must've got a hell of a discount. The men inside the jackets were government issue, too. Clean-shaven, boring hair, and stern expressions. All so familiar. They could've been the FBI and the thought made me inwardly groan. I was never going to get free of their sort.

They flashed badges and introduced themselves. I wasn't really listening. It all just got more complicated and would take forever as all government-run things did.

"We will be interviewing you separately," said the lead. "Miss Watts, this way."

Jake leaned into me and I held him tighter. Hobbes got on the other side of Jake to make a united front.

"That's a hard pass," I said.

"Are you declining to be interviewed?"

"Nailed it."

"Why?"

"Because she promised to stay with me," said Jake, sounding stronger than I expected.

"We could skip the interviews and go straight to arrests," the CID agent said.

"Me or him?" I asked.

"Both."

"He's seventeen and a witness."

"To what?"

"Conspiracy, for starters," I said.

"He can tell us all about it in his interview," said the agent.

"No. I have to talk to my mom," said Jake. "And Mercy's staying with me or I won't tell you anything."

Look at you kicking ass.

"I'd listen to him," I said. "He's a fount of information."

"How are you involved in all this?"

"I'm the victim."

Both agents crossed their arms and the second one said, "We were told you were here investigating."

"The two aren't mutually exclusive," I said.

"I wouldn't be so snotty if I were you," said the lead. "You used illegal means to investigate."

"Says who? I came to investigate my own crime because nobody else was. I asked questions. I got a lead. That took me to a café where Anton Thooft was extorted and blackmailed into kidnapping me. That led me to Jake here and the truth. You could've done that, but you didn't. Don't cry about it now."

Both agents swallowed hard, probably to keep from yelling at me. My mother would've been appalled at my impolite behavior and Dad wouldn't be thrilled, either. He was always more charming than me. He'd have made friends. I wanted to kick them in the junk and get the hell out of there.

"We need to interview you separately," said the lead.

"Jake needs to tell his mother what happened," I said. "We have no objection to you hearing it."

"The FBI international unit is on its way."

"The more the merrier."

That took them back for about three seconds, but they came back swinging.

"You have compromised this investigation with illegal tactics and you will be charged."

I laughed. "What investigation?"

"Our chances of a conviction of our suspect are materially damaged."

"You don't have a suspect," I said. "Go ahead. Tell me who got Madison Purcell to do everything. Who is it? Enlighten me."

Oh, they hated me so hard and I did enjoy it. Not a good angel moment, but I was tired, and yet another headache was blooming in my brain.

"What you got can't be used against those parties."

"How come?" Jake asked. "She knows stuff. You don't."

The agents gritted their teeth and then the lead said, "As an agent of law enforcement, Miss Watts can't use illegal means to get information."

"I'm not an agent of anything, except myself and my client, who is Kimberly Thooft Stackhouse by the way."

"As a consultant for the FBI—"

"Hold the phone," I said. "I'm not a consultant for those douchebags. That's my dad."

They frowned and checked their phones. "We were told you are on the FBI payroll and that's how you got out of the *Polizei's* grip."

"Nope. My dad's been angling for a consultant's fee, but I dipped on it and came here instead."

"Why would you do that?"

"Because they wanted me to have a bunch of chats with serial killers. The last time I played that card, I got bit on the face." I indicated my scar.

"Dude, you are badass," said Jake.

"If I was badass, I wouldn't have been bit on the face, but let's not quibble," I said. "Take us to his mom. I've got a headache and I need coffee in a huge way."

"We want everything," said the lead.

"He'll give you everything." *I won't.*

The lead took a breath, and I could see him thinking about how this was against the rules or regulations or whatever. That fought against getting the job done. A pretty good tug of war or so I've been told. Rules have never been my thing.

"Alright," he said at long last and turned to the MP, who was fascinated by the exchange. "Where is the mother?"

"Right this way," he said, and I turned to call for Moe, but my bodyguard was yakking it up with a couple of younger MPs. He'd pulled his VFW hat out of somewhere and popped it on. They were discussing a sniper's life in-country and I decided to leave him to it. The old guy was having a ball.

Jake, Hobbes, and I followed the MP through a warren of hallways to a plain door with a placard that said occupied. He knocked and opened the door. Before I could blink, Lisa Purcell was slobbering all over her son and momming it up real good. It was work to get them back in the interview room, but the CID did a good job of it.

Lisa tried to pull Jake to the other side of the narrow table in the center of the room where a cup of coffee was sitting with her purse, but the boy pushed her off and got back to me.

"What is she doing here?" Lisa demanded with a red face and swollen eyes. "It's her fault we're here. My son could've been killed."

I pulled out a chair and resisted the urge to Bogart her coffee, germs be damned. "Your son has been suicidal for weeks. Please, sit down and we'll tell you everything."

"You chased him." She pointed at Hobbes. "He said...he said..."

Hobbes went around the table to take Lisa's shaking hand. "I said that Jake was suicidal and running. She went after him. The news said she talked him down." The counselor looked at Jake, who was pale as paper, and asked, "Is that true?"

"Yeah. I was totally going to jump."

"Why?" Lisa wailed. "I don't understand what's happening."

The CID agents moved in and got her calmed down with the help of Hobbes, but she still said, "It's her fault you almost died. If she hadn't come here..."

"I was going to do it anyway," said Jake softly. "Because of what happened to Mr. Thooft."

"That's got nothing to do with you."

Jake looked at me and I said, "Madison blackmailed him into coming after me. Your son figured it out and it's been tearing him apart." I told her the timeline and the CID took notes and recorded me. I think they expected me to object, but I couldn't have cared less.

"It's not true," said Lisa. "Madison wouldn't do any of that. She only had that boyfriend for a little while. A month at most."

"It was a lot longer than that, Mom," said Jake.

"She would not do those things. She's just a kid."

"I don't think it was her idea, but she did do it," I said.

Lisa scoffed. "You really think my daughter stole her father's SGLI money? You must be nuts."

"She did," said Jake.

His mother pointed at him and yelled, "Do not lie!"

Jake shuddered and I grabbed his hand under the table. "Check your account. It's empty."

"How do you know?" the CID lead asked.

"A little bird told me," I said.

"Illegal—"

"I told her," said Jake.

"Jake," said Lisa. "Don't protect her. Don't lie."

"I'm not lying."

He was lying his face off and I loved him for it. The pleasure of seeing the sucking lemon expressions on the agents' faces was enough to make my headache better. No coffee required.

"Seriously," I said. "Check your account."

"It's utterly ridiculous," said Lisa.

"Madison stole the money, Mom," said Jake. "She was going to steal our college funds, but I told her that I knew the codes for our accounts and I'd tell you if she did."

"Oh, my God," said Lisa. "So she took Dad's money."

"I didn't think of that. I would've stopped her if I had." The boy got teared up. "You can't retire now. I'm so sorry, but Mercy's going to try to get it back."

"Are you now?" asked the CID lead.

"Somebody has to," I said. "What are you going to do?"

"We will follow the law."

"Awesome. I'll follow the criminal and we'll see who gets there first."

He muttered something unintelligible under his breath and Hobbes suppressed a smile before saying, "You should check your account, Lisa. To confirm."

Lisa got her phone out and in a matter of minutes did just that. Then through sobs, she called her daughter, who still wasn't answering. The CID started asking questions and although Jake was upset he answered everything, but he didn't let out the name. Sebastian Nadelbaum was mine and he knew it on instinct or maybe he just didn't like the CID. That was also possible.

It took quite a while to go through everything twice, which the agents insisted on. I did get some coffee. It was terrible, but I was desperate.

"What was the point of all this?" asked the lead. "What do you think Anton was going to do with you?"

"I don't really know, but it has something to do with The Klinefeld Group," I said.

"Who?"

I explained about the Bleds' issues with the not-for-profit group, but they weren't convinced until I brought up Lester's murder. That got them on their phones to check it out and were quickly shocked to find I was telling the truth.

"The group was never charged," said the second agent.

"Nope. They're good. I'll give them that."

"If they could pull that off, why use a high school teacher to do this?"

"This wasn't their idea," I said.

Lisa stood up. "I have to go home. She won't answer. Maybe she left a note."

"We're not done, ma'am," said the lead.

Hobbes stood up and put a big hand on Lisa's shoulder. "You have enough for now, don't you? They're not going anywhere."

I am.

"Yes, time to go," I said. "Jake needs to talk to his counselor, I'm sure."

"Definitely," said Hobbes. "I've got the rest of the day and we're going to work through everything you're ready to discuss."

Jake nodded and stood up.

"Hold on," said the lead and his partner showed him his phone. Neither was happy and they both glared at me.

"You haven't given us a name," said the lead.

"What name?" I asked with batting eyelashes.

"Don't give me that," he said. "You know who the boyfriend is." He turned on Jake. "Or he does."

Lisa came around the table and grabbed her son. "Don't you talk to him like that. It's not his fault."

"She called him Mr. Big," said Jake.

"Like *Sex in the City*?" Lisa asked. "Gross."

I had to agree, but that wasn't going to be enough. The agents were looking pretty shifty and I had to tell them something to get out of there. Novak's train would be arriving in Gare de l'Est any minute.

"I suggest you talk to The Klinefeld Group," I said. "Unless I miss my guess, he's an employee or contractor for them."

I described Nadelbaum, but they weren't soothed.

"That could be anybody and if they did what you claim they're not going to tell us anything," said the lead.

"You know..." said Jake.

Don't do it. Don't do it.

"How about we go and get you home," I said, and the agents lit up, smelling a withheld clue.

"It's cool, Mercy," said Jake. "They're going to find out."

He squeezed my arm and I had to trust him. "Go ahead then."

"Madison did call him something else one time. It might be his name. I don't know."

The agents leaned forward and I have to admit, I did too. Where in the heck was Jake going?

"What was it?" asked the lead.

"Evergreen," said Jake with satisfaction.

Holy crap! Good call.

"Evergreen?" I said, faking bewilderment. "I guess that could be a name."

"Or a code," said the second agent. "Anything else?"

Jake shrugged. "Nope. It was just the one time and I didn't ask her about it."

The agents conferred about the name and we went for the door. I expected protests at the very least, but they just let us leave, hustling out as fast as we could.

Moe was still in the same spot with a bigger audience, holding them enthralled with a description of the Mekong Delta. He had a way with words and I wanted to hear what happened. We all did, but then he saw me, and said, "Oh, Mercy. All done?"

"For the moment," I said. "Go ahead."

Moe finished his story and I'm not going to lie, it was gruesome. I wished I hadn't heard it. His words made me think of Grandad's scarred back and I tried never to think about that.

"You have to write it all down," said one of the MPs.

"I might just do that," said Moe. "Thanks for listening."

They all shook his hand. Brothers in arms. Different generations but still the same in a way. We walked out and Moe chuffed Jake on the shoulder. "So you did alright and your mom hasn't lost her marbles."

"I don't know about that," said Lisa. "What do we do now?"

"Ask Mercy," said Moe. "She's the girl with a plan."

"Actually, I don't pl—"

"Mercy can find her," said Jake. "You find her and then find that dirtbag. Or find the dirtbag and find Madison. They'll be together, won't they?"

"But all you have is Evergreen," said Lisa.

"Get a grip, Mom." Jake rolled his eyes.

"You lied to CID?" She put her head in her hands. "I don't know what they'll do to you."

"Nothing," I said. "He didn't lie. The name is Evergreen."

"Is it?" Moe asked.

"If you translate it."

Jake grinned at me. "Pretty good, huh?"

"Excellent," I said. "Your son has serious smarts."

"It's not working out for me," said Lisa. "They're both smart and look where we are."

Jake took his mom's hand and said, "We're going to get that guy and Madison, too."

"She's not going to go to him. He ruined her life."

"But she doesn't know he set her up," I said. "She thinks the loss was a trick of the market. She'll go to him if she can." My phone buzzed and I glanced at the screen. Novak. "Pulling up to the station."

"We don't know where she is," said Lisa. "I've been calling and calling. The *Polizei* said her car is gone."

"We know where she is," said Moe.

"She could be going to Paris," I said. "That's where he is."

"You know that?" Lisa asked.

"We do. Madison might know as well."

"Let's see, shall we?" Moe took out his phone, pressed a few buttons and said, "Would you look at that. Heading for Paris." He held up his phone to show a map with a red dot moving along a highway.

"What in the world is that?" I asked.

"I put a tracker on her car."

"When?"

"After we tailed her to Pizza Hut. You were talking to the coworker and I snapped a device on. I figured she'd book it at some point. Why make things difficult?"

Lisa grabbed the phone. "She's not that far. What are all the points?"

Moe took back the phone. "Looks like she was looking for him in Stuttgart. She drove to two apartment buildings and a couple of bars. Now she's on the A8."

"You are a genius," I said.

"I learned from the best," said Moe with a grin that made me think of a pirate. He only lacked the eyepatch. "Let's have the *Polizei* grab her up."

"Yes." Lisa looked frantically around for a car, but hers had been towed.

"No," said Jake. "She's going to that guy. We should follow her."

"We're going to Paris one way or the other," I said to Lisa. "As for Madison, it's your call. The *Polizei* could get her in a matter of minutes."

Lisa thought for a moment. "She's going to him and he's in Paris..."

"He is," I said. "But we've got people on him already, so—"

"No, you don't," said Moe.

"What?"

"Call Novak."

I checked my phone and saw a text. "He got past us."

"What the—" I called Novak and my exhausted hacker answered with an apology. "Sorry. The bastard jumped off the train."

"Well, then he's dead," I said. "It was high speed."

Novak sighed. "No, unfortunately. He pulled an emergency door when we were coming into the station and jumped out. Low risk. A man matching his description was seen running on the tracks. It's my fault. I fell asleep. I texted you and looked for him when I woke up, but he was gone."

"He's got a few skills," I said.

"We will get him. Where are you?"

I told him about Jake and our interview.

"You've got the mother?"

"Yeah," I said. "Why?"

"Does she like you?"

I looked at Lisa. "Do you like me?"

"I haven't decided," said Lisa with total honesty.

"Mom!" exclaimed Jake. "She's helping."

"I'm okay in her book," I told Novak.

"Get her to search the house for that burner."

"Now you're cookin' with gas," I said.

"You've spent too much time with old people," said Novak.

"You are not wrong, but that's been my whole life." I hung up and said, "We lost him in Paris. What's your decision?"

Lisa took a breath and held tight onto her son. "I want that bastard. Follow her."

"Can you do me a huge favor?"

"Anything."

"Madison had a burner phone to talk to him with," I said. "I need you two to search the house for it while we go to Paris."

I could tell that was a struggle. She wanted to go and be there to see Madison and possibly to strangle Nadelbaum, but Jake convinced her to go home.

"Alright," she said and turned to Hobbes. "Can you give us a ride?"

"Absolutely and for the record, it's what I would do," said Hobbes.

"What do we do if we find the phone?" Jake asked.

"Plug it in, turn it on, and have it use your Wi-Fi," I said.

"That's it?" Lisa asked.

"We'll do the rest."

"You really are doing the stuff the CID thinks," said Lisa. "I wasn't sure. It seemed so high tech."

"I don't have to be high tech to know high-tech people," I said. "Now we've got a plan."

I looked at Moe and he said, "Execute."

So we executed as fast as we could and in a Mercedes, that's pretty damn fast.

CHAPTER TWENTY-FIVE

We caught up with Madison just before crossing the border at Strasbourg. I wasn't sure we would, since she had a good head start. But Moe and I jumped into the car and were zipping along the A8 in no time. We had a shot and I was feeling pretty good until I wasn't.

"Um...Moe?" I asked.

"We'll get her. Don't worry," he said with his moist eyes pinned to the road.

"We left Grandma and Aaron at the school."

For a scary second, I thought he was going to slam it into reverse or do a U-turn. He did start doing deep breathing and announced we would be getting off at the next exit.

"We can't," I said. "We'll lose her."

"Then we'll lose her. I'm not leaving Janine. She's been left enough."

I'm not gonna lie. My heart seized up a little at that, but we were on a job.

"I'll fix it with her."

He growled and I got to work. It wasn't easy. I had a feisty grandmother to contend with and one that had never seen Paris thanks to that grandfather of mine. I noticed that Grandad was getting lower on her list, not higher. Moe was looking good, tracking down Jake and not getting a scratch on the Mercedes in the process. I did everything I could to convince her that they should stay in Stuttgart, pack up, and get on the direct train tomorrow, but she wasn't buying.

I argued that all her products, i.e. Noxzema, were in the hotel and that woman did not want to be seen in the City of Lights without good skin and lipstick. We didn't have time to go to the hotel.

"What about all your clothes and your laptop?" Grandma asked. "You'll look like a mess."

I didn't care what I looked like and it was a good thing, too. The wind on the overpass had swirled my hair so bad I looked like a used Q-tip.

"It's fine. You can pack it up."

"I'm not missing out on the big get," she said stubbornly.

That's when it came to me. "But what about Anton's cat? We can't leave the cat."

That did it. Vanity zero. Fat tuxedo for the win.

"Alright, fine," she said. "I will get that health certificate thing and pack up Aaron and Isolda."

"Isolda?" I asked.

"You don't think she wants to miss out, do you?"

"Guess not. See you tomorrow." I turned to Moe. "She's saving the American meow from abandonment in a foreign country."

"You got lucky," said Moe, still unhappy, but he whipped out a small black device and booted it up.

"Radar detector?" I asked.

"And so much more."

"Illegal?"

"What do you think?" he asked.

"If we get caught after everything else—"

"What will happen? Nothing. You've got friends, remember," said Moe.

"I can't think who. The CID wanted to know who intervened, but I have no idea. It wasn't the FBI. They hate me hard right now. Mom said the agents I met were seething."

"Their own fault. They should've known not to test you." Moe zigzagged through cars with ease and we got up to a good 160 KPH, blowing by everyone through the eighty zones that the Swabians were famous for. Flipping slowpokes. The speed limits opened up after we got out of the Baden-Württemberg region and Moe was truly enjoying himself.

"They've gotten me to do things before," I said.

"When it was in your own best interest."

"You make me sound totally self-involved."

"When it comes to psycho serial killers you get to be," he said.

"I like you," I said.

He grinned. "Fats knew we'd be a good match. Have you talked to her lately?"

"Texted before it all broke loose this morning. She's good and getting jazzed about the five-month ultrasound."

"Ah, yes. Going to find out the sex."

"Don't have to," I said. "She's sure it's a girl."

"She was supposed to be a boy. We Licatas never like to be predictable," he said. "Check the app. Let's see how our girl is doing."

Madison was doing just fine, pointing like an arrow right at Paris, and we settled in for a long drive. I thought it would be boring, but Licatas didn't do boring, either. We plotted out Uncle Moe's memoir of Vietnam and I have to say that's not usually my thing, but I was totally buying that book.

An hour later, we saw Madison's Kia and Moe pulled up behind her, leaving only a crappy Fiat between us.

"We shouldn't get so close," I said.

"She's never going to spot us," he said. "Leave the driving to the expert."

"Snotty."

"Cupcake."

"I will fight you," I said.

"Haven't we just been talking about hand to hand in Vietnam?"

"Never mind."

"That's what I thought," said Moe.

We drove over the Rhine river and directly into Strasbourg but not the picturesque part with the cathedral. We looped around in a big half-moon following signs for Paris.

"Nothing to see here," said Moe. "I was hoping to spot the spires at least."

"We're not that close," I said.

"Maybe on the way back."

"I doubt we're coming back."

"No?"

"Everything we need is in Paris."

He smiled. "I bet a lot of people have thought that."

"Madison included," I said.

"Your phone is buzzing."

I checked the screen and it was Lisa. Even her texts came across as frantic, so I called her.

"Everything's fine," I said.

"You still have her?"

"Right in front of us."

She took a ragged breath. "I should've come with you. I don't know what I was thinking about."

"Your son, for starters," I said. "It's fine. I will handle it and Madison will be fine. Did you find the phone?"

"We did. Well, Jake did. It wasn't until we stripped the bed that Jake noticed some foam sticking out of the mattress. She'd cut a hole in it and the phone was in there."

"Did you plug it in?" I asked.

"We had to find a cord that fit. It was dead and the service lapsed. I re-upped it about forty-five minutes ago. I should've called you before, but the MPs showed up."

"Everything okay?"

"They want to know where you went?"

"Did you tell them?" I asked.

"Not a chance. What now?"

"I'll tell my guy and we'll see what we can see. Thanks, Lisa."

I was about to hang up, but she asked, "What if he's violent?"

I glanced at Moe and found I wasn't worried about that in the slightest. "We can handle Nadelbaum."

"I'm so worried. He could shoot you or Madison."

"We could shoot him and frankly that's more likely," I said.

"Is it?"

I thought about Richard Costilla as he tumbled backward down the stairs. "Google me," I said.

"I did. It's mostly bikini shots."

"Most of those aren't me."

"Really?"

"I can handle myself and Moe can handle anything twice over," I said.

She took a breath and said, "Okay. Call me right away when something happens."

I promised her and called Novak immediately, but it wasn't necessary and I should've known that.

"Got it," he said.

"The burner?"

"The second it got on the Wi-Fi and we're in luck. He's both a bastard and a cheap bastard."

"Still using his same burner?" I asked, giving Moe a thumbs-up.

"It's not a burner. Well, the first phone he used with Madison wasn't. Looks like he changed to a burner after he stole the money. That one isn't accessible, but the first phone is still live."

"Tell me he's on it right now."

"He is not, but I've got all the data. The contract is under Sherwood Dankworth."

"You're joking," I said. "That is a terrible name."

"And fake, but with a sizable history. Sherwood's been busy. It's going to take a while to unravel this, but it looks like Nadelbaum, that is his real name, was running some kind of Ponzi scheme and may have taken a very wrong turn."

"What do you mean by that?"

"You know how you wouldn't want to steal hundreds of thousands of dollars from Calpurnia Fibonacci?"

"Dude *is* in trouble," I said. "Who did he steal from?"

"I'm not positive, but I think it was The Klinefeld Group."

I gasped. No joking. I really did. Moe glanced over. “Everything okay?”

“I was a trade, a get out of jail free card,” I said.

“Looks like it,” said Novak. “Nadelbaum was an employee of the group, a kind of contract player. He’d been with them for years, working in several capacities, including security and finance. He’s also a licensed pilot under the name Dankworth.”

“He was one of the two men at the airport waiting for me.”

“Reasonable to assume,” said Novak. “I have been poking around in his rancid little life and he’s got some computer skills, but I doubt he was the one who put the plants on Anton’s computer. My money is on his wingman. He’s based in Berlin. No name yet.”

“Do you think Spidermonkey can...steal Lisa’s money back?” I asked.

Novak chuckled. “He can do anything.”

“I love you guys.”

“You should, considering what you’ve put me through,” he said, suddenly very grumpy.

“I am sorry about your head,” I said.

“Not my head. My mother. So far, I’ve been soaked in some kind of medicinal bubble bath, had my hair trimmed, and got half my wardrobe thrown out.”

“Which part of that is bad?”

“All of it. Express sympathy or you may never see that money,” said Novak.

“Your mother is evil and must be stopped,” I said.

“And you will have dinner with her and tell her I’m a fabulous boyfriend.”

“Er...”

“This is still free if you do.”

“I think I’d rather pay,” I said.

He gave me my total cost.

“What time’s dinner?”

“I’ll let you know.”

“Swell.”

I hung up and heaved a sigh. “Now I’m having dinner with Novak’s mother.”

“I saw that coming from a mile away,” said Moe.

“You should’ve shared that with me.”

“And miss seeing your face? Never.”

I wadded up my coat and leaned against the door. “You kinda suck.”

“I’m awesome and you know it.”

“Keep dreaming,” I said.

“About Janine,” he said.

“Stop it!”

Moe laughed and put on classical music. “Go to sleep, cupcake. Four hours to go and then it’s back to detecting.”

I closed my eyes, thinking I couldn’t possibly sleep with the image of Moe and Grandma smiling at each other imprinted in my brain, but I did and it was a good thing, too.

CHAPTER TWENTY-SIX

I woke up hours later when Moe gave me a hard jab in the hip and said, "Look at that. It's the Seine."

"Exciting." I sat up and yawned. "Are we there?"

"I don't know where there is," Moe yawned with his whole body and I took a good look.

"You should've woken me up," I said. "You needed a break."

"I like driving and you like sleeping."

Not wrong there.

"You look exhausted," I said.

"This is nothing. Remember that march I told you about?" Moe asked.

"I'm trying to forget it."

"We all are."

Moe's face grew more weary and I didn't know what to say so I looked out ahead of us. There was Madison zipping along.

"She never stopped?"

"Once for gas, but you didn't wake up," he said. "She's getting nervous though."

"How can you tell?" I asked.

"The driving's getting more erratic. She keeps changing lanes, speeding up and then slowing down."

"She's probably exhausted."

He nodded. "She's been on her phone, but not for long. I think she's been trying to call Nadelbaum."

I searched for my phone and found it on the charger. "Thanks. I didn't think of that."

"It's been going off. Spidermonkey and Novak. I told them you were asleep."

"What did they find out?" I asked.

Plenty was the answer. Nadelbaum had taken company funds from The Klinefeld Group and used it to pay off investors in his Ponzi scheme. There were still plenty of investors screaming bloody murder, but Nadelbaum wasn't worried about them. He'd borrowed a large unspecified amount and guess what? The Klinefeld Group noticed. Promises were made and not kept. Nadelbaum had stolen Lisa's money, but he didn't use it to pay off his debt. It was still sitting in a bitcoin wallet.

"I don't get it," I said. "What was the plan?"

Moe shrugged. "They can't tell. He kept giving The Klinefeld Group promises and working unpaid, flying them around and chauffeuring."

"While hatching a stupid plot to kidnap me."

"It could've worked. It would've worked if you hadn't been you and Thooft had tied you up."

"He tried," I said. "The cast was the problem."

He smiled. "I didn't know that. Who would've thought an entire plot taken down by a cast?"

"A lot of variables and Anton panicked."

"And Madison's another variable," said Moe as we exited the highway. "Where do you think we're going?"

"Beats me, but she clearly has a plan," I said as we drove through a complicated set of streets to the Bastille area. We ended up on a wide avenue, watching Madison pull into a small parking garage across from a really cool church that I'd never seen before. It had the pre-revolution style I liked, all curves with a big dome and a red door.

"We have to go in that church," said Moe.

"We have to park," I said. "But we can't go in there. She's not that oblivious."

"I'll wait a minute." Moe waved other drivers around our car. "You get out and tail her, just in case she's speedy. No fiking."

"No problem." I got out and shivered at the cold. I'd gotten too used to my lovely heated seat. Moe drove into the parking garage and I dashed over to a clothing store to casually look in the window while I pulled my poofball hat down low.

It took a few minutes, but Madison was out and moving down the street at a good clip. Her phone wasn't out. She knew where she was going and I had to nearly break into a jog to keep up with her long legs while texting Moe our direction.

After walking several blocks, we ended up in a residential area on a one-way street. There wasn't much to recommend it, a couple of restaurants, one was shuttered, and a small hotel. It was not touristy, but the buildings were old and a few had the typical Parisian ironwork on the small balconies.

I thought Madison would go into the hotel, but she turned to a small set of wooden doors opposite. On second thought, they weren't really small in a normal sense, only small for Paris with big brass knobs in the center of each door and encased in some nice stonework.

Madison peered at a panel next to the door and I crossed the street to the hotel. They had their prices on a placard next to the door under a certificate of excellence from Tripadviser. I pretended to study it and texted my location to Moe while keeping a side-eye on Madison who had chosen a button and pushed it repeatedly. Nobody answered and she chose another button. This time someone answered and I could make out Madison asking in rudimentary French if they knew Sebastian Nadelbaum. Since she pushed another button, I guess the answer was no. There had to be a reason Madison was there and thought Nadelbaum would be, too, so I googled the address.

"Oh, Madison," I whispered.

Moe arrived at my side and handed over my purse. "What's she doing?"

"Getting a wake-up call."

"I imagine so but give me the skinny."

I gestured with my head and said, "I think she thinks he has an apartment there."

"Spidermonkey didn't mention any property," said Moe.

"It's an Airbnb."

"That pretty little fool."

The pretty little fool kept pushing buttons until a woman dressed for a party came out. Madison chased her down the street, pelting her with questions and getting an irritated shake of the head before the woman dashed away. Madison stood on the sidewalk with her arms limp at her side.

"Do you want to talk to her?" Moe asked.

"Let's see what she does," I said and on cue, Madison took off with a purposeful walk and after a couple of turns, I knew where she was going.

We were well into dusk when we walked into the square where the Bastille once stood. There were only some stones marking the perimeter to disappoint the unknowing tourist who expected a prison. There was also a metro stop and that's where Madison was going. We followed her at a decent distance, but she never once looked back at us or at her surroundings. If Nadelbaum knew anything, he hadn't taught it to her.

The station was an outdoor one and super easy to access and see everything. Madison checked a map and then her phone. I was close enough to see her using a metro app, but I couldn't tell what our destination was. She bought a ticket and we did too. I was getting closer and closer to her. I guess I just wanted to see if she would notice. In a way, I wanted it to be over so I could start asking questions and tell her mother we had her.

But Madison took no notice of me, walking right onto the train car directly behind her. It was pretty packed, but I mean, come on, who stands out more than Moe Licata. Half the car was looking at him, but not Madison. She was in her own world with a deep frown on her face and clenched fists.

We traveled on two different lines to end up at the Abbesses metro stop in Montmartre where Madison got off and bypassed the elevators to climb the long spiral stairs up to the street. Moe was not thrilled. I thought he would love the gorgeous paintings on the curved walls, but it was hard to get a good look with all the people and he was getting more and more tired. If I could've left him behind to rest, I would've.

He was muttering as Madison picked up speed and squeezed past hordes of people coming through the station's narrow entrance after a day's work. She cleared the beautiful Art Nouveau structure and I expected her to dash off to be lost in the crowd while I waited for Moe, who'd gotten stuck behind a woman with three children and a pile of Christmas shopping.

But Madison didn't dash off. She stood next to the carousel all decked out for Christmas and wrapped her arms around herself as the children went round and round. We were right in the middle of a Christmas market. Stalls crowded the small area, selling everything from nougat cut off huge blocks to Christmas ornaments.

"Churros," said Moe as he came gasping up beside me. "I need a churro."

"I need a bathroom," I said.

"And a comb. What is going on with your hair?"

I reached up and sure enough, the part that had come out under my hat had gone all frizzy. "It doesn't like Paris."

"Your hair has an opinion?"

"Always." I stuffed it up in my hat and Moe nodded approval. "You should talk to Fats. She could fix it."

"I know, but this particular thing is only in Paris," I said.

Moe wasn't buying that, but he said, "How long do you think she'll—"

Madison was off again. She had her phone out and it was giving her directions rather loudly. Very tourist. She rushed past a stand done up like a train that had the most wonderful smell coming from it.

Moe groaned. "I'll catch up."

"They're chestnuts," I said.

"Dammit. Why do they smell good and taste like grainy—"

"Pus?"

"God no," he said. "Why would you say that? Now I'm thinking about it. Oh God I can taste it."

"Bet you're not hungry anymore," I said.

"Bet you still have to pee. Waterfalls. Dripping faucets."

"Shut up."

"You shut up."

We followed Madison through the colorful streets of Montmartre, passing everything from shops selling all their food in pitas to a funky vintage store that I longed to shop in but in which nothing would fit me. And people think breasts are so great, not if you're dying to buy the Pucci dress in the window they're not.

And to Moe's dismay, there were hills everywhere. Paris always seems flat until you got to Montmartre. Maybe that's why all the artists lived there. Everyone else said screw it and went for convenience and high prices.

"I will kill that girl," muttered Moe and that's when she turned on a side street that was a little rundown and sad. She turned around and backtracked to go down another street and I was sure she saw us, but nothing happened. She just kept looking at her phone and following the directions until she got to a plain building with an equally plain door. I don't mean plain for Paris. I mean plain for anywhere and pretty crappy. The door was a 1970s metal job with frosted windows and it didn't seem possible, but there were seven apartments inside that building. It was only three stories and four windows wide. Maybe it was the modern version of the storied Paris garret.

Moe and I ducked behind a van parked haphazardly to watch Madison pick out a buzzer. She hesitated, took a breath, and then pushed. It was a long push. A you-better-answer-the-damn-door push, but it didn't work. No one answered. She tried again, pushing so hard her finger must've hurt. I could see her face past the van's side mirror. Her lip was quivering and her eyes overflowed. She pushed again. Nothing. She tried the other buzzers and did get a couple answers, but no one knew Sebastian Nadelbaum.

Then Madison looked at her phone, pressed it to her chest, and it seemed like she would call someone, but instead, she did a long press, a press that lasted until the curtains were drawn aside in one of the windows above. A woman, around thirty-five and pudgy with a phone to her ear, looked out, saw Madison, and then yanked the curtain back over the window. She didn't answer Madison's desperate buzz.

"Out of options," said Moe.

"One would think," I said.

Madison stepped back and looked at the window in question. No one appeared and her shoulders sagged. My phone buzzed. Spidermonkey. Nadelbaum had taken money out of an ATM, but no hotel or airline charges. Airlines didn't take cash. I wasn't so sure about trains. Maybe. I texted Lisa that we were about to approach Madison. I got a thumbs-up as I watched Madison spin in a circle and then take off up the street.

"Why did it have to be uphill?" Moe asked

"It's us," I said.

"It's you, you mean."

"Pretty much."

We continued on until the street split.

I know this area.

"There's a park in about half a block," I said. "I'll follow. You cut her off. I don't want to lose her."

"I'll follow. You cut," said my geezer bodyguard.

I nodded and raced down the other road to the small park past a lovely café with heaters and blankets in the outdoor seating. They probably had a bathroom.

Don't think about that.

I dashed through the little park, if you want to call it that. It was completely paved with cobblestones, but it did have trees and people. A few Christmas stands were set up, selling *vin chaud*, and people were getting tanked. I pushed my way through and burst onto the other street ramming right into Madison, who, to my amazement, still didn't recognize me.

"Pardon," she said and sidestepped me.

This is harder than I thought.

I grabbed her arm and said, "Madison, pay attention."

Even that didn't get much reaction. She pulled away, but she wasn't serious about it and I dug my fingernails in. I was so over it. Done.

Moe got on the other side of her, in case she bolted and got out of my grasp, but she just looked at me and stopped pulling.

"We need to talk," I said.

Now I was ready for anything, a throat punch, weaponry, she could've peed and it wouldn't have surprised me, but what she did do shocked the hell out of me. Madison Purcell threw her arms around my neck and sobbed like her brother had taken a header off that overpass. I patted her back and gave Moe the big eyes.

"Well, that was easy," said Moe. "Let's eat."

"And pee," I said.

Madison made a horrible snuffling snorting noise and I did not want to look at my shoulder. It was wet in a bad way.

"What are you doing here?" she asked through sobs.

"Looking for you," I said. "There's a café. I have to go there."

"Um...okay."

I dragged Madison by the arm through the park back to the café. We got a table by a toasty heater and I parked Madison next to Moe saying, "If I have to chase you down again, I will shoot you. Don't leave."

I took off and heard Madison say behind me, "She doesn't mean that."

"If she doesn't, I do," said Moe.

There was a bathroom and they let me use it. That's not always a given, believe it or not. I've been denied bathrooms on three continents. Maybe it's me. That time I got in and when I went back to our table I found Madison crying into her napkin with a waitress nervously hovering beside her.

"*Ihr geht es gut*," I said. "*Danke*."

The waitress frowned and gave me a menu before hoofing it away from the juicy Madison.

"That was German," said Moe.

"Something is wrong with me."

"I don't disagree." He looked at his menu. "Do you think they have churros?"

"No, I don't." I got a tissue pack out of my purse and gave it to Madison, who looked up, seemingly surprised to find us still there as if sobbing could get rid of me. The Corsican hitman couldn't get rid of me, but that's another story.

"My mom does that," she said between sniffing and gulping for air. "Always the wrong language."

"I'm in good company," I said.

"You are." And the tears began afresh.

The waitress came back and I ordered, in French or something like it, quiche, salads, and a bottle of wine. I needed wine, but it wasn't the best choice.

While we waited, I filled Madison in on what we thought and the tears stopped.

"Is he okay? I didn't think Jake would do anything like that," she said.

"He's alright for the moment, but you are going home to face it, all of it."

"I know," she said with fresh tears.

The waitress came and Moe checked the wine like a sommelier while I did my best not to fall on my quiche like a jackal.

"Why did you take your mother's money?" Moe asked as he swirled a glass of wine looking for something as he held it up to the light. I didn't care if it was halfway to vinegar and had a beetle floating in it. I was drinking. He gave me the glass and I didn't bother to sip.

"I thought it would be easy. Sebastian made all his money that way. He said I could double the insurance for my mom." She shook and wine spilled on the tablecloth. "But then there was this freak downturn in the market and—"

"He stole it," I said.

"What?"

"He set you up and stole the money."

Madison stared at me with a crumb of quiche on her lip. "That's not...no, that's not what happened."

"We know where it is. He has it," I said.

"That's his money. He's an investor and brilliant at it."

"He's a criminal and a douchebag."

Madison couldn't believe it. Nadelbaum had cried with her when the money was lost. He was investing some money for her to earn it back. The fact that that money was never seen or in her name didn't cause any concern. He was rich and handsome so he simply wouldn't do anything bad. They were in love.

"You know that first apartment you went to," I said, getting out my phone.

"That's his apartment. We stayed there. It's so beautiful. He said I could move in," said Madison.

I showed her the Airbnb page and the thread of faith snapped. She told us everything and it was a pretty good hustle, but I must admit I don't think it started out like that. It sounded like Nadelbaum liked Madison, but then his scheme went south and he needed cash.

"How did he know about Anton?" I asked.

She swallowed hard and said, "I told him. It was just gossip and kind of cool that Jake figured it out."

"But then he wanted to use that against him."

She nodded and told us the tale that Nadelbaum had woven for her. I had something that belonged to a charity, The Klinefeld Group. The Bleds had stolen it and I was keeping the charity from getting it back. Only I knew where it was.

"I'm the bad one?" I couldn't keep the sarcasm out of my voice.

"He said you didn't understand what was going on. He said you were kind of a..."

"Drug-addled nitwit?"

She shrugged. "Basically."

"I get that a lot," I said. "What was supposed to happen?"

"You weren't going to get hurt," she said. "Mr. Thooft was just going to go get you and put you on the plane."

Moe topped up my wine and said, "By smothering her with insecticide and throwing her in a trunk."

"I don't know anything about that chemical," said Madison.

"Where did he get it?"

"Sebastian must've given it to him before he left."

"They met?" I asked.

"Just once." She gripped the table. "You weren't going to get hurt and I had to get that money."

"There was no money," I said. "He was going to use me to pay off a debt."

"I...but he said there was a reward for that thing you have," she said. "I could pay back my mom and it would all be fine."

Madison looked at me with wide blank eyes and I questioned her sanity. How would this be alright? Freaking how?

"How did you get Anton to do it?" I asked.

She looked away. "I told you."

"Jake says there was something else."

She glanced back at me. "He did?"

"Your brother is very bright," I said. "What else did you have on Anton?"

"Nothing. We didn't have anything."

Moe finished his quiche and asked, "Why did Jake have to be in the café?"

Nice one.

Her eyes got all shifty. "No reason."

"You wanted Thooft to think your brother was in on it," said Moe.

She nodded. "That's right. I told Mr. Thooft that Jake would tell people about his family."

"That's cold-blooded," I said. "What did he ever do to you?"

The tears came again. "Nothing. I really liked him, but I had to get that money back for my mom. I didn't think anything would happen to him."

I could tell she believed it or maybe she had to to do what she did.

"What else did you threaten him with?"

"Nothing."

Something wasn't right. I could feel it. Anton Thooft would not have kidnapped me over Kimberly. I thought he did, but that wasn't right. He did a lot of things to hide what his mother did. He gave up the love of his life. He left the country for crying out loud, but no one ever said he was violent. He'd have to be pushed hard for that to happen.

"What else did you threaten him with?" I asked.

"Nothing."

"Look, little girl," said Moe, "I've had just about enough of you. I'm tired and I'm old and this is bullshit. It's about Jake. Did you say that Jake would accuse him of molestation?"

I gasped and she cried.

"I did, but Jake would never have done it."

"Jesus Christ, you are a piece of work," said Moe.

"I was desperate. Sebastian said I had to or we couldn't get the money. I swear I wouldn't have done it."

"But Anton believed you." I couldn't look at her. "You were going to ruin his family and brand him as a child molester."

"I thought it would be alright," said Madison. "Sebastian said it would. Mr. Thooft just had to get you to the plane. That's it."

"And Mercy would just tell The Klinefeld Group what they wanted to know?" Moe asked, shaking his head in amazement.

"Well, yeah." Madison looked at me. "It's not yours or the Bleds. You have to give it back to the charity. It's not fair to keep it."

I leaned back and looked at her young face, wondering if I was ever that dumb. I hoped not.

"I don't have it, Madison, and neither do the Bleds. We don't even know what it is."

"But you have to. Sebastian said that his friend at the charity said you know all the stuff, but you just won't tell."

"I know some stuff, but I don't know that. Your boyfriend is an idiot. If The Klinefeld Group wanted to get ahold of me, you don't think they would've done it themselves?"

"I...I don't know. I mean they're a charity," she said. "Do you think he made up everything? All of it?"

"Now you're cooking with gas," said Moe and he signaled the waitress for the bill.

"I think I want to kill him," said Madison. "For real. I want to kill him."

"Get in line," I said.

"Let's start with that crappy apartment you were just at," said Moe. "Who lives there?"

"His friend Josephine. We had dinner with her. I thought he might go there since he wasn't at his apartment."

I thought about the woman in the window. On her phone. Calling Nadelbaum?

"Hold on," I said, and I called Spidermonkey. "Where was the ATM?"

"Hello. How are you?" he asked.

"I'm sorry. It's been a long day."

"You're forgiven. Let's see. Nadelbaum took cash out of a Crédit Mutuel about an hour ago. Why?"

"Where is it?"

"On the Rue des Abbesses. Does that help?"

I wanted to scream and I may have squeaked. "Yes. It does."

"Are you okay? I transferred the money back the way it came into Madison's original wallet. I can't put it in the bank. The mom's got a two-factor system for security. I can see in the accounts through the bank, but I can't move anything. A complete pain."

"At least something is."

"I could do it, but why bother with the effort."

I thanked him and hung up. "He took cash out of an ATM across from the metro stop an hour ago," I said. "We were right there."

"He *is* here." Madison jolted to her feet, knocking her chair over. "He *was* at Josephine's, that witch. Come on."

She bounded out of the café and Moe said, "I guess we're leaving."

I was already gone.

Madison banged on Josephine's crappy front door, yelling, "Open up, you piece of trash!"

I caught up and grabbed her. "They could call the police."

"Freaking call the police!"

"Madison!"

The girl turned and grabbed me. "She told me that he was a bitcoin genius. Then she came to Stuttgart and backed up all that crap about you. She said the plan was flawless and nobody would get hurt!" She was screaming again. "You got hurt. Everybody got hurt. Now she's getting hurt! I'm going to hurt you, Josephine, you sack of shit!"

Moe caught up and said, "Someone's mad enough to eat nails."

"No kidding," I said.

Madison banged on the door so hard she cracked the glass. "Open up so I can kill you, Josephine!"

A crowd was gathering and a woman started yelling. We backed up to see the doughy Josephine pointing her phone at us. "I'm calling 112! You are crazy!"

"Call them!" screamed Madison. "I can't wait to tell them what you did."

"I didn't do anything."

Madison started to scream again, but Moe grabbed her and I yelled up, "You're harboring a fugitive!"

"I am not!"

"Sebastian Nadelbaum stole 300 thousand dollars from this girl and orchestrated a kidnapping and a murder. You want us to tell the gendarmerie that you helped him? Do you? Because we will."

Josephine's face went red and then pale. "I didn't do that, any of that."

"Oh, yeah? Tell us where he went. Right now, and maybe we'll leave you out of it."

"Hey!" yelled Madison.

"Shut up," I hissed. "Josephine, tell me or I will turn you in. I know the FBI. Surely you know who I am."

She started to close the window and I yelled, "I've got all night to talk about how the woman who lives in this apartment helped get a man murde—"

Josephine threw open the window. "He went shopping for Christmas, you crazy bitch."

"Where?"

"On the Champs Élysées. Where else? He likes the finer things!" she yelled. "Go the fuck away!"

"Not good enough! What store?"

"I don't know!"

"You better figure it out!" I yelled.

Josephine was shaking with rage and the crowd was pointing. "Louis Vuitton for me and Disney for my daughter."

"He's buying you Louis Vuitton with my mother's money, you whore?" screamed Madison. "I will—"

Moe whipped Madison around and marched her away and I yelled up one more time. "If we don't find him, we will be back!"

"Fuck you!"

My mother would be proud. I kept my dignity and only gave her the finger. Trust me. I wanted to say a lot more than that, but who had the time? I had a Disney store to get to.

CHAPTER TWENTY-SEVEN

There are Disney stores everywhere and I do not get it. Even on the Champs-Élysées, there was a line to get in and it wasn't a good thing. Madison was losing her mind. She'd started mumbling on the metro and I don't know what language it was or if it even was a language. People near us appeared to think she was speaking in tongues. When people start crossing themselves, you know you've got trouble.

"Call your mother," I said in yet another attempt to distract her, but she ignored me and pushed up against a woman in front of us like a true European. Personal space? What personal space?

Moe pulled her back and apologized. "Call your mother. Now."

Madison obeyed him and texted the relieved Lisa. On the way to Paris's swankiest shopping street, I had Madison send her mother all her bitcoin wallet information, and Lisa used it to transfer the money into her savings account.

"She's got it," said Madison as we moved from the elegant avenue to the super crowded store. I had hoped we'd catch a break and find Nadelbaum in Louis Vuitton. It wasn't so popular with the masses, but no such luck. A haughty salesman deigned to look at a photo and said Nadelbaum might've been there. He wasn't about to swear to it with so many handsome men wearing black wandering about and we were invited to leave. No loitering allowed in Louis Vuitton.

"I don't see him," said Moe up on his toes to look through the Disney store.

It was so crowded and there were barriers, pillars and displays.

"He could be—"

"Upstairs," Madison said and jetted toward the spiral blue staircase with crystal-lined spindles.

"Wait!" I cried out, but she was pushing past moms to get to her quarry.

Moe went to follow. "Come on."

"I'm going to clear the back," I said, and he stopped.

"Are you going to Fike me?"

"He could be up there," I said. "Do you want her to toss him over the balcony?"

"It's not the worst idea I've heard," Moe said.

"Just go. I'm not going to Fike you." I worked my way through the rest of the store past little girls holding up princess dresses and trying on tiaras and fathers looking like they were ready to lay down and sleep right there on the floor. Nadelbaum was nowhere to be found.

I texted Moe and started up the staircase when I heard a shout. "I see you, you crap weasel!"

"Get away from me, you stupid little bitch!" a man yelled, and a shocked gasp rose from the crowd.

"I'll show you stupid!"

Nadelbaum and Madison were on the stairs. He was shoving people and they were going down like dominoes. Security ran up but got tangled in customers. They were coming around the curve and she did it. Madison launched herself at Nadelbaum, using the bannister to kick off and come at that guy like a rabid flying squirrel. It was a thing of beauty, if insanity. Fats would've been impressed, except for one thing. She missed.

Nadelbaum ducked to the left and she sailed past, nailing security and me. I fell backward, tumbling down the stairs amid so many other bodies. It didn't hurt. I was well-cushioned.

"*Arrête*! Stop!" screamed security.

I looked up to see Nadelbaum slamming into a customer coming in the door. She slowed him just enough for me to scramble to my feet.

"Mercy! No!"

I glanced back at Moe on the stairs above the fray.

Sorry. Gotta go.

I ran the obstacle course to the door and juked around security who were helping the woman to her feet. Then I was out on the avenue, running full out behind Nadelbaum. The trees beautifully strung with red lights showed him off. He darted into the Christmas market; upsetting cups and powdered sugar went everywhere. He was so much taller and faster, but he plowed into everyone. I ran through his wake, undeterred and apologizing. Yes, it was in German and possibly Italian. I don't know. I was apologizing. It was a reflex my mother ingrained in me.

I thought for sure Nadelbaum would go for a metro station, but instead he ran for the river. I was not thrilled. It wasn't that far, but by the time he turned to run down the path beside the river, I was ready to pull out the Mauser and shoot him. Unfortunately, there were tons of tourists getting on and off boats. I couldn't take the chance and they did slow him down. That guy could not corner. It was all straight lines for Nadelbaum and right into everyone in his path. I almost caught up to him when he turned to run across the Quai d'Orsay, but a car almost took me out and he dashed out of sight.

Straight line. Straight line. Straight line. Invalides.

I ran for the Invalides metro stop. From his trajectory, that was the goal.

Please, let this be right. Please.

There he was at the entrance, bent over and holding onto the pole. Idiot.

I kept running, sounding like a beleaguered water buffalo and he heard me, staring in astonishment at my persistence before running down into the metro with me not far behind. He jumped a turnstile with ease. I did not. I tumbled over that thing with all the elegance of a baby elephant and staggered down into the station sucking wind and once again thinking about shooting him.

Nadelbaum didn't go into the metro. He probably thought I would assume that. I did, but I saw a woman exclaim and drop her bags. I knew that would be him. Sneaky he was not. I chased him into the RER and right onto a platform with a train waiting. He ran down the length. I thought he was going to run right back out again. That's what I would've done, but at the last car, he juked inside. The closing door alarm went off and I had no choice. I darted into the first car to my left, almost getting caught in the door. The train left the station and I started working my way toward Nadelbaum's car. The train was packed and it wasn't easy. I thought he would get off a the Musée d'Orsay and he did, but I managed to hide behind an enormous Swede at the door to my car and watch. He looked around at the crowd leaving. There was such a rush of people and I wasn't the only short woman with a poofball hat on. I could've been one of them going for the stairs. Several were in a Mercy-like hurry. I watched him bite his lip and then dart back on the car.

I worked my way up three more cars until I was in his. He saw me as we rolled into the Saint-Michel station. He shoved some women away from the door.

"I'm calling the gendarmerie!" I yelled. "You can't get away."

People grabbed at him. The word gendarmerie was magic. He threw a punch and a man's nose exploded. Blood spattered against the windows and the doors opened. He ran out through the cacophony of screams and I was right with him.

Everyone was so shocked on the platform that no one stopped him and there were no gendarmerie or national police as there often were. He ran through the station and shoved through an exit gate with some poor woman who was screaming as he stumbled over her body.

"Stop him!" I screamed.

People rushed to help the fallen woman, but a man next to me stood stock still, mouth open with his ticket in hand. I snatched it and shoved it in an exit slot.

Score!

"Hey!" the man yelled. "*Mon billet*!"

I tossed the ticket toward him and ran past the woman, catching sight of Nadelbaum as he rammed a kid into a wall. It was like chasing a wrecking ball with legs. I dashed past the kid and his screaming parents up to the street and there Nadelbaum was running toward Notre Dame and the cranes repairing it.

What is the damn plan? Are we going to run through all of Paris?

Nadelbaum jumped off the sidewalk and for a sweet second, I thought he was going to get hit by a car. Instead, the bastard snatched a man off his bike. It happened so fast the guy just came off and landed on the sidewalk before he even screamed.

I guess not.

I looked for my own bike. No such luck, but a scooter rolled up and started to get off to help the bicyclist.

It's worked before.

I ran to him and yelled, "We have to get him!"

The scooter guy looked at me and then the bicyclist, who yelled, "*Va*! *Va*!"

Without asking, I leapt on the back to his surprise and pointed at the bike passing Shakespeare and Company. He hit the gas and we zipped through the traffic after Nadelbaum, who looked back and nearly took out a trashcan. I thought we had him, but he sped off, squeezing through hordes of tourists. We took a safer, longer route, but kept after him, zigzagging through the streets until we reached one with an incline up between tall buildings made of creamy stone on either side. It seemed familiar, but I didn't know where we were until I saw the building where the road ended in a T at The Panthéon.

Nadelbaum was almost at the intersection, struggling on his bike, and we were right behind.

"Stop!" I screamed and he looked back but kept going, t-boning a black taxi and launching himself over the hood.

The scooter guy skidded to a halt and shouted, "Woohoo!"

I jumped off the scooter to hurry around the taxi, totally expecting Nadelbaum to have hit one of the stone benches that lined the walkway, but Nadelbaum had come up running. He looked back and I automatically dropped down, peeking past the taillight. The driver was out of the car and shaking a fist. People were yelling and pointing. Two scooters collided and took out some pedestrians enjoying *Vin Chaud*. People were yelling into their phones for ambulances and sirens erupted in the distance.

Nadelbaum didn't see me and stopped running. He pulled a cap out of his pocket and pulled it low over his eyes before he straightened his coat, tucked his scarf up around his ears, and melted into the frantic crowd all dressed in black coats.

I stayed with him to the square in front of the Panthéon. It had a beautiful display of Christmas trees that was kind of ruined by the tremendous number of sirens going off and bouncing off the stone buildings surrounding it. Nadelbaum shoved his hands in his pockets and scanned the area. Then he went between the trees and the Panthéon. I decided to stay tucked up behind a square pillar at the edge of the Panthéon grounds to see where he went. I didn't have a plan, as usual, but pulling a weapon on a panicked, packed square didn't seem like a good idea, and I didn't know how else I could subdue him.

I waited and Nadelbaum hesitated, looking around for an out, but then a group of national police came running from a side street, hands on weapons.

Yes!

Nadelbaum hung a left into the Panthéon entrance.

No!

That douchebag casually walked up the stairs to security, averting his face and showing his empty hands. The guard barely glanced at him. Now I could've gone to the police and pointed out where he went, but let's face it, if Nadelbaum was all over their radios, so was the crazy blonde in a pink poofball chasing him. They could arrest me and let Nadelbaum get away.

I took a breath and trucked inside the gate, trying not to look frantic to catch up, which I certainly was. The guard was focused on the crowd down in the square and waved me past. I walked into the checkpoint where another distracted guard was up on her tiptoes trying to see what was happening. I opened my purse and said, "There was an accident."

The guard nodded, but was so distracted by the sirens and her own radio, squawking non-stop, she barely looked. Hello. I had a Mauser in there under the remaining tissue packs and wallet, but she didn't see it and waved me in.

I came into the grandiose interior, expecting to see Nadelbaum buying a ticket, but the area was empty. He wasn't anywhere in sight. I brought up his picture on my phone and asked the man inside the glass booth, "Did you see this man come in here?"

He dragged his eyes from his own phone and nodded, saying in lightly-accented English, "Yes, he just went in."

"Did he buy a ticket?"

"No. He had a pass."

Bastard.

I bought a ticket and went through the ticket gate to rush over to the exit guard with my phone up. "Did this man just leave?"

The guard glanced at my phone and then me, did a double-take and stared.

I said something about a friend in clumsy French. I was panting a little and it was hard to think.

"I speak English," he said.

"Oh, thank goodness," I said, getting more breathless. He'd like it. I could tell. "My friend, have you seen him?"

The guard looked at Nadelbaum's picture and shook his head. "He hasn't been by me. What is the matter?"

I considered my options and went with the most dramatic. "I'm supposed to meet him here and I think he's off his meds. I need to find him immediately."

He reached up and clicked his walkie. "*J'ai une situation.*"

Too dramatic.

"No, no," I said. "It's fine. He just gets emotional and he'll...cry if I'm not here."

The guard made a face and asked, "What do you wish me to do?"

"I'm going to look for him. Can you call me if he leaves, so I can catch up?"

He agreed and I gave him my phone number. "This man," he asked, "he is your boyfriend?"

"Absolutely not," I said and asked for his phone number. He liked that and I was sure he'd call me if Nadelbaum scooted out.

I dashed into the nave past the paintings depicting the life of Joan of Arc to find a few tourists inside, milling around and craning their necks to see the super-sized statues and austere stonework in soft grey all leading up to the paintings under the enormous dome. I hurried around the perimeter over the marble floor done in geometric designs. It deserved more pictures than it got. Everyone was looking up.

So many columns. So many statues. Nooks and crannies galore, but I didn't find Nadelbaum in any of them while keeping an eye on the front. I didn't think he'd gone out. Right after I came in, a couple of national police entered, scanning the area and speaking on their walkies. Nadelbaum was clearly a chance taker but trying to get past them would've been a huge one to take and I didn't think he had the balls to try it. He wasn't that kind of criminal.

Where would I go? Where would I go?

I stopped at Foucault's pendulum under the dome, standing at the thick tape measure that blocked off the swinging gold ball, and watched it gently come to me and then away.

I wouldn't have come in there at all. It was a dead end. It was stupid. But he was stupid. What was the stupidest thing to do? What would I never do?

"The crypt." I did an about-face and walked back toward Marianne the revolutionary goddess of liberty standing stern above all the men struggling below. The Girls liked that statue. I always wondered where the women were.

I bypassed Marianne and the Panthéon model to go down the stairs to the world's most exclusive graveyard. A few people were coming up, but I was the only one going down, which was weird because the crypt was the best part. Where else can you be in such good company?

Rousseau and Voltaire didn't get a second glance on that visit. A first glance was enough to see that Nadelbaum wasn't there. I slipped my Mauser into the pocket of my jacket and strolled through the vestibule, looking behind each pillar holding up the beautifully arched ceiling before climbing the curved stairs to the rotunda. I called it the donut when I was little. I loved the smooth walls, curved like a donut.

From there I went for the first passage to the crypts on the right. It was an obvious place to hide. The right passage had one open door and I checked inside. It was empty of both Nadelbaum and honored dead. The other doors were closed and locked. I went back to the center hall and started at the beginning of the left passage. I knew that one well. Jean Moulin, The Veils, and Germaine Tillion were honored there. Stella was supposed to have known them during the war and The Girls thought Stella's time in Ravensbrück probably coincided with Germaine's, so we always visited her, too, even though she wasn't really there, just some dirt from her grave. It's the thought that counts, Millicent would tell me, but at that moment I was having no thoughts other than that the crypts were darker than I remembered with more shadows and lonely without any other visitors in the area. I'd never been afraid there before. It was a new and unpleasant sensation.

I held my breath as I looked in each vault, but Nadelbaum wasn't in with Jean Moulin or the Veils and I was starting to think I'd picked the wrong section. He might be in with Victor Hugo or the mathematicians or the banker. I hurried toward third door, the one that contained the Curies, the scientists shared a hall with the resistance fighters and a holocaust surviver, appropriate, I always thought.

I hadn't really walked in any of the vaults. They were narrow with just enough room for two people to pass comfortably. I didn't think there was a good place to hide from view, but I was wrong. There on Pierre Curie's vault was a smear of red on the pale stone. The vault looked clear. I slipped out my Mauser and put my back toward the open black gate-like door, sliding myself sideways inside.

"You don't make good choices," I said.

Nadelbaum looked down at me from where he'd wedged himself on top of Marie Curie's tomb. "Shit."

"You disgust me. There are five women in this place and you had to squat your rank butt on one of them. I ought to shoot you just for that."

"She's dead. She doesn't care," he said with a sneer.

"Pay attention. I care," I said. "Get off."

"You have no authority over me."

"This," I shook the weapon, "says I do. Get down, now."

"You won't shoot me." He wasn't looking all that confident when I clicked off the safety, but he didn't budge.

"I shot Richard Costilla in the face so you might want to move along."

Nadelbaum scampered to the end of the tomb. Then he climbed down as he cradled one arm, leaving more smears of blood, and knocking off the flowers. He had scrapes like rug burn down one side of his face and a lower lip that was swelling to epic proportions. He pressed himself against the back wall in the dimmest part, looking back like he thought he might be able to climb out the small, barred window.

"What are you going to do?" he asked.

I used my casted hand to pull out my panic button and pressed it.

"What's that?"

"It alerts the cops if something's happened to me," I said. "You happened to me."

He flushed with anger and he was pretty good-looking. Better in person than in photos and I was starting to see what Madison fell for. That deep melodious voice, cultured, even when whining about his predicament. The good clothes and expensive watch. Such a good way to suck a girl in.

"Why did you chase me?" he demanded.

"So I would catch you."

That was apparently confusing and he dithered for a minute before tilting his head and saying, "What do you want?"

"I've got it."

Nadelbaum fumbled in his pocket and I got ready to fire, but he didn't pull out a weapon. He pulled out an opaque green bottle, yelled, "Ha!" and threw it with gusto at my feet where it landed with a thunk.

We both stared at it for a second until I said, "What was supposed to happen?"

"I thought..."

"What? I'm *dying* of curiosity. Would it explode, so you could escape through a plume of green smoke like the Wicked Witch of the West or something?" I asked, barely containing my urge to laugh.

He didn't answer, staring down at his failure, a bottle that had a skull and crossbones and the words, "*Vorsicht*" and "*Gift*" on the label. *Gift* meant poison as if the skull and crossbones weren't enough to give it away. Underneath that was piece of paper with a handwritten note that I couldn't make out.

"Why didn't it break?" he asked finally.

"You're an asshole and fate hates you," I said.

He stared at me like I was serious, so I said, "It looks like Bakelite, you moron."

"Bakelite?"

"Plastic."

"It's not plastic," he said with considerable umbrage. "My great-great-grandfather made that in the war."

"Wait a minute," I said. "Is that the insecticide you gave Anton to knock me out?"

His eyes got all shifty. "No."

"It says poison. You could've killed me. The Klinefeld Group wouldn't give you money for my body, idiot."

"I'll...give you the money," he said. "As soon as you let me go, I'll give it to you."

"Who do you think you're dealing with? You tried to kill me," I said and pointed at the bottle. "Twice."

"I have the money. You want it, don't you? Let me go and I'll give it to you."

I rolled my eyes. "We already have it, moron. Done and dusted. Back where it belongs." I glanced back. "Where are the cops? I'm ready for some creme brûlée and a hot bath."

"You're lying," he hissed.

"Nope. Lisa Purcell was transferring it back into her account about the time you were in Louis Vuitton," I said.

He balled up his fists and said, "What do you want?"

"You don't have anything I want."

Nadelbaum pointed a shaking finger at me. "I'll tell the cops that it was all Madison's idea. The kidnapping, everything. Let me go or I'll say it."

"What about the money you stole from The Klinefeld Group? Was that Madison's idea, too?" I asked.

He pressed back hard against the stone and pulled out a wallet. "I've got some money here. You want it?"

"Not even a little."

He fumbled the wallet and it fell at his feet. "You've got to let me go. They'll kill me if I don't pay them back."

"And that bothers me because?"

"You don't want me to get killed," said Nadelbaum. "You don't."

I tilted my head. "Well, I'm willing to see how it goes."

"I...I have information about them."

"The Klinefeld Group? Sure, you do."

"They're Nazis and they're into all kinds of, you know, Nazi stuff."

I yawned. "Shocking." I pulled out my phone and pressed the emergency button, so much for the stupid panic button.

"Don't do that," he pleaded.

"Too late."

"I know about Berlin."

"I know about Berlin, too," I said. "Love the Thai ladies in the park. The broth is so good."

He stared at me like I was an idiot, but I was just having fun. The broth is magical though.

"The murder. They did it. You were investigating it. I know about what happened."

You've got my attention.

"The powers that be told *you* they killed someone in Berlin?" I asked. "Get real."

"You *do* want to know. Let me go and I'll tell you."

"Tell me and I'll let you go," I said. *Liar, liar, pants on fire.*

"Okay," he said coming forward. "So the Mossad knew about him and he knew that they knew. Nobody gets away from the Mossad."

"Who are we talking about?"

"Jens Waldemar Hoff, the real one. He was going to cooperate and tell them information."

"So..."

"They killed him and then they killed the cop."

"I know all that," I said. "Tell me something I don't know."

"They're money laundering through the charity. That's how they're funded."

"Now that is interesting," I asked. "Who are they working for?"

"I only saw them once. I think they are with the—"Nadelbaum

flew back against the wall blood spraying against the stone. I shrieked and a man grabbed me, tossing me in the crypt. He pointed a 9mm with a silencer at me. It's a misnomer to say that thing was silent. I flipping heard it. I just didn't hear him.

"Thank you, Miss Watts," he said. "You've saved me time and effort."

I pointed my Mauser at him and asked, "Who the hell are you?"

"Can't you guess?" He smiled but with no warmth whatsoever and I gave him the once over. Generic guy, on the small side with a tight, mean expression in his eyes. That stood out, the intensity of the meanness, but no bells were rung, and I said the only name that came to mind.

"Jens Waldemar Hoff?"

"Very good."

"Not really," I said. "You're all called that. Not very inventive, if you don't mind me saying."

Hoff jerked his head toward Nadelbaum who had a hole dead center in his forehead. "He wasn't."

"*He* wasn't one of you," I said.

"No, he wasn't."

"So your own people killed the first Hoff," I said. "Wasn't he one of you?"

He frowned and then said, "He was and then he wasn't. One must do what is necessary for success." He advanced on me and I slipped in Nadelbaum's blood and nearly went down. "Where is it?"

"What?"

He smiled again and a chill went down my spine. "Let's not play games. The package. Where is it?"

"Beats the hell out of me," I said.

"I will shoot you," he said.

"Right back at you." I glanced at my phone. I pressed emergency but the screen was blank. Of course, it was. We were underground in a vault. Idiot.

"They are not coming," he said. "I have done my civic duty."

"Oh, really?"

"I helpfully pointed out where the man you were chasing went. I'm sure they will have a fine time searching the Luxembourg gardens."

"Swell, but you forgot some things," I said.

"I don't think so. I'm not known for failure."

"For starters, you let that dingus over there steal from you and find out about that Mossad thing. I call that a failure."

"Not my doing although I was quite efficient at cleaning up that mess. All I had to do was follow you," he said with another chilling smile. "Very little effort on my part."

"Did you really kill Werner Richter, too?" I asked.

"Me, personally?"

"I meant your people, but I'll take that as a yes."

"Take it any way you want," he said. "Where is the package?"

"I don't know," I said. "Ask again The answer will be the same."

Hoff showed his teeth. They were very white and kinda pointy. "You *are* going to tell me."

I might pee.

"I might if I knew, but I don't, so I can't."

It could've been the tone of my voice or my expression. Something made him think again.

"You found something in that dead woman's purse," he said.

"Her name was Agatha and your people murdered her."

"It was about something in your parent's house."

I could lie, but why bother. "The liquor cabinet. Stella shipped it back in 1938."

"Liquor cabinet?" He frowned again and his mind started working. So did mine.

"Tell me where it is." He extended his arm, pointing the 9mm at the center of my chest, but I had no fear. It just drained right out of me. It took some of my sense with it.

"Tell me *what* it is," I said.

His mouth worked a little and I laughed.

"You don't know, do you?"

"Do you?" The question was surprisingly innocent.

"No, I don't. The liquor cabinet had a secret compartment, but it was empty," I said.

"It couldn't be," he said.

"Okay. You're right. I'll tell you what *was* in it," I said. "A page ripped out of a Shel Silverstein book. Poetry. That's it."

"Poetry." His voice was flat.

"I guess Josiah Bled liked it and we're all screwed. By the way, they're closing."

"What?"

"That's another thing you forgot," I said, keeping the Mauser on him. "The guards will be checking for lingering tourists and here we are."

Voices echoed down into the vault. Young voices.

He stepped back and looked. "You're right. Someone is coming. A family. Do you want me to shoot them?"

"Do you want me to shoot you?" I asked.

"Legend has it you can't," he said.

Astonished, I asked, "What?"

"Not with that weapon anyway. It belongs to us. Nice to see it in person. I would like to have it for my own, but I suppose I will leave empty-handed."

"I suppose you will," I said.

He turned the 9mm and held it against his stomach pointing it under his other arm in the direction of the donut and gazed at my Mauser with longing. It was creepy, in case you're wondering.

"Aren't you going to shoot me?" I asked genuinely curious.

"You shouldn't give men like me suggestions," he said.

"I'm incorrigible," I said.

"That's why I won't. You will find the package someday and I'll be right behind you."

"Sounds like a plan."

The smile came back and I felt oddly light. There but not there under his nasty gaze.

He turned his weapon back on me. "You have been a problem for some time now. Perhaps I will save myself the trouble of killing you later."

"How will you find the package?" I couldn't tell if he was just toying with me or not.

"There are always other avenues to pursue," he said.

"Then why haven't you pursued them? It's only been like eighty years."

Hoff's mouth twitched and he extended the weapon to the perfect firing position. "On second thought, tell me about that poetry."

"Nothing to say," I said.

His trigger finger moved ever so slightly and someone yelled out, "Hey!"

Hoff looked to the left, a gun went off, and his head snapped back, his gun arm swinging wildly, firing one shot into the ceiling. I screamed and slipped around in Nadelbaum's blood as Hoff fell out of sight. Then I scrambled for the entrance to the vault to find him sprawled out with a shot through one eye.

Moe walked up, holstering his weapon, and said, "Aren't you glad you couldn't Fike me?"

I found myself sinking down into the floor, melting like warm jelly. People were running toward us. A family. I pointed, yelling something about staying back. Unfortunately, I pointed with my gun hand, Mauser still in it. The family scattered and Moe took the Mauser and shoved it in his coat pocket before hoisting me to a seated position.

"You're alright," he said, stroking my hair and tucking my panic button inside my coat. "It's over."

"I don't know if he was really going to kill me," I whispered.

"Now he'll never have the option."

CHAPTER TWENTY-EIGHT

So they arrested us. I don't blame them. Found in the Panthéon crypt with two dead guys and multiple weapons. It didn't look good. But neither did my blood pressure. It was so low, I passed out. The police cuffed me and took me to the hospital under guard. Sometimes things just work out. I was in the same room as last time, so Jean-Yves Thyraud knew just where to find me.

The French spymaster, if indeed that's what he was, walked in looking identical to the last time I'd seen him with his rumpled cheap suit and round, smiling face. He had a coat this time that looked like he'd robbed a homeless person to get it and the smell of a full ashtray filled up my small room.

"Miss Watts, lovely to see you again," he said, pulling up a chair.

"Is it?" I jangled my cuff that was attached to the bed rail.

He produced a small key and released me. "Better?"

"Much. What about Moe?"

"He's been released."

"What happens now?" I asked.

"You're both free to go," he said, steepling his stubby fingers under his chin and I knew that wasn't all there was to it.

"Yeah, right."

"I'd like a full statement," Thyraud said with a smile.

"I made a full statement."

"No, you didn't."

I didn't. Of course, I didn't. I wasn't going to tell the Paris cops about my connection to The Klinefeld Group and Stella Bled Lawrence. That was on a need-to-know basis and they didn't need to know.

"You were in that crypt a long time," he said. "What did you discuss?"

"My kidnapping and whatnot."

"I'm interested in the whatnot and I believe you owe me."

I sat up and folded my hand in my lap. "Thank you for getting the *Polizei* off our backs."

"Twice," he said.

"Oh, that was you," I said.

He put his palms out. "Who else? And let's not forget the US Army."

"I thought that was too easy. How do you have pull with our military?"

"I don't. My government has an interest in letting you do what you do," he said.

"Because of The Klinefeld Group? You said you have an interest."

"I do. We do. What did Nadelbaum tell you?"

Because I did owe Thyraud, and because I couldn't think of a reason not to tell, I spilled it. "They're Nazis."

He blew out a breath in irritation. "Of course, they are. What else?"

"They murdered one of their own in the 60s because he was going to cooperate with the Mossad."

"Now we're getting down to it," said Thyraud and he took out a notepad. "Names?"

"I thought that might interest you." I told him everything that I had on the murder. For me, it was done, so why not? "Also, Nadelbaum says they're laundering money through the charitable works."

"Ah, yes. It's nice to have that confirmed. They've been able to cloak themselves in charity for far too long. Who is funding them?"

"We didn't get that far," I said.

He tapped his lower lip and said, "I suspect, you wouldn't be here if you had. Mr. Licata got there remarkably fast, but..."

"But?" I pulled the blanket up around my chest. So close. Too close.

"But," Thyraud said, "there must be another factor in your escape."

"Other than Moe killing him?" I asked.

"What did that Jens Waldemar Hoff want from you? It saved you until Mr. Licata arrived. Using the panic button to locate you was brilliant by the way. "

"And here I thought it was useless."

"It told him you went in the Pantheon," said Thyraud. "He didn't need more. So? What was Hoff after?"

"You're not the only one that thinks I'm useful." I told him about Stella's package and the dead end, leaving out the clues that Josiah Bled had left. Need to know and all that.

"You don't look surprised," I said. "Did you know about Stella?"

"We knew that they were after something from the Bleds. What it is remains a mystery," he said. "Unless..."

"Sorry. Not a clue."

"Small enough to be inside a liquor cabinet," said Thyraud, his brow furrowing. "A work of art?"

"A small one." I showed him the dimensions of the cabinet.

"Very intriguing. Why would the family leave this object hidden for so long?"

"No one knows, not even the living Bleds. Agatha and Daniel knew about the liquor cabinet and were bringing the knowledge with them to the Bleds. When The Klinefeld Group killed them, the chain was broken."

"So the location of the object was passed down through your mother's family, not the Bleds, but the Bleds, and then your parents had the object," said Thyraud, tapping again. "A kind of double security."

"I think so, although my father may know something. He was the last person to see Josiah Bled alive, but he's never going to say anything. He has an NDA."

"Your father wouldn't betray a confidence anyway," said Thyraud.

"Very true. He's made close to the vest a lifestyle," I said. "What about the Hoff that killed Nadelbaum. Who is he really?"

"We have no idea. He had no identification and his fingerprints aren't on file with anyone anywhere. He was a professional hitter. We can tell that from the Panthéon video.

"There's video?" I asked.

"Yes, that's how we verified your story and Mr. Licata's." He paused and then said, "You look concerned."

"Moe really isn't going to have any trouble?"

"None whatsoever."

"The video is definitive?"

"We have chosen to see it that way. Hoff was going to shoot you and Moe Licata, the elderly American sniper, shot him. It didn't hurt that Hoff had already shot Nadelbaum and misdirected the police in order to pursue you. No one is questioning if it was necessary."

"You've seen to that?" I asked.

"I have," said Thyraund. "We've put Hoff's picture out through Interpol and all other channels for identification," said Thyraud.

"Are you confident?" I asked.

"No. If he has turned up on anyone's radar, he will have looked completely different."

"Swell."

My monitor started dinging as my pressure got dicey again. Thyraud reached over and pressed my call button. "Until we meet again, Miss Watts."

"You sound so sure," I said.

"I've been doing this a long time." He nodded at me and turned to go, crossing paths with Moe, who burst in with one hand on his weapon under his coat. "What happened? Who are you?"

Thyraud calmly stepped into the doorway and said, "She will explain."

He slipped out and Moe came to my bedside. "So?"

"That was our get out of jail free card," I said.

"He smells terrible."

I started laughing and my pressure popped back to normal just as a nurse rushed in. I calmed her down while Moe loitered by the window, up to something no doubt.

When the nurse left, he handed me an envelope. "From Madison. She copped to everything. Full confession. The embassy is handling her transfer back to Germany."

"What's this?" I asked.

"An apology."

I laid it on my lap and pushed it away.

"You're not going to open it?" Moe asked.

"Maybe later."

"Understood."

He stayed by the window, watching me with a kind of evaluation in his eyes. "How are you feeling? Not forgiving, I take it."

"That's going to take a while," I said.

"Not for everyone though."

"What are you getting at?"

"You have a visitor," said Moe. "But I'm worried about your blood pressure."

"Do they want to kill me?" I asked.

He smiled. "That's the very last thing on his mind."

"Do I want to see them?"

"Hard to say, but I recommend it."

I crossed my arm over my cast and braced myself. "Let's do it then."

Moe opened the door and said in a very gameshow-type voice, "Disgraced boyfriend, come on down."

Chuck popped his head around the door frame. "Surprise."

I was shocked into silence for a long moment and then said, "How did you get here so fast?"

"I was over the English Channel when you were being held at gunpoint," he said, still not coming in.

"He comes bearing gifts," said Moe.

I gave my boyfriend the stink eye but said, "Bring it on."

Chuck came in just like his poodle did after he'd stolen something off the table. He was a bad boy and he knew it, but he came with flowers, so that was something.

"I'm going for coffee," said Moe. "Anything I can get you?"

"Can you see if they'll take this cast off? I'm over it," I said.

Moe nodded and closed the door behind him, leaving me and Chuck eyeing each other.

"I'm sorry," he said.

"You shouldn't have sent me to your girlfriend's house without a warning and then tried to say she wasn't a serious girlfriend," I said. "You were engaged."

"I completely own that." He gave me the flowers. "I was afraid you wouldn't talk to her if I told you and I knew you needed that in."

"You're not wrong." I smelled the flowers and they were pretty fragrant considering it was the dead of winter.

"Am I forgiven?" Chuck asked, trying not to give me that big cheesy smile of his.

"Are you going to stop eating eggs and taking supplements and gassing me out of the house?"

Chuck put a hand on his chest and feigned dismay. "Are you putting a price on forgiveness?"

"You bet."

"Okay. I'll stop it."

"It's not working anyway," I said, keeping my joyful smile to a minimum.

"Way to rub it in," he said. "Are we good?"

"I heard you came bearing gifts," I said. "Plural."

"I was wondering if you noticed that."

I held out a hand and he opened the carryon he'd dragged in. "I thought you'd want to see this ASAP." Chuck got out a folder and set it in my lap. "Stevie's doing better and you got him to thinking."

"About what?" I asked with fingers dancing along the edge of the thick paper.

"His grandfather. When he got home, he went and found all those dragon books he told you about. There were ten in all and that was in one of them."

I opened the folder and the breath just whooshed out of my lungs. Constanza Stern, Big Steve's mother, looked up at me. Like the painting of Stella in the Bled Mansion, the portrait was done in rough quick strokes but the style was wholly effective, showing her thin, starved face in painful angles, surrounded by thick, tangled dark hair. Her eyes, like Stella's drew me in. They were haunted but defiant. Constanza was not beaten, far from it.

"I had it scanned," said Chuck. "The Girls have the original for safekeeping."

"Why not Stevie?" I asked without thinking.

"It's Stevie. He forgot about it for twenty years. He's afraid he'll forget again."

I held up the thick card stock the portrait had been printed on. "It's the same artist, but watercolors."

"That's what we thought, too," said Chuck. "Check out the flowers she's holding."

I already was. Stella had been holding an Arbutus flower, unusual to say the least and it meant I love only you. Constanza held a bunch of what looked like wildflowers, nothing that I recognized. It couldn't be easy like a rose or something.

"What are they?" I asked.

"Wait for it." Chuck paused for effect until I smacked his leg. "Tarragon."

"No. Really?"

Tarragon was the name embossed on Stella's scrapbook, the one The Girls' mother Florence had kept on all her war activities. No one knew why in the world an herb was on there instead of her name.

"Do tarragon flowers have a meaning?" I asked.

"Not like other flowers, but sometimes the meaning is said to be little dragon, a sort of messed up version of an Arabic word for tarragon."

"What's the Arabic word?"

"Tarkhum," he said.

"Look at those eyes," I said. "Little dragon isn't far off."

"You could say the same about Stella and Tarragon is on her album."

"Code name?"

"Sounds right to me," said Chuck and he got a twinkle in his eyes. I waited for the sleazy smile that sometimes followed it, but it didn't show up.

"What? Oh!" I flipped the paper over. It was blank, but there was another sheet, mostly blank, except for the faint scrawl of Sinclair and the year 1944.

"Sinclair again," I said. "Who is he?"

"Beats me. Look at the flower again."

I flipped back to the portrait and looked closely, squinting. It took me a minute to find what was hidden there, but I did find it. Stella's portrait had DH8, which was the code for Berlin's notorious House prison, but this was a name. Lilliana was written in the petals of the tarragon flowers.

"What does Stevie think?" Then I laughed. "I never thought I'd ask that."

"Lilliana's her name, her real name. He thinks his grandfather told him that, but he'd just forgotten," said Chuck.

"Lilliana and tarragon. The same person? Two people?," I asked. "What did Big Steve say?"

"Stevie didn't tell him. He's afraid it'll ruin their fresh start."

"I don't blame him. How's he doing?"

"Okay. Can't remember to take his pills without being reminded, but he's trying," said Chuck. "Our vermin love him and he's staying at our place."

I made a face. "Do you think he'll remember to feed them?"

"Mr. Cervantes is going to help. When I left, Aunt Miriam was there and they were all going to watch some horror flick," he said.

"Better them than me," I said.

Chuck brushed a frizzy curl off my cheek. "Am I forgiven?"

I grabbed his jacket and pulled him down for a kiss. "Absolutely. But no more springing old girlfriends on me. Tell me about everyone."

"That could take a while," he said and was a little embarrassed about it.

"Don't I know it. You were a slut."

"I was not."

"Oh, come on. You dated everyone I know."

"Only because you wouldn't go out with me."

"You were irritating," I said.

"I'm still irritating and yet here we are," he said, breaking into the sleazy smile I knew so well.

The door opened and a pretty nurse, who couldn't take her eyes off my boyfriend asked, "You would like your cast off?"

"Yes, please."

She put me in a wheelchair while Moe came in and started plotting our evening in Paris.

"Don't get too excited," I said. "I've got a plan."

Chuck sighed. "I was afraid of that. Can't we just go to the Eiffel Tower like regular people?"

"We're not regular people," I said.

"You got that right," said Moe and he rubbed his hands together. "Where are we going?

"Elias Bled's apartment."

"Oh, God," said Chuck. "Why?"

"I have to check something," I said.

"Call Monsieur Barre. He'll do it."

The nurse pointed my wheelchair at the door and Moe hurried to open it. "Why doesn't the slutty boyfriend want to go see Elias Bled?" Moe asked.

"I'm not slutty and nobody wants to go to that apartment," said Chuck.

"Why?"

"Because," I said with a smile. "Elias is dead and still hanging around."

"Haunted apartment in Paris," said Moe. "I didn't have that on my bingo card. Let's do it."

"No," said Chuck, but I was out the door. It was a done deal.

Monsieur Barre was not happy with me. The old guy did his best not to let us inside the elegant address on the Île Saint-Louis. I had to threaten to call Isolda and that did the trick. He opened the enormous door and stepped back, eyeing my clothes and hat. I'd never known

Monsieur Barre to be anything less than perfect. All three of his hairs were perfectly placed on his bald head and his three-piece suit immaculate. I sometimes questioned whether the building manager slept in a suit. The Girls and I had roused him at all times of day and night over the years and he was always wearing one.

"You decorated," I said, peeking behind me.

"Naturally," he said primly. "It is Christmas."

I hooked arms with Moe and left the unwilling Chuck behind as I crossed the grand foyer with its beautiful tree done up with all silver decorations. Evergreen garlands were roped around the staircase's wrought iron and there was mistletoe hanging from the chandelier. Perfect. Storybook.

Monsieur Barre did his best to get in front of us but couldn't quite make it. I wasn't sure how old he was, but he knew Stella during the war, so that tells you something.

"Mademoiselle, what happened to your beautiful clothes?" he asked. "Madam Ziegler worked so hard to make you presentable."

"It didn't take, my friend," said Moe.

"Yes, I see this."

We reached the stairs and Monsieur Barre poked the arm of my puffer coat. "What is this thing? Why do you wear it?"

"It fits," I said.

He frowned.

"It's supposed to look like this."

"This is a terrible thing that you are wearing. You are a Bled. Appearances matter."

"Huh?" Moe looked at me.

"I'm not a Bled," I said quickly. "I'm a goddaughter. It's not the same."

"It is the same and why are you here? You will only make him angry," said Monsieur Barre. "We had such trouble the last time you came."

"Ghosts don't like you?" asked Moe. "Why am I not surprised?"

"Elias likes me just fine. Nothing happened."

Monsieur Barre started wringing his hands. "There was such

banging and wailing. It went on and on. Our other residents threatened to leave."

I rolled my eyes. "Nobody's moving out of this address. You've got a waiting list for buyers. People have been on that for twenty years."

"Thirty," the manager said smugly.

I held out my hand. "Key please."

"You will not rile him up?"

I had no clue what riled up ghosts or Elias in particular, but I said, "I will not. Ten minutes. Fifteen tops."

Monsieur Barre pulled out the big brass key but held it out of reach. "You will go shopping and rid yourself of that hideous coat?"

I will not.

"Yes."

"I do not believe you."

"That is because I'm lying." I grabbed the key and dashed up the stairs, leaving the men complaining in my wake.

I made it to Elias' round foyer on the third floor, gasping, to face the two doors. They were both Elias'. Like any Bled, he took up all the space, whether it made sense or not.

I stuck the key in door A and turned it before I changed my mind. Elias had been fine last time. I'd seen him on the bridge below, where he was rumored to have thrown himself in over the loss of the prostitute, presumably Giséle aka Gladys, my great-great-grandmother. It'd been a surreal experience, but not threatening. Chuck had seen him in the apartment and had never quite gotten over it.

"Elias," I called out. "It's me again. Don't freak out. I'm just going to look at something."

Silence.

I heard Chuck call out for me to wait, but I didn't wait. I never wait. I walked in and was amazed at the transformation. All the stacks of art that had been leaning against the walls were gone. Elias was an avid collector and had money to spare. When he disappeared, his mother Brina ordered the apartment left intact for when he returned. He never did, but the family honored their matriarch's wishes, until I got into the act. A Bled family friend, Serge Dombey of the Orsay museum, and I cooked up a plan to catalog Elias' collection and look for early sketches of the impressionists. Then The Girls decided to have the entire collection looked over. There was quite a bit of work to be done, conserving and cataloging. As far as I knew Serge was still at it.

Without all the art, I could see the space better. The sunburst pattern from the foyer floor was repeated inside and gleamed with a fresh cleaning. The walls had marks where all the canvases had been and nothing was going to get a hundred years of stain out of the silk wallpaper.

"Wow. This is different," said Chuck, coming in behind me.

"Different than what?" Moe asked. "This is...like stepping back in time."

"You are," I said. "1910 original condition."

"The rich are eccentric. Why keep it all here?"

A tremendous banging erupted in the kitchen and Moe jumped a foot.

"Who's that?"

"Guess," I said with a smile.

Moe put his nose up and sniffed. "Is that...bacon?"

"Not real bacon. More like a memory of bacon."

"This I've got to see." And my bodyguard was off.

"You won't like it," said Chuck.

"You young people can't handle anything!" yelled Moe as he disappeared through a doorway.

"So?" Chuck looked at me.

"So let's go to the bedroom."

"Alright. That's what I'm talking about."

"Gross," I said. "Elias is here."

"Sort of," said Chuck.

"Moe definitely is."

"Good point."

I led him into Elias' bedroom and there was the picture I'd come for. It was in a silver frame on Elias' dresser. The woman I'd noticed the last time I'd been there was as I remembered her. She was Gladys without a doubt and wearing a rather formal Edwardian high-necked dress. Not the picture of a prostitute in my opinion or at least not a currently working one.

I turned to the wardrobe and looked through the clothes. One side was women's and the other men's. Perhaps not a full-time resident, but Gladys spent some serious time in the apartment.

Chuck hovered by the door and asked, "What are we here for?"

"Her," I said and pulled up the photo on my phone from Grandma's family tree and held it out to him.

Chuck looked back and forth between the pictures. "It's her. Where in the heck did you get that?"

"My family tree. Grandma J made it on Ancestry."

"This is...who is she?"

"Gladys Watts, my great-great-grandmother," I said.

He picked up the silver frame. "She's the—"

"I think so."

"Check this out." I picked up the other photo from the dresser. It was of the Bled family in the 1880s. Elias would've been in his twenties in that photo and he was standing next to his mother in the back row, smiling awkwardly.

"What am I looking for?" Chuck asked.

"That's Elias." I pulled up another photo from the tree. "And this is Elijah."

"Whoa. They look exactly alike. Who's Elijah?"

"My great-grandfather," I said.

To my surprise, Chuck's blue eyes filled up. "You are a Bled," he whispered.

"It's true. I think it is."

"But why not just tell you, tell all of you?"

"I don't know. Maybe something to do with the rumors about Gladys. Her real name was Giséle by the way."

He smiled and gathered me into his arms. "There's a story behind that, I assume."

"Oh, yeah."

"Were the rumors about her true?"

"I don't know, but I won't judge her harshly even if they are. She had to do what she had to do and she's family," I said. "Grandma J said she was wonderful and Elijah adored her."

Chuck started to speak, but then he pulled back. The scent of roses filled the apartment. Wild roses. Hothouse roses. Heirloom, climbing, tea, Bourbon. The scent was everywhere, thick and warm, filling my heart and opening passages to my family's past, both my families. I can only say that it smelled like love.

CHAPTER TWENTY-NINE

I woke up the next morning to the smell of hot chocolate and fresh croissants. Hands down the best way to wake up. No contest.

We'd gotten permission to take the Montorgueil apartment from The Girls, who were more than happy to have us safe in one of the company properties. I stretched out on the comfy bed and then felt a prickle of intuition. Someone was watching me.

"Creepy," I said.

"How'd you know I'm watching you?" Chuck asked.

I rolled over and saw him lounging in the doorway, wearing only pajama bottoms and holding a cup of coffee. It was the kind of image that ought to be on a poster. It was that perfect with the light angling in from the window and the old, elegant woodwork framing his perfect body. Sometimes I questioned keeping him. In that moment, I couldn't remember why.

"I can feel you."

He gave me his sleaziest smile. Oddly, it didn't ruin the effect. "Any time, my beloved."

At that moment, a fat tuxedo cat sauntered in like he owned the place and leapt up on the bed to begin the most serious four-pawed knead I'd ever witnessed. Skanky kneaded, but he was half-hearted in comparison.

"He's adjusted," I said.

Chuck laughed. "He's a chill cat. This is what we're doing now and he's good with it."

I gave Porky Boy a scratch and said, "So they're here."

"In a huge way."

Grandma came up behind Chuck, ducked under his arm, and bustled in with a tray. "Finally. I thought you'd never wake up."

"What time is it?" I asked.

"Time to go. Get up." She set the tray on the bed and put a latte in my hands. "You showered last night. That's good, but what happened to your hair? My goodness. It's like Medusa with garter snakes."

"Thanks."

"Isolda," called out Grandma, "you weren't kidding about the hair."

The next thing I knew, Isolda was in the bedroom, evaluating my hair and wardrobe. Monsieur Barre had called her about us going in Elias' apartment and informed her of my tragic state. Bastard.

"So shopping first thing," she said.

"Didn't you bring my clothes?" I asked.

"We did, but those aren't clothes for Paris."

"They're fine. We're not staying very long."

Isolda and Grandma ignored that and decided shopping was on the menu.

"We don't have time for Madam Ziegler, but Moncler will do," said Isolda.

"I can't shop at Moncler," I said.

"Why not?" Grandma asked.

"Because they charge two hundred bucks for a tank top."

Isolda waved that off. "It's winter. You don't need tank tops."

Grandma wrinkled her nose. "You shouldn't wear tank tops, dear. They don't really work for your figure."

"That's not the point, and thanks for reminding me that I'm too booby for tank tops."

"It's just a fact, dear," said Isolda. "I'm too tall for stilettos. It is what it is."

Chuck sucked in his lips and barely kept himself from laughing as the old ladies discussed what I might be able to pull off. Not much was the assessment. They totally ignored my contributions and lack of money. Isolda said I should put it on my account. I don't have an account at Moncler or anywhere in Paris. I was lucky to pay off Madam Ziegler and that stuff, while gorgeous, was living in the back of my closet. Where am I going to wear it? On a stakeout? Chasing criminals? Blood draws? I don't think so.

They started discussing my shoes as Aaron trotted in with hot chocolate and asked, "You hungry?"

"Yes. I'm planning on eating my feelings all day."

Moe came in with damp hair and a half-eaten croissant. "When do we leave?"

"Is anyone left?" I asked. "Would anyone else like to come in?"

"Don't be silly," said Grandma. "There's no one else here."

"Well, that's a relief." I took the hot chocolate from Aaron and let it course through my body, soothing me even as Grandma started listing our stops for the day. In short, everything. If it was in Paris, we were seeing it.

"That's a lot for two days," said Chuck, his amusement gone.

"True. The Louvre can't be done properly in less than two alone and we have to start at the Orsay," said Isolda.

"Can you call him?" Grandma asked. "We're going to be late."

"We'll change it to tonight. Serge won't mind. He's lovely."

I waved at them. "What are we doing?"

"We've made arrangements to see Elias' collection. Serge Dombey is very excited about what he's uncovered," said Isolda. "I will call and change the time. He'll understand. He knows Mercy."

Chuck shooed them all out and pulled me out of bed. "It'll be an adventure."

"Isn't it always?"

"Get dressed in your garbage clothes and let's do this thing."

He laughed even as I was chasing him around, trying to give him a good smack. My clothes were fine. My hair wasn't, but that's what hats are for.

We managed to get out of the apartment in less than a half-hour and start Aaron's food tour of Paris, mixed with the sights. We started with the Eiffel Tower because that's practically a requirement and worked our way across the city, ending up at the Orsay as dusk was setting in.

"It's just beautiful," Grandma said. "I knew it would be, but it's better than I imagined."

We crossed the Pont Royal with a gorgeous view of the glorious train station that now housed the Orsay Museum. It was hard to believe, but at one point there had been a plan to tear down the building with all its stonework and arches. I couldn't imagine what horror would've been put up in its place. Paris wouldn't have been the same with some modern monstrosity on the Seine.

"I'm just so excited," said Grandma, hooking her arm through Moe's. "Aren't you?"

Moe smiled at her. "These last few days have been some of the most exciting of my life."

They hurried off ahead with Isolda and Chuck pulled me close. "What's going on there?"

"I'm afraid to ask," I said.

We followed the trio along the river to the museum entrance. There was no queue since it was closing time, but Serge Dombey was outside waiting for us with a glowing smile. He dashed across the pavers to exchange cheek kisses with Isolda and then me before taking Grandma's hand for a kiss and patting it.

"It is a pleasure to meet any member of Mercy's family." Serge's big hands enveloped Grandma's. His charm and joy were infectious and I forgot the miles we'd logged.

"This is Moe Licata," I said. "He helped me with my latest case."

"I heard about that," said Serge, shaking Moe's hand. "You must tell me more. The city is buzzing about fresh bodies in the Panthéon. That doesn't happen every day." Then he turned to Aaron. "My friend, it has been too long."

He and Aaron exchanged cheek kisses and began discussing a new technique for duck confit as we went in the reserved entrance.

"Oh, Moe!" Grandma exclaimed. "Look."

Coming in the Orsay always felt like a revelation, an opening of the soul. The huge curved ceiling with the glass showing off the night sky above the sculpture gallery made me feel like a bird. I could just take flight and soar through the beauty.

"Would you like your tour first?" Serge asked. "Or perhaps Elias' collection?"

"Oh, the collection," said Isolda. "I can't wait to see what you've accomplished."

Elias it was and we left the showy section of the museum to go to the working part. Inside a room the size of my apartment was Elias Bled's collection on easels, tables, and the walls.

Serge took me by the arm and led me to a section filled with sketches. Even my untrained eye saw the significance.

"They're here just like Alice Monet said in her letters." Serge showed us with growing excitement a dozen sketches by Monet, Degas, and others. "Elias had a better eye than I gave him credit for. He bought so many artists that weren't in the styles I associate with him."

"Like who?" I asked.

Serge brought me over to where Isolda, Moe, and Grandma were admiring a set of canvases in brilliant colors with geometric shapes blended with soft flowing ones.

"These are by Delaunay. They show he was moving into Orphism earlier than we knew. These are the only examples of this blend between his earlier Neo-impressionist period and his later Orphism. This is a portrait of his soon-to-be wife in the brief period between her divorce and their marriage."

"What's Orphism?" Chuck asked.

Now you've done it.

Serge got going on the differences between cubism, Neo-impressionism, and Orphism. I'd heard it all before, but his enthusiasm drew me in anyway and I listened as he showed us different examples until there was a soft touch on my arm. Aaron drew me away from the lesson and took me to a corner of the room where there were several racks that included paintings in watercolor and oils, sketches, and sculptures. I didn't see the significance until he pulled a piece off a rack. It was Giséle in a reclining nude pose in charcoal. It was by

Matisse and I'd seen something similar by him before, but it wasn't as delicate.

Aaron put that piece back and showed me another. This one wasn't nude, but of a smiling Giséle pulling up her skirt to wade in a lily pond. I didn't recognize the artist. There were more, many more. I counted twenty and we weren't done.

"They're all her," I said.

Aaron touched my arm and quickly put a watercolor out of sight before Grandma came up. "I think we'll go up now for a coffee before the café closes."

"I'll be right there," I said.

She looked around at Elias' collection, missing his true passion completely as we all had for the last one hundred years. "So sad what happened to him. He was a great collector. Serge says he was amazing."

I was choked up but managed to squeak out, "I think he was."

"But sad."

I thought of seeing Elias on the bridge and of him seeing me, a moment I couldn't shake. "Very."

Serge escorted everyone, except Aaron and me to the door, leaving us briefly alone with greatness and I don't just mean the artists.

"How did you know?" I asked Aaron.

"You saw the cat last time," he said.

"Oh," whooshed out of me. I had seen the family apparition in Elias' apartment. My mother had named the black cat with startling green eyes Blackie and he only showed up on family property in times of tragedy for Mom's side of the family. Mom had seen him before Aunt Tenne's terrible car accident and of course, right before Agatha and Daniel were murdered. I'd seen him at Nana and PopPop's house before Richard Costilla had tried to kill me and in Elias' apartment before nearly getting killed by Poinaré when he tried to kill Angela Riley. Family property. Always on family property.

"It's family property," I said. "It never occurred to me why I could see him there. Why didn't you say something?"

Aaron shrugged. "You needed to figure it out for yourself."

I gave him a hug and pulled out the nude again. It wasn't unseemly or porn-like. It was beautiful. Was Giséle a prostitute or simply an artist's model people decided to see in a bad light? I might never know.

"I see you've found one of our mysteries," said Serge, coming up behind us. "I should've known you would."

I wasn't ready to give anything away and I knew Aaron wouldn't. It was impossible for the little guy to go against me.

"It was Aaron actually," I said.

"Well spotted, Aaron," said Serge. "I saw this nude first. A Matisse and rare, of course, but I didn't think anything of it until we started uncovering the other works featuring this particular model. She was obviously a favorite. There are thirty pieces in all featuring her during a one-year time span and by multiple different artists, but I've never seen her before."

"How unusual," I said.

"All artists have their favorites, but she wasn't unique to one artist."

"Maybe she was Elias' favorite."

He rubbed his big hands together. "The mysterious woman that drove him to despair. Yes, I can see it. A beauty and such a smile."

Serge showed us everything with Giséle in it and nothing I saw changed my mind about her. It was love. I was sure of it. The artists saw her with Elias' eyes. He was a terrible artist, so he had them immortalize Giséle for him.

"We should go." Serge took us back up to the museum café where Grandma surprised me by sitting alone with her coffee. She waved me over and I sat down with a grateful sigh while Aaron and Serge went in search of the others.

"Where is everyone?" I asked. "Are you getting tired?"

"I've never been less tired," she said. "I wanted to talk to you."

"I'm still not buying clothes at Moncler"

"I know. It's not that."

An attendant brought me a latte and I sat back with it warming my hands. My mind was only half there. Elias and Giséle took up most of the space in my brain. "You look serious."

"I've made a decision," said Grandma. "And it is final."

Elias and Giséle vanished.

"About what?" I asked, taking a big drink.

"I'm not going back."

"To the apartment? Would you rather go to a hotel?"

She shook her head and a strand of silver hair got stuck in her lipstick. "I'm not going back to St. Louis."

"What do you mean? You have to go back. We have tickets," I said, sounding silly even to myself. *Tickets. That's all you've got?*

"Tickets can be changed and they have been. It's done."

"I don't understand what you're going to do."

Grandma brushed the hair away and smiled. "Anything I want. Isolda's in search of her father. Moe and I are going to tag along. She's got a lead in Berlin. We'll do that and then we'll go somewhere else. Maybe Denmark or Norway. I've seen nothing of the world and I want to see it all before it's too late."

I drank my latte to delay and then said, "But it's Christmas.

She reached across the table and took my hand. "I've spent the last fifty years and more doing for everyone else. I've missed nothing that anyone else needed or wanted. This is just for me and it's only one Christmas. Do you have any idea how many Christmases your grandfather's missed?"

It's not a small number, I know that.

"A few," I said.

"A lot. It was his work and I admire that commitment, but I was never first." She twisted in her seat and pointed out into the gallery at Chuck standing with Aaron and Moe, laughing with Isolda and Serge. "He came. He made a mistake with you and dropped everything to make it right. You forgave as you should. I always forgave, but your grandfather never made it right."

"He loves you. Grandad loves you," I said.

"I know, and I love him." She smiled. "But I'm not going to wait for him to make me happy anymore. That's my job and I'm going to do it. You've taught me a lot during this trip."

Don't say that.

"I don't think so," I said.

"You don't wait for something to happen. You just go out and do whatever needs doing," said Grandma with pride. "You really are my favorite."

"Are you sure about that? Isn't there a neighbor you like better? One that isn't weepy, snotty, spoiled, or ya know, me."

"I'm sure. I wasn't until this trip. I didn't know you very well and I regret that. I let The Girls take you over. I thought they needed you, but I missed out." She stood up and came over to kiss the top of my head.

"I guess I'll take Porky Boy back with me, unless you're planning on traveling with a cat," I said.

"I am not, but it's all arranged," said Grandma. "Aaron will take him."

"Where am I going to be?" I asked.

She drew me to my feet and said, "Ask the one that puts you first." With that, my grandmother sashayed out into the grand hall of the Orsay to be escorted on the best tour possible.

Chuck went to follow but then turned to find me. He was always turning to find me. I smiled and he came over. "What's up? You've got a look."

"She's not going back," I said.

He nodded. "I had a feeling. Are you upset?"

"I don't think so. It's her life and who knows maybe Grandad will wake up."

"I don't know about him, but I'm very awake," said Chuck.

"I know you are," I said.

"This may not be the right time to say this, but we're not going back, either."

"No?"

"Nope. You and me. Christmas in Switzerland," he said with a grin. "Good present, huh?"

"Nice try," I said with a little elbow to the ribs.

Chuck got all shifty-eyed. "Whatever do you mean?"

"I appreciate the trip, but it doesn't negate our bet."

"Bet. What bet? I recall no bet," he said.

"Good thing we put it in writing since your memory is clearly failing," I said.

"I remember the important things."

"Like how to wield a toilet brush?"

Chuck grabbed me and squeezed until I squeaked. "I come halfway around the world and I get no quarter from you. None at all."

"A bet's a bet," I said. "You'd have made me eat that crab."

"Never."

"Oh, yes, you would."

We bickered our way through the museum until we reached the clock overlooking the Seine and we stopped to gaze past the hands slowly marking time. Chuck and I looked out at the lights. So many lights. So many lives.

"Are you going to tell them about Elias and Giséle?" he asked.

"Not yet. I want DNA confirmation first."

He wrapped his arms around me and said, "Everything's going to change."

I thought about Grandma and The Girls, Elias and Elijah. My father and his father. I wasn't Mercy Watts. I'd known it for a while, but now it was real.

I turned around and pressed into him, holding on with all my strength to his steady support. I needed it like never before.

"Everything already has."

The End

PREVIEW

Silver Bells at Hotel Hell (Mercy Watts Mysteries Book 13)

Somebody up there likes me.

Those are words you should never say. To be on the safe side you should never even think them. It's straight up tempting fate. You're asking to get your butt kicked. Don't do it.

If I'd known that, I'd have stopped him. I'd have clamped a hand over his mouth or screamed. But I didn't know and the rest is history.

"Don't worry," said Chuck as he hunched over the steering wheel, glaring out into the blinding snow. "Somebody up there likes me."

I had one hand on the dash of our rental car and the other on the 'Oh Shit' handle of my door. It made me feel better even though bracing for impact wasn't going to help when plunging to your death over a guard rail in the Swiss Alps.

"Oh yeah?" I asked. "What about me?"

"What about you?"

"I'm in here. What if somebody up there likes you, but they don't like me?"

My boyfriend hazarded a grin in my direction. He was enjoying the drive from Paris to a Swiss hotel buried in the Alps, and I do mean buried, in the worst winter storm in decades. I was not. He promised a getaway. A relaxing getaway and I needed one. I'd been on the go since

Anton Thooft kidnapped me three weeks earlier. I figured out why he did it and who made him do it. I was down to the occasional headache from my concussion and the rash from the insecticide he knocked me out with was finally gone. I was ready to kick back and relax.

So was Chuck, or so he claimed, but we clearly had different ideas of what relaxing actually meant. I would've loved it if we'd stayed in Paris, eating at swanky restaurants, and walking along cobblestoned lanes soaking in the atmosphere and enjoying Christmas markets. Instead, we were risking our lives, driving in white-out conditions along mountain passes that would scare the crap out of billy goats.

"Everybody likes you."

"That is demonstrably not true," I said, holding up my arm that recently been broken and healed.

"Even if you're right, somebody up there *does* like me," said Chuck.

"We've established that, although I don't know why you think that."

"Because it's true. And if they like me, they're not going to want to kill me to get to you. We'll be fine. We haven't died yet."

"I'd like to kill you right now."

"Your grandmother wasn't worried. She thought this was a great idea."

"Grandma J has adventure on her mind. She wasn't thinking about the weather."

My grandmother had recently surprised my entire family by heading off to Germany to help me with the Thooft case during which she'd bonded with my geriatric bodyguard Moe Licata. We ran into Isolda Bled and as soon as my case was resolved the three of them decided that they'd go off exploring Europe. Grandma J would be missing Christmas with the family for the first time ever and she didn't give the smallest crap. My grandad, never the most observant of husbands, hadn't noticed yet, but when he and the rest of the family realized she wasn't coming back, it would be my fault. I think they might be right, but I'm not sure how. No one could've predicted that my prim grandmother would have so much in common with a hoodlum from the Fibonacci crime family. I sure didn't.

"Hold on," yelled Chuck and he did a controlled braking maneuver that kept us from ramming into the back of a Ukrainian tractor trailer. We did do a three-sixty and then shot past the truck on the wrong side of the two-lane road to somehow get in front of the truck intact.

"You can stop screaming now," said Chuck.

I wasn't aware that I was screaming. Pure terror was like that.

"Pull over," I said, gasping.

"I'm not pulling over. Where would I pull over to?"

"There was a sign. I saw it right before I thought we were going to die. It was for a hotel. There's an exit coming up."

"We're not stopping at some random hotel," said Chuck. "We should be clearing the storm any minute. Check the weather tracker. It's beautiful on the other side of this."

"Exit. Hotel."

"For crying out loud, Mercy. It's fine. You've been risking your life on a regular basis since birth. This is just weather."

"Not since birth," I said still trying to catch my breath.

We fishtailed past the exit sign, and I watched my last chance fade into whiteness.

"Okay. When? When was the first time you nearly got killed or whatever? I know Tommy has had you tailing suspects since you could drive."

"Since before that," I said.

A deep frown creased Chuck's high forehead. "How long before?" Chuck idolized my father, the great Tommy Watts. Dad was a legend on the St. Louis Police Force and then in his so-called retirement as a private investigator. Since Chuck and I got together, I'd begun to see some cracks in the hero worship. Tommy Watts could do wrong. Who knew?

"I remember hunting for some guy in Babler State Park when I was eight."

"What were you doing there?"

"Dad promised Mom he'd spend some time with me, and we were supposed to be horseback riding," I said.

"Whose idea was that?" he asked.

"Dad's."

"You never got near the stables, did you?"

"Nope. We did find a mini meth lab and Dad arrested the guy. I think his name was Cooter. He smelled terrible and looked worse. If I had ever had an inclination toward drug use, that guy cured it. He had one tooth and that is not an exaggeration."

"He is never babysitting," muttered Chuck.

"Babysitting?"

"Nothing."

"You know the stuff that's happened wasn't always my fault," I said.

"Someone else had you set fire to the Bled's garage?"

"I'll cop to that one."

He cast a blue eye on me and seemed to consider something.

"What?" I asked.

"You were basically a good kid, right?" Chuck asked like it was important. Really important.

No.

"Basically," I said.

"What do you mean by that?"

I spotted some blue up ahead. There was a break in the storm. I relaxed and shifted in my seat to face him. I had settled down, but he was more tense than ever, despite the snow getting considerably lighter.

"I got good grades," I said. "I didn't rob liquor stores or anything."

A muscle twitched in Chuck's cheek. "What about when you were little?"

"Why are you asking?"

"You told me about Tommy. I mean, what your grandmother said," he said.

"Oh, yeah. Dad was a nightmare."

"You weren't like that, right?"

Well...

"I was adorable," I said.

"What did you do?" he asked in a rush. "You didn't escape and run into traffic or anything, right? You were so tiny. I've seen the pictures."

It was still snowing pretty hard, and I didn't want the man freaking out and he was already kind of freaking out. About my childhood, for some reason.

"I was pretty good. I cried a lot, but you know that."

"Crying's not so bad." He glanced over. "Nothing like Tommy or your uncles. That's good."

I nodded, but it was a big fat lie. My earliest memory was being at Grandma J's house. She was babysitting me on a Saturday during her book club meeting. I must've been driving them nuts because she insisted I take a nap. I tried crying and yelling, but Grandma could not be moved. I had to stay in the rickety crib that had once belonged to my father and uncles.

Grandma J clearly didn't know who she was dealing with because she didn't lock the wheels on the crib. I used my bodyweight to rock the crib along the wall until I got to the window that was left open. I pulled the shade down and then worked on the screen until I got it loose. It's not as impressive as it sounds. The house was built in the sixties and the windows were the original cheap metal things. Then I stood on the bedding, shade, and screen and proceeded to boot my two-year-old self through the window.

Lucky for me, Grandma J's favorite son, who wasn't her son at all but a neighbor, happened to be walking his prize Pekinese at the time. He saw my blonde head come out of the window and rushed over to catch me as I shot out, headfirst over an eight-foot drop to concrete. No wonder Kevin is Grandma's favorite.

"Maybe someone up there does like me," I said.

"Yeah?" Chuck asked.

"I keep not dying."

"You worry me."

"Join the club."

Somebody up there likes me. Those are words you should never say. To be on the safe side you should never even think them. It's straight up tempting fate. You're asking to get your butt kicked. Don't do it.

If I'd known that, I'd have stopped him. I'd have clamped a hand over his mouth or screamed. But I didn't know and the rest is history.

"Don't worry," said Chuck as he hunched over the steering wheel, glaring out into the blinding snow. "Somebody up there likes me."

I had one hand on the dash of our rental car and the other on the 'Oh Shit' handle of my door. It made me feel better even though bracing for impact wasn't going to help when plunging to your death over a guard rail in the Swiss Alps.

"Oh yeah?" I asked. "What about me?"

"What about you?"

"I'm in here. What if somebody up there likes you, but they don't like me?"

My boyfriend hazarded a grin in my direction. He was enjoying the drive from Paris to a Swiss hotel buried in the Alps, and I do mean buried, in the worst winter storm in decades. I was not. He promised a getaway. A relaxing getaway and I needed one. I'd been on the go since Anton Thooft kidnapped me three weeks earlier. I figured out why he did it and who made him do it. I was down to the occasional headache from my concussion and the rash from the insecticide he knocked me out with was finally gone. I was ready to kick back and relax.

So was Chuck, or so he claimed, but we clearly had different ideas of what relaxing actually meant. I would've loved it if we'd stayed in Paris, eating at swanky restaurants, and walking along cobblestoned lanes soaking in the atmosphere and enjoying Christmas markets. Instead, we were risking our lives, driving in white-out conditions along mountain passes that would scare the crap out of billy goats.

"Everybody likes you."

"That is demonstrably not true," I said, holding up my arm that recently been broken and healed.

"Even if you're right, somebody up there *does* like me," said Chuck.

"We've established that, although I don't know why you think that."

"Because it's true. And if they like me, they're not going to want to kill me to get to you. We'll be fine. We haven't died yet."

"I'd like to kill you right now."

"Your grandmother wasn't worried. She thought this was a great idea."

"Grandma J has adventure on her mind. She wasn't thinking about the weather."

My grandmother had recently surprised my entire family by heading off to Germany to help me with the Thooft case during which she'd bonded with my geriatric bodyguard Moe Licata. We ran into

Isolda Bled and as soon as my case was resolved the three of them decided that they'd go off exploring Europe. Grandma J would be missing Christmas with the family for the first time ever and she didn't give the smallest crap. My grandad, never the most observant of husbands, hadn't noticed yet, but when he and the rest of the family realized she wasn't coming back, it would be my fault. I think they might be right, but I'm not sure how. No one could've predicted that my prim grandmother would have so much in common with a hoodlum from the Fibonacci crime family. I sure didn't.

"Hold on," yelled Chuck and he did a controlled braking maneuver that kept us from ramming into the back of a Ukrainian tractor trailer. We did do a three-sixty and then shot past the truck on the wrong side of the two-lane road to somehow get in front of the truck intact.

"You can stop screaming now," said Chuck.

I wasn't aware that I was screaming. Pure terror was like that.

"Pull over," I said, gasping.

"I'm not pulling over. Where would I pull over to?"

"There was a sign. I saw it right before I thought we were going to die. It was for a hotel. There's an exit coming up."

"We're not stopping at some random hotel," said Chuck. "We should be clearing the storm any minute. Check the weather tracker. It's beautiful on the other side of this."

"Exit. Hotel."

"For crying out loud, Mercy. It's fine. You've been risking your life on a regular basis since birth. This is just weather."

"Not since birth," I said still trying to catch my breath.

We fishtailed past the exit sign, and I watched my last chance fade into whiteness.

"Okay. When? When was the first time you nearly got killed or whatever? I know Tommy has had you tailing suspects since you could drive."

"Since before that," I said.

A deep frown creased Chuck's high forehead. "How long before?" Chuck idolized my father, the great Tommy Watts. Dad was a legend on the St. Louis Police Force and then in his so-called retirement as a private investigator. Since Chuck and I got together, I'd begun to see some cracks in the hero worship. Tommy Watts could do wrong. Who knew?

"I remember hunting for some guy in Babler State Park when I was eight."

"What were you doing there?"

"Dad promised Mom he'd spend some time with me, and we were supposed to be horseback riding," I said.

"Whose idea was that?" he asked.

"Dad's."

"You never got near the stables, did you?"

"Nope. We did find a mini meth lab and Dad arrested the guy. I think his name was Cooter. He smelled terrible and looked worse. If I had ever had an inclination toward drug use, that guy cured it. He had one tooth and that is not an exaggeration."

"He is never babysitting," muttered Chuck.

"Babysitting?"

"Nothing."

"You know the stuff that's happened wasn't always my fault," I said.

"Someone else had you set fire to the Bled's garage?"

"I'll cop to that one."

He cast a blue eye on me and seemed to consider something.

"What?" I asked.

"You were basically a good kid, right?" Chuck asked like it was important. Really important.

No.

"Basically," I said.

"What do you mean by that?"

I spotted some blue up ahead. There was a break in the storm. I relaxed and shifted in my seat to face him. I had settled down, but he was more tense than ever, despite the snow getting considerably lighter.

"I got good grades," I said. "I didn't rob liquor stores or anything."

A muscle twitched in Chuck's cheek. "What about when you were little?"

"Why are you asking?"

"You told me about Tommy. I mean, what your grandmother said," he said.

"Oh, yeah. Dad was a nightmare."

"You weren't like that, right?"

Well...

"I was adorable," I said.

"What did you do?" he asked in a rush. "You didn't escape and run into traffic or anything, right? You were so tiny. I've seen the pictures."

It was still snowing pretty hard, and I didn't want the man freaking out and he was already kind of freaking out. About my childhood, for some reason.

"I was pretty good. I cried a lot, but you know that."

"Crying's not so bad." He glanced over. "Nothing like Tommy or your uncles. That's good."

I nodded, but it was a big fat lie. My earliest memory was being at Grandma J's house. She was babysitting me on a Saturday during her book club meeting. I must've been driving them nuts because she insisted I take a nap. I tried crying and yelling, but Grandma could not be moved. I had to stay in the rickety crib that had once belonged to my father and uncles.

Grandma J clearly didn't know who she was dealing with because she didn't lock the wheels on the crib. I used my bodyweight to rock the crib along the wall until I got to the window that was left open. I pulled the shade down and then worked on the screen until I got it loose. It's not as impressive as it sounds. The house was built in the sixties and the windows were the original cheap metal things. Then I stood on the bedding, shade, and screen and proceeded to boot my two-year-old self through the window.

Lucky for me, Grandma J's favorite son, who wasn't her son at all but a neighbor, happened to be walking his prize Pekinese at the time. He saw my blonde head come out of the window and rushed over to catch me as I shot out, headfirst over an eight-foot drop to concrete. No wonder Kevin is Grandma's favorite.

"Maybe someone up there does like me," I said.

"Yeah?" Chuck asked.

"I keep not dying."

"You worry me."

"Join the club."

Somebody up there likes me. Those are words you should never say. To be on the safe side you should never even think them. It's straight up tempting fate. You're asking to get your butt kicked. Don't do it.

If I'd known that, I'd have stopped him. I'd have clamped a hand over his mouth or screamed. But I didn't know and the rest is history.

"Don't worry," said Chuck as he hunched over the steering wheel, glaring out into the blinding snow. "Somebody up there likes me."

I had one hand on the dash of our rental car and the other on the 'Oh Shit' handle of my door. It made me feel better even though bracing for impact wasn't going to help when plunging to your death over a guard rail in the Swiss Alps.

"Oh yeah?" I asked. "What about me?"

"What about you?"

"I'm in here. What if somebody up there likes you, but they don't like me?"

My boyfriend hazarded a grin in my direction. He was enjoying the drive from Paris to a Swiss hotel buried in the Alps, and I do mean buried, in the worst winter storm in decades. I was not. He promised a getaway. A relaxing getaway and I needed one. I'd been on the go since Anton Thooft kidnapped me three weeks earlier. I figured out why he did it and who made him do it. I was down to the occasional headache from my concussion and the rash from the insecticide he knocked me out with was finally gone. I was ready to kick back and relax.

So was Chuck, or so he claimed, but we clearly had different ideas of what relaxing actually meant. I would've loved it if we'd stayed in Paris, eating at swanky restaurants, and walking along cobblestoned lanes soaking in the atmosphere and enjoying Christmas markets. Instead, we were risking our lives, driving in white-out conditions along mountain passes that would scare the crap out of billy goats.

"Everybody likes you."

"That is demonstrably not true," I said, holding up my arm that recently been broken and healed.

"Even if you're right, somebody up there *does* like me," said Chuck.

"We've established that, although I don't know why you think that."

"Because it's true. And if they like me, they're not going to want to kill me to get to you. We'll be fine. We haven't died yet."

"I'd like to kill you right now."

"Your grandmother wasn't worried. She thought this was a great idea."

"Grandma J has adventure on her mind. She wasn't thinking about the weather."

My grandmother had recently surprised my entire family by heading off to Germany to help me with the Thooft case during which she'd bonded with my geriatric bodyguard Moe Licata. We ran into Isolda Bled and as soon as my case was resolved the three of them decided that they'd go off exploring Europe. Grandma J would be missing Christmas with the family for the first time ever and she didn't give the smallest crap. My grandad, never the most observant of husbands, hadn't noticed yet, but when he and the rest of the family realized she wasn't coming back, it would be my fault. I think they might be right, but I'm not sure how. No one could've predicted that my prim grandmother would have so much in common with a hoodlum from the Fibonacci crime family. I sure didn't.

"Hold on," yelled Chuck and he did a controlled braking maneuver that kept us from ramming into the back of a Ukrainian tractor trailer. We did do a three-sixty and then shot past the truck on the wrong side of the two-lane road to somehow get in front of the truck intact.

"You can stop screaming now," said Chuck.

I wasn't aware that I was screaming. Pure terror was like that.

"Pull over," I said, gasping.

"I'm not pulling over. Where would I pull over to?"

"There was a sign. I saw it right before I thought we were going to die. It was for a hotel. There's an exit coming up."

"We're not stopping at some random hotel," said Chuck. "We should be clearing the storm any minute. Check the weather tracker. It's beautiful on the other side of this."

"Exit. Hotel."

"For crying out loud, Mercy. It's fine. You've been risking your life on a regular basis since birth. This is just weather."

"Not since birth," I said still trying to catch my breath.

We fishtailed past the exit sign, and I watched my last chance fade into whiteness.

"Okay. When? When was the first time you nearly got killed or whatever? I know Tommy has had you tailing suspects since you could drive."

"Since before that," I said.

A deep frown creased Chuck's high forehead. "How long before?" Chuck idolized my father, the great Tommy Watts. Dad was a legend on the St. Louis Police Force and then in his so-called retirement as a private investigator. Since Chuck and I got together, I'd begun to see some cracks in the hero worship. Tommy Watts could do wrong. Who knew?

"I remember hunting for some guy in Babler State Park when I was eight."

"What were you doing there?"

"Dad promised Mom he'd spend some time with me, and we were supposed to be horseback riding," I said.

"Whose idea was that?" he asked.

"Dad's."

"You never got near the stables, did you?"

"Nope. We did find a mini meth lab and Dad arrested the guy. I think his name was Cooter. He smelled terrible and looked worse. If I had ever had an inclination toward drug use, that guy cured it. He had one tooth and that is not an exaggeration."

"He is never babysitting," muttered Chuck.

"Babysitting?"

"Nothing."

"You know the stuff that's happened wasn't always my fault," I said.

"Someone else had you set fire to the Bled's garage?"

"I'll cop to that one."

He cast a blue eye on me and seemed to consider something.

"What?" I asked.

"You were basically a good kid, right?" Chuck asked like it was important. Really important.

No.

"Basically," I said.

"What do you mean by that?"

I spotted some blue up ahead. There was a break in the storm. I relaxed and shifted in my seat to face him. I had settled down, but he was more tense than ever, despite the snow getting considerably lighter.

"I got good grades," I said. "I didn't rob liquor stores or anything."

A muscle twitched in Chuck's cheek. "What about when you were little?"

"Why are you asking?"

"You told me about Tommy. I mean, what your grandmother said," he said.

"Oh, yeah. Dad was a nightmare."

"You weren't like that, right?"

Well...

"I was adorable," I said.

"What did you do?" he asked in a rush. "You didn't escape and run into traffic or anything, right? You were so tiny. I've seen the pictures."

It was still snowing pretty hard, and I didn't want the man freaking out and he was already kind of freaking out. About my childhood, for some reason.

"I was pretty good. I cried a lot, but you know that."

"Crying's not so bad." He glanced over. "Nothing like Tommy or your uncles. That's good."

I nodded, but it was a big fat lie. My earliest memory was being at Grandma J's house. She was babysitting me on a Saturday during her book club meeting. I must've been driving them nuts because she insisted I take a nap. I tried crying and yelling, but Grandma could not be moved. I had to stay in the rickety crib that had once belonged to my father and uncles.

Grandma J clearly didn't know who she was dealing with because she didn't lock the wheels on the crib. I used my bodyweight to rock the crib along the wall until I got to the window that was left open. I pulled the shade down and then worked on the screen until I got it loose. It's not as impressive as it sounds. The house was built in the sixties and the windows were the original cheap metal things. Then I stood on the bedding, shade, and screen and proceeded to boot my two-year-old self through the window.

Lucky for me, Grandma J's favorite son, who wasn't her son at all but a neighbor, happened to be walking his prize Pekinese at the time. He saw my blonde head come out of the window and rushed over to catch me as I shot out, headfirst over an eight-foot drop to concrete. No wonder Kevin is Grandma's favorite.

"Maybe someone up there does like me," I said.

"Yeah?" Chuck asked.

"I keep not dying."

"You worry me."

"Join the club."

Read the rest in Silver Bells in Hotel Hell (Mercy Watts Mysteries Book Thirteen)

A.W. HARTOIN'S NEWSLETTER

To be the first to hear all about the A.W. Hartoin news and new releases click the link or scan the QR code to join the mailing list. Only sales, news, and new releases. No spam. Spam is evil.

Newsletter sign-up

ABOUT THE AUTHOR

USA Today bestselling author A.W. Hartoin grew up in rural Missouri, but her grandmother lived in the Central West End area of St. Louis. The CWE fascinated her with its enormous houses, every one unique. She was sure there was a story behind each ornate door. Going to Grandma's house was a treat and an adventure. As the only grandchild around for many years, A.W. spent her visits exploring the many rooms with their many secrets. That's how Mercy Watts and the fairies of Whipplethorn came to be.

As an adult, A.W. Hartoin decided she needed a whole lot more life experience if she was going to write good characters so she joined the Air Force. It was the best education she could've hoped for. She met her husband and traveled the world, living in Alaska, Italy, and Germany before settling in Colorado for nearly eleven years. Now A.W. has returned to Germany and lives in picturesque Waldenbuch with her family and two spoiled cats, who absolutely believe they should be allowed to escape and roam the village freely.

Made in United States
North Haven, CT
30 May 2023